ST. MARTIN'S

MINOTAUR

MYSTERIES

D1024605

PRAISE FOR KJ ERICKSON'S
THIRD PERSON SINGULAR

third
person
singular

KJ ERICKSON

St. Martin's Paperbacks

THIRD PERSON SINGULAR

Copyright © 2001 by KJ Erickson.

Excerpt from *The Dead Survivors* copyright © 2002 by KJ Erickson.

ISBN: 0-312-98213-5

Printed in the United States of America

St. Martin's Press hardcover edition / January 2001
St. Martin's Paperbacks edition / March 2002

St. Martin's Paperbacks are published by St. Martin's Press, 175 Fifth Avenue, New York, NY 10010.

10 9 8 7 6 5 4 3 2 1

For
JEB & JEG
Past, Present, and Future Tense

AUTHOR'S NOTE

Author Richard Price, in describing the relationship between facts and imagination in fiction, said his objective is to establish parameters of reality, within which parameters he makes stuff up. This is as good a description of writing fiction as I've found. While the places and police procedures in *Third Person Singular* are, for the most part, based on actual sites and practices, the people and institutions (particularly the Minneapolis and Edina police departments and the Hennepin County Attorney's Office) within *Third Person Singular* are fiction.

third
person
singular

PART 1

MINNEAPOLIS

THURSDAY, APRIL 3

CHAPTER

1

The Father Hennepin Bluffs rise on the east side of the Mississippi River, facing the Minneapolis skyline. Below the bluffs is St. Anthony Falls—the only falls on the more than two thousand miles of the Mississippi. It is at the falls that the Mississippi gives up its casual, low-banked meandering and begins to take itself and its journey to the Gulf of Mexico seriously.

Evelyn Rau pulled up and parked on the railroad tracks that ran in front of the historic Pillsbury A Mill on Southeast Main Street. The mill's windows—opaque with milled flour dust—stared out blindly over the cobbled street, toward the river. Directly across from the mill was the west trailhead for the paths that crisscrossed the bluffs below.

Evelyn would have liked to keep the car running. She'd been cold since waking. But sitting alone in a car with the engine running on a nearly deserted street might draw attention. So she stayed cold and got in position, adjusting the seat back so she could lie low enough to avoid being seen by someone looking in, but still able to catch any action from behind in the rearview mirror.

Two months from now, and a block or so farther up on Main, the street would be swarming with people wandering between the bars and restaurants that filled the warehouses facing the Mississippi. But before noon on a cold, damp April weekday, the street was empty. Which was good. What was better was that Main was neither residential nor were there small business. Homeowners and small-business owners were the worst when it came to people with their noses up for deals going down.

But her real risk was always the buyer. That he'd been hustling stuff to get money and the cops had turned him. So she always gave the buyer a short rope for getting the deal done. She'd called this morning's buyer from a Super America where she'd stopped for a coffee. He had less than a half hour if he wanted to make a buy.

Remembering the coffee, she leaned forward for the cup she'd wedged between the gear box and the seat. The heat of the cup in her hands felt good. On reflex, she glanced at the side-view mirror—and froze. A dark green BMW had made it within a half block of where she was parked. The car moved slowly. It wasn't the buyer. She knew his car and his license plate. And there were two people in the BMW. She wouldn't sell to two people. Her buyers knew that.

The Beemer slowed to a stop maybe thirty feet behind her, then pulled in and parked. The front parking lights flashed and died, and from the driver's side, a tall, good-looking guy eased out. His eyes took in everything as he moved to the backseat door, opened it, leaned in and took out a narrow brown bag. A young girl—younger than the guy—came from the other side of the car. He wasn't paying much attention to her. He was paying attention to the street, his eyes landing for a moment on Evelyn's car, then darting up at the mill, across the road toward the river.

Another dealer? The guy wasn't a cop, she'd put money on that. But he was thinking hard about something. The couple crossed Main to the trailhead. In moments they'd disappeared down the trail. A shudder hit Evelyn before she

4

knew it was coming. Without knowing why, she was spooked.

Something wasn't right. Reaching down to the side of the seat, she flipped the seat back into position, let it push her upright, and cranked the ignition. She stopped just long enough to take a deep gulp of the coffee. Then, rolling down her window, she dumped what was left, throwing the empty cup on the floor.

Without turning her head, she pulled out, hung a right on Third, and drove up the hill above Main, then circled back to Main to come up behind the BMW. With the car idling, she focused for a moment on the plates: VSW 341. An association from her past life entered her consciousness like a ghost. *Virginia Stephen Woolf.* A twinge of emotional pain twisted in her gut, and she pulled back out onto Main, away from ghosts, buyers, and mystery couples.

Back at the apartment, Evelyn sat in the underground garage for almost ten minutes. With any luck, Gary would either be sleeping or would have gone out after she left. Scooping up crap from the car floor, she dumped it in the barrel by the elevators on her way in. Keeping the car neat was one of the things she did to create the illusion that her life was under control.

She held her breath as she turned the key in the apartment door. No luck. The door wasn't half open before the sound of the TV from the living room told her Gary was in and up.

He was standing directly in front of the TV. Shirtless, watching cartoons and drinking a can of beer. His hair, long and shapeless, hung forward over his unshaven face. He had on a pair of unzipped jeans; the skin of his belly looked soft and white.

He didn't look up from the TV or say anything as she walked through the living room into the kitchen. She was bent over in front of the open refrigerator when he called to her.

"Where you been?"

She straightened up and shut the refrigerator door without taking anything out. She didn't move from where she was standing. "I was supposed to do a deal down by the river. The buyer didn't show."

Gary walked into the kitchen, crunched the empty beer can with one hand and dropped it on the counter. It rattled briefly, the only sound between them. He leaned against the wall and fixed his eyes on her.

"How much cash we got?"

She shrugged and turned away. "I don't know exactly. Seven, eight hundred, maybe."

She heard him blow air through his lips in contempt.

"Eight hundred does diddly if I'm gonna get more stuff from Howard, which I need to do pretty quick, or he's gonna start treating me like a stranger. Meanwhile, we're sittin' on practically everything we bought last month, which I don't much like having around. What's the problem, Evie?"

She hiked herself up on the edge of the counter and concentrated on a rough cuticle. "I told you. The buyer didn't show."

Gary left the room, leaving her sitting on the counter edge. He came back in with a pack of cigarettes. Holding his hair back from his forehead, he flicked on one of the gas burners on the stove, bent forward, and lit a cigarette. He inhaled deeply and blew smoke directly at her. Picking tobacco off his tongue, he said, "Far as I can tell, you haven't sold hardly any stuff in the past two, three weeks. The deal we had was, I handle wholesale, you do retail. Now, anytime you want to trade places, say the word."

She knew they were both thinking about the one time she'd gone with him to buy from Howard. In a downstairs room of a ramshackle duplex, Evelyn and Gary did business with four black men and one woman. The woman was grossly overweight and had no upper teeth on the right side of her mouth. Two thin, ill-tempered German shepherds could be seen down the hallway, tied to doorknobs with ropes.

Howard and Gary sat on a couch that was missing a front leg and two seat cushions. In front of the couch, a board had been propped up on cardboard boxes. On the board were maybe a dozen brown paper bags, the kind kids used for school lunches. Gary and Howard were counting capsules into piles, after which they'd dump them into one of the bags. When they'd finished with the capsules, the woman brought in a cardboard box filled with plastic bags of coke. With surprising delicacy, Howard would open a bag and offer it to Gary, who'd touch his finger to his tongue, dip the finger into a bag, and touch it again to his tongue. He made a small sound of acceptance after each of these gestures.

Gary put the bags of capsules and powder into a canvas bag. "Give me the money," he said, without looking at Evelyn. Evelyn, who'd left her jacket on, reached inside the jacket to pull out the thick rectangle of cash Gary'd given her to carry. Gary passed the cash to Howard.

Howard's eyes went from the cash to Evelyn.

"You wanna throw in piece a tha for a one-day-only discount, Mistah Gare-uh Say-hen?"

Gary joined the others in snickering at Howard's suggestion. He glanced over at Evelyn, not to let her in on the joke but to suggest to the others that she was his to do with as he pleased.

He was slow in answering. Then, as if it didn't much matter, he said, "We got our deal, Howard. Leave it like it is."

7

"You member tha woman wit you first time you an me did business?"

Gary sucked on his cigarette, blew out, and looked up at Evelyn. He looked at her without meeting her eyes. He tapped the ash off his cigarette and with great concentration, eyes downward, ground the ash into the bare wood floor with the heel of his boot.

"Yeah. Romona," he answered.

"Thas it. Rah-moe-nah. Big titties on tha Rah-moe-nah girl. Member I tol you five hunnert off for a squeeze on Rah-moe-nah's big titties and what she done when I says tha?"

Gary gave no sign of answering. Howard looked around at the others with a wide grin. "This Rah-moe-nah girl, when I says I wanna squeeze on her big titties, she come over, pull her shirt off, sits right down on my lap, pulls my face down on them big titties and says, 'You give me ten dimes worth a coke an I fuck you right here, right now,' and she did. She did Eli for nuthin, too. But then she'd blown through so much stuff, I doan think she knew no more wha she's doin. Wha ever happened to tha Rah-moe-nah girl, Mistah Say-hen?"

"I had to cut her loose," Gary said, standing. "She was doing more stuff than she was selling. Come on, Evie. We got places to go and people to see."

"You come see me again, Mistah Gare-uh Say-hen, and bring some other big-tittie girl. I like this Evie all right, but she ain't got them big titties like I like. You see that Rah-moe-nah girl, you tell her come see Howard."

Evelyn couldn't remember how she got out of the house and back to the car. Sitting next to Gary in the front seat, she hissed, "*You shit!* You let them think I was some piece of crap that'd do whatever you said. You *jerk-off!*"

Gary hadn't answered her. He'd reached into his jacket to a paper bag he'd stashed separate from the canvas tote and pulled out a handful of colored capsules and bags of coke. He'd dumped them in her lap and kept driving.

More or less like he'd done the first time they'd met.

A friend asked her, "For God's sake, Evelyn, what do you see in him?" The question had come soon after she'd started seeing Gary Sehen, when she thought the answer was simple.

The first reason: he wasn't an academic, a qualification of some significance to Evelyn after four years as a floundering Ph.D. candidate.

The second reason: he'd been kind to her, and she wasn't used to people being kind to her. "Are you okay?" he'd asked, looking at her through the rearview mirror where she huddled in the back seat of his cab. His voice had been quiet, respectful.

Surprising herself, she'd answered honestly. "Not okay. But I'll survive. Thanks for asking."

"You've got a west bank address—teach at the U?" He kept his eyes on her in the mirror.

"Sort of. I'm a graduate student."

"Really? Maybe that's why you look familiar. What's your degree in?"

"English literature." She paused, then tested him a bit, the way academics always did in social situations. She disliked herself even as she did it. "Early-twentieth-century English novelists. The Bloomsbury group is my specialty."

He smiled at her, shaking his head. "Definitely not why you looked familiar. One of the reasons I haven't finished my econ degree after six years is I've still got the English comp requirement hanging over my head. That, and driving a cab full-time."

Pass. He hadn't pulled any phony bullshit to try to impress her.

She tried to think of something to say in return, but she was too tired to be clever, and nothing came. "Sorry," she said, "I'm not much for chat tonight. I've had a long trip and I've got a stack of midterm papers to correct before lights out . . ."

He held up a hand in response. "No problem. Take it easy." And he'd been quiet the rest of the ride, talking in a muffled voice into a handheld mike now and again and scribbling on a clipboard lying on the seat next to him.

At the apartment entrance, he'd hopped out of the cab and carried her luggage into the lobby before she had a chance to get out of the backseat. When she handed him cash for the fare, he'd held up a hand in resistance and instead put an envelope in her hand, pressing her fingers closed around it.

"You look to me like somebody who could use a good deed. Let me recommend my little friends. I couldn't get through finals without them."

In her apartment, with the door closed behind her, she'd opened the envelope to find a couple dozen red-and-orange capsules. *Speed*. Evelyn's undergraduate roommate sophomore year had relied on these guys to stay thin and get through finals. There was a message scrawled on the envelope: "Take two as needed. Call me if I can help again. Gary Sehen, 331-8979."

Evelyn looked at the capsules in her hand and then at her watch. She contemplated her briefcase, stuffed with the ungraded midterms, due to be returned to students in less than ten hours.

What the hell.

Within a half hour, a smooth, internal warmth was moving through her veins, into tight muscles, through frazzled nerves. She'd expected—what? Maybe frenetic energy. What she felt was a calm intensity. She worked through the night with a concentration she'd not been able to muster since her first year of graduate school. Her comments on the midterms were detailed and on point. She felt confident about the grades she assigned.

She completed the last paper just after dawn, stacked it neatly with the others, and decided to shower and change. She could have gone to bed for a catnap, but the prospect of an early start had an inexplicable appeal.

Coming out of the shower, she realized the effect of the capsules was wearing thin. She felt jangly, warm, and slightly dizzy. She walked back to the desk where she'd left the envelope. She took one capsule out, went into the kitchen to make a pot of coffee, and washed the single capsule down with hot coffee. By the time she left the apartment for campus she was back on track.

The English Department office looked and felt like a high school principal's office. The de facto principal of the department was its senior secretary, Rita Hoehne. Rita was a squat, tightly permed divorcee who'd worked in the department for more than twenty years. Her dominance of the department was founded on a genius for organization, abundant energy, a self-defined sense of moral purpose, and a deeply rooted anti-intellectualism. In combination these qualities had the effect of making the faculty and students she served feel incompetent with respect to the basic functions of daily living. Their resulting insecurity kept them slightly off-balance and squarely under Rita's thumb. Which was just where she wanted them.

Among the current crop of graduate students, all of whom depended on Rita in important ways, only Evelyn escaped Rita's contempt. Evelyn chalked this up to Rita's recognition that, like Rita, Evelyn was an outsider in academe. And Evelyn knew that being a graduate student wasn't really important. Evelyn's self-knowledge relieved Rita of her duty to remind Evelyn of these truths on a daily basis.

"So. You're back." Rita greeted Evelyn without looking at her.

"Yup," Evelyn said, and walked over to her mailbox. "Back last night, after midnight." She grabbed the mail from her box, dumped it on a table, and helped herself to coffee from the department pot. Then she opened her briefcase and removed the midterms, plopping them on the counter next to Rita.

"For John. He in yet?"

Rita pulled a face and looked over the top of her glasses at Evelyn. "At eight-thirty in the morning? You *have* been out of touch." She scooped up the term papers. "When did you find time to get these done?"

"I didn't go to bed last night. I expect John's nose is sufficiently out of joint, my being gone for almost three weeks in the middle of the term, much less my coming back without the midterms graded."

"You got that right. Dead dads don't count for much with our John Oswald. He came close to doing an honest day's work once or twice while you were gone. Made a lot of noise while he was at it. Drove us all crazy. When was the funeral?"

"Thursday. I finished going through my dad's things on Saturday and got a cheap flight back last night. So I take it I still have a job? I called John from Texas just after Dad died to say I'd be a week longer. He all but told me I needn't bother to come back."

Rita snorted. "Ha. Fat chance. You don't come back and he's got to finish the research on his MLA paper, write the final for the senior seminar, and grade the honors papers. I won't live long enough to see him do as much as that for the rest of his life, much less between now and the end of the quarter."

Rita's recital of what Evelyn had left to do for John Oswald—not including Evelyn's own work—deflated the thin layer of control the pills had laid on her psyche. As she loaded up her mail and walked back to her desk, a familiar sense of dread began to gather. Standing over the disorder of her desk, she doubted she had the energy to get through the day, much less the term. Most pressing was the as-yet-undone research for John Oswald's MLA paper. *The Decline of Literature: Galsworthy and the Masses.* The paper's theme grated on Evelyn's intellectual soul. It had been her enthusiasm for Galsworthy in a graduate seminar that had confirmed her as a heathen in the groves of academe. During a discussion of character development, she had used a Galsworthy character as an example of complex, multilayered personality development. The professor leading the seminar had looked slowly around the circle of aspiring intellectuals. An uneasy silence gathered heavily in the room. Then, with a glance at his wristwatch, the professor said, "Well, Miss Rau. It's almost two-thirty. We must be keeping you from your soap operas." Her fellow graduate students had laughed loudly, nervously. The experience was the starting point of a cynicism that took on ever larger proportions in Evelyn's life as a graduate student.

Damn. Why had she left the pills at the apartment? Why, for that matter, had she taken just one before leaving?

The third reason Evelyn had gotten involved with Gary Sehen, and the one she was least willing to admit to herself, was that she wanted more orange-and-red capsules. What she told herself was that if she hadn't gotten sick two weeks after getting back from her father's funeral, she wouldn't have noticed that she didn't have any pills left.

It had been almost two days since she'd taken the last pair of pills when she woke with a stiff neck. Her throat was sore by the time she got to campus. At the end of the day her eyes were bright with fever and a cold had turned the inside of her head into wet cement. The thought of being sick threw her into a dead panic.

The empty envelope with Gary Sehen's note and number was still in her desk drawer. She sat at the desk with the envelope pressed against her warm forehead for a long time. Then, reaching for the phone, she punched the seven digits.

An answering machine picked up. "Hi, it's Gary. Leave your name and number and I'll get back to you."

So she did. And so he did.

PART II

MINNEAPOLIS

SATURDAY, APRIL 5 TO
           SATURDAY, JULY 12

CHAPTER

2

"Nice signal, fuckhead!"

Mars Bahr glanced down at the small, curly-haired boy next to him in the car's front passenger seat. Chris's eight-year-old face was screwed into an expression of self-righteous indignation, his attention riveted on the Ford Tempo directly in front of them.

The Tempo's driver had committed a cardinal error in the Bahr family book of driving etiquette. The driver had failed to turn on his left-turn signal until after the light had turned green, leaving Mars and Chris locked behind the Tempo while traffic to their right flowed smoothly through the intersection.

Mars frowned. Chris had a litany of passenger-side impatience he'd begun chanting at age four. His phrasing and inflection were precise copies of what Mars said and how Mars said it since Mars had gotten his driver's license twenty years earlier. The "fuckhead" stuff was something else. Chris's language was getting as bad as the Minneapolis Police Department squad room. Mars made a mental note to add a discussion of language to their breakfast agenda.

Saturday morning breakfasts—and garage sales May through September—were routine for the two of them. They'd started by going to restaurants. Al's in Dinkytown, the Modern in Northeast Minneapolis, or the Perkins on Riverside. When Chris had turned five, he'd started Cub Scouts, where he's he'd learned to make baking powder biscuits. Mars ate maybe two hundred biscuits after the first batch came out of the oven. When Chris learned how to make scrambled eggs, they usually skipped restaurants and Chris made breakfast at Mars's apartment.

Mars would pick Chris up around nine at Denise's. Chris would come out to the car carrying a big paper bag full of his own cooking gear, most of which had been bought at garage sales. If they needed groceries, they'd stop on the way to the apartment. Mars had offered early on to get groceries in advance, but Chris got as interested in grocery shopping as he was in cooking.

"So. What's for breakfast?"

"Cheese omelettes. You want sautéed onions in yours?" Chris said, saw-*teed*.

"Saw-*taid* onions would be good." Mars said saw-*taid* carelessly, as if that's how he'd heard Chris say it. "Where do we stand on groceries?"

Chris narrowed his eyes in deep concentration. As he thought, he bounced his head back and forth off the seat. "We need cheese, of course. And onion—you got any onions?"

"I've got nothing except Coca-Cola and ice cubes. *Maybe* half a dozen eggs left over from last week. I've got a quart of milk left from . . . Well, we probably need milk, too."

"Okay," Chris said. "Then we need milk, cheese, and onions. Half a dozen eggs should be enough, but I'd like some good bread, too. You know how when you make an omelette and the butter and the juice from the omelette is still on the plate? I'd like some French bread to mop that up with." Chris's head flopped sideways to look up at Mars. "Could we get to Surdyk's to get cheese and bread? And go to Cub for

18

the other stuff? If we go to Cub we could get extra eggs for next time. And oranges. I know I used all the oranges last week, so we'll need oranges. And Cub's the best place to get oranges."

Mars swung the big, standard-issue Pontiac into the Cub parking lot and got the best spot in the lot, a piece of luck that brought a big grin to Chris's face. It was the kind of thing Chris cared about.

"Dad? 'Cause you're a cop, could you park in a handicap spot and not get a ticket?"

Mars gave a push down on Chris's head. "Yes, I could, but no, I wouldn't. Come on, let's shop."

Chris was a serious shopper. His mother's genes. He smelled and squeezed produce. Counted pieces of fruit when it was sold by the bag. Took out the pocket calculator Mars had given him and figured unit costs. Checked expiration dates. He saved all their grocery receipts and compared prices of what they'd spent with the Sunday paper ads, a task that involved a mix of moans and cries of triumph.

This Saturday he spent a long time with the oranges. "Four bucks!" he said, holding up a bag in disgust. He looked at Mars for approval.

Mars shrugged. "Wouldn't be breakfast without fresh orange juice. Maybe cut down from four oranges apiece to three."

In the dairy section, Chris found a milk carton in the back with an expiration date that was almost a week later than the ones in the front. This was the equivalent of getting the best parking space in the lot. On their way out and back to the best parking space in the lot, Chris said with satisfaction, "Next stop, Surdyk's."

The counter staff at Surdyk's looked like art students, and they took cheese seriously. Mars wouldn't have known where

19

to start with them. But Chris, after pulling a wheat-and-herb baguette from a basket and sliding it into a narrow white bag, grabbed a number and began an undaunted consideration of the yards of cheese.

"Number thirty-six?" A pale young woman with blue-black hair and a stud in her nose walked toward the number Chris held up. Chris didn't look at her, keeping his eyes on the cheese. "I need some cheese for omelettes. Cheddar, I think."

"I've got a Wisconsin white cheddar on special that would be nice."

Chris followed her to the far end of the refrigerated cheese case. With a gesture graceful enough to be part of a dance, she swiped a stainless tool across a block of white cheese and dropped it on a piece of cracker. Chris chewed it slowly, nodding only slightly.

"It's okay. On the cracker. You got a yellow cheddar?"

She smiled at him. A smile of respect, not condescension. "Let's try an aged Vermont cheddar. A bit pricey, but I think it's going to be what you want." Another artful swipe, dropped on a cracker and barely in Chris's mouth before his nod was decisively affirmative.

"How much is it?"

She turned the card, which was stuck in the cheese. "Five ninety-eight a pound. I think you'll like the texture of this cheese in the omelette. It holds up well under heat." Mars made a slight face, but nodded his agreement.

"We'll take half a pound," Chris said, clearly pleased.

To call where Mars lived home was to suggest a degree of domesticity that exceeded reality. Mars had a single standard for a place to live after the divorce: cheap. He found what he was looking for in a three-story red-brick walk-up on the outskirts of downtown. The apartment was a studio plus-bath.

The kitchen was laid out against one wall, single bed under the windows, futon rolled on the floor for Chris. A row of steel frame shelves lined the wall opposite the kitchen. Mars's clothes were folded on the shelves. The only other furniture was a table with four chairs. The only decoration was a movie poster for *The Usual Suspects*. Chris had bought the poster at a garage sale because he thought Mars looked like Kevin Spacey.

In the four years he'd lived there, Mars never had a rent raise. He understood why. First, he paid his rent on time, which wasn't the neighborhood standard. Second, it was clear the caretaker liked having a cop living in the building. For Mars, keeping his rent low meant he'd been able to maintain Chris and Denise's lifestyle at the same standard as when Mars and Denise had been married.

Chris began preparations for breakfast with precision. Their mutual roles were firmly established. Mars set the table with the odd bits of tableware he kept at the apartment and took directions from Chris.

Chris pulled a yellow onion out of the bag. "You can slice the onion. Real thin is best." Chris dug around in the bag and pulled out a knife and a cutting board. He'd asked to get pieces of Trident cutlery for Christmas last year, after the previous summer's garage sale expeditions had failed to produce anything up to his standard. The cutting board he'd made in Scouts.

Mars was aware as he started on the onion that Chris was glancing over now and again to be sure the onion was getting sliced thin. Without turning around, Chris said, "You know what those Salad Shooter things are really good for?"

"Making salad?"

"Making shredded cheese." Chris stopped whisking to extract a complicated-looking hunk of white plastic from his bag. He assembled some funnel pieces, and placing the Salad

Shooter over an empty plate, pressed their pricey cheese through one end. It took less than seconds, after which Chris held up a plate of perfectly shredded aged Vermont cheddar. Mars had enough experience with Chris's newfound enthusiasms to be fairly sure their menus for the foreseeable future would be dominated by entrees that used shredded cheese.

"*Carl* gave it to to Mom for Valentine's, and I used it to shred cheese for some tacos I made for dinner Thursday night."

Chris had looked over his shoulder at Mars as he said Carl. Mars made it a point not to react. What he thought was that Carl was lucky to have found maybe the one woman alive who'd be pleased to get a Salad Shooter for Valentine's Day.

As the omelette sizzled in the cast-iron pan Chris had bought at a garage sale and seasoned himself, Chris squeezed orange juice. "You know how you always say, 'The sweeter the juice, the less juice you get'?"

"How're we doing this morning with those overpriced suckers?"

Chris handed Mars his glass of juice. Mars tossed back half a glass in a single gulp.

"I got almost twelve ounces out of three oranges. Just about a record. And it's sweet, right?"

Mars nodded with genuine appreciation. "Sweetest so far this year."

Chris brought the omelettes to the table. They were perfect. Crisply browned skin, light and fluffy inside, a first-class cheddar cheese, and delicious wisps of saw-taid onions.

Chris's attention was evenly divided between his pleasure in eating and watching Mars for his reactions. "How's your omelette?"

"Outstanding. Just the way I like it. Crisp on the outside. Great cheese."

"What do you think about the onions? Maybe we shoulda had them across the top, instead of inside?"

Mars shook his head. "No, they're fine inside. Of course, nothing to say next time we can't have the onions in the cheese *and* across the top. How'd I do on the onions? Thin enough?"

"Perfect."

Mars tore off a hunk of French bread and dabbed at his empty plate. "We should get some business done. You need to be Scouts when?"

"Eleven-thirty. We're leaving from Grace Lutheran Church."

"We'd better get going on our agenda, then. Whatcha got?"

Chris pulled out a spiral-bound notebook and folded it open. Across the table, Mars could see the carefully block-printed list.

"Mom says we gotta talk about summer vacation. Soccer camp's in July. It costs a lot. And if I go to soccer camp, and go to the Black Hills with Mom, plus going camping with you, it doesn't leave much time to do stuff with James."

A sharp, thin pain shot through Mars. A kid shouldn't have to feel guilty about arranging a summer schedule to accommodate divorced parents. "Look. In my book, hanging out is what summer vacation is all about. Why don't we plan on taking a couple of short trips during the school year—like out to Blue Mounds State Park or do some hiking on the Lake Superior Trail. How would that be?"

Chris smiled with pleasure. And relief. "That'd be good. How about the money for soccer camp? Mom says she'll try and come up with half. She's making some stuff for Aunt Gwen, but she's not going to get paid till later, so you'd have to pay the whole thing, then she'd pay you. . . ."

Mars shook his head. "Tell your mom to let me know

23

how much, and I'll pay. I appreciate knowing in advance so I can plan to get it together."

Chris smiled again, and, looking a little shy, said, "Mom says you don't leave enough money for yourself. Brent Rice's dad, who's a big shithead anyway, yells at Brent all the time about the support money he's gotta give Brent's mom, and Brent's dad doesn't give Brent's mom even half as much money as you give Mom. Brent says so."

"Your mom and I have a deal. She gives you time, I give money. We talked about it when we got divorced. Your mom wanted to be able to stay home, and I wanted her to be able to keep the house. With my job, I can't count on being around when you need me. It's what we agreed on a long time ago, and I think it works pretty good. What else on your list?"

"Know what my health science teacher said about smoking and taking drugs?"

Mars shook his head and waited.

"He said that if you haven't started smoking or taking drugs by the time you graduate from high school, chances are something like ninety-nine point nine-nine-nine-nine you never will."

"I think that's probably right."

"I was really glad to hear that. I thought, like, I was going to have to worry my whole life that I might be a junkie or something."

"I'd say that's a teacher who knows what he's talking about."

"Dad?" Chris was looking at the tattered box of Camels next to Mars's plate. "Tell me again about when you quit smoking."

"I quit the day your mom told me she was pregnant with you."

"Because . . ."

"Because I knew that if I smoked, you'd be at a higher risk for smoking."

"And . . ."

"And because I didn't want Mom breathing smoke when she was pregnant with you."

"Tell the part about why you still buy cigarettes."

"Well, when I stopped smoking, I felt sort of lonely. Like I'd lost a good friend. I'd go in to pay for gas, or whatever, and I'd see all those cigarettes, and I just missed having that pack. So then I thought, what's to say I can't buy a pack of cigarettes and carry it around with me? Put it on the table in the morning when I'm having my first can of Coke, which is when I really missed smoking. So I've been buying a pack and carrying it around ever since. It helped."

"How long you had that pack?"

Mars picked up the pack and rotated it in his left hand. "Well, let's see. I bought this pack in . . . February. I bought it the day Latisha Williams's body was found in the trunk of Duwayne Turner's car. So that was February eighth, and this is April fifth—just about two months." Mars changed the subject. "That it for you?"

"Yup." Chris slapped his notebook shut and straightened up. "What's on your 'genda?"

Mars looked at him directly. "Language. Fuckhead. Shithead. I think we need to think about some guidelines for using swear words."

"Mom says it's against the Ten Commandments to say goddamn."

Thin ice, here. "Okay, for some people that would be one reason not to swear. For me, it's not that simple." Mars sat back and thought about it. "I know one thing I don't like about swearing is that a lot of people use swear words because they're too lazy to think of a better word to use. Being lazy

25

when you talk makes you sound stupid. So that's rule number one: Think before you talk."

Chris said, "Y'know what Dennis Engstrom does? He makes lists of all the swear words he knows. He's got two hundred seventy-three words so far. Then he sees how many he can say without taking a breath. On the bus Tuesday he got to forty-seven."

Mars held up two fingers. "Rule number two: Don't use swear words to try and gross other guys out. People who are impressed because you've got a foul mouth aren't the people you want to impress, anyway."

"What else?"

"Well, in my book, using any word too much, swear word or not, is bad, so that would be rule number three. A guy I work with begins every other sentence with, 'The way I see it . . .' Second or third time in the space of five minutes you hear 'the way I see it,' you're ready to grab the guy by the throat."

"You say 'in my book' a lot."

The kid was quick. "Point taken."

"So it's okay to swear sometimes."

"For me, there're times when a good, hard, flat *damn* hits the spot."

"Dad? Know what we could do? If I swear, you say, like, 'Number one' if you think I'm being lazy. Or, 'Number three' if you think I'm using a word too much. Okay? Then if you don't say anything, I'll know you think it was okay that time. You wanna do that?"

Mars smiled at Chris. "Sure. Let's try it. Keep us both on our toes."

They were doing dishes when Mars's beeper went off. Chris's face glowed. More than good parking spots, Chris liked police action.

Mars handed Chris the towel. "You finish up, and I'll catch my beeper." He walked over to the wall phone and punched the Homicide Division number.

The assistant division chief answered. "Mars? A girl's body's been found down on the Father Hennepin Bluffs, just below the A Mill. Chief says he'd like you to have a look."

Mars glanced at his watch. "I was just about to take Chris to Scouts. I could get down there in a half hour. Maybe less. Who's down there now?"

"Some guys from the Second Precinct who took the call when the body was found. I think they've called the ME, but I don't know if he's there yet."

"Tell them I'm on my way."

Chris's eyes were fixed on Mars's face. "Somebody dead?" The question contained no remorse.

"Yup."

"Can I come?"

"Nope. You get to go to Scouts."

"Shit."

They looked at each other. Mars said nothing. He dumped Chris's jacket hood over his head, gave the kid a quick, affectionate butt slap, and said, "I'll call you later and let you know what's up. Now let's get our shows on the road."

CHAPTER
3

The city of Minneapolis was founded near the Father Hennepin Bluffs, drawn, as nineteenth-century settlements were, to the convenience and natural power of the river and St. Anthony Falls. The city's milling and lumber industries used the cascading water power to transport logs and grind grain. When the milling industry changed and moved on, and when the trees had been cut, what was left behind was a damaged and deformed landscape.

Mars stood at the top of the stairs leading down the bluffs. Behind him, the Pillsbury A Mill—the only mill still operating on the river—rose in monolithic splendor. The mill's massive limestone face towered over the bluffs, facing the river. Mars winced as he looked at the mill. Its windows looked directly down on the crime scene. But they were frosted with flour dust. So much for getting lucky with what a casual witness might have seen from the mill.

The cobblestone road of Southeast Main Street—some of which was original to the 1800s and which ran between the mill and the bluffs—was barricaded with police stands. Three police squad cars were parked at random, arrogant angles within the barricaded area. The flashers over one empty car rotated with ominous self-importance. Black-lettered yellow tape roped the steps off.

Mars ducked under the tape and walked to the trailhead. Looking down the railroad-tie stairs that led to the river, Mars saw a gaggle of cops at a clump of bushes near a path. There were uniforms, some Crime Scene Unit guys and Dr. Denton D. Mont, the city's chief medical examiner.

It was inevitable that Dr. Mont would be called Doc D, with reference to death rather than his initials. He was a short, wiry, buttless man who smoked cigarettes down to the filter, owned no suits, and kept his only sports coat in the trunk of his car, just in case. Rolled in the pocket of the sports coat was a maroon-and-navy striped tie, which he unrolled and tied on for court appearances. Sartorial standards aside, Mars liked working with Doc D for three reasons: Doc D was fast, careful, and curious.

Mars headed down the stairs, passing a small, well-dressed woman struggling to restrain a handsome yellow Labrador retriever. These two, Mars guessed, had found the body.

John Roseman, the CSU supervisor, greeted Mars. "Hey. Candy Man. Thought they might send you down on this one. Has a lot of front-page potential, is my guess."

Mars made it a point not to take the bait. He was used to cynicism from his colleagues about his role as a special investigator reporting directly to the chief of police. Anytime he got called Candy Man, he knew the implied reference was not a play on his name and a candy bar. The reference was to candy ass.

Roseman made a motion to Mars, and they walked around the bushes and down the trail a bit before Mars caught sight of the girl's body, her pink windbreaker standing out on the dull ground.

"We got an ID on her yet?"

Roseman nodded. "Yeah. She had a driver's license in her purse. Mary Pat Fitzgerald. Lives out on Cornelia Drive, west of Southdale."

"Edina?"

"Yup. Just what we need, huh? Some little princess from lotus-eater land comes into the city to get offed. Don't know how a kid like that ends up dead on the bluffs. Unless it's drugs."

Mars moved closer to the body. She wasn't what he'd been expecting. There'd been a group of Indians living under one of the bridges just up the river, and Mars had noticed a girl traveling with them for the past three, four months. When he'd gotten the call about a girl dead on the bluffs, his mind's eye had seen that girl: short, potbellied, drunk. *I'll be scraping her off the sidewalk before long* is what Mars had thought the last time he'd seen her weaving down Hennepin Avenue with three men. The group had stopped inside a bus shelter in front of the Minneapolis Public Library. One of the men had held a bagged bottle to the woman's mouth.

Nothing like the girl lying maybe three yards away. Even in death this girl didn't look like she belonged on the bluffs. Her hair was white blond. One arm was extended, the hand cupped, nails clean. An expensive-looking leather-banded watch on the fine bones of her extended wrist. Crisp white sneakers, creased khaki pants, a pink windbreaker. This kid was clearly a long way from home.

The only thing that looked off was her clothes. Her pants, which zipped in the front, were unzipped, the belt undone. Her shirt had been pulled up, as if she'd been about to take it off over her head. Her butt was slightly elevated, as if she'd been on her knees, then fallen forward. Mars couldn't see any blood. He turned sideways to look for Doc D.

"Hey, Doc. Whatta ya got?"

Doc D walked over. Standing next to Mars, he held the filter of his cigarette between his thumb and index finger as he took a deep drag. He was careful to drop the ash from his cigarette into the Styrofoam cup he carried. Peering through his exhaled smoke at nothing in particular, he answered.

"Let us just say that this scene does not speak to me."

"Meaning?..."

"Meaning there isn't a lot here and what there is doesn't tell much of a story."

"You at least know how she died?"

"Got a pretty good guess. Puncture wound to the chest. Probably took out her aorta."

Mars looked at the body again. "The aorta? She took a stab wound to the aorta and we're not up to our knees in blood?"

Doc D dropped the cigarette butt into the cup, giving it a little swirl. "I said *puncture* wound to the aorta. Remember how when you were a kid your mother warned you if you stepped on a nail you had to wash it out real good, 'cause the wound closed on itself when you pulled the nail out? And blood couldn't flow out to wash the wound? Well, that's what happened here. There's blood all right. All pooled up inside her chest cavity."

"So what would the perp have used? What kind of weapon are we looking for?"

Doc D didn't hesitate. "A screwdriver, an ice pick, something like that. I should be able to tell when I open her up."

"Any evidence of sexual assault?"

"First guess, no. Given the state of her clothes, she might have been in the middle of something with a boyfriend...."

Mars walked closer to the body, dropping down, sitting on his heels, to get a closer look. "No tears or anything around the zipper. Looks like she undid it herself."

Roseman came over. "Well, we're about finished up. Gonna head back downtown. Talk to you tomorrow?"

Mars stood up, grimacing at how stiff his knees felt after

thirty seconds in a crouch. "You've got video and thirty-five millimeter?"

"Does a bear shit in the woods?"

"She have any valuables on her?"

"About seventeen bucks. Two credit cards. If it was a robbery, someone got scared off before he got what he was after. Same goes, I'd guess, if he was trying to get in her pants."

Mars turned to Doc D. "I'm going to want to do the family notification. Kid like this, I'm going to look real close at everybody she knew. I'd like to see their reaction. Anything on the line about her being missing?"

Doc D answered. "Doubt anyone's had a chance to check. Took the wallet off her maybe an hour ago. Time of death is going to be a bitch." He lit up again, glancing over at the body. "Between Monday and now, there hasn't been more than six, seven degrees variation in the temperature, day or night. And the temp's been between, say, thirty to thirty-eight degrees. Pretty near perfect conditions for maintaining a dead body." Doc D kicked at the ground, glanced around, and shook his head. "Well, I'm as done as I'm gonna get. When you expect I can bring her downtown?"

Roseman glanced at his watch. "Like I said. CSU guys are done now. Take her."

Mars said, "I'm going to talk to the woman who found the body." He looked back at the woman, who was still struggling with the dog. "That's her with the dog?"

"Yeah. I'd like to let her get going pretty quick. She's sorta shocky. The guys from the Second did an interview with her."

"All the same, I'd like to talk to her. Shouldn't take more than a few minutes—assuming she's not involved."

"Not a chance."

To Doc D, Mars said, "I'll be down here another half hour or so. I'll make a stop in the squad room, then I'll come over to the morgue. Why don't you start without me, I'll be along as soon as I can. Probably won't hang around long with you. I'm going to track down Phil Keck in Edina, take a run out to Cornelia Drive."

Mars walked over to an officer who was on the scene from the Second Precinct.

"What's the woman's name?"

"Linda Mistad. Lives a few blocks up, Southeast Fifth."

Mars approached the woman, flashing his badge. The dog took an exuberant leap toward him.

"Robin! Stay! I'm sorry, he gets so excited around new people. It would help if I was stronger and better coordinated...."

Mars took hold of the dog's collar with both hands and gave the dog a firm shake. "Sit!" he said. The dog did a couple of quick, nervous gulps and sat. Mars stroked the dog's head. "Good boy. Mrs. Mistad? I'm Special Detective Marshall Bahr with the Minneapolis PD Homicide Division. You found the body when?..."

Mrs. Mistad brushed her well-cut hair away from her face, holding it back from the wind. "It's maddening how Robin always obeys men and totally ignores me—you asked when I found the body? I couldn't say exactly. It's been over an hour now, maybe longer." She looked at her watch. "Good grief. It's been almost two hours. My husband's going to kill *me*. He's told me not to come down here alone with Robin. But it's usually pretty much deserted down here, so I can let Robin off the lead, and he can get a good run, burn off some energy without running me ragged." She stopped, shivering, and folded her arms across her middle, sliding her hands deep into her jacket sleeves. "I'm sorry—I can't stop shaking—"

Mars called to one of the Crime Unit technicians. "You guys got a blanket?" A technician came over with a heavy,

33

rough, dark green wool blanket. Mars hoped Mrs. Mistad wouldn't give much thought to where the blanket had been before he draped it around her.

"You were saying you got down here when?"

"The blanket helps—thanks. Let's see. I left the house around ten A.M., and it wouldn't have taken me more than, say, six or seven minutes to get from there down here, especially with Robin knowing he was coming down to the river. When we got to the bottom of the steps, I let Robin off the lead and he started running for the rapids that come down just the other side of the power plant."

Mars's authority with the dog was short-lived. Robin bolted again, dragging Mrs. Mistad back toward the steps. Mars jogged forward to catch up, took the lead from Mrs. Mistad, and pulled the dog up short. "Come on, let's sit down on the steps. I'll hang on to this guy. So Robin was off the lead, headed in one direction, then he started off to where the body was?"

"When he got by the bushes, he stopped cold. Something he's not done before, not ever on this path. He started, well, it was like he was tiptoeing. And his hackles went up. It frightened me. I thought there might be vagrants who'd made a camp in the bushes. That wouldn't be unusual down here, which is why my husband . . ."

"Do you walk Robin here every morning?"

"No, Bob—my husband—is on vacation this week, and he's been taking Robin out. . . ." She stopped, pulling the blanket tighter, and drawing a deep breath. "It's just that he's got a trip later today that he's getting ready for, so I took Robin this morning. Last time I was down here was Sunday. Robin was fine. No problem."

"And your husband wouldn't have brought the dog down here between Sunday and yesterday?"

"God, no. He had a fit, as I said, about my coming here."

"And when you found the body. You didn't see anyone else in the area?"

She shook her head. "I went over to pick up Robin's lead, to try to get him to move on. I didn't want him antagonizing anyone who might be back there. When I approached Robin he ran farther into the bushes. I had to go after him, and I saw the pink of her jacket. At first, that's all I saw. I thought someone had dropped a jacket in the weeds. Then I noticed her hand, her hair. My first thought was that she had fallen asleep. That's not as far-fetched as it sounds. Kids do sometimes come down here for parties. They drink too much, God knows what else. It's not inconceivable someone would have ended up sleeping down here after a binge."

She stopped, breathed deeply, and removing leather gloves, rubbed her hands over her face. "I'm sorry. I'm rambling. It was just such a shock. . . ."

Mars put his hand on her shoulder, squeezing lightly. "You're doing fine. So you thought she was sleeping?"

"Yes, at first. But there was something about the position she was in that didn't seem right. And Robin was terrified of her. He didn't really want to go up to her. If she'd been all right, he would have been bounding up to her begging for attention. I called out—asked if she was all right and . . . I don't know how to explain this . . . but it was the silence after I called out. I just knew she was dead."

She stopped again, readjusting the blanket. In a voice that was more controlled, she said, "Once I realized it was a body, I just tore up the steps to the pay phone down by the theater. To tell the truth, I don't even remember getting from here to there. And I waited up at the top of the stairs until the police came. It's silly, but I was afraid the body would be gone when they got here. That people would think I was crazy."

"You did fine," Mars said. "Look. Anything else you remember—it doesn't matter how small a detail, or if it makes sense to you—anything at all, just give me a call." Mars handed her a card and called over one of the uniform guys from the Second Precinct.

"Officer, could you take Mrs. Mistad and her dog home? Just a couple blocks up the hill, other side of University Avenue."

The cop, Mrs. Mistad, and the Labrador headed back up the steps. Mars grinned. If you'd put wheels on Mrs. Mistad, the Lab would have gotten her home ahead of the squad car.

CHAPTER
4

An hour later Mars made it down to the morgue. He was feeling behind the curve, having gotten hung up in the squad room. While the autopsy was usually time well spent, from what he'd seen at the crime scene, Mars wasn't expecting much. Where he wanted to be was out on Cornelia Drive. He'd spend no more than half an hour with Doc D. Then he'd try to get a hold of Phil Keck, chief of police in Edina, to coordinate a visit to the Fitzgerald family.

Entering the autopsy room at the Hennepin County Morgue, Mars was always conscious of his own smell: faint sweat, warm blood. The autopsy room air was perpetually cold and damp, punctuated with a chemical smell that felt like it could turn the inside of your nostrils to corduroy. The chill was intensified by the hard, shining surfaces of tile and stainless steel. Even the fabrics in the room—stiff white sheets and Doc D's ice-green scrubs—looked cold.

Mary Pat Fitzgerald's white blond hair spilled out from under a cover sheet and over the edge of the autopsy table. Seeing her bare foot at one end of the sheet covered autopsy table, Mars guessed she'd already been stripped and scrubbed. Doc D was shaking his hands over a stainless steel wall sink as Mars came in. To Mars he said, "Prettiest corpse I've seen in a long time. And clean. I'm gonna be real surprised if the

Trace Unit finds anything. Whatever it was happened to her on the bluffs didn't dirty her up any."

Mars walked over to the body and pulled the sheet from the girl's face. Her beautiful bone structure was even more evident, Mars guessed, in death than in life.

Doc D called Mars over to a countertop where he'd laid out a number of objects removed from the body. "Take a look at this." He handed Mars a tank watch with a tan leather strap. "She was wearing a Weissie wrist watch. You notice it on her arm at the scene?"

Mars nodded.

"My dad collected watches when I was kid. Sold most of them to send me to college." Here Doc D stopped to light another cigarette. He drew deeply on the cigarette and looked at Mars as he exhaled. "A Weissie? Well, my dad could have paid for a couple of years of medical school back in the sixties if he'd cashed in what the kid was wearing on her wrist. Solid gold case, hand hammered. Hand-stitched leather band— original, in good condition."

Mars waited for Doc D to make his point.

"The Weissie's got a month and a date calendar built into the face, and the interesting thing about a Weissie is that it has a very tricky setting mechanism. To wind the watch, you pull out of the stem and wind, pretty much like you would for any watch that isn't digital. But if you want to reset the calendar, you pull the stem out and—very slightly—give it a half turn counterclockwise, which stops the works—time, calendar, everything. It's not the kind of action a person could do by accident. You'd have to think about doing it, *intend* to do it.

"The Fitzgerald girl's Weissie was stopped, with the stem pulled, at eleven-oh-five on April third. This tells me that at eleven-oh-five last Thursday, she knew she was in trouble. And goddamn it, knowing she was in trouble, she had the presence of mind to send us a message. I tell you, Mars, I got tears in my eyes when I figured out what she'd done with that watch."

Mars said, "It's not the kind of evidence that holds up very well in a courtroom. But for investigative purposes, it'll help."

"This, too," Doc D said, holding up the girl's khaki pants. He pointed to the knees on the pants. Dirt stains were visible. "At some point she was on her knees, but it wasn't a fall. Her knees look fine. No bruising, which would have shown up even if she died a few minutes after falling."

Mars said, "At the scene, the way her butt was sort of up in the air, it looked like she'd been kneeling, then fallen forward. You opened her up yet?"

"Just about to start. Got her scrubbed, and my first guess, that she took a shiv to the aorta, looks like it's gonna hold up. She's got a puncture wound in the right place. Nothing else that looks probable for cause of death. One thing's a little odd. There's a slight trauma over the skin of the pubis—and she's missing pubic hair in that area. Hard to say what's going on there. Say she's about to have sex with someone, and he's over her, pants unzipped. Gets interrupted, starts to zip up fast. Catches her pubic hair in his zipper, pulls away, taking some pubic hair with him. That's what it looks like."

Mars said, "But she was in the wrong position for that to be the murder scenario. I mean, he's not gonna be interrupted, zip up, get her on her knees, then stick her with a screwdriver. He's gonna zip up and get the hell out of there..."

Doc D nodded. "I take your point. Thing is, there's evidence of very slight bleeding in the area where pubic hair is missing. Takes a magnifying glass to see it, and I haven't done run any tests yet, but my guess is we've got pinpoint bleeding."

"But you didn't find any blood on her panties."

"None. Remember, her pants were down, so if the trauma

occurred in connection with the murder, that fits. But I agree, it's hard to figure a scenario that fits the pubic trauma with the murder. I don't know. Just strikes me as odd. Probably doesn't mean anything."

Mars said, "So, if we find a suspect, we should check pant zippers."

Doc D snapped on powdered latex gloves. "That's what I'd do. Well, might as well get on with the main event. You staying around?"

Mars shifted. "I'd like to, but frankly, I'm thinking my best shot is getting out to Edina as fast as possible. I'm not feeling particularly good about what's coming out of the crime scene. I'd like to be the first to deliver the news to the family, check out their reactions, start interviewing people. You available sometime early tomorrow to go over what you find?"

"You gonna be around, say, eight tomorrow morning?"

"Sounds fine. You want me to come over here?"

"Nah. I'll come over to the squad room. Your domestic arrangements are superior to mine."

Back in the Pontiac, Mars switched on the ignition and cranked the heater. Then he dug around in the glove box for his phone directory. The Directory of Metropolitan Area Law Enforcement Officers was a much-abused object: bent, torn, coffee stained. Chris had colored on more than one page and as many pages were missing as remained.

Mars thumbed through the Cities index and found Edina. He was in luck, the page listing the Edina Police Department was intact. Pulling up the antenna on his mobile phone, he punched out the numbers and tucked the phone between his ear and shoulder.

"Edina Police Department. This is Chief Keck's Office. How may I help you?"

Now, there was a difference right off. Three sentences to answer a phone.

"This is Special Detective Marshall Bahr with the Minneapolis Police Department. Is Chief Keck in?"

"I'm sorry, Special Detective, but the chief is out of the office at the moment. May I have him return your call?"

Mars hesitated. "Well, I'd like to talk to him sooner rather than later. Any chance you could give him a page and have him get back to me within the next fifteen minutes or so?"

This time it was Edina that hesitated. "I'm sorry to say Chief Keck is involved with a family friend whose daughter is missing. I will certainly interrupt him if you think it necessary. I'd prefer to wait until Chief Keck returns later this afternoon. What would be best for you?"

Mars looked out the car window. There were maybe ten miles between where he was sitting and the Edina Police Department. But at that moment, he had no doubt they were on the same page.

"Is Chief Keck with the Fitzgerald family?"

"Why, yes. Forgive me. I hadn't understood that you were returning the chief's call."

"I'm not. But I do need to talk to the chief about Mary Pat Fitzgerald. Why don't you go ahead and page the chief." Mars gave his mobile phone number, then settled in to wait for the return call.

Keck had started his police career in the Minneapolis PD as a patrolman. He'd done well, put a lot of effort into career training, and had been a good PR guy who'd moved off the streets fast and into department administration. He'd been a deputy division director when he was picked to head up the Edina PD. Mars had run into Keck at the Southdale Target maybe two years ago. You didn't see much of your inner-city colleagues when you were chief of police in a suburb where a typical felony was a set of golf clubs getting stolen out of the trunk of a Lexus sedan.

In less than three minutes the mobile phone rang.

"Mars. Phil Keck. I got a call from my office saying you wanted to talk to me about Mary Pat Fitzgerald. How did you guys get in on this?"

Mars made a face to himself. "We found her body, Phil."

Keck didn't say anything for a count of five. "Wait a minute. What body? Mary Pat ran an errand over at Southdale Thursday and didn't come home. But we've got no reason to expect that she's in any big trouble. In fact, her boyfriend's been out of town since Thursday morning, and what we think is she hooked up with him. He's due back tomorrow morning.

"I mean, *what* body?"

CHAPTER
5

Cornelia Drive was not the typical venue in which Mars paid visits to victims' families. The lawns on Cornelia Drive got more attention than most of the kids Mars saw in city neighborhoods. The curved street was lined with 1950s-style ramblers, many of which, like the Fitzgerald house, were white brick.

Mars rang the doorbell. Phil Keck came to the door. He shook Mar's hand too hard and then held on to keep Mars in the entryway. In an artificial whisper, standing too close, Keck said, "I think we should go slow on this with the family. You know, until we're sure. Absolutely sure. I was thinking after I hung up with you that maybe what's happened is that Mary Pat's ID got stolen. That the girl you found on the bluffs had ripped it off."

"That would be a long shot," Mars said. "The ID the vic was carrying fits the body. What have you told the family about my coming out?"

"I just said that in a missing-persons case having other jurisdictions involved is helpful. That you were somebody I knew and trusted, that you'd be helping out. I haven't said anything about your being Homicide or about the body you found on the bluffs."

"One thing I can't figure, Phil. What are you doing here?

Even in Edina, a missing teenager can't be something the PD pays much attention to right off. What gives? You do home visits on all these cases?"

Keck shook his head with his eyes closed. "You can't imagine the kind of kid Mary Pat is, in addition to which her dad, Doc Fitzgerald, delivered both my kids. When Mary Pat was in junior high, she baby-sat my kids. Her parents are beside themselves and my being here helps. And I know this is what people always say in these situations, but in Mary Pat's case, it's really true: her being gone without telling her parents just isn't in character."

"I thought you said on the phone you were pretty sure she was with her boyfriend."

"Well, I did—and I do think that's where she's going to turn up. It's just that it doesn't really fit, so I'm playing it safe."

"Okay. This is how I want to handle things. I want a description from her parents of what she was wearing when they last saw her, and I want to see a recent picture. If either of those fits with what we found on the bluffs, that's it. I'm going to tell them we've found a body that matches her description."

"Hold off, would you? If at that point it looks like this really might be Mary Pat—good God, I can't believe I'm even saying this out loud—but if it sounds like it might be her, I'll drive downtown myself to identify the body."

"That's fine. But I'm not dinking around to make you feel good, Phil. I need to get going on this. You know as well as I do that time is critical, and I wouldn't be out here in the first place if I wasn't pretty sure."

"No problem. My God. If this is Mary Pat, I'm as hot as you are to get going. I just don't want the Fitzgeralds to suffer that kind of shock unless we're sure. C'mon in and I'll introduce you."

44

The Fitzgerald living room was large, with a picture window at the back of the room facing Lake Cornelia. The furniture was heavily upholstered in floral prints, with lots of highly polished end tables and tassle-shaded lamps. It looked like it had been delivered en masse from Grand Rapids, Michigan, maybe twenty years ago, and taken good care of since.

Doc Fitzgerald was standing when they entered the room. A tiny woman, wearing sunglasses and hanging on to a mug of coffee like it was life's blood sat beside him in a chair that probably weighed four times what she did.

Keck put a hand on Mars's shoulder. "Doc, Mrs. Fitz, this is the guy I told you about. Special Detective Marshall Bahr from the Minneapolis PD. Mars and I worked together years ago. He's first class, and we're lucky he's able to help out."

Doc Fitzgerald stepped forward with energy to shake Mars's hand. "I—we—do appreciate this very much, Special Detective. A bit embarrassed, of course. I'm sure Phil's told you we think this is a goose chase. If Mary Pat wasn't so conscientious, I doubt we'd think twice about her being gone two days. She's almost nineteen—but it's not like her. . . ."

Mars held up a hand. "No problem. Just a couple of things that would help me out. Do you have a recent picture of Mary Pat?"

Mrs. Fitzgerald spoke without moving. "Her senior picture's in our bedroom on the dresser—" She stopped and her face tightened slightly. "Doc. The picture of you and Mary Pat that was taken down at the Biltmore, in Phoenix, in February. It's in your study. That one's more recent, and more like she has her hair now."

Doc Fitzgerald returned with two photos. One was a portrait in a nine-by-twelve frame. The girl in the picture had close-cropped white blond hair. The other was a snapshot. Father and daughter looked out from the frame, smiling into the camera against bright sunlight, each with a golf club in hand. Doc Fitzgerald had a sun visor on. Mary Pat Fitzgerald was bareheaded, her pale blond hair blowing across her forehead and onto her father's shoulder.

Doc Fitzgerald handed both photos to Mars. "Like Mother said, the snapshot down at the Biltmore is more like her hair is now. Her senior picture was taken when she still had her hair cropped for swimming."

Mars turned away from Fitzgerald as if to look at the photos in better light. He faced Phil Keck, giving him a slight nod, which caused Keck to change color.

Mars said, "She's a beautiful girl. It would help if I could take the photos with me. I'll see that you get them back. Would you happen to know what Mary Pat was wearing when you last saw her on Thursday?"

Again, it was Mrs. Fitzgerald who spoke. "I remember she wore her Ralph Lauren windbreaker, because I told her it wasn't warm enough, that she should wear her down jacket. But she said she was just going over to Southdale to get fitted for her prom dress and it would be fine."

"The windbreaker. What color was it?"

"Pink. The windbreaker was pink."

They took the news about the body quietly. Doc Fitzgerald moved away to stand in front of the picture window, staring out at the lake. Mrs. Fitzgerald rose abruptly. "I'm sorry. I should have offered you coffee when you came in." She walked quickly but unsteadily toward the kitchen. Mars and Phil Keck stood awkwardly in the center of the living room until she returned, carrying in shaking hands two mugs of steaming black coffee. She didn't ask if they wanted cream or sugar, and after putting their cups down on an end table, she went back to the kitchen.

From the window, and still facing the lake, Dr. Fitzgerald

spoke. "I don't mean to suggest that what you've said isn't based on good police work. Far from it. I have the highest regard for law enforcement in this community. But I can't help feeling—and Phil, you can bear me out on this—I can't help feeling that if you knew Mary Pat, you'd know how unlikely it is that she could be the unfortunate young woman you've found . . . where is it you said? . . ."

Mars answered. "The Father Hennepin Bluffs. Just across the river from downtown."

"Well, there it is. I've never heard of the place and I'm sure Mary Pat hasn't either. It doesn't make any sense, not any of it, and with all due respect, I think you've got the wrong girl."

Keck spoke, and for once he was helpful. "My idea, Doc, is that I can get this straightened out. I'll drive downtown and—" Mars caught the brief halt while Keck stopped himself from saying he would identify Mary Pat's body. "—I'll meet with the medical examiner and get this business straightened out. Mars can stay here and get more information we can use in finding out exactly where Mary Pat is."

Dr. Fitzgerald turned from the window. He'd pushed his glasses up on his forehead and was rubbing his eyes with the heels of his hands. "I hate to keep imposing, Phil, but—well, Mother and I'd appreciate it." Keck was out the front door when Dr. Fitzgerald went after him. "One more favor, Phil. Call from the medical examiner's office, will you?"

A phone rang in the kitchen, twice, without Mrs. Fitzgerald picking up. Dr. Fitzgerald scurried toward the kitchen as if he expected that she wouldn't answer. Mars could hear him on the phone, his voice briefly effusive, then subdued, but Mars could not make out what was being said.

Within minutes Dr. Fitzgerald came back into the living room. "That was my son Robert. We tried to get hold of him yesterday, but he's been out of town. He lives in Boston . . . teaches English at the university there. He wants to come out, which doesn't really seem necessary . . . but . . ."

"The more people who knew Mary Pat, the better." Mars winced when he realized he'd used the past tense. But the doctor didn't seem to notice. "If you don't mind," Mars said, "I'd like to ask you and Mrs. Fitzgerald a few questions. Do you think you're up to it?"

"Of course. Yes, of course." He hesitated. "I'll just get Mother." He walked back to the kitchen. When he returned, Mrs. Fitzgerald was at his side. Her gait was more unsteady than before. She clutched her coffee mug with both hands.

Ah. The dark glasses, the trembling hands, the ever-present mug. It wasn't just grief Mars was seeing. Mrs. Fitzgerald was drunk.

Mrs. Fitzgerald took her place in the overstuffed chair. Doc pulled a hassock up, sitting down a little to the front of his wife. He leaned forward in an attitude of eagerness, as if his answering Mars correctly would guarantee the outcome he wanted.

Mars began. "Tell me what happened on Thursday, including anything that might have upset Mary Pat before she left the house, and what's happened since then."

Doc looked to his wife and back at Mars. "I'm going to have to ask Mother Fitz to begin. I was at the hospital from early Thursday morning until late that night. I'd had two breach deliveries and a C-section on Thursday. I didn't know of any of this until I got home just before midnight—"

"It's just like I said before." Mrs. Fitzgerald's voice was too loud, with the slightly arrogant tone that some drunks adopt. "Mary Pat was just going to run over to Southdale about her prom dress." Mrs. Fitzgerald made a harrumphing sound, which turned into a cough.

"Do you remember when she left?" Mars could see that Mrs. Fitzgerald was made uneasy by the question.

Doc interrupted in a gentle voice. "I called home just after Carol Givens had delivered her baby—which was about nine-thirty A.M. You said Mary Pat had just left to run an errand over at Southdale. Do you remember, Mother?"

Mother Fitz took another swig from her mug and shrugged.

"And you didn't hear from Mary Pat again?"

Dr. Fitzgerald answered. "As I said. I got home just before midnight and noticed that the station wagon wasn't in the garage." He paused, glanced briefly at his wife. "Mother doesn't drive, so I assumed Mary Pat was out. Mother was already sleeping when I got in, so I just sat up for a while in my study, doing some reading. I turned in around one A.M., I'd guess."

The doorbell rang, startling the three of them.

"I'll go." Dr. Fitzgerald rose abruptly and started toward the front door. Mars held up his hand to stop him.

"You're expecting somebody? Any chance this is the boyfriend?"

"Brian? No, I don't think so. We're not expecting Brian back until tomorrow. It could be anybody—people have been calling and dropping by pretty steadily since yesterday morning."

"Go ahead, answer the door."

Doc returned with a girl Mars guessed to be about Mary Pat's age. She walked in with an assurance that came from the near certainty that she would be the best looking person in any room she entered, in combination with the natural arrogance of adolescence.

"Special Detective Bahr, this is Becky Prince. Mary Pat's best friend."

Becky Prince looked at Mars, but neither spoke nor

smiled. Mars noticed she didn't bother to greet Mrs. Fitzgerald, but turned to Doc Fitzgerald abruptly.

"Have you heard anything?" She spoke only to Doc.

Doc glanced at Mars. It was clear he didn't want to say anything about the body on the bluffs. "Sit down, Becky. We haven't heard anything since you were here last night. Phil Keck's asked his colleague here to help out, and we were just telling him everything we know about what happened Thursday, which isn't much."

Becky crossed her arms over her chest in a gesture of frustration and tension. "Has anybody tracked Brian down yet?"

The phone rang before Doc could answer Becky. "That'll be Phil," he said, heading to the kitchen at a slow run. Mars braced himself for what he knew would be bad news for the Fitzgeralds.

When Doc came back, he moved slowly, but did not seem unduly upset. He glanced at his watch. "That was Bobby, calling with his flight time." He jingled change in his pocket and glanced at his watch again. "I really was expecting we'd have heard from Phil by now. It's been..." He looked at Mars. "How long would you say before we could expect to hear from Phil?"

"I wouldn't guess, if I were you. Any number of things could have slowed him down. We'll hear from him when we hear from him. Right now—"

The phone rang again, causing impatience to override Mars's sympathy for the Fitzgerald's situation. He clutched at Doc Fitzgerald's arm as Doc headed off to answer the phone.

"You got an answering machine?"

"Yes, but if it's Phil—"

"If it's Phil, we'll hear his voice. Right now what I really need is a basic picture of where we are, which I can't get if we're interrupted by every phone call. Let's just sit down, all of us, and get some facts straight."

Doc stood momentarily to listen to the answering machine, but whoever had called hung up before the recorder started. He sat reluctantly. Becky Prince turned to stand in front of the picture window, her back to the rest of them. But Mars had no doubt she was keeping track of what was going on.

Mars began again. "You were saying you went to bed around one A.M. on Thursday ... well, actually that would have been Friday morning."

Doc nodded.

"So you went to bed around one A.M. Friday and Mary Pat wasn't home yet. Was it usual for her to be out until after midnight on a weeknight?"

Becky answered, her back still turned. "It was a weeknight but it wasn't a school night. It was staff development for teachers, Wednesday through Friday, so we had off. Which is why Brian went up north to his cousin's to cut wood, which he does every staff development break in the spring."

"Up north to his cousin's to cut wood?"

Becky turned to face him. With her back to the light of the window, she appeared as a silhouette. "He's got a cousin who owns a lot of land up in Itasca County. He lets Brian come up every spring and thin out some of the forest on his land. Brian cuts the wood in spring, leaves it to dry out, then goes back up over Columbus Day weekend in the fall. He picks the wood up and brings it back to the cities to sell. Drives around in his pickup looking for houses with chimneys and asks if they want to buy wood. He makes a couple thousand every year doing that."

"What was unusual was for Mary Pat to be out that late without leaving word." Doc drew his index finger across his lower lip. "I just assumed she'd told Mother she was staying with Becky, or . . ." He trailed off.

"So you realized she hadn't come home when you got up yesterday morning?"

"Well, it was on my mind, I guess. Because I checked the garage first thing when I got up. The station wagon was still out. That was just after six. I wasn't comfortable calling Becky that early, so I waited until about seven-thirty to call."

"Mrs. Fitzgerald . . ." Mars turned his attention back to the mother. "Mrs. Fitzgerald, when did you tell your husband you hadn't heard from Mary Pat on Thursday night?"

Again, Doc answered for his wife. "Special Detective, Mother has suffered from migraine headaches for years. She's had a bad week and has been taking medication off and on. The medication pretty much does her in, so I didn't wake her when I got home Thursday night. She was up around seven o'clock Friday morning. That's when I asked her where Mary Pat was, and when she didn't know, I called Becky."

"And you called Phil Keck when?"

"I called Phil right after I talked to Becky."

Doc paused, his gaze caught by something behind Mars. Mars swiveled to see Phil Keck standing silently in the front hallway. Mary Pat's father rose slowly, without speaking.

Without coming fully into the room, Phil Keck spoke. "It's bad news, Doc. It's bad news."

CHAPTER
6

Phil walked Mars back out to the Pontiac. Mars had left him with a substantial amount of investigative work to handle on the Edina end, but Keck wasn't focusing. Getting into the Pontiac, Mars said, "Look, Phil, just get your best investigators going on the things I asked you to do. We'll get together again after I've met with the chief and the mayor."

Mars didn't bother going into the squad room when he entered city hall. He headed directly to the mayor's office on the second floor.

At one time the office would have been an impressive space. The red granite Richardsonian city hall had twelve-foot windows facing the county courthouse across the street. It was a large room with space for the mayor's desk, bookcases, couches, a full-size conference table, and eight chairs. But there had been no room—fiscally or politically—for official grandeur in the city's budget for the last three administrations, and the room had a haphazard air.

Mayor Alice Geff and Chief of Police John Turner sat at the table. Both looked liked they'd come in from Saturday night functions that didn't have much to do with dead bodies on the Father Hennepin Bluffs. Mars had a measured amount of respect for the mayor. Unlike other mayors Mars had worked under, Alice Geff knew by instinct when the police department had a case she should be involved in. And once involved, she was a force to be reckoned with.

Chief Turner was something else. Mars had almost left the department shortly after Turner became the city's first black chief of police. Mars had been through a series of tough cases, had taken a lot of administrative heat, and his partner was set to retire. Turner's appointment hadn't done anything to make Mars optimistic about things getting better. Turner was a big man, always formally dressed and mannered. Mars had first seen him as a politically correct appointment who'd provide the mayor with a shield against minority community complaints. A chief who'd play it safe and be a weak chief at precisely the moment the department, and the city, needed a risk taker. Mars had made the mistake of reading the chief's quiet good manners as weakness.

A couple of months after Turner's appointment, Mars had been on his way out of city hall when the chief's administrative assistant had called out to him. "Marshall? Glad I caught you. The chief wants a minute—"

Mars had knocked on the chief's door, which was partially open, before going in.

The chief was sitting at his desk, his hand cupped over his mouth, reading a file. He wore a plain black suit, a stiff white shirt, and a nondescript tie. The suit looked a little tight on the chief's bulky body.

The chief didn't look up as Mars entered, but said, "Good afternoon, Detective Bahr." It was the first time Mars had been alone with Turner, but the man's tone was as formal as it had been in the news conference when his appointment was announced. He made a small gesture toward a chair in front of his desk. "Sit down." The chief closed the file he'd been reading, smoothing it with big, hammy hands. There were no other papers on the chief's desk.

"You've heard, I expect, that I've been meeting with senior sworn staff in the divisions?"

"Yes, sir."

The chief was quiet a moment. "A difficult thing, gettin' a handle on who's who. What's what. People tell you what they want you to know. What is in their interest for you to know. I suppose that's to be expected. . . ."

Mars had been surprised by the casual sound of "gettin'." It stood out like a piece of white lint on the chief's perfectly pressed suit. Mars knew the chief was giving him an opening, but he purposely ignored it and sat silent.

"You have any idea what I hear about you, Detective Bahr?"

Mars smiled. "I could guess."

The chief fixed Mars in his sights. "I hear you're not one of the boys. Not among those who adjourn to The Little Wagon when their shift's over. That you don't drink." A small glimmer of something—amusement?—flickered in the chief's eye. "Kind of a tight-ass, is what I hear." The last was said with the same sort of intentional irony with which the chief had said "gettin'."

"True, for the most part." Mars held back again.

"I hear you're a good dad. Maybe more unusual, that you're a good ex-husband. And when I ask officers, 'If your wife or mother had been murdered, who would you want leading the investigation?' Of course, they always say, 'Me, my partner.' When I say, 'Who beside yourself, your partner.' They think about it, then—most of them grudging it—they say, 'Probably the Candy Man. Yeah, probably the Candy Man.' Then I ask, if your son was accused of murder, and there's no question he's innocent, which officer would you want to head the investigation? Right off the dime—not even grudging it—they say, 'The Candy Man. Absolutely the Candy Man.' "

This time the chief had him. Mars was surprised and it showed.

The chief said, "You ask yourself, what would make a bunch of guys pay a high compliment to somebody they don't much like? I think the answer is with cops there's a loyalty that goes beyond ego and friendship. It's loyalty to the profession, and it's that loyalty that keeps them from denying recognition to a fellow officer who deserves it. Even if that officer is too much of a tight-ass to go over to The Little Wagon for a drink, now and again."

"It doesn't work that way. Going over to The Little Wagon 'now and again.' You're either a regular at the Wagon, or you're not there. That's the way it is."

"I know that. In case you hadn't noticed, I'm something of a tight-ass myself."

"I had noticed, as a matter of fact."

"What else I hear is that you're thinking about leaving the force."

Mars shifted uneasily. He wasn't prepared to put his professional future on the table without having made the decision to leave or stay. His answer was ambiguous. "Well, I've been on the force, one way or another, for almost twelve years. I suppose everyone asks himself now and again if this is what he wants to do for the rest of his life."

The chief nodded. "I can understand that. I just wanted you to know that I need you to stay, so if there's anything I can do to make you stay, I'd like an opportunity to do it."

Mars stared at the chief blankly. "I must be missing something here. Apart from the fact that I'm a great ex-husband and I don't hang out at The Little Wagon, why is it you care if I go or stay?"

"Why don't you start by telling me why it is you're thinking of leaving. Unless I'm missing my bets, the reasons you want to go and the reasons I want you to stay are gonna be more or less the same thing."

"As long as it's understood I haven't actually made a decision to leave or stay . . ."

"Of course," the chief said.

"My issues are simple. Last couple of big cases we didn't get the support we needed. The division all but had us punching clocks to make sure we weren't logging any overtime. You can't clear homicides working a shift. And it doesn't seem to me that we're organized right. We're getting blown away by drug- and gang-related cases that really need someone who's wired in tight to those scenes. But we keep shifting people between those cases and murders that *aren't* related to drugs and gangs. It's just not efficient, and it keeps us from developing the kind of expertise we need. Other thing is, my partner retires early next year. I really can't think of anybody I'd want to partner with, or, for that matter, who'd want to partner with me. Goes back to my being a tight-ass."

The chief didn't look at Mars when he said, "Pretty much what I was expecting you to say. The way I see it, we could use a few more tight-asses in the department. And I can't afford to lose the ones I got. You notice it or not, younger guys comin' up pay attention to a guy like you. Down deep they don't want to be one of the guys sitting over at The Little Wagon with their guts hanging over their belts. If I'm gonna turn the department around, head it in the direction it needs to go, I've got to start bringing new types in, and I need someone like you to show 'em what being a cop means."

He tapped the file he'd been reading when Mars came in. "You know you're the only officer with more than ten years on the force who hasn't had a single citizen's complaint filed against him?"

"That's not necessarily a good thing. And I've been lucky."

"Maybe so, maybe so. But I put that together with what else I see in the file and I don't think it's all luck. Fact is, this city's about to hit some rough road. If we're gonna get over it in one piece, the community's gonna have to have a higher level of trust in the department than it does right now. And that trust is gonna come from the character of the officers we put out there. That's my biggest challenge, as I see it. What I'd like to ask you is this: Give me a month or so to work something out with the division directors and the union. Then I'd like to sit down and talk again. Maybe I can put something together that'll make you want to stay."

And when they got back together five weeks later, the chief had put together exactly what it took to make Mars Bahr want to stay.

"Say it isn't so, Special Detective." The mayor's face was grim. The chief's face remained impassive.

Mars sat down at the table. "The best I can offer is I think we've got a good shot that the perp is her boyfriend—homegrown Edina boy, from what I understand. Nobody can offer any explanation why Mary Pat Fitzgerald would have been down on the bluffs. Her best friend doesn't know where the bluffs are, much less why she would have gone there. We getting any noise from the press?"

The chief shifted in his chair. "All we've released is that a woman's body was found on the bluffs and that release of her identification is pending. No one's nose seems to be up. Given the location, I think the assumption is she's a transient."

"The first transient homecoming queen in Edina's history," Mars said.

The mayor groaned. "You're serious? She was a homecoming queen?"

"She was everything. Homecoming queen. Class president. Valedictorian. A state high school golf and swimming champion. Beautiful. Her father has delivered half of the Catholic babies born in Edina in the last twenty years. She was going to be a freshman at Brown in the fall."

The mayor had removed her glasses. "My God. It's not like any kid dying this way isn't a tragedy, but this is my worst nightmare. The heat I took on the money we spent down there to try and clean the area up. And we're due later this month to find out if we're going to get a federal matching grant to do more development on the riverfront. Now this. Well, at least we've probably got another twenty-four hours before the press realizes this isn't just Jane Doe—which means I'm counting on you to nail the Edina homeboy between now and tomorrow afternoon."

The chief asked, "What does the boy say?"

"The boy," said Mars, "is somewhere up north cutting wood. I'm guessing he's a probable because"—Mars paused, holding up one finger—"first, as we all know, the boyfriend is never a bad guess, and, second"—his second finger went up—"Mary Pat Fitzgerald's best friend is clearly antsy about the boyfriend. Before she knew Mary Pat was dead, she kept asking why we weren't tracking Brian down. And, when she found out Mary Pat was dead, she clammed up. Now, this kid—the best friend, Becky Prince—is a class A bitch princess, but she's no fool. If she's worried about the boyfriend, I'm betting there's a reason to be worried."

"How *are* you doing on tracking the boyfriend down?"

"All we've got to go on is that he's up in Itasca County. Nobody's been able to tell us where. And a description of his truck, which we've asked the Itasca County Sheriff's Department to keep an eye out for. Apparently he's on a relative's property, but there's no phone on the property."

"That's just fine, Special Detective. But like I said, let's wrap this up fast and send it back to Edina. The last thing the city needs now is Terror on the Bluffs." The mayor stood.

"Well, gentlemen, I need to get back to a banquet where I'm the guest speaker. I trust you all understand my agenda: I don't want Minneapolis taking the rap on this case. Damn suburbanites want to get killed, they should do it in the suburbs."

Mars and the chief headed back toward the police department offices. "What do you need?" the chief asked.

"Well, I've got Keck's people working the Edina angle. Southdale, high school teachers and counselors, friends. You know what that asshole did? Keck's people find the car Mary Pat drove to Southdale—which for all we know, may be the last place she was seen alive—sitting in the parking lot at Southdale with a flat tire. They call Keck, and Keck tells them to change the tire and drive the car back to the Fitzgeralds. As a *courtesy*, he says. My God. Probably the best piece of evidence we had at this point, and three thousand people have driven in and out of that spot in the last forty-eight hours and the car is sitting back in the Fitzgerald garage. 'So I didn't know she was dead then,' Keck says to me."

"You trust him to carry out the investigation in Edina?"

"Keck? No. But Keck isn't going to be the one doing the investigating. He's got a couple of pretty good investigative detectives out there. They mostly work robberies, penny-ante drug stuff, but they're plenty smart. Know the drill. And they've got their fur up on this one. Probably see it as the opportunity of a lifetime. Soon as I get hold of Nettie, I'll have her coordinate their activities. They'll do fine.

"What I will need is some uniforms to check out the Bluff area for any witnesses and to follow up on anything I turn up with the boyfriend or that comes out of the Edina side of things. Three, four guys should do fine. And Nettie will need some help putting together the routine record search stuff. She'll nail down what she needs there. Doc D and the crime-scene guys are getting together with me first thing tomorrow, so I'll touch back then, let you know how things stand. After I meet with them tomorrow A.M., I'm going back to the Fitzgerald's. The boyfriend's due sometime tomorrow morning, and I want to be there when he shows up."

Back in the squad room, Mars sat down at his desk and put his feet up. He punched out Denise's number. As the line rang, he glanced at his watch. Good grief. It was already almost 9:00 P.M. Chris would be in bed, but Mars was sure he'd be awake.

Simultaneously, Denise and Chris said, "Hello."

"Keep it short, kiddo. Hi, Marshall." Denise hung up her line.

"Dad? Who's dead? Can I stay up to watch the ten o'clock news?"

"A girl who should have lived a long, happy life. And there won't be anything on the news. You can stay up to watch the ten o'clock news tomorrow night. How was Scouts?"

"Boring. Did she get shot?"

"Nope. Stabbed."

"You call Nettie yet?"

Mars smiled. Nettie and Mars had been partnering since Mars had taken on his new assignment as a special detective. And Nettie and Chris had become soulmates shortly thereafter.

"I call Nettie as soon as I hang up with you."

CHAPTER
7

Her given name was Jeanette.

If she'd gone by Jean, it would have fit. But she went by Nettie. Nettie Frisch. A name that gave rise to the image of a plump woman with frizzy hair, padding around in Birkenstocks.

Nettie Frisch, in the flesh, didn't fit that image or any of its parts. She was sleek and glossy, with high-shine, precision-cut black hair, chalk white skin, and sharply angled features. She wore only black and white clothes because, she said, it made life simpler.

She got stared at by people trying to reason out the unusual combination of her features. Individually those features were not attractive, but as the result of some mathematical law of aesthetics, in which negative values combine for a positive result, Nettie was, at a minimum, striking. There were many who confused Nettie's style with beauty, which in Mars's judgment was a mistake.

When Mars and Chief Turner met after their first conversation about Mars's future in the department, the chief gave Mars an attractive option. The chief proposed a plan for two special detective units within the Homicide Division. He wanted Mars to head what he called the First Response Unit, which would report directly to the chief. The FRU would focus on high-profile cases that didn't have drug or gang connections, could log overtime without prior approval, and could draw resources it needed from anywhere in the department. The chief had informal approval from the police union for the plan and the mayor had committed funding. The second unit would focus on drug- and gang-related homicides and Jim Risser, an officer Mars respected but didn't much like, would be asked to head that unit. It was a savvy strategy. Mars being given a plum assignment on his own wouldn't have been doable politically. But Risser was popular on the force and with him as part of the package, it flew. That—and the fact that both jobs were jobs anyone in the division would want to aim for—got it through.

For Mars, it was close to a perfect job. Not just because it gave him access to resources when he needed them, but because it kept him out of the management side of things, which had always been part of other promotion opportunities he'd considered but passed up.

The one thing the chief's proposal didn't resolve was Mars's partner problems.

Mars thought about it and came back with a request. He wanted to pull Nettie Frisch from the division's administrative section and have her assigned as his partner.

"Why Nettie?" the chief had asked. "I'd give you anybody you wanted. Henderson. Couldn't do better than Henderson."

"Because," Mars said, "I want what I don't already have. Henderson would just duplicate me. I want somebody who'll stay on top of the paper, who'll develop databases, keep track of where we are on different stuff. Nettie'll do that. Besides which, Nettie thinks real close to the ground. I'll go off doing what I do, making assumptions that get me in trouble, that lead me off the path, and Nettie will ask a simple question. Exactly the *right* question. Plain commonsense kind of thing. It'll bring me right back where I need to be. Henderson—

he'd be off making the same assumptions I'm making. To-gether we'd get ourselves so deep in the woods we'd never find our way back."

The chief frowned. "Problem is, I'm gonna have a hell of a time getting the union to go along with pulling someone out of the admin pool and making them a detective. She's got no training credentials, no uniform experience—"

Mars interrupted. "I'm not suggesting Nettie would be a sworn officer. Not even sure that's something she'd want. What I'm saying is, instead of putting me with another sworn officer, just give me the administrative support."

The chief shrugged. "It's your call. That's what you want, go get it."

Nettie came into work every day with a liter bottle of Evian water. She'd walk into the squad room and head straight for the fridge, which sat next to a row of file cabinets on the far wall. She'd put the Evian bottle into the freezer for a couple hours, until it was partially frozen. Then, taking it to her desk, she'd slam the bottle bottom on the top of her desk—causing anyone in the squad room at the time to jump off their chairs. Then she had a bottle of chipped-ice drink she'd swig from for the rest of the day.

When Mars sat down to talk to Nettie about the change, she looked at him hard and without pleasure. "I don't think that would work for me," she said.

Mars felt a little silly at his disappointment that she wasn't sputtering with gratitude at what he offered. Then he realized it wasn't just a crazy scheme he'd pulled out of the air in response to the chief's open-ended offer. He'd been counting on her to take the job to make his own new job work.

He tried to stay calm. "Why not?"

"What about my Evian water?"

"Your *Evian water*? What does your Evian water have to do with you getting promoted as my partner?"

"Unless you're willing to put a freezer in the backseat of the Pontiac, I don't see how it would work. I really need ice-cold Evian to get through the day."

"You're not listening, Nettie. I don't want a partner riding around with me in the Pontiac holding on to a lukewarm bottle of Evian. I want you right here. Holding down the fort, doing your thing on the computer. Keeping the investigation organized. Pretty much what you do now, except you'd be dedicated to the investigations I'd be working on. I wouldn't have to stand in line to get you to do stuff. We could work whatever hours we needed to."

"Oh," she said. "Well, that would be okay. I guess. As long as I don't have to run all over town dealing with the scum of the earth."

"I'll even move your desk right next to the fridge, if that'd make a difference."

"No, that won't be necessary."

Mars called Nettie at around 9:30 P.M. There was no answer first time around, but she picked up on the first ring when he called at 9:45.

"Hello?"

"Chris said I needed to call."

"Did he say why?"

"Dead girl found down on the Father Hennepin Bluffs."

"I bet it was that girl—what was her name, the one the detox crew thought was dead when they picked her up last week—Wanda something. The Indian girl."

"Nope. Near as I know, Wanda still walks the earth, although probably not in a straight line. The girl we found was a beautiful blond from Edina. I spent most of the afternoon with her folks, trying to get them and Phil Keck to believe something this bad could be real."

"Oh, my God. Her Honor must be having a cow."

"Her Honor is counting on me, and by association on you, to pin this one on a fellow Edinan. Wash our urban hands of the mess, so to speak. I trust you had no more compelling plans for the remainder of the evening?"

"I'll be down in about a half hour."

By the time Nettie showed up in black jeans and a black cotton V-neck over a starched white shirt, Mars had three possible lines of investigation worked out. Flipping his cigarette box back and forth between his right and left hands, he laid it out.

First, that Mary Pat Fitzgerald had either planned to meet her boyfriend at Southdale or he planned to run into her there. That the boyfriend had talked Mary Pat down to the bluffs and killed her—for whatever reason.

Second, that Mary Pat had run into someone she knew at Southdale—other than the boyfriend—and for reasons unknown, the two of them had decided to go to the bluffs. And *that* person had, for whatever reason, done the deed.

Third, when Mary Pat went out to the parking lot and found her car with a flat tire, she started to walk the seven, eight blocks between Southdale and Cornelia Drive. On the way, someone offered her a ride that ended with Mary Pat dead on the bluffs.

Of the three possibilities, the logical one was the first. The one that felt right to Mars was the third. But it was too early to say why.

He and Nettie worked out what Nettie needed to do over the next forty-eight hours. Nettie would start putting together the case profile they'd run through the FBI's database. Nettie would maintain contacts with the Edina investigators doing basic legwork with the folks at Southdale. Nettie would work up and assign interviews to patrolmen to conduct along the bluffs. Nettie would work with the Public Affairs Office to get a statement ready for the press, making sure it got cleared first through the chief's office, and in this case, the mayor's office as well.

That sorted out, they sat back and took stock of where they were. Mars said, "You've got fifteen seconds: 'God forgive me, but I love it.'"

"*Patton.* George C. Scott is standing on the battlefield looking at a bunch of dead bodies."

Mars snapped his fingers. "Bingo."

Nettie said, "Now that the games have begun, what's first on your to-do list?"

"I need to start lining up what we've got on each of our three theories underlying the investigation so I can start proving—or disproving—the theories. Once we can narrow down the investigation to one of the three, it's going to help a lot. And I've got to pin down what we know, what we don't know, where we can find out what we need to know."

Nettie stretched and yawned. "Well. I think I'm ready for tomorrow. You going back to your apartment at all tonight?"

"Nah. Think I'll keep going while I've got adrenaline working for me. *Oh, geez.* I told Phil Keck I'd call him about six hours ago. I wonder if the asshole has moved from the phone since then."

"It'll keep him out of trouble if he hasn't. I'm shoving off. See you in the A.M."

"It *is* the A.M., Nettie."

"So? I'm still right."

When the adrenaline ran out, Mars couldn't have said for sure. But he'd been sleeping with his head down on his desk when something caused him to wake with a start around 7:00 A.M.

Doc D was sitting at Nettie's desk, reading the Sunday paper. In violation of all city administrative policies, Doc D held a burning cigarette in his right hand.

"You were up all night?" Mars asked, rubbing his eyes.

Doc D continued reading the paper. "No. Wasn't much of a job. Like we were saying at the scene, there's not a lot coming out of this one." He drew the pages of the paper together, flapped it shut, and pulled a narrow notebook from his back pocket.

Squinting at the notebook, he said, "Couple of things, though."

Mars smiled. "You want some coffee?"

"If it's being offered, I wouldn't say no."

Doc D started talking while Mars walked over to the coffeepot Nettie'd left on. Mars sloshed the dregs of the pot into a paper cup and carried the cup back to Doc D.

"What I find most intriguing—apart from the fact there's so little of the kind of thing you'd *expect* to find in a violent death—is that the kid had a belly full of gin. Blood alcohol was high—point two-one—but nothing like it would have been if what was in her stomach had made it into her bloodstream before she died. If all that gin had made it into her bloodstream, the gin alone coulda killed her."

Half to himself, Mars said. "Like mother, like daughter."

"Say what?"

"I was just thinking that the kid's mother looked like an alkie to me." Mars got up and shook himself. Walked around to loosen up, get the juices flowing again. "You said at the scene that you'd thought you'd be able to tell better what the weapon was?..."

"Looks like, say, a three-eighths-inch screwdriver. A very clean entry wound, directly to the aorta, delivered with enormous force. No shoving in some, taking another draw and shoving again. Then, once it was all the way in, he did a nice little twist—holding the shaft pretty straight—that tore the shit out of the aorta but left the entry wound smooth. Very nice piece of work if you wanted someone to lose a lot of blood fast, and not make much of a mess while you were at it."

"How long would she have lived after she took the hit?"

"Given the hole in the aorta, she would have gotten light-headed within, say, fifteen seconds. Blacked out in another forty-five seconds. In combination with the alcohol, she wouldn't have been able to stand up after she got the shiv."

"No sexual assault?"

"Well, she wasn't the Virgin Mary, if you take my point. But there was no evidence of recent intercourse, no sperm or any trauma to the vagina. What I did find under the scalp was a very substantial cephalohematoma. Fresh. Someone had grabbed her good by the hair—so hard that the scalp separated from the cranium. The cephalohematoma was toward the rear of the cranium, on the right side, and under her jaw, left side, there was a puncture wound. Barely enough to draw blood, but enough to hurt. Remember the dirt on the knees of the pants? My guess is you had it about right. The guy had her kneel down, so he'd have real good leverage, then he grabbed her by the hair with one hand and stuck her under the jaw with the pick."

"I'm not getting it. What is it he wants her to do? She hasn't been raped, she wasn't robbed. What's the guy's motive to go for the aorta? She's got enough alcohol in her system to let him pretty much do whatever he wants anyway. If it's a rage killing, one jab isn't gonna provide much gratification." Mars sighed. "Or why, if she was as drunk as she was, would he have to use an ice pick to get her in line. I'm not liking this. What else have you got?"

Doc D stubbed out his cigarette and did not, as was his practice, immediately light another. He looked at Mars directly. "This is what I found most interesting. You remember the Weissie wristwatch? Stopped at eleven-oh-five on the third? With a blood alcohol of point two-one, she wouldn't have been capable of doing the fine motor movements she'd need to stop the watch. Especially if she was trying to do it without someone noticing her doing it. So when she did it, she was more or less sober." Doc D stopped, took out a cigarette, but did not light it.

"My guess is that—for whatever reason—the guy grabbed her hair, stuck her under the chin with the pick—and that's the moment she knew she was in trouble. That's when she stopped the watch. She started drinking, or at least started drinking heavily after she stopped the watch. Then you've gotta ask yourself, why would she start drinking with the guy after she knows she's in trouble? And not just have a drink to pretend to be sociable, to try and talk her way out of trouble. Drink enough to get her blood alcohol to point two-one. I mean, go figure. At eleven-oh-five she thought she was going to die. I'm guessing if you could find out why she'd get drunk once she knew that, you'd have something worth knowing."

CHAPTER
8

There'd been too much coming and going at the Fitzgerald house the day before to suit Mars, but when he turned down Cornelia Drive on Sunday morning around ten o'clock it was clear the traffic problem had gotten worse.

He was nearly a block away when he noticed that cars were parked solid on both sides of the street. Pulling up in front of the Fitzgeralds', he saw a cluster of high school girls standing on the lawn, eyes and noses red from crying. They hugged and cried more. Phil Keck was standing on the front steps, talking earnestly to a couple who looked like they were on their way to or from church. Another pair pushed their way out the front door, giving Keck a pat and a handshake as they left.

Mars double-parked, locking in a bright orange Saab convertible. He walked across the grass, royally pissed not only that Keck had allowed the house to turn into Grand Central Station, but that Keck seemed to view his role as social director. Keck should have been back at the station, working the investigation.

Mars was close enough to smell Keck's aftershave lotion before Keck noticed him.

"Mars! We need to talk. I've been waiting for your call. Come on over and meet..."

71

Mars nodded at the couple but kept walking, pulling Keck into the front hallway. A woman approached, dipping down to smooth her hair in front of a wall mirror. The kitchen was to the immediate left of the front hall. Mars could see a group of women standing in front of an open refrigerator. They were rearranging the contents of the refrigerator to accommodate a tableful of foil-covered dishes.

Mars said, "You've got to clear the house. All I want around is the Fitzgerald family and, if she's here, the Prince girl."

"Whoaaa . . ." Keck held up both hands. "This isn't some crack house in the inner city, Special Detective. Folks out here expect to be treated with courtesy, even when—I should say *especially* when—a family member has been murdered. If the Fitzgeralds want to be alone, we'll have the house cleared. But last I heard, this was their house, and I'm not about to tell them who can and can't be here."

Mars said, "Let's take a trip to the garage."

Looking confused, Keck followed Mars through the kitchen into the attached garage. They found three teenagers smoking.

"Excuse me," Mars said. "Chief Keck and I need you back in the house just now."

The girl spoke. "We can't smoke in the house."

"So put your cigarettes out. I need you gone. Now."

The girl twisted her mouth in an expression of resentment and brushed by Mars, knocking him slightly as she passed. The two guys were grinning and indifferent. *Better zip codes,* Mars thought, *don't make better teenagers.*

He turned to Keck.

"You're not getting it, Phil. This isn't an awkward social situation where you get points for good manners. We've got one of your kids dead on my ground. So Minneapolis PD is on the hook. If people are offended by what we have to do to get a handle on this case, I can't help that. But I can tell you this. You'd better brace yourself. I've never seen a murder investigation where the family didn't find out more about the victim than they wanted to know. And I damn well don't want to spend the rest of the investigation butting into you because you're worried someone's going to feel bad. It comes with the territory. Somebody's been murdered, and everybody's going to feel bad. Now, you can go back in the house and clear it out, or I'll do it. What's it gonna be?"

Keck had turned away from Mars. In profile, his face was tight with the tension of indignation and uncertainty. He stubbed the cement floor with a highly polished tassled loafer once or twice before answering. "You say you want *our* support. *I* haven't heard anything since you left here yesterday. I've got the family and half the population of Edina banging on my door and I don't know anything more than they know. I've got the management of Southdale breathing down my neck wanting to straighten out their involvement. You want our cooperation, it's got to be a two-way street."

Mars grimaced inwardly. Keck had a point. Mars finessed. "I'd like to sit down with you and the family. Talk about what we know so far. I can't do that with a house full of people. Let's get this situation under control." Then, pausing, "I apologize for not getting back to you yesterday. Fact is, I didn't know much of anything until early this morning, after I met with the ME. One thing: I'm gonna want your investigators to follow up on people Mary Pat partied with, people she spent time with when she was going to tie one on."

"I don't need to talk to my investigators about that. I can tell you here and now that Mary Pat Fitzgerald didn't drink, didn't do drugs, didn't smoke. That's a given."

"And I can tell you that it's a given that Mary Pat had a

blood alcohol of point two one at the time of death, with enough gin still in her stomach to kill her if she hadn't died first from a puncture wound to the aorta."

Phil Keck stared at him. "That's not possible. Not Mary Pat. She fucking *hated* drinking." Keck looked back toward the house; Mars knew he was thinking about Mother Fitz. "If Mary Pat had a blood alcohol of point two one, someone was forcing her to drink. She wouldn't have done it on her own."

"It's like I said, Phil. Every murder investigation, you find out things you'd rather not know. You and the family are going to have to remember everything you know about Mary Pat down to the smallest detail. And you're going to have to be open to the possibility that there was a side of Mary Pat you didn't know. That's what's needed if we're going to figure out what happened. Okay?"

Keck looked subdued. "Let's go back in," he said. "I'll talk to Doc about having people leave. I think it'll go better if he asks, rather than having me order people around."

And easier on your image, Mars thought. He followed Keck back through the kitchen into the living room. Within fifteen minutes the crowd had cleared, and Mars sat with Keck, Doc, and Mrs. Fitzgerald in the living room. Becky Prince, they said, had been over first thing that morning, but had left to pick up Robert Fitzgerald, Jr., at the airport. They were expected momentarily.

The Fitzgeralds were existing in the high-oxygen interlude that follows tragedy, when normal activities and responsibilities become irrelevant. Mother Fitz's reactions were hard to gauge behind the dark glasses. Doc's face looked strained, but he continued to play the role of gracious host.

Mars was gentle, choosing his words carefully. He spoke of a quick death, assuring them that Mary Pat had not been mutilated or sexually assaulted. And then, in a quiet voice, "I think you should know that Mary Pat's blood alcohol level was high. Can you think of anything that might have upset her, that might have caused her to drink more than she usually would?"

Mother Fitz's cup stopped midway in the air. Doc's face froze in an expression of disbelief. "Blood alcohol level? Mary Pat? This just isn't possible. Mary Pat wasn't a drinker. Wouldn't even go out with anyone who drank. If she went to a party where the drinking got out of hand, she'd come home early. When she was a sophomore, she broke up with a boy she liked because she thought he drank too much. You remember, Mother . . . that Kerry boy, Don and Elise Kerry's oldest boy—"

Mars interrupted. "I know from what everyone's said that it wasn't typical behavior. But the simple fact is that her blood alcohol level was very high. And precisely because it wasn't usual for her, it's important to know why she was drinking on Thursday morning. If there was something that upset her, that made her act out of character. *Someone* she might have hooked up with if she was going to drink. It might have been someone she wouldn't have spent time with. . . ."

Doc got up and paced the room. "This is a nightmare." He stopped suddenly, covered his face with his hands. A wrenching, sharp cry came from under his hands. His shoulders shook. Phil Keck rose and put an arm around Doc. Mars noticed that Mother Fitz didn't move from her chair or change her expression. As he thought about it, he realized he hadn't seen Mother Fitz and Doc touch during the past two days.

They all started when the front doorbell chimed.

Mars walked to the bay window that faced Cornelia Drive. There was no sign of the blue Ford pickup they were expecting Brian to be driving. He couldn't see who was at the front door, so he told Keck to get it, adding, "I don't want anyone else coming in. No more hot casseroles." Mars moved

75

near the front hallway to listen as Keck walked to the door. The visitor was one of Keck's investigators, a tiny, freckle-faced brunette Mars had met the day before.

"Sorry to butt in, Chief, but something's come up I thought you should know about right away."

Keck stepped back to let her in. Lt. Toni Andorf noticed Mars and gave him a crisp nod, flushing slightly. Mars could tell she cared about making an impression.

"A counselor at Edina mentioned that one of her coun-selees—Erin Moss—was unusually jealous of Mary Pat. So I followed up by going over to talk to Erin, and she said some-thing I thought you should know before you interview the boyfriend. She said it was common knowledge around school that Brian had been physically abusive to Mary Pat. Erin saw Brian and Mary Pat at a basketball game earlier this year, saw him hit Mary Pat so hard she fell to the floor." Lt. Andorf stopped and waited for a response.

"Have you talked to anyone who confirms that?" Mars asked.

"That's just it. It's like everybody clams up when I ask if Brian and Mary Pat had any relationship problems. They don't say no, they just look away and shrug. The Moss girl is the only one who'll say anything, but like the counselor said, she's more than happy to say something negative about Mary Pat."

"You talk to the Prince girl . . . Becky?"

Toni Andorf made a face. "*Her*. Like she's going to give me the time of day. Everybody says, 'Talk to Becky,' but no-body says how I'm gonna get Becky to talk. She's a spoiled brat, if you ask me."

"Keep talking to the other kids. It may be important to have more than one person document the abuse angle. And one other thing. Push on whether people knew that Mary Pat occasionally got stone-cold drunk."

Mars returned to the living room before Keck came back. He faced the Fitzgeralds' expectant faces. They didn't need to hear Andorf's news. "Nothing. Just one of Phil's officers, checking in."

It wasn't more than a half hour after Toni Andorf left when Robert Fitzgerald, Jr., and Becky Prince arrived. Even Mother Fitz got up when Bobby Fitzgerald came into the living room. For the first time, Mars felt he was seeing a family as he watched the mother and father embrace what was now their only child.

Bobby's face had the same look of blank disbelief as his father's, but a sense of deep emotion was much closer to the surface. He wasn't in the same state of denial as his parents. In a few moments he turned to Keck.

"What do you know? What happened? Do you have any idea . . ."

Keck looked sideways at Mars, not certain that he should answer. When Mars stayed silent, Keck said, "We don't know very much. We're anxious to talk to Brian. We hope there'll be some answers there."

"Why Brian? You're wasting your time if you're checking out Brian. He's a good kid, he wouldn't do something like this."

Mars and Keck exchanged glances. Mars spoke. "In a situation like this, it's more likely than not that Mary Pat was killed by someone she knew. That's why we have to check all of you out pretty carefully, not just Brian. Statistically, that's just the way it is."

Bobby Fitzgerald sputtered. "So. While you're spinning your wheels chasing statistical probabilities, whoever did it gets harder to get, right?"

"I can understand from your perspective it looks like all we're doing is focusing on the obvious. But between Phil and me, we've got almost two dozen officers working this case. We've got people combing Southdale for witnesses who saw Mary Pat while she was there. We've got people checking out anyone who might have seen her walking back to Cornelia Drive after she found the flat on her car. We're working with Edina administrators to identify who Mary Pat spent time with at school. I've got officers down on the bluffs interviewing vagrants who live under the bridges and interviewing people who worked in the buildings on Southeast Main above the bluffs. I've got people down at city hall running computer searches based on what we know about what happened, running down creeps who get involved in this kind of thing and might have been around. The point is, we're not just kicking back and waiting for Brian to show up."

Hands on his hips, Bobby paced. Mars's answer may not have satisfied him, but it shut him up. Watching him, Mars decided Bobby looked like his sister. Their coloring was different. Bobby had a head of curly auburn hair, but the bone structure and the perfectly proportioned body came from the same genetic stuff.

"Brian's here."

Becky Prince had been staring out the front bay window since she'd come in. She made an immediate move toward the front door.

Mars said sharply, *"No!"* He turned to Doc. "Dr. Fitzgerald, answer the front door without saying anything to Brian. Just ask him to come into the living room." Mars half turned to the others. "The rest of you. Please, say nothing until I've told Brian about Mary Pat."

Mars moved quickly to the side of the picture window to watch Brian. The kid was still in his truck, with the driver-side door ajar. He slid out of the front seat, started to shut the door, stopped, leaned across the cab, pulled back, and shut the door, taking a skipping jump across the curb and onto the lawn. He caught himself short and detoured to the sidewalk, a longer path to the front door. The kind of move a kid who cared what his girlfriend's parents thought about him would make.

Every muscle in Mar's body tightened, and the poison juice of doubt shot through his gut. Not doubt. Certainty. The kid didn't have a clue. There was not a hint of self-consciousness, wariness, or tension in Brian Peterson.

So much for moving this mess back to Edina fast, was what Mars thought.

CHAPTER
9

There was a full cast of characters in the mayor's office by the time Mars arrived, the mayor, the chief, Nettie, and Glenn Gjerde, an assistant prosecuting attorney from the Hennepin County Attorney's Office. Mars was running late, and they were pushing hard against their 3:00 P.M. target for releasing Mary Pat's ID.

The mayor looked up as Mars came in. She did a quick double take. Looking at her looking at him, Mars remembered that he hadn't shaved or changed clothes for two days.

"My oh my. Don't we look cute, Special Detective. Do you intend to wear that outfit for the duration of the investigation?"

"Phil Keck is in charge of cute on this one," Mars said, pulling up a chair.

"And doing a fine job, I'm sure," the mayor answered. "Now that we've got cute covered, why don't we put you in charge of good news. Let's have it."

"You must know something I don't," Mars said.

The mayor groaned. "So what happened to our great white hope, the boyfriend?"

"Well, I think he's going to do just fine for us on limited circumstantial evidence for the next day or two, until we get his alibi sorted out. But even without the alibi, I'm pretty sure he's not our guy. Not a trace of guilty conscience in sight. Genuine shock when he got the news. He's asthmatic. So when he gets the news, he has an attack—I mean he turns blue. We came close to calling nine-one-one. We get him stabilized, and he keeps processing the information and slipping back into 'She's not dead.' If it was an act, he had me fooled."

"How's his alibi?" the chief asked.

"Like I said before, he goes up to Itasca County every spring, cuts wood to bring back to sell. He left Thursday morning—he thinks about eight-thirty. He talked to Mary Pat on the phone just before he left. No problems there. Said he'd stop by when he got back Sunday.

"When I first asked him if anybody could verify his whereabouts between nine A.M. and one P.M. on Thursday, he says *no*. That he didn't see anyone on Thursday at all, that he got up to his cousin's place around one, chopped wood until dark, then slept in the cousin's cabin. Friday he went into Chisholm, had breakfast, same on Saturday. Sunday morning he loads the pickup with wood he didn't have room for a year ago. Figures he'll try and sell some yet this spring. Thinks he left Itasca County around nine-thirty, maybe ten o'clock. Gassed up the truck at a station in Chisholm before heading back to the Cities. So what we've got as far as the investigation goes—is that he was in his truck, heading north on Thursday morning, with nobody who can ID him during the critical time period. So far, so good.

"But when I push him on how long it took him to get to Itasca on Thursday, he says he got there around one-thirty P.M., maybe a little after. I say, 'Why's that? Can't be more than a two-and-a-half, three-hour drive and you said you left at eight-thirty.' He shifts around, looks blank, then remembers he stopped on Highway Two, just north of the Fond du Lac

Indian Reservation to help a woman with three kids who was having car trouble. He figures that was around eleven-thirty, noon.

"I look at him. He looks at me. He says, 'Oh, right. I forgot about her.' But he doesn't know her name or anything. Says she looked like she was Indian, probably was heading to the res. Said the car was a big old gas-burning Buick. Junker, rusted out, two-tone. Doesn't recall the plates. So, as soon as we find that woman, our great white hope is off the hook."

Glenn Gjerde stood. "This doesn't much sound like you're going to need me anytime soon."

The mayor held up a well-manicured hand. "Hold on. Mars, you said we had some good circumstantial evidence on the boy. Wouldn't it at least be prudent to take him into custody, get the truck impounded—pending our getting the alibi pinned down?"

Mars, Nettie, the chief, and Gjerde all exchanged glances. No one missed what the mayor was up to. In a measured voice Mars answered, staring directly into her eyes. "I said we had some *limited* circumstantial evidence. What we've got is a critical time period not pinned down—but a pretty plausible story—and one witness who saw Brian hit Mary Pat. . . ."

"He's *hit* her? And you're calling that limited circumstantial evidence?"

"We don't know if he did for sure, and we don't know what the circumstances were if he did."

"Oh, I get it," the mayor said. "If he had good reason for hitting her it doesn't count?" The mayor was not much of a feminist, but she knew an opportunity when she saw it. She turned to Gjerde and the chief. "Am I missing something here, or do we have a basis for bringing the kid in until his alibi pans out?"

The chief was off the mark before Gjerde could weigh in. "I agree with Mars. There's not a lot to go on here. And

I trust Mars's judgment. If the kid seems credible, that counts. Either way, the kid is going to take a beating on this deal, and I don't want to expose him to unnecessary speculation."

To Mars he said, "Am I right that we *have* impounded the pickup?"

Nettie unscrewed the cap of her Evian bottle and took a deep swig before she said, "It was picked up from the Fitzgeralds. The Peterson kid signed a release for a search on the spot. But based on what we got from Doc D and the crime-scene guys, even if Brian did it, I don't think the truck is going to tell us much. I got the Crime Scene Unit's preliminary report just before I came up here, and they haven't found any evidence she was killed anywhere but on the bluffs. Fact is, they don't have much of anything: no prints, no body fluids, nothing on the ground. But in looking at Doc D's report, he noted that after she took the shaft to the aorta, the pooling of blood in her chest cavity was consistent with her falling forward and staying in that position until we found her. So it's pretty clear Mary Pat got stabbed and died at the same place. That being the case, we're not going to find any blood in the truck. And even if we find her prints, she must have ridden in the truck a thousand times, so her prints are going to be all over anyway."

Mars said to everyone in general and the mayor in particular, "I don't want it released that we've impounded the truck. That's just normal investigative procedure. We release that and it's the same as saying we think Brian did it."

The mayor's face set. She didn't look at Mars. Looking at the chief, she said, "I'd like to know how we'd be handling this if some black guy on the near north side had just shot his girlfriend. Am I wrong, or would he be sitting in a cell on the third floor as we speak?" The mayor was no more a civil libertarian than she was a feminist, but once again, she wasn't about to miss an opportunity.

The chief didn't flinch. "Madam Mayor, I want to assure you it would depend entirely on the circumstances of the case. If the suspect's girlfriend was dead and all we had was he couldn't prove where he was at the time of death, I'd like to think he'd be exactly where Brian Peterson is under the same circumstances."

"Except he probably wouldn't be in Edina," Glenn Gjerde said, moving toward the door. "Why don't you call me if something comes up and you need some legal papers fast. Nettie's got my pager number." He waved as he walked out.

The tension was thick as Mars, Nettie, the chief, and the mayor went over the statement that would accompany the release of Mary Pat's ID. The mayor and the chief debated having his name on the release as the contact person rather than listing the department's public information officer. The chief had a lot of confidence in the IO and saw no reason for departing from standard procedure. The mayor wanted to send a signal that the city was pulling out the stops to clear the case. In the end, the chief convinced the mayor that the IO could be trusted to bring him in on any sensitive inquiries and that they'd take heat for handling a white suburbanite's murder differently than a city resident's. It was a message the mayor didn't miss.

"Do we need to schedule a news conference?" Nettie asked.

"We'll probably want something tomorrow," the chief said. "By then there'll be a herd of reporters trampling all over the bluffs and Southdale."

Mars and Nettie walked back with the chief to his office after they left the mayor. Mars was still ticked. He didn't trust the mayor to play fair with Brian Peterson. The chief tried to play peacemaker. "I don't agree with the mayor that we're giving the Peterson kid special treatment just because he's a white guy from Edina. Based on what we've got so far, his not being in custody is perfectly reasonable. But it's also true—even if it isn't fair—that in a situation like this, the boyfriend is gonna get tarred. Just the way it is."

Mars said, "I understand that. I just don't want us doing anything to set him up. The media knows all the key phrases: 'Investigators are interviewing individuals close to the Fitzgerald family,' 'Investigators have not ruled out that the victim's boyfriend, Brian Peterson, may be involved,' or 'Police sources say Brian Peterson has not been able to account for his whereabouts during the critical time period on Thursday, April third. . . .' You know how that kind of stuff plays as well as I do."

"Why aren't you comfortable with what we agreed to in the statement?" the chief asked.

" 'Minneapolis and Edina police are pursuing all normal lines of investigation at this time.' . . . Couldn't be more boilerplate. . . ."

"I'm fine with that, as long as the mayor doesn't go further with a few comments of her own. That's all I'm saying."

Mars went back to the squad room to go over reports that were in so far. Like Nettie said, the Crime Scene Unit guys had turned up zilch. The ground was still too hard to yield anything by way of footprints, and it was clear the perp had had limited physical contact with Mary Pat. It being a weekend, the file of interviews with people who worked in the Pillsbury A Mill or in the converted warehouses along Main Street was still pretty thin. Nettie had half a dozen guys lined up to comb those sites starting first thing in the morning. She'd had photos of Mary Pat duplicated from the picture Mars had taken from the Fitzgeralds. Doc Fitzgerald had been cropped out of the photo. Mars held up the eight-by-ten black-and-white glossy of Mary Pat and stared at it. Mrs. Fitzgerald said the picture had been taken in February. Just a couple of months earlier. The haphazardness of life always struck Mars. The image of someone standing on a golf course in Arizona with a camera focused on a beautiful young girl and her father came into his mind. There was nothing to suggest that in two months the image the camera was capturing would be of a dead girl, that the photo would appear in Twin Cities newspapers. That the photo would be carried all over the Cities by cops asking if anyone had seen the girl in the picture on Thursday morning, April 3.

He turned to the files that Nettie had collected from the Edina investigators. No more statements from anyone saying that Brian had been abusive to Mary Pat. Two clerks at South-dale reported seeing Mary Pat just after nine-thirty. One had helped with the fitting of her prom dress. The second was a classmate who worked part-time at Dayton's. She'd seen Mary Pat walking through the store just before ten. *Jeez.* And an hour later, Mary Pat was on the bluffs, knowing she was going to die.

It was almost 9:45 P.M. when Mars had finished going through the files and making notes about things he and Nettie'd need to do next. He'd missed calling Chris. Then he remembered that he'd told Chris he could stay up to watch the ten o'clock news, so he called.

Chris answered.

"Dad? I told Mom you said I could stay up. You find who killed that girl yet?"

"No such luck. What you been up to today?"

"I was over at James's. We watched part of the Twins game and played Nintendo. Dad, can we watch the news together?"

"Sure. Only I'm still down at city hall. I'll have to go into the lounge and watch on that set. I'll finish up a couple little things and call you right back."

The employee lounge just the other side of the squad room had a pop machine, two plastic couches with metal tube arms, a floor lamp, and a small laminated wood table with an old black-and-white TV sitting on it. A wall phone hung to the side of one of the couches. Mars fiddled with the set, managing to bring up an image and acceptable audio, sat down, and called Chris again.

"Don't expect too much tonight. They've just got the ID and they're still getting their acts together on what they're covering. Tomorrow will be the first big day and, no, you can't stay up late to watch tomorrow. Tape it."

The faded image of Channel Four's two weekend anchors popped out. They chatted amiably about the weekend weather and professed curiosity about what the rest of the week would be. A third, sad face joined the anchors to lament a bad weekend for the Twins, promising details later in the program. The two anchors bucked each other up.

"Still early in the season, though, Bruce."

"That's right, Nancy, the Twins have a long way to go, and Larry has a preview later on in the program about new players on the team who are creating real optimism that this season could be a replay of nineteen eighty-seven and nineteen ninety-one."

The camera shifted to a tight front angle on the woman anchor. Her face became appropriately serious as she said, "On a tragic front, Bruce, and leading tonight's news, the Minneapolis police released this afternoon the name of a young Edina woman whose partially clad body was found on the riverfront yesterday morning. Let's go to Linda Ronay who's live on the scene. Linda, what can you tell us about the girl who was killed and what police know about her killer?"

Mars groaned.

Chris immediately said, "What?"

"Linda Ronay. She's the absolute worst. Always reports every story like it's the apocalypse. Quiet now . . . I want to hear this."

Ronay, microphone in hand, heavily lit by kliegs, was standing at the head of the stairs leading down to the bluff trails, just above where Mary Pat had been found.

"Nancy, shocking news this afternoon from the Minneapolis PD. The girl's body found on the bluffs Saturday morning has been identified as Mary Pat Fitzgerald. A senior at Edina High School, Mary Pat may have been the last person you'd expect to find dead under these circumstances." The scene shifted to a late afternoon shot of the Fitzgerald's house. Then, a shot of Phil Keck talking to Ronay. Mars suppressed another groan so as not to provoke a question from Chris. Phil went through the litany of Mary Pat's achievements. He had tears in his eyes as he talked.

The camera came in tight again on Linda. "Bruce and Nancy, investigators say it's much too early to say yet what happened to Mary Pat Fitzgerald, but Edina police chief Phil Keck says early indications are this was a random event and that Mary Pat Fitzgerald did not know her attacker."

"Fuck!"

"Dad? Number one?"

"No. This fuck doesn't have a number. Chris, I've gotta go. Talk to you tomorrow."

Mars's phone was ringing by the time he got back to his desk. He was expecting it to be the chief, or worse yet, Her Honor herself. It was Phil Keck.

"Mars? Jesus Christ, Mars. I didn't say what that woman on Channel Four said at all. Honest to God. She kept pressing me on what we thought happened and all I said was, at this point, as far as we knew, it could be anything. It could be a friend, it could be a complete stranger. Honest to God, Mars—"

Mars said, "Keck. At this point it doesn't matter what you

did or didn't say. The damage's been done. I spent a half an hour this afternoon trying to get the mayor to cool off on Brian Peterson, and I can tell you after the news tonight she's gonna go after him hard. You'll have yourself to thank for that."

"But Mars. Put yourself in my place. What could I have said that would've been okay? I swear, I didn't—"

"It's simple Phil. All you had to say was, 'Sorry. If you've got any questions call the information office at the Minneapolis PD.' Write that down, Phil. This isn't gonna be your last opportunity to screw up before we're done."

By Monday morning, the media swarm was in full swing. Mars knew personally most of the print and TV reporters who covered the police beat, so he made it a point to stay away from city hall. He called in to pick up messages, and Nettie said he had twenty-one pink slips from eight reporters. "I'm just telling them to call the IO, which is making them mad as hops."

"They scheduled a press conference yet?"

"At five o'clock. It'll run live on the five o'clock news shows. The chief and Her Honor are giving a bunch of interviews afterwards that'll run on the six o'clock and ten o'clock news."

"What's the *Strib* up to?"

"Something, for sure. They've been asking for details on how many people we've got working on the case and how many were assigned to Deanna Rae Cater's case in March. My guess is, they're gonna run a comparison of how the two cases were managed."

"Predictable. Any progress on pinning down the kid's alibi?"

"Nothing yet. I've actually got Edina following that up. Figure they're motivated. They've called the tribal office and asked them to get the word out—they've faxed a notice for the tribe to put up. I've seen the mayor's statement, and she's not saying anything about looking for someone to come forward—which is good news, bad news. It at least means she isn't identifying Brian Peterson as a suspect."

"Yeah. Well, what's in her statement and what comes out of her mouth tonight are apt to be two different things. She's still doing a slow burn about what Keck said yesterday. I'd love to tie up the alibi before the mayor's news conference. Keep on that, will you?"

"So. What're you doin'?"

"Well, I had coffee with Mary Pat's brother, Robert, Jr.— Bobby. Nothing much there, other than he's as sure as I am that Brian isn't our guy. The brother and Mary Pat were close, but the fact is they haven't seen much of each other in the past eight or nine years, which is when he left home to go to college. He was in graduate school after that, teaches college English in Boston now. But the big news is I got a call from Hal Willens. He's working for the Prince family. Apparently Hal and Jack Prince were at law school together, and Jack Prince asked Willens to contact me. They've finally agreed to let me talk to Becky Prince. I'm meeting with them tomorrow afternoon. Anything turning up on our Main Street interviews?"

"Zilch. I'm running down the other alibis right now. Doc Fitzgerald clears easy. He was in the delivery room or thereabouts at Fairview Southdale Hospital all Thursday. Like three blocks away from where Mary Pat parked the station wagon. A pile of people can verify that. Robert, Jr., isn't clear yet, but I should be able to confirm his alibi by this afternoon. Ma Fitzgerald isn't gonna clear, but she just doesn't fit. She doesn't drive, she can barely stand up, much less drag her daughter down to the bluffs and stick a screwdriver in her. . . ."

"Agreed. Look. I'll come back downtown before the news conference. Beep me if you get anything in the meantime."

As Mars put down the phone, he felt discouragement rising. It had surged on his first sight of Brian Peterson. And as each lead spun out, thin and empty, discouragement began to take solid form. He knew the effect that feeling would have: it would make him dull, inattentive, drain his energy. What he needed was a piece of luck with enough charge to get him going again. Did it feel like he was going to get lucky?

Not at all.

CHAPTER
10

Dakota Trail in the Indian Hills section of Edina bore no resemblance to the stolid permanence of Cornelia Drive. It was a more fashionable address than Cornelia Drive, being farther from commercial centers and because of the wooded hills where houses nestled, most on lots substantially larger than those on Cornelia Drive.

Indian Hills had its share of split-level ramblers, but there were also many aggressively contemporary homes that clung precariously to the hillsides. Hal Willens had given Mars directions to the Prince house as if he were directing him to a location outside the solar system. Initially offended by the detailed directions, Mars found himself grateful as he wound the Pontiac up and down hills where street names changed every few blocks and where house numbers were not easy to spot from the street. He took a right on the last leg of Willen's directions, ascending a steep incline to make a sharp left up a private drive. The drive ended in a wide circle, with the Prince house—of the aggressively contemporary school—hanging over the drive.

While the Fitzgerald house looked like a house that was maintained with affection by the owners, the Prince house had a professional spit and polish. There was little lawn and the shrubbery was lush and abundant. A white Mercedes with vanity plates—HJWWINS—was idling, its taillights lit, as Mars drove up. Mars swung the Pontiac into place along the edge of the circle and watched in his rearview mirror as Hal emerged from the Mercedes. Willens was dressed in white pants, a white cable-knit sweater, and a navy golf shirt under the sweater. No other cars were in the drive, but tucked under the overhang of the house was a four-car garage.

Willens stood waiting for him. "Mars. The Princes appreciate your coming out." His hand was outstretched for moments before Mars was within range. Hal Willens was a very good-looking, middle-aged guy. Always tan and always just a little too well dressed and groomed.

Mars shook Willens's hand, withdrawing before Hal had released his grip. "Tell me, Harold. Why does someone call the most expensive defense attorney in the Cities before passing information to the police?"

Willens shook his head at Mars. As they walked toward the house, Willens said, "I forget how it is with you downtown guys. You are to be forgiven for your innocence. These are people who, from the first day of their offsprings' births, devote substantial resources to their children's present and future well-being. They are careful people, Mars. And they believe, as if by creed, in using who they know to protect themselves in situations like this. I went to law school with Jack Prince. I'd have been surprised if he hadn't called me under these circumstances."

Willens tapped Mars on the chest with a tanned hand. "Which is not the same thing as saying there's anything you're going to hear this afternoon that in the remotest sense implicates anyone in the Prince family with respect to the Fitzgerald girl's death. When Jack called, he simply explained that some information has come to their attention that they feel may be relevant in the investigation, and they wanted me to arrange a meeting. That's all there is to it."

Carol Prince held open a broad teak door that was covered with brass fittings. In the crook of her left arm she balanced maybe eight pounds of dachshund. "Maggy" was hand embroidered on the dog's red velvet collar.

As they entered, Mrs. Prince flicked a brief smile at Hal, looked at Mars without saying anything, and called to her husband. Maggy fixed Mars with a look, her upper lip trembling slightly before it rose above a row of small, sharp teeth. A growl befitting a rottweiler oozed out of the dog. Mars thought about it and decided if he had a choice between meeting Maggy or a rottweiler in a dark alley, he'd take the rottweiler.

Jack Prince came into the hallway at a trot, his enthusiasm a shallow cover for his wife's hostility.

"Hey-ya, Willy."

Willens turned and swept his arm in a gesture of introduction to Mars. "Carol and Jack. Special Detective Marshall Bahr from the Minneapolis PD." Maggy's growl erupted into aggressive yapping.

Jack Prince clasped Mars's hand. "Appreciate it, Special Detective. Spoke with Phil Keck this morning. He told us we were lucky to have you involved."

Mars gave a quick nod to both Jack and Carol Prince. Carol Prince was looking him over. "Just doing my job. Your daughter at home?"

"Becky cut out early from dance line practice to join us. She's upstairs taking a shower and will be down in a minute. C'mon. Let's go out to the solarium and have coffee."

Mars shot a look at Willens. Hal made a small gesture to encourage patience as they moved down a marble hallway and into a very white, bright room, the cathedral ceiling and north wall of which was triple-glazed glass. A large glass block sculpture sat in the center of the room, colored lights glowing softly under a thin veil of running water. They sat at a glass

94

table and within moments a Hispanic woman in a white uniform came in with a tray of espresso and small, crustless sandwiches.

Carol Prince seemed unconnected to the food. Her manner became even colder and more hostile. She made no gestures of hospitality and got up and left the room moments after they sat down, the dachshund still tucked under her arm. She returned with a cup of black coffee.

"Where *is* Becky?" She directed this question at her husband in a tone of accusation. He answered her without making eye contact.

"Like I said. She was upstairs taking a shower when I came down. I'm sure she'll be here shortly."

The air bristled with Carol Prince's annoyance. She said nothing, but gave her husband a look of contempt. She pulled an ashtray toward herself across the table and fumbled in her sweater pocket, bringing out a gold cigarette case. She dropped the case on the table with a gesture calculated as an affront to her husband, drew out a cigarette, tapping it against the tabletop. Her glare at her husband held as she accepted a light from Hal Willens.

Jack Prince changed the subject. "Hal. We don't see enough of you and . . ." He struggled to remember Hal's wife's name, a momentary lapse that apparently was understandable. Willens was on his fourth wife. ". . . you and Madelyn," he finished, sounding reasonably confident in his choice of names.

"It's the truth," Willens said. "The people you care about, those are the people you never see. And Maddie . . ." He rolled his eyes to the ceiling. "This is a woman who never sits still. Up to her eyeballs at the club, and she's serving as chairman of one of the major committees for this year's Symphony Ball. Next year she's co-chair of the whole damn shebang. Which is fine, of course. I'm not complaining. Carol? You been involved in the Symphony Ball?"

Mars shifted in his chair, tapped his fingers on the table, and fixed Willens with a look that made clear he was getting tired of small talk. Then he caught a glimpse of Becky Prince coming down stairs from another level of the house. She was barefooted, wearing a man's oversized white terry cloth robe.

The bitch princess descends.

Mars had seen Becky before the other men, but not much before her mother saw her. Carol Prince's jaw tightened at the sight of her daughter. She drew a deep drag on her cigarette. Becky came into the solarium, and picking up on Hal's question about whether Carol Prince had been involved with the Symphony Ball, said, "Could she do it from a golf cart?"

She stopped by her father's chair, gave him a brief kiss on his forehead. Hal almost fell over shoving back his chair to stand up. Carol Prince took this in and her resentment at her daughter became palpable.

"Becky! Good grief. I haven't seen you since . . ." Willens turned toward Jack Prince. "Jack, I don't think I've seen this beautiful daughter of yours since the two of you were over at Interlachen to play tennis with Peter McLeod and his daughter—we ran into you out in the parking lot—when was that?—two years, maybe more than that? Excuse me, Becky, I was so surprised to see you so grown up, I didn't hear you come in. You were saying? . . ."

"You asked if my mother had been involved with the Symphony Ball, and I just asked if she could do it from a golf cart. Because, if she can't, forget it."

"What, young lady, do you think you're doing coming down dressed like that?" Carol Prince blew smoke.

Becky Prince didn't look at her mother. She picked over fruit in a bowl on the table. "You said you wanted me downstairs immediately and not to fool around getting dressed. So . . ."

"I didn't say to come downstairs half-naked. Jack. Are you going to speak to your daughter?"

Mars interrupted. "Could we get going? There isn't a dress code for this meeting. I just want to know what it is you want to tell me. Who's gonna start?"

Becky concentrated on her fingernails. She's drawn her legs up, balancing bare feet on a rung of the chair. The robe had slid open, revealing a smooth, tanned thigh.

Carol Prince said, "We were having dinner at Edina CC last night. Everyone, of course, is talking about Mary Pat. And it's no secret that the Peterson boy is involved. Becky, mind you"—here she swung her glance toward her daughter— "didn't want to go to the club for dinner. She and Brian, of all people, go over to Sidney's for pasta. So, while we're having dinner at the club, Lyle and Janice Flynn say that it's common knowledge that Brian had beaten up Mary Pat..."

"The fucking Flynns don't know anything about anything. *Why are you repeating this shit?*" Becky slammed out of her chair and headed back upstairs.

"*Jack...*"

Jack Prince followed his daughter, saying over his shoulder, "Let me handle this."

Hal Willens said, "The kid's upset, which is understandable. Her best friend dead in a situation like this..."

"The kid is a spoiled brat, is what the kid is." Carol Prince lit another cigarette "Which, as should be evident to everyone at this point, is because her father's been giving in to her since day one."

Mars stood. "I really need to get going. Either I hear what you want to talk about in the next five minutes, or I'm going back downtown."

Hal Willens rose and took Mars's arm. "I'm sorry about this, Mars. But people are upset. Let's give this a couple more minutes."

97

Jack Prince returned, running the palm of his hand across his hair. He looked directly at Mars. "Becky says she'll talk to Detective Bahr, but she doesn't want the rest of us around. Hal . . . I guess I don't see any problem with that. Certainly no offense intended to you, but Becky's very emotional about this. You and I know the substance of the information, and I don't see that Becky's at risk here, you agree, Hal?"

Willens shifted, jangled change in his pants pockets. "I agree, of course. But I'd prefer to be on hand. Does Becky understand I'm here on her behalf?"

"What you should have said is you *wanted* her to meet alone with the police, then she'd have insisted on our staying." Carol Prince rose. "I'm going upstairs. You handle it." She left the room without saying good-bye to Willens or Mars. The dachshund's butt stuck out under her arm, its tail wagging in response to some personal sense of triumph.

There must be a bitch gene, is what Mars thought as Carol Prince stalked from the room.

Mars glanced at his watch. "Either Miss Prince is down here in the next three minutes, or I'm on my way back downtown."

Jack Prince and Hal Willens looked at each other. Willens said, "Why don't you bring Becky down. Tell her we'll be in your study if she needs us. I've every confidence Mars will handle this in a satisfactory manner. Special Detective, I want it on the record that Becky is talking with you voluntarily."

When Becky Prince came back to the solarium she was wearing jeans and a T-shirt, penny loafers without socks. She didn't look at Mars, but for the first time since he'd met her at the Fitzgeralds, four days earlier, she seemed vulnerable. When she did look at him, her eyes glistened with tears.

"I don't know how to say this without making both Brian and Mary Pat sound awful."

"Something you should understand, Becky. There's stuff

nobody wants anybody else to know about them. Most people can live their lives without that stuff getting out. But when someone is murdered, one of the lousy things that happens, that has to happen, is that the victim's privacy is destroyed. The choice we've got is that we can find out the bad stuff, which is usually connected to why someone got murdered in the first place, or we can protect the victim and let the person who did it get away. Or even let someone else look like he's guilty, when he's not. And I can guarantee there isn't anything you can tell me about Mary Pat that will be even half as bad as what I hear every day on this job. Besides which, no matter what the bad stuff is, the good stuff is pretty damn good. No one needs to be a saint, alive or dead."

Tears had started running down Becky Prince's face. Her nose dripped, and her black hair, which had been slicked back from the shower, began to fall forward over her face as it dried. Her voice escaped from a deep trap of grief. "I miss her so much. Already. I can't imagine the rest of today, much less the rest of my life, without Mary Pat." She gulped, her words tripping over the sobs. "And worst of all, as if Mary Pat being dead wasn't already the worst thing in the world, people are saying all this *crap*. I mean, I think most people are actually enjoying saying bad things. They were all so jealous of her anyway. Now that she's dead, they're all standing in line to say bad stuff." She rubbed the palm of her hands over her face, across the slick wet of tears and mucus, without a trace of self-consciousness. She made a loud snuffing noise, sighed deeply, and sat silent for a moment. Then she started to talk.

"I don't know how to explain this to you, except to say that Mary Pat took risks. She took risks because she had a hard time feeling *real,* feeling deep emotion. . . ."

"Did Mary Pat tell you why she didn't feel emotion?"

Becky was still before answering. "I suppose there were a

lot of things. Maybe because things were easy for Mary Pat, in a lot of ways. She was beautiful. She was smart. Really smart. She was great at math. She was taking trig at the U three days a week and getting A's. She took advanced-placement French and German. She was really talented athletically. I mean, she could have excelled at any sport. State champion in the butterfly event, three years in a row...."

"Let's go back to what you said about the risks Mary Pat took."

"Well," Becky hesitated. "Sometimes it was just really pushing herself when she was doing sports. But what she would do sometimes that scared me was to just go off with some stranger...."

"Tell me about that, especially anything you can tell me about any of the people she went with, where she met them, where she'd go with them, if she'd drink with them—"

Becky looked up at him. "No, not drinking. Mary Pat wouldn't drink. You know, don't you, that Mother Fitz is an alcoholic."

Mars decided not to say anything about Mary Pat's blood alcohol level. He said, "I thought she might be."

"Well, I think that was a lot of why Mary Pat hated drinking, doing drugs, all that stuff. But she also said she thought doing drugs or whatever would just make it harder to connect emotionally. Make her more numb. So she'd put herself in really scary situations, situations that made her heart pump, where her adrenaline would get going. She said that made her feel more real than anything else."

"Like I said, tell me about what she'd do."

"The last time it happened, Brian found out. We'd gone up to Duluth for a swimming meet, and Mary Pat had gone for a walk along the lake. She'd met some guy, and they went up to Gooseberry Falls. The thing is, Brian had come up to Duluth to surprise Mary Pat. He'd come over to the hotel to

100

see where she was, and I told him she'd gone for a walk down by the lake. He saw Mary Pat with the guy, and followed them. He didn't do anything then, he just drove back to the Cities. They had a fight at the basketball game the next Friday, when Mary Pat didn't want to meet Brian after the game. That's what everybody's talking about. I know you're assuming they were sleeping together. But they weren't anymore. Not since last fall. Mary Pat just wanted them to be friends. That was making Brian crazy, too. Like I said, he shouldn't have hit her. It wasn't okay. But he was really upset. I mean, he was already having a hard time with the fact that Mary Pat wasn't really his girlfriend anymore. She was going to Brown in the fall, and he knew that would pretty much be it for them. Then she'd gone off with some stranger. . . ."

Becky stopped. She made a face of frustration, then said, "I know this makes it sound like he could have killed her in a jealous rage or something. I guess I can even imagine Brian *could* do something crazy. But when I heard how she'd died, that someone had just stuck a knife or something into her, well, that wasn't how Brian would have done it. He would have done something like hit her, and she would have fallen and hit her head. Like that. Not just taking her to some weird place and sticking a knife in her. Do you know what I'm saying?"

Mars nodded. "Yeah, I do."

She gave him a small smile.

"And what about these guys Mary Pat went off with, Becky? Did she see them more than once? Did she ever go down to the bluffs with any of them?"

Becky shook her head. "Part of the thing with her and these guys was that it was, like, anonymous. No names. No *relationships*. She was careful about that. She didn't want them turning up later. Like I said, Mary Pat was smart. She took risks, but she was careful to build walls around those risks."

"One of the walls wasn't high enough, Becky. Just give me your gut feeling. Do you think one of Mary Pat's pickups killed her?"

Becky looked up at him. Her eyes were dry. She nodded. "But I'll tell you something. You'll never get him. If he was smart enough, *evil* enough to fool Mary Pat, you'll never find him."

CHAPTER
11

Mars was in the Pontiac on the way back downtown when the mobile phone rang.

It was Nettie.

"Mars? I've got a woman here from the Fond du Lac Reservation. And her three kids. She says she saw Brian Peterson on the news last night, being interviewed after the mayor's press conference, and that he's the guy who stopped on the road last Thursday and helped her with her car."

"She seem credible?"

"Very. We've got an alibi even the mayor isn't going to be able to take shots at. So what turned up in the Prince interview?"

"Nothing solid, but it gives me a handle on how Mary Pat could have gotten herself down on the bluffs. I'll tell you about it when I get downtown. Keep our Peterson alibi on ice. I'll be back in about fifteen minutes."

"Don't worry. This little lady isn't going anywhere till she speaks her piece."

Renee Boudreau was a small, pretty woman who could have passed as a teenager. She and her kids had taken over the lounge. Renee and the oldest kid were watching TV. The two youngest were sprawled on the floor, drawing on paper Nettie'd given them.

"Mrs. Boudreau?" Mars held out his hand as Renee stood to greet him. She began talking before he could get a question out.

"Officer, I seen this guy on the TV last night. They was saying he was a suspect in killing some girl down here in the Cities, but that he said he'd been up in Itasca County last Thursday. I seen that lady, the mayor, what's her name, say that nobody'd came forward to back up his alibi. Well, I says to my cousin Helen, 'cause, see, we was at her place, which is how I happened to see the Channel Four news, which I don't get on our set. Helen, she's got a dish, so she gets everything. Anyways, we was sittin' in her living room with the TV on, and I see this kid, and I say, 'That's the guy who helped me last week....' "

One of the kids on the floor rolled over and lay flat on his back, looking up at his mom and Mars. "Mommy? I seen Brian too, didn't I?"

The girl who'd been sitting next to her mom on the couch said, "Shut up, Jimmy. We all seen him."

"Yeah, me too," said the other boy on the floor. "Brian gives us quarters."

Renee Boudreau said, "He was a really nice guy. Like Terry says, after he helped get the car goin', he gave the kids quarters."

"Seeee," said Jimmy, still on his back on the floor, holding up a quarter.

"Put that dumb quarter back in your pocket before you lose it, you little baby." The older girl had inherited her mother's authoritative manner.

Mars turned to Renee Boudreau. "We really appreciate your coming forward like this. If I can ask you to stay around for another hour or so, I'll have my partner take your statement and track Brian down. I think it would help to have in-person identification, long as you're down here. Can you stick around for another couple hours?"

"Your partner Nettie?"

"That's her."

"Well, she already took my statement while we was waitin' on you. And she got a hold of the guy and he's gonna be here pretty quick, I think. I can't stay too long. I barely had enough cash on me to get gas for the car, and I had to pay parking besides. And my car's makin' weird sounds, so I wanna make sure we get back home before it starts gettin' dark."

"Mommy? You said we could get a hamburger. Mommy, I'm hungry, and you said we could get a hamburger." Jimmy had risen from the floor and was tugging at the pocket of his mother's jeans.

"I know I says that, Jimmy, but I didn't know I was gonna have to spend like ten bucks to park, and even with that, I'm not sure I've got enough gas money to get home. You kids are gonna have to wait to eat till we get home."

Jimmy started a soft whimper at which the older girl picked him up and carried him back to the couch, where she held him, rubbing his forehead.

Mars said, "Hey. Do you know what? You guys get a reward for being good citizens." He pulled a twenty from his wallet and walked them over to the county courthouse cafeteria.

Mars went back to the incident room, where he found Nettie at the computer.

"She was sorta cute," Nettie said.

"More than sorta."

Nettie gave him a look that combined disdain and amusement. Then, "She remind you of anybody?"

105

Mars thought about it. Somewhere in his subconscious there was something. But he couldn't find it.

Nettie said, "Like, Denise, maybe?"

Click.

Not physically, not at all physically. But the energy. The self-assurance. The straight-ahead-let's-wrap-this-up kind of approach to life.

Mars frowned. "Jeez. Why do I always go for that?"

Nettie gave him a look. "As if you don't know."

Mars blinked. "No. No, I *don't* know, as a matter of fact...." Nettie was still giving him a cool, condescending smile. "But I'm pretty sure you're gonna tell me."

Nettie busied herself pulling files. Her back to him, she said, in a bored voice, "Denise, Renee Boudreau—and that woman from the County Attorney's Office you went out with last winter...."

"Connie—uh—Connie what's-her-name..."

"Connie-Who-You-Went-Out-with-for-Three-Months— and whose last name you can't remember—"

"Cunningham. Her last name was Cunningham."

"Whatever. The point is—Denise, Renee, Connie—they're all low-maintenance women. They don't expect you to talk about their problems, and they're not interested in what's on your mind. No feelings, just-the-facts, keep-it-simple kind of babes. *Perfect* for you. Intimacy, partner, ain't in your bag of tricks."

Mars opened his mouth to defend himself, but no words came. Instead, he wadded up a piece of paper and threw it at her.

Nettie ducked the paper wad and changed the subject. "You haven't forgotten we've got a status meeting in a half hour, have you?"

Mars sighed and rolled back on his chair, stretching full

length. "No. I'll be there. Is it down here or up in the department?"

"Most of the team is coming in. So it'll be in the department conference room."

"Her Honor gonna be in attendance?"

"I called her office. My guess is her nose has picked up the smell on this one, and we'll be seeing less of her from here on out."

"Shoot. I wanted to watch her face when we announced we nailed the Peterson kid's alibi. Well, if our luck keeps up on this case, we should have plenty of other chances to see the mayor mad before we're through. See you upstairs."

Nettie was right. The mayor didn't show up at the status meeting. Mars led with the news about Brian Peterson's alibi, news that prompted a chorus of groans. He noticed that Toni Andorf, the Edina PD lieutenant, had come in for the meeting. Seeing how bright Andorf's eyes were with the adrenalin of being downtown on a big case made Mars feel old. He went over the interview with Becky Prince, asking Lt. Andorf to go back over her Edina interviews and press for specific details on any men Mary Pat had associated with over the past year.

Steve Patterson from the Second Precinct was there. He'd been in charge of a team of four uniformed patrolmen who'd conducted interviews in the bluffs area. They'd come up empty. Not a scrap of new information to follow up. Nettie summarized where they were with phone reports and computer file analysis. It could have been a one-word report: nowhere.

Lt. Andorf, her voice shaky with nerves, went over the Southdale area interviews in excruciating detail. Andorf had set up a screen on Sixty-sixth Street, the road Mars had guessed Mary Pat would have taken if she'd tried to walk home after finding the flat tire. Andorf had stationed officers at the intersection of Sixty-sixth and France between 8:00 and 10:00 A.M. Monday morning and today. They'd held large photos of Mary Pat and a telephone number to call if drivers had seen Mary Pat on the road the previous Thursday morning. Like everything else in this investigation, the effort had panned a lot of gravel and no gold.

Bottom line was that the Edina end of the investigation was running as dry as downtown's.

After the status meeting Mars felt at loose ends. On an impulse, he went down to the garage and drove the Pontiac out on Fourth Avenue, then around the block to Third Avenue. He crossed the Third Avenue Bridge, which curved across the Mississippi, maybe five hundred feet up river from the Falls. On the other side of the bridge, Third Avenue became Central Avenue. Mars turned right off Central at the first light, drove three blocks, turned right again and parked the Pontiac on Southeast Main in front of the Pillsbury A Mill.

He got out on Main and did a slow jog across the cobblestones. The barricades from the previous weekend, yellow-and-black tape wound loosely around the boards, were still there, piled on the boulevard.

Damn. It was cold for April. He jammed his hands deep into his pockets and moved slowly down the wooden stairs at the west end of the bluff trails. He tried to see the trail ahead as Mary Pat would have seen it. Nothing came.

From the scene where Mary Pat's body had been found, the trail branched off in two directions. One trail turned across a wooden bridge to a small island in the main channel of the river. The other crossed another bridge to a large, hilly island that connected to the east end of the bluff trails. He followed the east trail to the steep wooden staircase that led up the bluffs at the opposite end of the trail from where he'd come down.

The tension—the *aura*—of the site where Mary Pat's body had been found was sustained. It was something all investigators knew. There was an energy that attached to a crime scene, as if the crime had created a magnetic field of its own. Coming up the stairs into a park area at the east end of the trail, the aura remained. Mars would bet money that when the killer left the scene, he had returned to the street via this route, separating himself from the crime scene near the other end of the trail.

At the top of the stairs, Mars turned right toward the east-bank end of the James J. Hill Stone Arch Bridge. A railroad bridge built in the late 1800s, it had been at least ten years since it had been used for rail traffic. It had been renovated as a pedestrian bridge the previous year. The aura evaporated as he walked down the bridge away from the bluffs. Mars kept walking until he was halfway across the bridge. He faced upstream, downtown Minneapolis on his left, the bluffs to the right. St. Anthony Falls thundered before him. He looked to the right. Toward the spot on the bluffs where Mary Pat's body had been found. He remembered Doc D's words: *Let us just say this scene does not speak to me.*

Eloquent.

CHAPTER
12

"So, Gloria asked me to go with her. Can I?"

Mars looked at Chris across the table at Perkins. They'd skipped breakfast at the apartment to get a jump on weekend garage sales. The Fitzgerald investigation had kept them off the garage sale circuit for most of late spring and early summer. By July the investigation was in full stall and except for the Fourth of July weekend, they hadn't missed a Saturday.

Mars said, "Gloria?"

Chris's face struggled for control against the powerful forces of pleasure, embarrassment, and confusion as he waited for Mars's response.

Gloria. Mars remembered who she was from Parents Career Day last spring. A birdlike eight-year-old with a precocious heap of curly black hair and dark brown eyes. Long lashes. Quick as a flea, but no beauty. Mars had observed that kids often confused pieces of beauty—Gloria's glamorous hair and dazzling eyes—with *being* beautiful. Gloria's eyes were too close together, set in a long, narrow face that was dominated by a nose that wouldn't have been out of place on a prizefighter. But Chris saw only the eyes and the hair.

"So, what happens if you say yes?"

A quick look up from Chris to Mars. "So I can?"

"You can *what*? I don't have a clue what *going with* someone means if you're eight years old."

Chris thought about what "going with" meant. Then he said, "I don't know either."

"Well, maybe the way to look at this thing is to agree on what 'going with' *isn't*. Like, 'going with' doesn't mean that Gloria would be more important to you than your other friends."

Chris was quick to take the point. "No way. James is my best friend. I like him a hundred times better than I like Gloria."

"Oookay. And 'going with' doesn't mean you can't be friends with other girls, besides Gloria."

Chris was uninterested in this issue and raised no objection.

"And I don't think 'going with' someone means you're ready for a big physical relationship."

"A what?"

"A physical relationship. Kissing, hugging, feeling each other up. Stuff like that."

Mars could almost feel the heat coming from Chris's blush. Chris was too embarrassed to answer. It was evident that the allure of Gloria's black hair and brown eyes had not yet given rise to lust.

"I guess I don't think you and Gloria are ready to go out on dates, either."

"No way. I'm not gonna go out on dates until I can drive, anyway."

Mars suppressed a grin. Age eight, and the kid decides romance requires wheels. Touchingly wide of the mark and yet exactly right. Did girls think about the rites of sexual passage in connection with a driver's license? Had boys ever separated attraction from mobility?

"Well," Mars said, "that pretty much does it for me. If 'going with' someone doesn't mean you spend time only with Gloria, or that you can't be friends with other girls, or that you're going to mush around or go out on dates—I guess it's okay with me if you want to go with Gloria."

Chris pushed back in the booth and smiled with deep satisfaction.

It was the last Mars heard of Chris's romantic life for several years.

Garage sales were symbolic of what had been wrong with Mars and Denise's marriage. Denise would spend an entire weekend shopping garage sales in a random, compulsive style. He remembered Denise and her sister, Gwen, standing out in the driveway on a Sunday afternoon unloading stuff from the rear of Gwen's van. "The whole thing—less than twenty-five bucks," Gwen said when Mars came out. They were surrounded by neatly folded piles of clothes, kids' toys, dishes, and a homemade pot with dried weeds that had been spray painted gold.

Denise patted a four-foot stack of kids' clothes. "This will get Chris through the whole school year. And I got it all for less than four dollars."

"If that's what you got paid to haul it away, I'd say you got the short end of the stick."

The only real source of contention between Mars and Denise in the divorce was Mars's demand that Chris would never wear secondhand garage sale clothes. Lawyers on both sides had been flummoxed by the heat this point generated. Mars had agreed to give Denise 60 percent of his gross income as child support to assure that she could keep the house and not work until Chris was twelve. But Mars wanted Denise's promise that she wouldn't buy clothes for Chris at garage sales, and Denise wouldn't give it.

"It goes against my grain," Denise said, sitting in her lawyer's office. "I just can't walk into a store and put down good money for clothes that I could get for five cents on the dollar at a garage sale."

Mars's lawyer ruffled his hair with both hands and removed his glasses. "My client was raised in foster homes. A fact of which both parties are aware. He never had new clothes as a kid, and it's important to him that his son not wear secondhand clothes. He has been more than reasonable in his child support commitment. He's providing almost three times the state support guideline. If he wants the boy to wear new clothes, I don't think that's an unreasonable request."

Denise had tears in her eyes. "I'm just saying that it would make me physically ill to walk into Dayton's and spend fifteen dollars for some little sweatshirt that I could get, just as good, for seventy-five cents. I'd rather give up half of what Mars is giving me than do that."

Denise's attorney snapped to attention. "My client is not making an offer to change the stipulated support agreement—"

Mars interrupted. "Denise? Would it help if we just agreed that I'd take Chris shopping for his clothes, and you'd agree not to buy him anything to wear at garage sales?"

Everyone looked at Denise. Denise looked at Mars. "You'd take the tags and everything off before Chris brought the clothes home?"

"If that's what you want."

"That would be fine," she said.

Mars's lawyer said, "I'll want to amend the support stipulation to reflect Mr. Bahr's responsibility for clothing the child—"

Mars interrupted again. "That won't be necessary. Money isn't the issue here—" He held up a hand as his lawyer began to protest. "I said, money isn't the issue. I'm satisfied with this arrangement, and I want it left as is."

When Mars and his lawyer left the conference room, Mars's lawyer blew air and shook his head. "Man, you could have saved my fee. I can't imagine a client making a worse deal on his own than we've just put together."

"In my book, this isn't a bad deal. You just don't understand my priorities."

"Well, lawyers keep saying we wish clients in divorce cases cared more about their kids' well-being than killing each other. Then you get clients that see things that way, and it seems crazy. But I'll tell you one thing. Your soon-to-be-ex-wife doesn't have a clue. I mean, 'Earth to Denise?' You can't touch a kid's sweatshirt at Dayton's for anything less than thirty bucks."

So it had chilled Mars's heart when, at age six, Chris had asked Mars to follow homemade garage sale signs to a driveway in Northeast Minneapolis. Chris jumped out of the car, walked around for maybe forty-five seconds, smiled politely at the woman sitting in a lawn chair with a shoe box full of bills and coins, said thanks, and climbed back into the car.

"Junk," he said.

"You go to garage sales with Mom?"

Chris nodded. "Sometimes. If I'm home on Saturday afternoon."

"You buy stuff at garage sales?"

Chris shook his head. "It's mostly junk—Dad?"

"What?"

"Is there some way I could find out about when rich people have garage sales?"

Mars thought about this. "I guess you could look at ads in the newspaper. I think most of the garage sale ads must run Thursday, Friday. Look for Kenwood, Linden Hills, Edina addresses."

The next Saturday Chris had turned up for breakfast with a garage sale notebook. Pasted on each page, in an order that corresponded to the route they would drive, were ads Chris had cut from the paper. Nettie had gotten a look at the garage sale notebook when they'd stopped down at city hall before setting off one Saturday.

"How'd you pick where you go? You know what you're looking for?"

"Well, I figured rich people would sell better stuff. So I put in ads from neighborhoods Dad says are where rich people live."

"Know what we could do? I could get a printout from the County Assessor's Office of home sale prices for your target neighborhoods. Then you could check the garage sale address against the printout to make sure you're only going to high-end neighborhoods."

This was an innovation for which Chris had great enthusiasm. Mars was unsure that it materially improved the quality of their garage sale stops, but was pleased at Chris's enthusiasm for precision, which marked him as a very different shopper from his mother.

By the end of their first garage sale season, Chris had refined his techniques to include limiting stops to moving sales only. This refinement was based on Chris's accurate observation that people moving were more apt to get rid of good stuff cheap. "That's what I'd do, if I was moving," Chris said.

They left from Perkins shortly after 9:00 A.M. It was warm already, with a promise of deep afternoon heat.

"So. Where are we headed today?"

Chris unfolded the notebook. "Forty-two hundred Browndale. Edina. All the stops today are Edina." Flipping the pages of his computer printout, he said, "None of the streets we're going to today have had any houses that sold for less than three

115

hundred thousand dollars—except five-oh-two-four Windsor. I want to go there because it says 'quality kitchen equipment.' "

It was the first time Mars had been to Edina since they'd cut back on the Fitzgerald investigation. He still spoke by phone with Bobby Fitzgerald in Boston because in June Doc Fitzgerald had had a stroke. He was in a nursing home, expected to survive, but it was unlikely that he'd ever walk again or that his speech would return to normal. Mars could not imagine how Mother Fitz was making do in the wake of her husband's illness. The last time Mars spoke with Bobby, Bobby said he'd be in England for most of the summer and would get in touch with Mars when he returned.

Browndale Avenue was as different from Cornelia Drive as Cornelia Drive had been from Dakota Trail. If Mars had money, he wouldn't have chosen to live on either Cornelia Drive or Dakota Trail. But Browndale Avenue would have been a temptation. The houses, broadly spaced between one another, were on flat lots with tall trees. There were no ranch-style houses here, nor were there flashy contemporaries. These were houses of tradition, built in brick, two stories. There were dormers and shuttered windows. The front doors would open into center halls with polished parquet floors and graceful staircases, the dining room to the left, living room to the right, and a long hallway leading back to the study, kitchen, pantry, and a mudroom. At the rear or to the side would be a screened porch. There were no triple-glazed solariums with illuminated fountains in sight.

Chris's strategy served him well on Browndale Avenue. He bought a set of mixing bowls for a dollar fifty that would have sold at Williams-Sonoma for thirty-five or forty dollars. He bought a garlic press for ten cents. "I've already got one," he said under his breath to Mars, "but for ten cents, I'll buy it to keep at your apartment." He was sorely tempted by a handsome Christmas crèche that he knew his mother would like. Her birthday was in November, and Chris knew she'd be pleased not only by the crèche but that he'd found it at a garage sale. The price on the crèche was fifteen dollars, which Chris felt was too much. Mars estimated it would have been over a hundred dollars new, but Chris was firm. He took his bowls and the garlic press over to the trim woman wearing Bermuda shorts and a polo shirt who was running the sale. Putting his things down on the card table, he said, "Can you do any better on the price of the crèche?"

This was a standard line for Chris to use, and one that usually produced the desired result. His success, Mars guessed, was more attributable to people being charmed by seriousness in an eight year old than by Chris's bargaining skills. In this instance, the seller's face softened and she smiled, but she was hesitant. Moving or not, she was clearly ambivalent about giving up the crèche.

Shamelessly, Chris added, "I wanted to get it for my mother's birthday."

She settled for twelve dollars for all three items.

Windsor Avenue was the last stop. There was indeed much quality kitchen equipment and Chris spent a long time considering his purchases. Mars wandered aimlessly along a table covered with books. Lying on one end of the table was an Edina High School yearbook, *The Hornet*. What surprised Mars was that it was a yearbook for the past school year. He picked it up and went to the index. Predictable. The entries under Mary Pat Fitzgerald's name took up nearly four inches. He flipped to her senior picture and was startled to see, written under the picture, "Liz—Never again. You've been so brave. We're almost home free. Love, MPF."

Mars hadn't seen Mary Pat's writing, and the message, elliptical as it was, gave Mars a shock. He carried the yearbook over to the woman running the sale and handed her a dollar.

"Kind of unusual, selling a brand-new yearbook. Liz your daughter?"

The woman's face tightened with displeasure. "No, thank God. The book belonged to a girl who was over here with another friend. She left the book, and my daughter called her a dozen times, but she never came over to pick it up. It's been sitting on our bookshelf since last April."

"Your daughter didn't just take it to school with her to give back?"

"Liz left school shortly after her friend left the yearbook. I could say more, but leave it at that."

Mars tucked the book under his arm. "I feel kind of bad buying a kid's yearbook, but a buddy graduated from Edina, and I just thought he'd get a kick out of it. What did you say the girl's last name was? Maybe I'll give her a call to make sure she doesn't want it back before I give it to my buddy. Just to clear my conscience."

"Take it. I'll be glad to be rid of it. It belonged to Liz Wyman. Good luck finding her."

Mars went back downtown after dropping Chris at Denise's. He hoped Nettie would be in, so he could have her track down Liz Wyman. No Nettie. He'd have to do it himself. Doing it himself reminded him why it had been such a good idea to bring Nettie on as his partner. She was better and faster at this kind of thing than he would ever be. In addition to which Nettie liked doing it and he didn't.

The White Pages on his lap, he flipped to the back of the book. There was a half column of Wymans, but only one— T. R. Wyman—had a three-digit prefix that placed it in Edina. He punched the numbers.

"Hello?" A woman's voice, small and uncertain.

"Liz Wyman please."

Immediately, a man's voice answered. "Who is this?"

"This is Special Detective Bahr with the Minneapolis Police Department. I'm calling regarding the Mary Pat Fitzgerald investigation, I'd like to speak to Liz, please."

"Liz is no longer at this number. I'd would appreciate your not calling here again." He hung up.

Mars sat with the phone in his hand for a moment after the line went dead. He considered redialing, but decided against it. Looking again at the White Pages, he saw there was no street address with the number. He'd have to turn this over to Nettie. He plopped the White Pages back on the desk and picked up *The Hornet*. This time he looked for Liz Wyman in the index. He found her name, but that's all there was. A name with no entries after it. How did a kid like that end up with Mary Pat as a friend? He remembered that Mary Pat had been a peer counselor on a school-sponsored phone hotline, and wondered if she'd connected with Liz Wyman through the hotline. He scooted over to the case file on his wheeled desk chair, and pulled the file that included back ground interviews. Nettie had attached a printout of people who'd been interviewed. He ran his finger down the list. No Liz Wyman.

Then he remembered that at some point early on they'd had Mary Pat's address book. He found it in a sealed box sitting next to the file cabinet. Nettie had labeled the book: "Database entered April sixteenth." Which meant that if he'd thought about it, and if Liz's number was in Mary Pat's book, he could have looked for the number on the computer. He flipped through the book. No Liz Wyman under the *W*'s. He went to the *L*'s. There was an entry for LW with two numbers, one of which had been crossed out. The crossed-out number was the number Mars had called in Edina. The second number had a three-digit prefix that would put it in a south Minneapolis neighborhood near downtown.

Mars dialed the number. An Asian man's voice answered.

"May I speak to Liz Wyman, please?"

"Who's calling?" The voice was firm, but not hostile.

"I'm a friend of the Fitzgerald family. I'm calling about Mary Pat Fitzgerald."

Mars could hear the man talking to someone. Then a woman came on the line.

"Who's calling, please?"

Mars hesitated. Liz Wyman clearly had problems in her life. If he identified himself as a cop, he knew there was a good chance he'd lose her. He tried an oblique response.

"Liz, I'm investigating Mary Pat Fitzgerald's death, and I came across your yearbook. I was interested in the message Mary Pat wrote in your book. I wondered if we could meet. A half hour would do it."

"You a cop?"

There didn't seem to be much point in denying it. "I've been in charge of the investigation. Let me assure you there isn't any question of your being involved. I'm pretty much tracking down anything we've got, and not being able to figure out what her yearbook message meant, I thought I'd see if you could shed some light." He held his breath waiting for her response.

"What did she write?"

"You haven't seen it?"

"Mary Pat and I had dinner one night, the week we got yearbooks. After dinner, we went over to Laura Gleason's. Laura'd been out of school with strep, and Mary Pat was supposed to drop off her French notes for Laura. Somehow or other, I left my book there. Mary Pat had written in my book at dinner, but I didn't look at it then. And the next week I moved out from my parents. Week after that, Mary Pat was killed. The last thing I was thinking about was the yearbook."

"How would it be if I dropped by with the book? Like I said, a half hour would be all it would take."

"I don't think so."

Mars tightened and then took a shot. "Look. Liz. I've got no interest in messing up your life. I'm just looking for anything that will help us out on this thing with Mary Pat Fitzgerald. Now we can take care of this yearbook between the two of us, or I can get the County Attorney's Office involved, which will make things more difficult for both of us." He paused and on a hunch said, "You being underage, if I do that, I've gotta get your parents involved, which I guess, given your present circumstances, you'd just as soon avoid—"

"If my father finds out where I am, he'll kill me and my boyfriend. You want more murders on your hands?"

"Liz, give me a half hour. I don't want to involve your parents any more than you want me to." The line was silent. Mars said, "Somehow I thought you'd want to help Mary Pat, that you'd want to help us to find who killed your friend."

The line stayed quiet, but Mars could feel she was thinking about what to do.

"You promise you won't let my dad know my number or where I'm living?"

"Promise."

"Hold on a sec." Mars could again hear conversation in the background.

"Can you get here before five o'clock?"

"No problem. Give me your address."

She gave him the street address and the apartment number. Mars left immediately.

The guy who answered the door was a scholarly-looking young Korean, maybe twenty-two, twenty-three years old, wearing horn-rimmed glasses, khaki pants, and a striped, button-down Oxford-cloth shirt. He was pulling on a jacket as he opened the door. "You Detective Bahr?"

"In this neighborhood you should be sure before you open the door. Believe me."

"Come on in." He called over his shoulder, "Liz? The copper is here."

From the back of the apartment, Liz Wyman came forward. She was plain, but like her boyfriend, intelligent looking. She wore a University of Minnesota sweatshirt, jeans, white crew socks, and loafers.

She said, "This is my boyfriend. Jared." Mars and Jared shook hands.

Jared nodded, said, "I'm outta here." He looked closely at Liz. "You okay with this?"

She nodded. "Go. I'll get a bus and meet you over there around six."

Inside, Mars handed over the yearbook. "Tell you the truth, I'm probably going to have to take that back with me. I'll see you get it back eventually."

"It's okay. I don't want it back. I just want to see what Mary Pat wrote. Where was it?"

"Right under Mary Pat's senior picture."

"Sit down."

Liz sat lotus style on a rug on the floor. Mars eased down on a futon draped over a wood frame. The apartment was small but attractive. The wood floors shone, the furniture was simple. It appeared that, after a flying leap, Liz Wyman had landed on her feet.

She found the picture and the note and stared at it for much longer than it took to read. Her hand went to her mouth and she pressed her lips together. When she looked up, her eyes were wet.

Mars spoke first. "Can you tell me what the message means?"

"Haven't you figured it out?"

They maintained eye contact as Mars followed another hunch. "My first guess would be that you've been a victim of sexual abuse. Was Mary Pat your peer counselor in the hotline program?"

"Pretty good. You're smart, for a cop. Keep going."

"Well, that's as far as I got."

"My dad started having sex with me when I was five years old. I pretty much went on automatic pilot from then until I called the hotline when I was fifteen. I got lucky—for the first time in my life—when Mary Pat answered the phone. I was going to kill myself. I'd let myself into my dad's car in his parking space downtown. I was going to cut my wrists, then my throat. I wanted my dad to come out of his office and find me in a pool of blood. He had a mobile phone in the car, and I called the hotline. First time. Mary Pat sort of got me stabilized, asked if she could call me back, which she did in about fifteen seconds. What I didn't know was that she was calling me back on her cell phone. And while we were talking, she was driving downtown. Next thing I knew, she was at the car door. She didn't say anything. She just opened the door and hugged me, crying. She kept saying, 'You can't let him win, you can't let him win.' Mary Pat was the only friend I had for the next three years. But when Mary Pat Fitzgerald is your friend, you don't really need anyone else." Liz began sobbing softly, but continued. "*Was* my friend.

"Anyway, Mary Pat convinced me that I had to confront my father and get my mother's support to end what he was doing to me. I did that in March. My mother's always been totally under my father's thumb—I mean, totally—but she stood by me when I told her. I wanted both of us to leave him. But she wouldn't—or couldn't. She couldn't imagine life on her own. It's crazy to say it—because in different ways he's been as abusive to her as he ever was to me—but she loves him. And with my mother, she doesn't see a future for herself. She can't imagine getting a job, which she's probably right that she'd have to do. My dad is shrewd. He'd put every ounce of himself into making sure we got as little as possible. So I left. I'm still hoping she'll leave. I can't even call the house. I called at first, and it turned out he had a bug on the phone, and he beat the shit out of my mom. He almost found out where Jared and I are living, and I honestly think if he found us, he'd try to kill us."

"You want some help with this situation? We've got good people in the Domestic Abuse Unit. They could hook up with Edina PD. You and your mother shouldn't have to put up with this."

She shook her head. "I know what the police can and can't do. And I know my mother couldn't go through what would happen if I filed charges against my dad. It took everything she had to get me out." She stopped and looked at him. "You're not here about me."

He held her eyes. "No, I'm not."

"You want to know if Mary Pat's dad was abusing her."

Mars maintained eye contact but said nothing.

Liz looked away. "I always thought so. The way she supported me—it was more than compassion. But she never said. She never said, 'I know what you're feeling because it happened to me.'" Liz silently read the message in the yearbook again. "Actually, what she's written is as close as she ever got to admitting Doc abused her—'*We're* almost home free'—not '*You're* almost home free.'

"Is there anybody she would have talked to? Becky Prince? Her mother?"

"Becky? Maybe. But I don't really think so. Becky isn't exactly the soft-shoulder type. Besides, I don't think Mary Pat would allow herself the luxury of not being strong, of telling somebody she had a problem she couldn't handle. Her mother? I *doubt* it. I mean, Mother Fitz was a total wuss. Besides. One of the reasons I thought it was happening was that it seemed to me like Mother Fitz knew, whether Mary Pat told her or not. If you were ever in that house with the three of them together—well, it was in the air."

Mars thought about it, catching in his mind's eye the brief impressions of perpetual distance between Doc and Mother Fitz, even when they were in the same room. He guessed that Liz was right.

Mars couldn't get back downtown fast enough after talking with Liz Wyman. He wanted to go over to Doc Fitzgerald's alibi file. There had to be something there that he'd missed first time around.

Going over Doc's file, it struck Mars for the first time that the file was more substantial than what you'd expect for a guy who'd never been a serious suspect. Seven people had been interviewed to confirm Doc's alibi. The file included copies of medical records that Doc had signed on the day that Mary Pat was killed. Most unexpected of all, Nettie had rechecked all the interviews herself. A routine alibi check like this, Mars had assumed Nettie would have accepted whatever the Edina PD turned up, unless something looked off. Nettie had ideas about Doc, or she wouldn't have gone over his alibis herself.

He called her.

"Hey, Nettie."

"Hey, Mars."

"Guess what."

"I don't guess on my day off. Just tell me."

"I bought an Edina High School yearbook at a garage sale. I found something Mary Pat wrote that didn't make sense. I tracked down—without your assistance, please note—the kid she wrote it to and the kid tells me she thinks there's a chance Doc Fitz was sexually abusing Mary Pat. How's that for a nice bit of detective work?"

"So tell me something I don't already know."

"Whaddya mean, tell you something you don't already know? You *knew* Doc had sexually abused Mary Pat and you didn't bother to mention that little detail to me?"

"I checked his alibi first. It was tight, like I told you. Very tight. I interviewed every patient he was with that day—and we've got times he was with his patients in their charts—times entered by labor room and delivery room nurses, not Doc Fitzgerald—I interviewed delivery room staff, the guy who covered the gate in the doctors' parking lot—Doc was there. Like he said, from first thing sunup until after eleven. Besides which, I figure I tell you what I'm thinking about the sexual abuse, it would send you off on a goose chase. And I didn't have a lot to go on in the first place."

"And what, may I ask, *did* you have to go on?"

"The picture. The picture didn't look right to me."

"*What* picture didn't look right to you?"

"The one we cropped for Mary Pat's picture. The one where she was standing on a golf course with Doc."

Mars found the photo file and pulled the five-by-seven-inch snap he'd taken from Fitzgerald that first Saturday. He looked at it hard. Nettie was right. If you looked, it was there. The father's hand on the daughter's waist. You could see the pressure on her shirt from her leaning away from him. The fa-

126

ther's sideways glance, a look that carried traces of guilt and anxiety in the eyes above the smile. And the daughter's eyes. Fixed. Not smiling above the posed, camera-ready lips.

It had been there all along.

So. What to do? What he had was the possibility that Doc had abused Mary Pat, but no hard evidence. What hard evidence he had was that Doc was nowhere near the Father Hennepin Bluffs on the morning of April 3. And Doc himself, now an invalid in a nursing home. Put it all together and you had a lead that was a nonstarter. On an impulse, he looked up Bobby Fitzgerald's number in Boston.

"Bobby? Mars Bahr in Minneapolis."

"Mars—something new?"

"No. Just thought I should touch base. You said last time we talked you'd be going to England this summer, and I thought I'd try and catch you before you left. . . ."

"Your timing's good. I leave day after tomorrow."

"And you'll be back when?"

"End of the month, early August. So there's nothing new?"

Mars hesitated. Then he said, "One thing, and it's probably nothing. I'm sorry to have to bring it up, but I can't ignore it, either. . . ."

There was anxiety in Bobby's voice. "What?"

"I talked to a young woman Mary Pat had met when Mary Pat was volunteering as a peer counselor. That woman had an impression—and there was nothing definite to back the impression up—that Mary Pat's relationship with your dad had some problems—maybe even sexual abuse. I'm sorry, Bobby, but I'm sure you can understand. I can't let a detail like that pass without checking."

The line was quiet for a long time. When he spoke, Bobby's voice was tight. "*Christ.* You were the one who told me that the family's alibis were solid. What are you saying?

That my dad had been abusing Mary Pat and that he killed her because of that?"

"Not at all. I'm comfortable with the alibis where they stand. It's what I said: I came across one person who raised a question. I didn't feel I could let it go without checking. If your dad were well, I'd put the question to him. As things stand, I'm asking you."

Bobby's voice was hoarse with emotion when he spoke. "I never thought I'd be glad my dad is in the shape he is. But if being a physical and mental basket case protects him from that question, then I'm grateful he's in no shape to be asked. . . ."

"Good. That's what I wanted to hear. Listen, I'll let you go. Sorry to have brought this up. Do me a favor. Give me a call when you get back, so I know where to reach you, and if you'd leave a number where you can be reached in England, just in case."

"You've got my office number. They'll know where to get hold of me. I'll call when I get back."

Bobby hung up sharply. Mars sat silent for moments after the call. It was predictable that Bobby would be offended by the suggestion that his father had been sexually abusing Mary Pat. But there was a trace of defensiveness in Bobby's response that troubled Mars. He couldn't bring himself to let it go altogether. What he needed was a fresh perspective. That's why he called Karen Pogue.

He'd met Karen when he'd been an investigator in the Sex Crimes Division and she'd done an inservice on the emotional origins of particular types of deviancy. Mars kept up an association with her that he found useful. It had also occurred to him that Karen was close to being his best friend—if you could say that someone you saw only a half dozen times a year could be called a best friend. They both looked for opportunities to get together and while the time they spent together usually involved professional issues, there was a connection between them that only occurs between people who genuinely like each other. What was different between them was that Karen was someone who made friends easily. Mars didn't. Friends took time, and he never worked less than sixty hours a week and what time he had after work went to Chris. Those were true facts. Mars also knew that if he worked less and didn't have Chris, he still wouldn't have a lot of friends. And as long as Chris and his work were doing well, that wasn't something that bothered Mars.

He called Karen's university office and got an answering machine. He tried her home number and got her just as she was going out.

"Can I call you back? I was supposed to pick Ted up like ten minutes ago. I've been hoping you'd call to talk about this Fitzgerald girl—is that why you're calling?"

"You got it."

"Oh, good. Where are you going to be after six—or wait. I don't want to talk about this on the phone. Why don't you just come over for dinner. Anytime after seven. Ted's got a big case on, so he probably won't be able to join us, but I'll make you dinner and you can tell me all about it."

If Mars had had enough money and domestic talent, he would have lived exactly like the Pogues. It was a style of living, in a big frame house a couple blocks up from Lake of the Isles, that made him feel a little wistful. When he thought about it, the wistfulness was because he knew you didn't live like the Pogues just by shopping at Dayton's. You lived like the Pogues if you'd been born to well-to-do parents, gotten more than one degree from Ivy League schools, and had an IQ well above the national average.

Karen Pogue—she wouldn't allow herself to be called doctor by friends or patients—had an irreverent sense of humor Mars found particularly appealing and a gift for friendship that she extended to a diverse group of people she found interesting. He liked Ted Pogue much less than he liked Karen. Ted, he suspected, did not find Mars or what Mars did interesting. It also seemed obvious to him that Ted Pogue was used to liking people less than his wife did and that Ted's frequent begging off from social occasions was for that reason, not the burden of work.

So Mars was grateful when he walked into the front hallway of the Pogues' house on Humboldt Avenue to have only Karen there to greet him. She didn't make excuses for Ted, and Mars didn't ask. He followed her down the long book-lined hallway to the kitchen. Over her shoulder, she said, "What have you been doing with yourself? I haven't talked to you for ages. If I didn't know better, I'd say you'd fallen madly in love with someone. . . ."

Mars stopped flat in his tracks. "What's that supposed to mean—*if you didn't know better you'd think I'd fallen madly in love with someone?*"

"Just that in all the years I've known you, I can't remember a time when a woman knocked you off your blocks."

Mars groaned. "Oh, please. Don't you start. Nettie's been giving me grief about my 'relationships'—or more precisely, what she perceives as my lack of relationships—every chance she gets. Just for the record, I *do* have a private life and it's because it's private that you and Nettie don't know about it."

Karen grinned. "My final word on the topic: What I usually find when men talk about relationships is they're talking about sex. I'd be willing to bet that isn't what Nettie is talking about and it's not what I'm talking about. But enough on that. Let's talk dead teenagers."

The kitchen was at the back of the house. At a center-island counter, Karen had set two places. She poured white wine into a thin-glassed goblet without asking him what he wanted.

"Sit," she said, "and talk. It'll take me another five minutes with the pasta."

He took a quick sip of the wine. This was also the only house in which he enjoyed a glass of wine. He would have preferred Coca-cola, but at Karen's, wine was acceptable.

"Well. You've read what's in the paper about the Fitzgerald girl?"

"Of course. Every word."

"I'd be interested in your reaction. Off the cuff."

She didn't answer right away. She was chopping basil, but Mars could tell she was thinking about what she was going to say.

"Off the cuff, I'd say something doesn't make sense—or at least, there's something that's missing from what I know about the case."

"Unfortunately, there's something missing from what I know about the case, too."

"What *do* you know?"

He decided not to say anything right off about the possibility of abuse. He'd stick to the basics and see what Karen came up with on her own. "I know that Mary Pat took risks with strange men, which makes me think she took one risk too many and didn't get back alive. I know the boyfriend didn't kill her. I know she was dead drunk when she died and that it wasn't usual for her to drink. Her best friend told me Mary Pat had trouble feeling emotion, which was part of why Mary Pat would take risks, to try and get her adrenaline going. To feel something. I know that even though it looked like she had a strong family, her mother and father are estranged and her mother is a lush. I know that she was killed by one clean shiv to the aorta. No evidence that she had any physical contact with the assailant. Sometime before she died she stopped her watch, an action she would have had to plan. I know she wasn't sexually assaulted—which is one of the reasons I didn't call you first thing—"

"I wondered about that. I guess I assumed there wasn't a sexual assault or you would have called—but now?"

"Truth is, I've been off base on this case pretty much from day one. At first I thought—no, hoped—it was the boyfriend, and there were some incidental details that supported that. But from my first look at him—and his alibi—not a chance. What my gut was telling me from the start—and this is consistent with the risk-taking behavior—is that she met some-one she didn't know and went off with him. They found her car with a flat tire in the parking lot at Southdale. My guess is she started to walk home and got picked up. But I don't have one scrap of evidence to support that theory. The ME thinks the perp had her on her knees in front of him when he stuck her. What I've got is bits and pieces, but nothing that fits together. Which is why I'd like to know what you think."

Karen walked back to the counter with two wide-lipped white bowls filled with perfectly cooked fettucine, sprinkled with fresh chopped basil, ground pine nuts, and freshly shred-ded mozzarella cheese. The mixed-green salad had a thin veil of vinegar and oil. She opened a heavy white linen napkin, uncovering a basket of hot, crusty rolls. Before she sat, she stood with the heels of her hands against the counter, looking out the glass doors that opened on a small backyard. It had turned dark since Mars arrived, and the glass in the doors was black.

Then Karen said, "Two things. The risk taking, the lack of emotion. You checked the male family members out pretty thoroughly?"

Mars stared at her. "Keep going."

Karen took a forkful of pasta. With her mouth half-full, she said, "What you've said about the impulsive sexual behavior, the acting out with strange men, would be very consistent with a sexual abuse victim. Also the 'dead' feeling, the lack of emotion. Not being able to feel things. Very common in girls who've been sexually abused when they're young, before they have control over the abuser's access to them."

Mars shook his head. "I hear what you're saying, but the brother and dad's alibis were tight." It was his turn to talk with a mouthful of pasta. "Actually, that's what got me off the dime to call you. I found some very thin evidence suggesting that Mary Pat might have been sexually abused by her dad. But when I look at his alibi—which is as tight as anybody's—it doesn't fit. And ... at a gut level, it doesn't click for me, either."

Karen nodded. "Well, I'd have to say that while Mary Pat might fit the pattern for sexual abuse, the dad doesn't sound like the perp in her murder."

"Tell me why you say that."

"I'd say the perp has a sexual object-identity problem. You know, the use of the sharp instrument for penetration, the lack of direct sexual contact. This victim is sexually stimulating to him, but in his mind at least, the figure is verboten—off limits. For arousal, he recreates a provocative image and thrusts with the knife. There's anger, too. The alcohol involvement—especially with the kneeling behavior—is a form of degradation. He's angry that this image has aroused him and he wants to humiliate the object. I'd guess without the image of drunkenness, he couldn't achieve arousal or climax. He appears to have a highly organized personality. Very disciplined. He's managing his anger against the sexual object in a very controlled way. He's protecting himself from acting on that anger in a way that could trap him. Like shredding her to bits and covering himself with blood."

Karen stopped, getting up for more wine. As she sipped, she shook her head. "None of that fits with the father as perpetrator. You'll find a fair amount of dominance behavior, but degradation for its own sake, without there being physical contact, just doesn't happen all that much. And the drinking—it's not unusual to find adults using drugs or alcohol to induce sexual participation in children, but it's a very class-correlated behavior. You'll find it in families where there isn't a lot of order or structure, where children are left alone with the abuser for long periods of time. Where the children are unprotected. In a situation like the Fitzgerald family, it wouldn't be typical and it particularly wouldn't be typical for a child who is an adult. My guess is that if he were abusing his daughter, that if he murdered her, it wouldn't be this hands-off kind of thing you found down on the bluffs. And I'd have the same question about the site. It just doesn't make any sense that he'd haul her all the way down to the river, to a place he doesn't have any reason for knowing about. You also don't find murder at this stage of abuse. If it's going to happen, it will happen early in the abusive relationship, at the first flush of guilt and fear of discovery. Not after years of abuse, when the child is an adult with resources to protect herself. By the way, were you able to determine if anything that belonged to the victim was missing—jewelry, clothing— something he could use to reconnect emotionally with the murder?"

Mars rubbed his face hard with the heels of both hands. "We didn't find anything."

Karen walked over to a newspaper rack on the wall and pulled out a section of the newspaper. "This is reminding me of something I read in this morning's paper—about the tsunami that hit Peru a year or so ago...."

Mars said, "I can't wait to hear how you're going to link my perpetrator to a Peruvian tsunami."

She put half-frame glasses on and spread the newspaper open on the counter. "Here it is," she said, peering down her nose through the specs at the paper. "Listen to this. 'Scientists have concluded that many tsunamis originate in faults on the ocean floor. When earthquakes occur along those fault lines, they generate subsurface waves that migrate toward shore. As the subsurface wave enters shallow water, its volume achieves waves of extraordinary height, capable of reaching inland for distances of several miles." Karen looked up at him. "Your killer is like that, Mars. There's a fault line deep in his psyche. When something trips that line, he moves—silently, invisibly—toward his victim. And the victim doesn't recognize the danger until it's too late. And after a tsunami, the only evidence remaining is destruction—the wave no longer exists."

Karen folded the newspaper shut, and taking her glasses off, said, "That's the MO on your killer, Mars. Tsunami Man."

Mars swirled the wine in his glass, staring at it as he thought about what Karen had said.

Watching him, Karen said, "This isn't making sense to you?"

Mars responded slowly. "What you're giving me is a motive—which we've been missing all along. The problem I've got is—if you're right—our perp is a psychopath. Someone who acts out of a deep psychological flaw. A guy like that, he's gonna do this more than once. We've sent a wire out to other jurisdictions—twice, in fact. And nothing's come back."

For the third time that day, Mars drove back downtown. It was nearly 9:30 P.M., but there was something he needed to do.

He walked down the hall to the administrative support pool. His footsteps clattered in the empty halls. It was a quiet Saturday night and not much of anyone was around this end of city hall. Through the fogged windows of the chief's office,

135

he saw a light beyond the reception area, but there was no sign of activity. In the admin pool he found what he was looking for: a stack of reinforced storage boxes. Grabbing five or six, he made his way back to the squad room.

He'd been working for an hour when he looked up to see the chief standing in the squad room door. "You're here late, Marshall. I hope that doesn't mean an addition to our annual body count."

Mars sat back. He'd been so deep into his thoughts he hadn't heard the chief coming. Glancing at his watch, he saw that it was nearly eleven-thirty.

"Nope. Old ghosts. Keeping too much stuff around on cases we haven't cleared. Need to get some of this stuff boxed. Clear my head and the files."

The chief walked over casually and sat on the edge of Mars's desk. He picked up a thick black three-ring binder, glancing at it before dropping it back on Mars's desk. The binder was clearly marked "M. P. Fitzgerald."

"Little early to put this one to bed, wouldn't you say?" the chief asked.

"Not putting it to bed. Just getting it better organized, clearing my head, like I said."

"How's Nettie doing on getting these files automated?"

Mars leaned back and stretched. With his hands clasped over the top of his head, he said, "As well as can be expected. If people'd quit killing each other she'd be doing better. That, and better hardware and software."

"Ah. I should have mentioned. The mayor told me this afternoon we got the federal funding. Should be able to get you some new equipment."

"How about the funding for the riverfront?"

"That too, I understand. They're gonna start cleaning up the trails, build an interpretive trail on the history of the bluffs, the mills, all that. The mayor turned the Fitzgerald murder to the city's advantage. Used it as an example of why we needed to spend money reclaiming the riverfront for the public. She's a genius, that lady."

Mars didn't answer. He half stood to lean across the desk and scoop up another pile of paper.

"You figure on being here all night, Marshall?"

"This is the last box. Spent too much time rereading, instead of getting it into boxes. I'll be outta here in another half hour or so."

The chief stood. "Well, I'll be on my way. Managed to get caught up on a little paperwork myself. Never seems to be time during the day." He moved toward the door, turning back before he left. "You get home now, hear? You look beat."

"Like I said. Another half hour."

"Good health. The *most* important thing."

A small smile passed Mars's lips as he wished the chief a good night. After the chief left, Mars picked up the phone.

Nettie's voice was fuzzy when she answered.

Mars said: "You've got fifteen seconds: the chief just dropped in while I was working on some files. Before he left, he said, 'Good health. The most important thing.' "

"Oh—give me a minute . . . you woke me up, by the way."

"Sorry. The clock is ticking."

"*The Godfather, Part One*, Marlon Brando to Al Pacino. They're talking in the garden."

"Ha! Wrong. *The Godfather, Part Two*. Lee Strasberg to Al Pacino when Pacino goes to see him in Florida."

"Shouldn't count when you wake someone up."

"You're a sore loser."

"I suppose it makes a nice change, your being right about something."

PART III

EAST SUSSEX, ENGLAND

FRIDAY, AUGUST 1 TO
           MONDAY, AUGUST 4

CHAPTER
13

Bobby Fitzgerald stood on the cement platform at Glynde rail station in the state of disequilibrium that comes when you're motionless after prolonged, rhythmic motion. He had been the only passenger to disembark at Glynde from the Network Southeast train. While he was hardly more than forty miles from his starting point—Victoria Station in London—Bobby felt like he'd traveled a continent to get to Glynde. The gray, gritty, depressed landscape that surrounded London rail routes always depressed him, but never more than on this trip.

He had agreed to spend the weekend at his friend's family estate in East Sussex because he desperately needed the solace of green space and fresh air the English countryside offered. London had been filled with din and disappointment. His seminar had not gone well. The students had been uninterested, anxious to be done with ideas and words and out on the streets of London, full of themselves and pints of warm English beer. Bobby had always felt a sense of camaraderie with his students, but for the first time their blind enthusiasms and bottomless self-confidence made him feel separate and older.

He knew himself well enough to know that bad students weren't enough to spoil a trip to London. What really weighed him down was guilt. Guilt at having left the States with his sister's murder unresolved, with his father in a nursing home. And with his mother sitting alone, day after day, in an unlighted room with sunglasses covering her eyes and a mug of gin within easy reach of her right hand.

In London, the guilt had dogged him. But he had no sooner put foot on the station platform at Glynde than he felt the prospect of relief. He took a deep breath. Glynde was idyllic. East Sussex might not be the most spectacular scenery England had to offer, but its beauty was classically English. The rolling hills were a brilliant green, vines rambled on centuries-old stone and brick, and the quiet was profound.

His friend had warned him that while trains stopped at Glynde, the station itself had been closed for some years. But he'd promised Bobby a car would meet the four-thirty train at Glynde. Bobby looked around. He had his father's need for precise information: *where* would the car meet him? Walking a few steps down the platform, he discovered a Way Out sign partially obscured by shrubs. He followed a path around the old brick stationhouse, passing through two creaking gates. He came out into a deserted car park. This had to be it. He looked at his watch. The train had been on time; it was now 4:35. He forced himself to ignore the anxiety that always rose when he faced uncertain circumstances. Worse come to worst, he could always walk into the village and find a phone. He had been about to find shade from the warm sunshine when he saw—and heard—a station wagon roar over the bridge that crossed the rail tracks. The car made a sharp turn at the bottom of the bridge and rolled into the car park at a clip.

A tall boy with tousled blond hair bounded out of the car. "You're Mr. Fitzgerald, then?" He came toward Bobby at a quick jog, snatched up his weekend bag before Bobby had thought to pick it up himself, and started back to the car. He opened the back door of the station wagon for Bobby, but Bobby shook his head, entering the front seat instead.

"Yes. I'm Robert Fitzgerald. You're?. . ."

"William, sir. Sorry to be late. There was some confusion about the cars, there was. Mr. Owen Cook, he was going to come along to meet you. But him and Miss Amundsen went out for a walk earlier, and hadn't come back. I waited a bit, then started off in the Bentley. Then Mr. Pack says, 'No, the Bentley was needed to pick up Mr. Neville Cook at the station in Lewes.' So then I get the estate car here and am finally off. . . ."

"I'd only just arrived, William. I'd say you were right on time."

William grinned broadly. "Glad to hear that, sir. Would appreciate your saying as much to Mr. Cook, if he asks. He'd have my head, he would, if he knew no one was waiting when you arrived."

Bobby was surprised. "Owen would be angry over something like that? Doesn't sound like him at all."

"Oh, not Mr. Owen Cook, sir. Not him. Easy as anything is Mr. Owen. It's Mr. Neville Cook that likes things done just so. Keeps track of everything, does Mr. Neville Cook. We're all in terror of Mr. Neville Cook. Miss Cook's just the same, maybe worse. But Mr. Owen, well, he's an easy man to please."

Bobby had met Neville Cook only once. Owen and Neville had been in Minneapolis on a real estate investment deal the previous Thanksgiving. Bobby had been in Minneapolis over the Thanksgiving weekend, and as he had been Owen's guest more than once in Boston and in London on several occasions, he had invited the brothers to join his family for Thanksgiving dinner. Owen had been charming, but Neville, while polite, had left them all with the clear impression that family dinners bored him. Bobby had little difficulty believing that Mr. Neville Cook would be a difficult taskmaster.

He was curious about William's reference to a Miss Amundsen. He hadn't realized that Owen had invited a girlfriend for the weekend. "You said Owen has another guest here, a Miss Amundsen?"

William shook his head. "Wrong Mr. Cook again, sir. Miss Amundsen is Mr. Neville Cook's friend. But Mr. Cook goes into the city every day, and as Mr. Owen is at his leisure, so to speak, he's been entertaining Miss Amundsen." William gave Bobby a sharp look. "Easy duty that is, if you ask me. A real looker is Miss Amundsen."

Bobby smiled. He was beginning to realize that by choosing to sit up front rather than in the back, he'd given William a signal that personal observations on the Cook family were in order. He could only guess what Mr. Neville Cook would have to say about William's candor. For himself, as long as the comments weren't critical of Owen, he rather enjoyed the below-stairs gossip.

They drove for about ten minutes before taking a turn at a gravel drive. The drive wound through a wood, came out on a broad meadow, turned sharply across a clear, fast-moving stream, and then ran through yet another wooded area. Finally, on the far side of the wood, the road straightened and ran directly, for perhaps half a mile, toward a large, stone house.

Bobby had expected something rather grand, but his expectations were exceeded. The house was centered at the end of the road, with a massive double stone staircase to the entrance. Large windows paned with old glass shone against the mellowing light of the summer afternoon. Behind the house, low wooded hills rose.

William brought the station wagon to a halt on the gravel driveway at the front entrance. "I'll see your bag gets up to your room, sir." He looked around. "Looks like Mr. Owen's not back from his walk yet, or I'm sure he'd be here to greet you."

Just then the front double doors opened, and a severe man in a formal black suit and stiff, white shirt came down the steps. To Bobby he conveyed a sense of authority rather than welcome.

"Mr. Fitzgerald. Welcome to Charhill. I'm Mr. Pack, head butler. I apologize that no one from the house is here to greet you, but Mr. Owen will be back shortly. Do come in. I'm sure you'd like a drink?"

Bobby slipped out of his sports coat, handing it to William. "Tell you what. After spending a couple hours on the train, I'd like to take a quick walk around the grounds. . . ." He reached over, retrieving his weekend bag from William. "Just let me get my camera. If it's all right, I'd like to take a few pictures of the house."

"Very good, sir." Mr. Pack gave some sort of signal to William, who, taking back Bobby's bag, trotted off toward the house. "Just come in the front door when you're ready, sir, and we'll see to it that you get something to drink."

The air was absolutely still, the gravel drive crunched under Bobby's feet as he walked, and the late afternoon sun was benevolent, without the biting heat of earlier in the day. The sense of well-being that Bobby had felt at the train station came back. He turned slowly in a complete circle; at every point there was an ordered beauty. He was tempted to head off into the wooded hills behind the house for a longer walk, but uncertain as to when Owen would return and when dinner would be served, decided against it. Instead, turning off the road, he found a path that led toward the stream they'd crossed coming to the house.

He had walked about fifteen minutes when he saw a large black car coming down the road toward the house. This, no doubt, was the Bentley bringing Neville Cook home. Bobby turned back on the path to the house. When he came to the road, with the house straight ahead, he saw three people standing by the Bentley. He recognized Owen and Neville; the woman had to be Miss Amundsen.

At fifty paces it was clear that William had not overstated Miss Amundsen's attractions. She was rather too tall and too thin for Bobby's taste, but she was strikingly elegant. Most unusual was her coloring. Bobby would have described her as being uniformly beige. Her smooth, midlength, pale brown hair hung partially over her face. When she pulled it back with a nervous, repetitive gesture, she looked out with taupe-colored eyes. Her skin was a pale tan. She was dressed in a white cotton shirt and khakis.

Owen raised an arm in greeting as Bobby approached. "Glad to see you've been amusing yourself. I'm afraid I've been a derelict host. Ann and I were walking and lost track of time." As Bobby joined them, Owen said, "Ann Amundsen, Bobby Fitzgerald. You're neighbors, you know—Ann lives in Boston, too."

Ann Amundsen dropped her head slightly to acknowledge the introduction. Casually, but with the clear purpose of avoiding a handshake, she put her hands into her pants pocket. "Hello," she said in a soft, neutral voice. Her voice, Bobby thought, matched everything about her appearance.

Before Bobby could say anything to Ann, Neville Cook moved forward, holding out his hand. "I'm Neville Cook. Owen's elder brother."

Bobby was embarrassed. He took Cook's hand, and as casually as he could, said, "Good to see you again. We met last Thanksgiving in Minneapolis. . . ."

Quickly, Neville said, "Yes. Of course. How is your family?"

It was a question Bobby wanted to avoid at all costs. He had never spoken to Owen about Mary Pat's death and now was not the moment for candor. Instead, he lifted his camera.

"Please, the three of you. A picture in front of the house. I only have a couple of shots left. Ann, in the middle..."

Ann shook her head and moved back. Neville Cook had quickly stepped aside. "No need for me to be in the picture, I'm sure. Ann and Owen, go ahead—or, if you like, the three of you together, and I'll take the picture."

Bobby shook his head. "I don't want a picture of myself. This will take just a minute.... C'mon—Ann, if you would just move...."

Ann moved reluctantly between the brothers. Barely moving her lips, she said in an impatient voice, "Let's just get this over with."

Bobby held the camera up, focusing on them where they stood. Neville stepped slightly to the side, moving away from rather than toward Ann and Owen. In the viewfinder, Bobby saw Owen put his hand on Ann's shoulder, almost as a gesture of comfort. Bobby could also see that Neville's drawing away from Ann had upset her. Bobby quickly clicked the shutter, and at the sound, the tenuous trio instantly broke apart.

What was that all about? Bobby wondered as he flipped the film-forward lever. Behind him, he heard the sharp step of someone approaching from the side of the house.

Neville and Owen bore a resemblance to each other. Jocelyn Cook looked nothing like her brothers. While both Neville and Owen were handsome men, Jocelyn was not an attractive woman. Hers was a face which even pleasure did not grace. The broad smile with which she greeted her guests—a smile that seemed genuine only when resting on Neville—gave an awkward emphasis to her strong nose and teeth and added an unattractive ruddiness to a complexion that had naturally high color.

"Sorry to be late getting back." Jocelyn spoke generally, but she looked to Neville for forgiveness. "We have a problem with the herd down at Mill Pond."

To Bobby, Owen said, "Before you leave you must have a look at my sister's pet cows. Most amusing. Jocelyn, my friend Bobby Fitzgerald."

Jocelyn's hand shot out, giving Bobby a quick, unfriendly shake. "They're not cows, Mr. Fitzgerald. We're doing very important work on herd genetics. Britain's cattle industry has undergone devastation in the past—"

It was Neville who interrupted her, saying, "Why don't we go in. I think a drink is in order. I'm sure Jocelyn's dissertation on herd genetics will be infinitely more palatable with a dollop of gin."

Jocelyn's face fell at Neville's subtle ridicule. Recovering herself, she said, "I'll have Pack bring drinks to the library. And you will be spared further facts regarding the herd. I'm afraid it's a subject that doesn't lend itself to cocktail chatter."

"A truer word was never spoken," Owen said, being the first to make for the house.

The weekend, Bobby thought, was showing some dramatic potential.

Charhill's interior was cavernous, impressive, and uncomfortable. The stone floors echoed with voices and footsteps, the wood floors creaked. All of the wall hangings, furnishings, light fixtures, and portraits gave the impression of having been in the house forever, but bore no relationship to the current occupants. And, while it had been warm all week, the house was damp and cold—a circumstance that became relevant to an altercation between Ann and Jocelyn.

They had been sitting in silence in the library, nursing their drinks with the careful attention people pay when they can think of nothing to say to one another. Then Jocelyn said, "I meant to mention, Ann—and this is a bit awkward—but I understand from Pack that you asked Marjorie to lay a fire in your room last night?"

Ann looked up at Jocelyn sharply. It was clear that she took this question as a call to battle. With a challenge in the single word, she said, "Yes?"

Jocelyn settled herself a little in her chair and affected a look of friendly concern. "The thing is, it makes quite a lot of extra work for Marjorie—going all the way down to the back hall and bringing up wood to that wing of the house. It's not really something she should be expected to do, is it?"

Ann looked back at Jocelyn without blinking. "I'm not understanding you, Jocelyn. For the first week I was here you criticized me for doing things the servants should do for me. Now you're telling me I've asked something they shouldn't be expected to do. You'll forgive me for not being sure what it is I should or shouldn't ask."

Color had risen on Jocelyn's neck. Then, finding her tack, she said, "I should have anticipated your being confused. My mistake entirely. I keep forgetting that you really haven't been brought up . . . that you're not used to . . . well, that a house run like Charhill is something of a mystery to a girl like yourself. The thing is, we haven't had the chimneys in that wing of the house done out in ever so long, and I think as easily as not you could have run into a considerable bit of trouble. . . ."

"So, it's the chimneys I should have thought of, not Marjorie's labors?" Ann wasn't giving ground.

The color in Jocelyn's neck now suffused her face. She stood abruptly. "I'm sorry to say these things aren't written in a book for every-savage to read and ape. A little common sense, Miss Amundsen, is what I should rely on if I were you. Now, if you'll excuse me, I must see to dinner. At eight o'clock, then."

The scene amazed Bobby on a number of counts. That it had taken place at all was surprising. That it had taken place with a virtual stranger in company was amazing. And that it had taken place without Neville interceding on his guest's behalf was almost beyond belief. Bobby stole a glance at Owen, to find Owen looking back at him with an expression of amused smugness. Owen's look said more clearly than words could, *"Now do you believe the stories I've told you about my family?"*

What was most surprising was that the argument between Jocelyn and Ann had revealed a side of Ann Bobby would not have anticipated from their first meeting. He had seen her as reticent. But what he had just seen revealed Ann as an effective hand-to-hand combatant. With few words and no visible expenditure of emotion, she had vanquished the formidable Jocelyn—and on Jocelyn's home turf.

The battles continued at dinner, but the antagonists changed. Ann Amundsen, almost transparent in a floor-length, camel-colored cashmere sheath, entered the dining room after Neville had arrived. Neville had glanced at her as she came in, then, with a critical expression, looked again. Bobby was near enough to hear him say quietly, "You've forgotten your pearls. I particularly bought you this dress as I thought it would show the pearls I gave you to advantage. You've time before dinner is served—why don't you go back upstairs—"

Ann had made a small gesture of dismissal with her hand and moved to the table. Neville had not moved; Bobby had the distinct impression that Neville was not used to being dismissed by anyone and most particularly not used to being dismissed by Ann. Bobby saw something tighten in Neville's face before Neville turned to take his place at the table.

The dinner table brought out impulses of the hostess in Jocelyn. She carefully addressed each dinner guest with attentive, if impersonal, questions. To Bobby she said, "Tell us, Mr. Fitzgerald, how it is you and Owen came to know one another? Am I remembering correctly . . . it was something to do with Owen's publishing venture?"

"Yes," Bobby said, glancing first at Owen, whose expression was neutral. "I gave a lecture at Durham University that Owen attended. . . ."

"I was on a *scouting* expedition, don't you see," Owen said. "And I knew immediately that I'd like Bobby to do something on Henry James for my as-yet-unborn press. I still would, but it seems I'm not very convincing—" Owen glanced at Neville with an expression that combined resentment and trepidation. "With Mr. Fitzgerald *or* my brother."

Neville said, "Speaking only for myself, I would agree with that conclusion."

The subject broached, Owen couldn't resist carrying his point forward. "Now, *cows* on the other hand. For cows there seem to be unlimited family funds. . . ."

Jocelyn broke in. "You persist, Owen, in referring to the herd as if it were a hobby. It is, may I remind you once again, a business venture—"

"Oh, really, Jocelyn. I'm not a fool. Your cows have infinitely less chance of being a paying proposition than does my publishing venture. You forget: I see the annual statement for the trust. Not only do your cows fail to produce a profit in the estate's interest, they've become a bloody sink hole for capital." Owen turned full face to Neville. "I can't imagine why you allow it to go on. And at the same time you refuse me the bit of capital that I need for my press. *Unfair* hardly does justice to the situation."

"This is neither the time nor place." Neville's voice was flat, unruffled.

"I've yet to find a time or place you did find suitable. You've only to say to say where and when." Owen stopped and seemed to regain his composure, but the remembrance of a final injustice curdled his temper. "Moreover, not only am I not given the capital I need, I'm required to spend most of my time on the real estate development side of the business...."

"*Not* a requirement," Neville said quietly but firmly. "Your *choice*, Owen."

"A *choice* only to the extent that I could otherwise choose to live like a pauper on the trust's income."

"You have the same income from the trust as do Jocelyn and I—please, Owen. This is most inconsiderate to our guests...."

Owen was silent for a moment before he said, "You know the flaw in that logic better than I. The arrangement as is simply isn't fair. I leave it at that."

Owen's case was one Bobby had heard directly from Owen. In previous conversations on the subject with Owen, Bobby had always been skeptical that the injustices Owen suffered were quite as one-sided as claimed. He did not know Owen well. Their acquaintance had been more professional than personal, but Bobby had opportunity to observe Owen's sybaritic lifestyle in some detail. He had been inclined to discount Owen's complaints as at least partially the ranting of a spoiled child. But mere hours in the company of Neville and Jocelyn had brought Bobby completely over to Owen's side.

The rest of the dinner was comparatively uneventful, interesting only to the extent to which Neville concerned himself with Ann's eating habits. Neville's eyes went often to her plate, and he urged her to eat whatever was untouched. There was a brief skirmish over red meat, with Ann's resistance taking the form of silence and a refusal to meet Neville's stare. Bobby saw the same expression of tightening across Neville's face that he'd noticed when Ann had refused to fetch her pearls.

It was a relief to all when dinner ended. There was a

brief gathering for after-dinner drinks in the library, with Ann excusing herself first to "make an early night of it." Soon after, Neville and Jocelyn pleaded business to be attended to and made off to their respective studies, leaving Bobby and Owen alone, a decanter of brandy between them.

With an impish smile, Owen said to Bobby, "So. You've had a front-row seat. Have I in past conversations exaggerated my family's foibles?"

Bobby laughed. "It was what I was thinking at dinner. I *had* rather wondered if you didn't protest your circumstances too much. But that doubt has been laid to rest. You are, incontestably, the wronged party. One thing I didn't quite follow—how *is* it that Neville and Jocelyn live as well as they do if you all have equal shares of the trust?"

Owen shifted down into the leather club chair, lifting his feet to the low table in front of them. "Two answers to that question. First, Neville does benefit as chairman of Cook Limited with a substantially larger salary than I. I don't grudge him that. He works damn hard—harder than I do, truth to be told. And he's good at it. I do just fine crunching numbers and performing due diligence examinations on prospective acquisitions, but the enterprise is successful because of Neville. The difference is, it's an enterprise that Neville would choose to do, even if money were no object. My involvement is solely based on the need for additional income.

"Neville's other advantage is that as chairman of Cook Limited, he has a very liberal expense allowance. My expenses are limited to those incurred directly in the line of duty, so to speak. As for Jocelyn, she lives free of charge at Charhill. More to the point, she has no real interest in money. You saw what she had on at dinner? The long plaid skirt with a silk blouse she's had since I was a child? She's only interested in her cows and that because it creates the illusion that she's a fully vested member of the landed gentry. If we were to do

153

nothing other than to sell the herd, my income from the trust would double—that's how much it's costing to sustain her illusions."

"Why on earth *does* Neville allow it?"

Owen looked into his globe of brandy, then drank deep. He sighed, put the glass down, and said, "It all goes back to the terms of my father's will. On the face of it, they are wholly reasonable. All the interests of the estate are in trust, with the beneficiaries—Neville, Jocelyn, myself—sharing an equal annual percentage of estate income. Beneficiaries may, by majority vote, alter the distribution and dispose of assets. For as long as the trust has been in effect, Neville and Jocelyn have constituted a majority against my minority. My *theory* is that Neville doesn't challenge Jocelyn's prerogatives so as to preserve their alliance against me."

"What *difference* should it make to Neville if he gives money to Jocelyn for the herd or to you to establish a publishing imprint?"

Owen smiled again. "Ah. And now we come to the heart of the matter. No difference financially—in fact, as I suggested—Jocelyn's cows cost the estate a damn sight more than would my publishing venture." Owen sat up in the chair and looked squarely at Bobby. He spoke in almost a whisper, as if what he were about to say was too important to be heard beyond the two of them. "But it's a matter of *control*, don't you see. More than money, more than anything, Neville needs to be in control. And in the dynamic of our family, Jocelyn has always sided with Neville, always been his ally—and I have always been the outsider. I have always been the one who *needed* to be controlled."

"And there's nothing in the will that provides for any arbitration against a—what would you call it—self-interested majority?"

Owen shook his head with the weariness of someone who

had exhausted all consideration of the question at hand. "Oh, there's the standard, boiler-plate language regarding moral turpitude—meaning that if Neville shat upon the steps of Buckingham Palace, he could be excluded as a beneficiary of the trust—" Owen shrugged. "We both know I'm more likely to breach that clause than is our Neville."

Bobby smiled, paused, then said, "What's Ann Amundsen's story? I can't figure out her relationship with your brother."

Owen rolled his head sideways on the back of the chair and looked at Bobby with a devilish grin. "Oh, *good*. I rather hoped you'd take to her. It will make Neville utterly mad. She is something of a stunner, isn't she?"

"Agreed that she is a stunner. But my question wasn't selfish. I am genuinely curious about what she's doing with him."

"It is curious, I admit. I have an idea what's going on—but only an idea. Actually, when we walked today we talked about it a good deal. I suppose I'm breaching a confidence, but I can't see that it matters. . . ."

"Please, do."

"I really didn't know Ann well before she came to Charhill with Neville. She's a consultant with one of the big accounting firms, based in Boston. I met her only once there—Neville's never been inclined to share the possessions he values."

The word "possessions" triggered Bobby's recollection of what he had witnessed between Neville and Ann that night. The notion that Neville viewed Ann as his possession struck Bobby as exactly right.

"Anyway, I had dinner with Ann and Neville at her apartment in Boston once. My impression then—and this was, oh, sometime last fall—was that the interest was all on Neville's side. I was surprised to hear she was coming with him to England, I'd rather expected she'd break off with him.

When I saw her here a few weeks ago, I was surprised. She was greatly changed. Thinner, subdued—and completely under Neville's thumb. She'd moved into his apartment in Boston—something Neville had not bothered to mention to me—and is on leave from her job. To be frank, I was confounded. When we walked today, she said that there had been—" Owen hesitated. "There had been a family tragedy. I don't think I should say more than that. Neville had been extremely supportive and that she'd allowed herself to become more and more dependent on him in recent months. This of course, is precisely the sort of scenario Neville looks for in relationships. Indeed, he doesn't really want a relationship at all. He wants an object to control, a victim, if you will. . . ."

Owen stopped again and grinned. "This next bit is really quite funny. Do you know what more or less snapped Ann out of her state of somnolence?"

"Not a clue."

"Jocelyn. Jocelyn has been unspeakably rude to Ann ever since she's arrived. Jocelyn, of course, is pathologically jealous of Neville's relationship with Ann, and is doing all she can to make Ann unwelcome—all under the guise, of course, of being the perfect hostess. The way Ann puts it, the energy she used to stand her ground against Jocelyn more or less woke her up. She started seeing her relationship with Neville in a different light. I think she may well make a run for it. I think in his own limited way, Neville is really attached to Ann. It will hurt him very much if she does leave. And I shall enjoy seeing him lose something he wants—maybe almost as much as I want my press."

Ann lay in bed thinking, her thoughts not much different from those of Owen's and Bobby's in the library below. She had come to Charhill with the expectation that she did so as Neville Cook's prospective wife. And only weeks ago, that was what she wanted. Now she was only sure that she no longer knew what she wanted.

What kept her awake was not only uncertainty but the uncomfortable realization that in the space of less than a year she had allowed herself to descend from being an independent woman into being wholly dependent on Neville Cook. The initial comfort she had taken in his control and authority had outlived any useful purpose in her life. More than that—her dependence on Neville had evolved into a powerful malignant force that had robbed her of emotional, intellectual, and physical freedom. Knowing how that had happened did not justify allowing the dependence to continue. The question became, was a relationship with Neville possible without dependence?

Jocelyn's reception had forced Ann to think realistically about what a permanent relationship with Neville would be like. And while Neville's control of her life had for several months been a source of comfort, it was increasingly a source of irritation. She dimly recognized that the irritation represented the return of her old spirit.

Small things—things that had happened only today— were having an impact on how she felt about Neville as well. As she and Owen had started their walk earlier in the afternoon, they had passed through a courtyard at the rear of the house. The area had once been a stable yard, the stables long since converted to garages. As they passed through, Ann noticed a young man and woman standing just inside one of the garages. Ann recognized the young man as William, the boy who drove the estate cars on occasion. The girl she didn't recognize. What she did recognize—with a force that caused a sharp pain of recognition—was the profound sense of intimacy between the pair. William stood straight above the girl, looking down at her, without touching, but with a tenderness that was visible even at a distance. What caused Ann pain

157

was the realization that the intimacy between this young boy and girl was more intense than anything she had experienced in the whole of her relationship with Neville.

She had talked about Neville with Owen as they'd walked. Of everything that Owen had said about Neville, the thing that rang truest was when Owen said Neville had no soul. How could you marry a man without a soul? Then, as they returned to the house to find Neville back from town and Bobby Fitzgerald arrived, there had been Neville's response to having their picture taken. She remembered Neville moving—almost imperceptibly—away from her. It was a brief moment, a small gesture, but it was the sort of moment when, in the space of perhaps four or five seconds, lives change.

Deep in those thoughts and finally drifting toward sleep, Ann was startled by a quick knock at the door. The door opened before she could answer, and Neville stepped into the room. He was in his pajamas and a dressing gown.

So complete was his dominance of her that Ann's first response to his presence was of guilt at the disloyal thoughts she had been thinking. Caught off guard, she welcomed him with more friendliness than she felt.

He stopped beside her, untying his robe and hanging it on the bedstead. From the first, Ann had been fascinated by Neville's lack of declared or demonstrated emotion. It had taken her completely by surprise when, after their third dinner date, he'd returned without invitation to her apartment. As they'd entered the foyer, he'd kissed her artfully, then taken her to bed. His lovemaking was confident and silent. He did not break even a dew of perspiration. Nor did he make any gesture of real affection.

This night his lovemaking was no different from any other night, except that it was different for Ann. Something in her was beginning or ending. She couldn't have said which, nor could she have said why.

She lay awake long after he had fallen asleep. In her mind's eye, she was seeing herself with Neville over the past several months. It was like a silent movie, in which she was a robotic image, going through the motions of a life that was safe but empty.

Resolved to sleep, Ann rose silently and went into the bathroom for a drink of water. As she walked carefully and silently back to the bed, Neville's voice rose toward her in the dark.

"It's not like you to be up during the night."

A chill swept through Ann. How did he know if it was or wasn't like her to be up during the night? Did he lie in a half sleep, night after night, with a Cyclops eye fixed on her in constant observation?

She didn't answer him, but she answered her own silent question. Did she want to stay with this man for the rest of her life? The answer was no.

The next morning, Saturday, before going down to breakfast, Ann thought through the timing of when she would speak to Neville. She would say nothing until Sunday night. Fitzgerald would be leaving Monday morning, so he would be spared the aftermath of her announcement—should there be an aftermath. But first, she wanted to tell Owen what she'd decided. After breakfast, she asked him to walk toward the river with her.

Their path was through the property at the front of the house, down the main road, then a turn to the river. Not a word was spoken between them as they walked. Reaching the river, they sat.

Ann said, "I've decided. I'm going back to Boston ahead of Neville. Before I go I'm going to end our relationship."

Owen stared at her without speaking.

She was impatient with his reticence. "Well? Is it or is it not what you thought best?"

Owen's face and his voice were serious when he spoke. "I suppose I'm feeling a little guilty—have I been too much of an influence in your decision?"

She shook her head. "No. Not at all. You helped me—definitely helped me—see Neville more objectively. But even if you hadn't, I would have come to this decision. As things stand now, I can't imagine how I've allowed myself to continue with Neville as long as I have."

"When do you intend to tell him?"

Ann made a face. "Making the decision was the easy part. I won't pretend I look forward to telling Neville. I think maybe after dinner tomorrow evening. Your friend leaves Monday morning, so by waiting until after dinner tomorrow there won't be any need to involve him in any unpleasantness."

Owen frowned. "You'll think I'm being unnecessarily cautious—but I think you should tell Neville Monday morning. Then he'll have the day in the City to let the news settle."

"But that's exactly what I wanted to avoid—his leaving upset, having to deal with business all day having just been—"

"I can't tell you why I think it best. It's just something I feel very strongly." Owen hesitated. He looked genuinely upset. "I don't want to be overly dramatic, but sometimes I feel I don't know Neville—or what he's capable of—at all. I'm quite serious about this. I want you to promise me you'll wait until Monday morning to tell Neville. When you come downstairs ask to speak to him in the library. Quite simply, I don't want you to be away from others in the house when you tell him. Promise me that, Ann."

Ann was moved by Owen's concern. It even touched an ill-defined fear she felt herself.

"All right," she said. "Monday morning it is."

The remaining two days of the weekend were uncomfortable for everyone. Ann was tense and self-conscious. Knowing what he did of Ann's plans, Owen avoided being with Ann and Neville as much as possible. And Bobby, unaware of the pending drama, was more than usually perplexed at the interplay between Ann and Neville and Owen's sudden withdrawal from the social scene.

On Monday morning, Ann felt something like relief at being able to end the suspense. She waited inside her room on Monday morning to hear Neville's door unlatch. When she heard the latch, she opened her own door. Meeting Neville in the hallway, she said, "Before you leave, Neville—could we talk a bit, just the two of us, in the library?"

He hadn't looked at her as he said, "I'm a bit rushed this morning. Perhaps this evening." Without waiting for her to respond, Neville turned and started down the hallway.

It was hard to explain why the single word—"perhaps"—made Ann as angry as it did. But Neville's unwillingness to talk this morning, or to make a definite commitment to talk in the evening, made Ann grind her teeth. *Perhaps* this evening! All right, then. If a talk didn't fit his schedule, Ann would suit her own schedule.

She was relieved on entering the dining room to see that Bobby Fitzgerald wasn't down. With a quick, warning glance at Owen, Ann said, "I've been thinking I should go back to Boston next Tuesday. I haven't checked flights, but there shouldn't be a problem."

The room went completely silent. Ann glanced up at Jocelyn, rather than looking directly at Neville. Jocelyn was transfixed. Her eyes glittered, her skin was brilliant with suppressed exhilaration. Owen immediately leaped up to fill his plate at the sideboard.

Feigning a calm she did not feel, Ann looked at Neville. His expression was frozen in neutrality so rigid that his lips had gone white.

161

He spoke almost without moving his lips. "I don't believe this is something we've discussed."

"I'm not sure what there is to discuss. And I'm not leaving till Tuesday. So if there's anything before then . . . *perhaps* this evening?"

Neville dabbed at his mouth with the white linen napkin. He rose, his bearing more regimental than usual. "Owen, if you're going into town with me, you'll need to be at the car in fifteen minutes."

Owen stood with a plate heaped with breakfast. "Yes, of course," he said.

Ann excused herself and went to her room. It had not been easy, but it was done. Somehow she had to get through the next week, then she'd be free. She stood at her window thinking about the prospect of being on her own again. And then, without having heard him come in, something made her turn to see Neville standing behind her. She visibly started.

"Neville. You frightened me."

"I must say, that was damned awkward of you. Do you mind telling me what you're up to?"

She hesitated, wondering how far to go. Given her belief that beginning was the hardest part of doing something and that she had in fact already gotten past the beginning, she decided to go ahead.

"It's what I said downstairs. I've decided to go back to Boston." She paused. Then, reaching for Neville's arm—which he immediately drew back—"Look, Neville. I don't belong, do I? I decided that for both of us it would be best if I got my own place. Of course I'll always want to be able to—"

"*You've* decided? *You've* decided?" His voice was equal parts rage and contempt. The whiteness of his face was now broken by two intense red spots on each cheekbone. His eyes had gone black.

Ann saw Neville's hand coming toward her without an idea that he meant to hit her. So when the flat of his hand banged against her jaw, surprise, not pain, was her first reaction. Surprise was quickly replaced by embarrassment. The force of the blow caused her to stumble and, illogically, she was embarrassed at having Neville see her fall. She managed to check her fall by grabbing the bedpost, and it was while she was in that position, almost on her knees, hanging from a bedpost, that Neville spoke his final words to her.

"I want you out of Charhill by the time I return from London tonight. I'll leave it to you to sort out how you manage that." He turned sharply and left the room, taking care to close the door quietly behind him. His self-control in shutting the door was more frightening to her than the bang of a slammed door would have been.

Ann could not have said how long she remained huddled on the floor, afraid to move for fear that movement would bring Neville back. As time passed, she felt the numbness on her face turn warm with pain. When she did stand, she walked to the dressing table to examine herself in the mirror. Her face was already swelling and growing red. She could see the image of Neville's open hand beginning to glow across the left side of her face.

How to get away? Jocelyn would already be out of the house—not that Ann would have asked her to help. Owen was out of the question—he had probably already left with Neville in any event, and his relationship with Neville would be hopelessly compromised if she involved him now. Pack was her only hope. She rang for him without having thought through what she would say, and he appeared before she had time to construct her story. Which turned out to be a good thing. Of necessity, she kept it simple.

"Pack, my plans have changed and I need to get to the airport. Could I ask you to arrange a car?"

"Very good, miss. What time will your flight be departing?"

Hesitating, Ann said, "I'm going to be taking the first available flight. I just want to get to the airport as quickly as possible."

It was Pack's turn to hesitate. "May I suggest, miss, that we take you to Gatwick. Mr. Fitzgerald is leaving within the hour and I'm sure we can book you on the same flight. I'm sorry to say if that doesn't work we might have to delay your departure until the car returns from taking Mr. Fitzgerald, as Mr. Neville and Mr. Owen have just left in the Bentley. And as you don't have a reservation, I do think the earlier we get you to the airport, the better."

Ann thought about it. She did not welcome the prospect of sharing a car to the airport—and a flight back to Boston—with Fitzgerald. What she wanted now was to be alone. But when she contemplated staying at Charhill for several more hours, the choice was easy.

"That would be fine. And Pack, I won't need any help packing my things. Circumstances being what they are, I'm going to be traveling light. I'll just take a carry-on bag. I'll leave instructions with Miss Cook as to what to do with my other things."

"Very good, miss." Pack hesitated for a moment. "May I say, miss, that we'll be sorry to see you go. We've enjoyed having you here."

Pack's simple act of courtesy almost broke Ann's thin emotional control. She turned from him as she said, "My thanks to the staff, Pack. You've all been very kind." Remembering her manners, Ann said, "Has Miss Cook left the house yet, Pack?"

"Yes, miss. Directly after breakfast."

"I would appreciate your expressing my regret at not being able to say a proper good-bye and thank-you...."

Pack and Ann looked at each other for a moment. There was understanding between them. He said only, "Very good, miss."

Ann's snap decision to leave everything but what she could carry herself offered a number of advantages, not the least of which was that she could be gone within the half hour. As she opened the armoire, she realized that Neville had given her almost everything she'd brought. She wanted none of it, and could think of nothing better to do than to abandon it at Charhill.

When she left, she was dressed in jeans and a sweater, with a light jacket. She carried only her purse and a garment bag. Pack stood on the front drive, holding the rear door of the estate car open for her. William was at the wheel, Bobby Fitzgerald sat in the backseat. Ann shifted her bag to shake Pack's hand, shrugging off his effort to take her bag. Thanking him for his courtesy, she dumped the bag into the backseat next to Fitzgerald. Then she went around to the passenger side of the front seat. No longer a prospective mistress of the house, the front passenger seat was the position of choice.

She kept her eyes on the rearview mirror as they drove down the drive. Now that she was almost safely away, small shudders of relief shook her in waves.

William looked at her with curiosity, uncertain of what he could or could not ask of this unpredictable young woman. Finally he spoke. "You'll not be coming back, then, miss?"

They had just passed from the front drive into the first woods beyond the house. "No, William," she said. "I'll not be coming back."

CHAPTER
14

Gatwick was not as nice as Heathrow. It had a jerry-built look, and it was crowded with tired-looking travelers, speaking a dozen different languages, who looked as if they'd flown all night on economy flights where the toilets had reached capacity several hours before the plane reached Gatwick.

Ann felt safe amidst the rabble. It was not a place she could imagine Neville choosing to be. So here she was, in jeans, three thousand miles from home, with a single bag. She longed for the moment when the plane doors shut and she could be sure that she had escaped Neville.

She hadn't escaped Bobby Fitzgerald, who clearly viewed their shared travel plans as an opportunity. He arranged adjoining seats and stuck to her like glue until they boarded.

It was the first time in years Ann hadn't flown first class. But she couldn't remember a time when she'd been more comfortable. She and Fitzgerald had an entire center row on the 747 to themselves, and sitting in the center of the center row, they sprawled across the unoccupied seats to either side of them. She began to enjoy their conversation and to be grateful for the distraction his presence offered on the long flight.

They had been airborne for less than an hour when Fitzgerald, looking at her closely, said, "What happened to your face?"

Ann's hand went to her face reflexively. "An accident. Sort of."

He continued to look at her. "Mind telling me what you were doing with Neville Cook to begin with? I mean, sure, he was rich and good-looking—but for a woman of your character, those must have been trivial considerations...."

She leaned her head back and closed her eyes. Her eyes felt raw under her eyelids. "You say that as if it were a joke. But I *didn't* care—except, I guess, that I thought I needed the protection Neville's money gave me."

"That's an odd thing to say."

Ann adjusted the flimsy navy blue airplane blanket, wrapped it around her shoulders, and drew her stocking feet up under her on the seat.

"When I first met Neville, I didn't dream it would be a long-term relationship. He was interesting, I wasn't seeing anyone else, and it didn't take any particular effort on my part to see him. But after—I don't know, maybe a couple months—he started to bother me. He was very controlling with me, with the other people around him. It didn't take me long to decide 'enough already, who needs it'—and I more or less stopped seeing him, for a time."

Ann stopped. To Bobby it seemed that there was something she was considering saying. But when she spoke again, all she said was, "The thing is, something pretty awful happened, and I—well, I guess you could say I collapsed. Neville's good with collapsed. He just took over. Neville made me feel safe, and the trade-off—that I didn't even know had happened until it was too late—was that I became a sort of zombie."

"So what changed?"

"Different things. Some big, some almost trivial. The trivial things were maybe more important than the big things."

"Like what?"

Ann grinned. "For one thing, going to battle with Jocelyn Cook. It kind of shook me out of my stupor. I couldn't believe the way she treated me, but when I stopped to think about it, I realized that in most respects, Neville treated me even worse. And I'd put up with it. Once I stood up to Jocelyn, not tolerating Neville's behavior was a logical next step."

Bobby gave a low laugh. "She really is a piece of work, isn't she? And when you put her in the same room as Neville, you've got a lethal combination. So you broke up with him. I gather Neville didn't take the news that you were leaving gracefully?" His eyes were on her discolored, swollen face.

Ann touched her face again. She could feel hot skin. "I'll tell you something funny. It was the only time Neville showed any real emotion in all the time I've known him. If you'd asked me before this morning if I thought Neville could be violent, I would have told you it was the one thing I was sure he couldn't be. I didn't think there was anything in him that could produce out-of-control anger, much less physical violence. The real joke is that Neville was the only person in the world who made me feel safe. . . ." She shook her head at her own misplaced trust.

"Tell me what it was that scared you to begin with."

Ann took a deep breath. She looked at him, uncertain. "My sister, Holly, was murdered. In my apartment. I found her, and it just . . . it just destroyed me. I couldn't go back to the apartment. Everywhere I went I felt this terror that the person who did it was near me. . . ."

Bobby's face was frozen in an expression of horror or repulsion. Ann couldn't tell which. "I'm sorry," she said. "I shouldn't have said anything."

Bobby held up a hand. He sat forward, and said, "It's not what you think. It's just that it is the most extraordinary thing—"

She said, "It *is* extraordinary, and not just because this horrible thing has happened. It makes freaks out of the family members. How many people do you know who've had a sister murdered?"

Bobby said, "Only you and me."

Ann was too stunned by Bobby telling her that his own sister had been murdered to hear much of what he said about the murder. And she was too absorbed in the horror of the co-incidence to pay attention to what Bobby was saying. She stopped him. "I'm sorry, I haven't been paying any attention to what you said. Start again. I'd really like to know what happened."

"I was just saying," Bobby explained, "we still don't know what happened. My sister was a terrific kid. The only thing the cops could figure was that she went out with somebody she didn't know—we found out she was a bit of a risk taker along those lines—and that the guy was a creep. By the time she figured that out, it was too late."

Ann nodded. "It was the same thing with my sister—that she'd used bad judgment in letting someone into the apartment. He tried to rape her—she was partially undressed, but there wasn't any physical evidence that she'd actually been raped—and she'd been drinking. Which was kind of strange. It wasn't that Holly never drank, but she was such a scatterbrain, she'd never drink long enough to get drunk. She'd open a can of beer, take a sip, put the can down, and go into another room. An hour later, she'd come back out and take another can of beer out of the refrigerator. She was the kind of person who'd take a drink at a party, put her glass down, and not remember where she left it. Getting seriously drunk would have taken organizational skills and a level of concentration way, way beyond Holly's abilities.

"But what was strange was that when the medical examiner did the autopsy, the report showed a blood alcohol of point three-oh—and a lot of gin in her stomach, as if she'd been chugalugging. It just wasn't like her at all."

Bobby's face had a strange expression. "How did you say she was killed?"

"They never found a weapon. The guy used a long, sharp instrument—which was all the police told me. They said it wasn't an impulse murder, that the wound was inflicted in a 'purposeful manner.' Their words, exactly. The weapon tore the hell out of her aorta. She probably bled to death in minutes, but there was hardly any blood because the wound closed on itself after she was stabbed."

Bobby looked dazed. Ann guessed she'd been too graphic.

"I'm sorry. I'm telling you more than you want to know. The thing that you don't know about murders until they happen to someone you love is that there's more than one victim. That the family is never the same again. These guys who go around killing people, they do a lot more damage than just the murder."

Bobby spoke softly. "You've got the pronoun wrong."

"I've got the *pronoun* wrong? What—?"

"It's not *they*. It's not third person plural. It's *he*. It's third person singular."

PART IV

MINNEAPOLIS

TUESDAY, AUGUST 5 TO
        SUNDAY, NOVEMBER 23

CHAPTER
15

"Somebody's gonna have to explain Rene Russo to me." Mars squinted into the bright afternoon sunlight as he and Chris came out of the movie theater.

"What d'you mean?"

"I mean, she's got enough bone in her jaw alone to build three full-grown adults. She's a *terrible* actress. Where she gets off being the romantic lead in half the movies we've seen over the past couple years, I'll never know."

"I don't like her either," Chris said.

Mars's beeper went.

"Yippeee!" Chris did a little dance.

"Don't get your hopes up," Mars said, giving Chris a playful swat. "Nettie's covering for me this afternoon, your mom being out of town, so it's probably nothing special."

Chris sat on his knees in the front seat of the squad car watching as Mars phoned in on the mobile phone. Chris held his hands up, the index and middle fingers on both hands crossed, while Mars punched out the Homicide Division number.

It was Nettie.

"Mars? There's a girl down here on possession with intent to sell. She says she wants to cut a deal on something she knows on the Mary Pat Fitzgerald case. Glenn says to tell you we've got kind of a narrow window of opportunity on doing a deal with her. He's charging her tomorrow on possession with intent and as accessory to murder. He says he's got more than enough for the charge and to hold her without bail on the accessory charge, but he doesn't think what he's got is gonna hold up through a trial. He thinks—tops—we've got a couple weeks to do a deal."

Mars's breath caught. A light tingle started a zillionth of a fraction of an inch off the back of his neck. "What's she got to say?"

"What she's got to say is that she's not saying anything to anybody but you. Otherwise I would have handled it myself— except I probably wouldn't have. Kinda thought this was one you might want to follow up yourself. Chris still with you?"

Mars gave a heavy sigh to dampen the rising expectations he felt shooting to the surface at even the possibility of something breaking on the Mary Pat Fitzgerald case. One solid lead would be more than they'd had since the day her body was found on the Father Hennepin Bluffs.

He looked at his watch. "Yeah, Chris is still with me. Denise won't be back in town till almost ten o'clock tonight." In his peripheral vision, Chris waved exuberantly, mouthing a plea to go down to city hall with Mars.

"When do you leave on vacation?"

"Not until tomorrow morning. Bring Chris down with you. We'll do more bridge lessons until you finish with the doper."

Mars glanced over the file before going up to the interrogation room.

Typical drug crap. The woman had been in an apartment with her boyfriend and two other known suppliers. An argument ensued. The woman's boyfriend had one of the suppliers on the floor, holding him down with his foot on the guy's neck while he bashed the guy's head with the butt of a rifle. The guy on the floor had reached up, found the trigger, and pulled. It blew the right side off the boyfriend's head. The woman had been covered in blood and brains when they'd brought her in.

You'd expect a girl held on possession with intent to sell to be a tough cookie. The woman sitting in the interrogation room on the third floor of the Hennepin County Jail didn't look tough. She looked battered. She was small, not short, but fine-boned. Longish, light brown hair in need of a wash. She wore a slept-in-looking white men's dress shirt and jeans. On one side of her neck, under the open collar of the shirt, was a long, purple-colored bruise. It looked old.

Mars didn't say anything on entering the room. He scraped a chair back from the table, flipped it around, and straddled the seat, leaning forward over the chair back. Slapping the file, a tablet of paper, and a pack of Camels on the table, he said abruptly and with studied indifference, "I'm Special Detective Bahr. I understand you have something to tell me about the Mary Pat Fitzgerald case."

Her eyes fixed on his face. She was sitting sort of hunched, holding herself with her arms wrapped across her chest. Her hands, the fingers long and extended against the white of the shirtsleeves, were fine. The nails were square cut and clean.

"What I said to Detective Mandlebaum in Narcotics was that I wanted a deal."

Mars nodded slowly, without looking at her. He stretched forward to pick up the Camel pack. The box was fraying at the sides, starting to lose its shape. He needed a new pack.

"That's what we all want, Miss..." He flipped open the manila file again. It said Evelyn Rau. R-a-u? "Miss... Row? German pronunciation?"

"I pronounce it 'Raw.' Like, uncooked."

"Miss Rau. Like I was saying, what we'd all like is a deal. But what we'd like and what we get aren't always the same thing. Give me what you've got and we'll go from there." He started manipulating the Camel box in his right hand, waiting for her to talk.

She looked at the Camels. "I'd prefer if you didn't smoke. It said in the hall outside that this is a smoke-free environment. And I need to know why I should tell you anything if I don't know what's in it for me."

Mars looked back at her hard and straight, rising slowly, swinging a leg over the back of the chair. Standing over her, he said in a voice that grew progressively meaner, "Oh, really. Well. Let me tell you something, Miss Half-baked or uncooked or whatever. I'm not gonna smoke. Not because some two-bit dope pusher tells me I can't, but because, as it happens, I don't smoke.

"And, while I'm at it, let me set you straight on another point. I worked on the Mary Pat Fitzgerald case just about full-time for six weeks. I worked three, four days without sleeping in a bed when we first found her body. I didn't take a piss for the first twelve hours. I worked seven days a week, two months running. A lot of it on my own clock. I didn't watch TV, I didn't go to movies. And I like to go to movies. What I did was I checked leads. I sat in this room with the scum of the earth. I spent time with Mary Pat's family. I couldn't tell you how many pieces of useless evidence I booked, how many reports I filed.

"So. When you sashay in here and say you're going to tell me something about the case I don't know, I gotta tell you your chances are less than zero that you will. The chance that you're gonna tell me something that I don't know that is *worth* knowing is less than that. What you've got to understand is that I'm doing you a favor even being here. Get it? The idea that I owe you something for being here is nuts. As we say in the trade, lady, the burden of proof is on your lap. So start saying something worth listening to or stop wasting my time."

She hadn't blinked. For the first time, she looked him in the eyes. "Do you know about Mary Pat Fitzgerald and a guy on Southeast Main Street the morning she died?"

Mars's breathing stopped altogether, and the light electrical charge he'd felt at the back of his neck when he first got Nettie's call accelerated to a major jolt. Mars struggled to stay cool, but looking back at Rau, he could see that she knew she had him.

"Keep talking."

"You talk deal, and I'll talk about what I saw on the bluffs."

Mars let it go. Then, calmly, he said, "You give me anything that gets me even close to who killed Mary Pat Fitzgerald, and I'll bust my butt with the County Attorney's Office to get you out of here free and clear. You've got my word on that. Anyone around here will tell you my word is worth having. But I can't talk deal until I know what I've got. You want out? You've gotta talk."

She kept looking at him, wary. So he said, his voice soft, "You're going to have to trust me on this."

Their eyes connected again and held for a moment.

"I was down on the bluffs that Thursday morning, parked on Southeast Main. Right in front of the Pillsbury A Mill. But I was kind of back in the seat. Someone walking or driving by wouldn't have seen me...."

She hesitated a moment, waiting for him to ask her what she'd been doing down there, both of them knowing why she'd been down there and why she'd been waiting for someone. Mars stayed quiet.

Taking his silence as a vote of confidence, she started again. "While I was waiting, a dark green BMW came up from behind and parked. There were two people in the car. The girl I recognized in the paper the next week. It was Mary Pat Fitzgerald."

"What was she wearing?"

Rau thought for a moment. "A pink windbreaker. Looked like maybe it was Ralph Lauren. Khaki slacks, a tan Coach purse. Shoulder bag."

"And the guy she was with?"

"Older than the girl. I'm not great on ages—he could have been anything from say, late twenties to early forties Very good-looking. Well put together. I'd say he was a good six inches taller than the Fitzgerald girl. They were walking side by side at one point. They seemed—hard to explain. I'd guess they didn't know each other real well. Her movements, the way she looked with him—kind of flirtatious. Not the way you'd act with somebody you'd known a long time. He was paying a lot of attention to everything but her. He was carrying what looked like a bottle of wine, wrapped in a brown paper bag...."

Mars had broken into a light sweat. His voice broke slightly as he asked, "Why do you say wine?"

She thought for a second before she answered. "Good question. I guess what it looked like was the kind of narrow bag liquor stores use. I just assumed it was wine. Could have been any kind of bottle, I guess."

Mars didn't breathe when he asked her, "Do you think you could identify the guy?"

She didn't hesitate. "I'm sure I could."

"Describe the circumstances of your seeing him. The angle from which you saw him, for how long you saw him...."

"I can tell you pretty exactly. I parked the car just after ten-fifty-five—I'd checked my watch when I parked, and I checked it again when the Beemer pulled up behind me. That was ten-fifty-one, I left maybe forty-five seconds after they disappeared, going down the steps on the bluffs, and I checked my watch then—which was ten-fifty-four. So I watched them, first from my side-view mirror, then as they walked past my car and down the bluffs, for around two minutes."

"How are you remembering the detail? This was almost five months ago."

She shook her head in a slight movement. "Something didn't feel right." She looked at him. "In my business, you depend on how things feel a lot. And it didn't feel right. Then, four days later, I saw the Fitzgerald girl's picture in the paper, the story about her being murdered. I wrote down some notes about what I remembered."

Mars closed his eyes for a moment before he asked, "Still have the notes?"

"Not here, but at my apartment."

"Anything about the notes tie them to that period of time?"

"I wrote the time I saw the Beemer and the time I left on the news clipping about the murder. It was the article you were quoted in. I think the clipping had the date."

Mars pushed her. Not out of doubt, but to find out if she had the potential to be as good a witness as he thought she'd be.

"So. You see something nearly five months ago that made enough of an impression on you that you took notes. But you don't come forward and tell anyone what you saw?"

She shrugged. "I wasn't interested in initiating contact with cops. For all I knew, I could have become a suspect." She thought for a moment. "If I'd seen a photo of her in the paper saying she was missing, instead of saying her body had been found . . ." Rau shrugged again. "I don't know. I'd like to think I'd have come forward then. But I don't know. Maybe, maybe not."

"Maybe it would have done some good to get the guy who killed her off the streets?"

She gave him a look. "Let's just say it wasn't a time in my life when public service was a real high priority."

Mars sat down. "What I'm going to do is have you write out a formal statement. You'll get a chance to review it before you sign it. I'm gonna want to have you get together with a department artist who'll try and put together a sketch based on your description. Then I'm going to have you go through a bunch of photos—see if you can pick anyone out of the photos. I'll be honest with you. I believe what you've told me. And this is the best information that we've had in this case yet. But if I can't use what you've given me to ID someone who looks probable—well, it's not going to do either of us much good. But if you ID someone I can tie to Mary Pat's death, I'll go to bat for you with the County Attorney's Office. My word on that.

"In the meantime, if you remember anything else—anything at all—" Mars stopped and fished around in his back pants pocket for his wallet. He pulled out a card, wrote on it, and pushed it across the table to her. "If you think of anything else, call me anytime at any of those numbers. Anytime."

There was still a small smile on her lips.

"There was something about the plate number I remember—would that help?"

The jolt hit again, with twice the force. He should have asked her. *Geez.* He'd actually forgotten to ask her for the plates.

"This is going to be a little hard to explain, but when I looked at the plates the letters reminded me of something. The letters on the plates were *VSW.* I don't remember the numbers, but the plate letters were *VSW.*"

Having a partial on the plate letters didn't make it simple.

Nettie got the job of tracking down the plate. She canceled her vacation to do it. Mars had argued with her about that, but she'd said, "If it were the other way around, if you were scheduled for leave tomorrow, what would you do?" He didn't answer, and she said, "This may come as a surprise to you, but I care as much about my job as you do about yours."

Mars was embarrassed because he hadn't really thought that was true until Nettie said it.

A day and a half later, she'd nailed a probable on the plates. Sitting herself down on the edge of his desk, she said, "Good news, bad news. How do you want it?"

"Good news first."

"I found something on the plates that fits."

Mars groaned. "So the bad news is it was a stolen car, right?"

"Not quite. Stolen plates. I ran a list of all active plates in Minnesota with VSW letters. One of those plates popped up as reported stolen on April thirteenth. The date was close enough to our time period, so I followed up the owner." Nettie glanced down at her clipboard. "A guy named Raymond Bluin had plates stolen from his car parked at the airport from April first to the twelfth. First three letters on the plates were VSW. The car was a Chevy, not a Beemer. Whoever stole the plates—that's our guy."

"Bluin doesn't look like a possible?"

"Bluin is in his late fifties, short and balding. Nothing about him matches Rau's story. The plate story is tight. Bluin filed a report with airport security the day after he got back in town. He'd been in San Diego for an association convention—he sells some kind of digital printing service— and I've checked the hotel records. They match. I haven't gone through his credit card records for that period—"

Mars had rocked back on his chair as he'd listened to Nettie. He dropped down on all four legs, hard. "Forget it. He's not our guy. See if you can get a picture of him from back then and add it to the photo lineup we're gonna have Rau look at. Let it go at-that. You check his record?"

"Clean. A moving violation four years ago. That's it."

"The airport have any video surveillance where Bluin was parked?"

"Well, we were lucky there. Because he filed a report on the missing plates, there's a notation on where Bluin parked: green ramp, level three, space A-thirty-one. The spot was in range of the surveillance camera, but . . ."

"More good news, bad news."

"Yup. The bad news is the surveillance tape runs for twelve hours. If there are no reported incidents during that time, it rewinds and retapes. Tell you the truth, I had the impression airport security wasn't about to get off their butts to look at the tape even if Bluin had filed the report before the tape rewound. And they made it pretty clear they thought I was nuts to even think they might still have the tape five months later."

"A bunch of chair warmers. Always have been. Well, that leaves us with the Beemer. What've you got there?"

"There are fourteen hundred and seven Beemers registered in Minnesota. One hundred and thirty-three of them were dark green. State's supposed to have the list over to me"—Nettie glanced at her watch—"an hour ago. Soon as I get it, I'll start checking. I'll get Teresa to match driver's license descriptions with the owners' list, and we'll focus on anyone that looks close. Probably gonna take us the rest of the week just to run down the guys that are around—longer than that to find everybody."

"I'll want photos of all the dark green Beemer owners in the photo lineup."

"That *is* gonna take a lot of time. You want to wrap this up during my lifetime?"

Mars shrugged. "Whatever. Have you run a check on stolen Beemers around that time?"

Nettie nodded. "Did that first thing. But I couldn't find anything on a stolen dark green Beemer for three weeks either side of April third. So I'm guessing the guy with Mary Pat either owned or rented the car"—Nettie held up a hand to keep Mars from interrupting her again—"and I've started contacts with the three car rental agencies in the Twin Cities that do high-end, specialty rentals. Two of them might be able to produce records for that period. The other one, well, I'm not sure they could tell you anything about yesterday.

"Long and short of it is, partner, that this is getting to be a lot of work—and everything we come up with is gonna produce another pile of stuff we'll have to track down. We need something fast to focus this thing. There are a thousand directions we could go at this point."

Mars grinned, folded his hands behind his head and rocked back on his chair again. "Just the way I like it. And just the way we didn't have in April. God. We've got more to go on in the last two days than we had for the whole investigation. This feels better. Much better." Mars stopped. "What if the guy rented the car in, say, Wisconsin?"

"Don't even think about it. I suppose we could expand the rental car search—and the vehicle registration check—to surrounding states, but give me a break. I'd like to rule out Minnesota first. I haven't even started on lease deals yet."

Mars sat upright. "Yeah. That's fine, for now." He stretched. "What I've got to do is talk to the chief about freeing us up to focus. And getting a war room together. There's going to be a lot to keep track of, and we'll need to spread out some—"

"I've already reserved the small conference room over on three."

Mars bent over and kissed the top of Nettie's head.

"You sure the chief is gonna go for this?"

Mars got up. "No problem."

And it wasn't.

Mars knocked on the chief's door and stuck his head in. "Got a minute?"

The chief looked up at Mars, then at his watch. "Three minutes, to be exact. I've got a meeting with the mayor on the federal application for new hires. What's up?"

Mars moved into the room, but stayed close to the door. "Remember Mary Pat Fitzgerald? The Edina princess that bought it down on the bluffs last April? We've got an informant out of Narcotics who saw her down on the Father Hennepin Bluffs with a guy the morning she was killed. Probably about a half hour to forty-five minutes before she died. We've got a description of the suspect, a vehicle description, and the tag letters—"

"Sounds like you're about ready to go to court. What do you need me for?" The chief looked at his watch, pulled on his jacket, and started down the hallway toward the mayor's office. He motioned for Mars to follow.

"Problem is, the plates were stolen. We've got a pile of vehicle checks to do. And we've got to get a drawing together of the suspect and start all over interviewing people to see if anybody can give us anything on him. I need to reassign a couple of cases Nettie and I are tied up with right now—"

"What about the information? You know my feelings on narcotics cases that come in with a story to tell. We've been burned more than once by those guys."

Mars nodded. "Understood. But for a lot of reasons, this one looks solid. First off, coming forward almost five months later—it doesn't fit with the usual songsters that come crawling while a case is still hot. And she's got details that match—"

"She?"

"Possession with intent to sell. The other thing is, she seems smart. Not your standard-issue lowlife. Can't put my finger on it exactly, but this one feels like a solid citizen who took a wrong turn somewhere along the line. She'll make a first-rate witness, if it comes to that."

The chief stopped in front of the mayor's office. "What have you offered her?"

"Nothing. I told her I had to match up what she had to say with a strong suspect—and if I could, then we'd talk deal. She hasn't got any priors—I'm not sure how much stuff they caught her with, but from the report, there's enough there for the charge, but I doubt Glenn's gonna want to take her to court."

"Go ahead and do what you need to do." The chief tipped his head toward the mayor's office. "I trust we're not getting anyone else's hopes up on this one just yet?"

"God, no. That's all we need to jinx it."

"Let me know how it goes." And with that the chief broke into a rare, broad grin. "My oh my. Would be satisfying to bring that one home." He gave Mars a light slap on the arm and walked into the mayor's office.

By the end of the week Nettie had completed the vehicle checks and gotten through most of the rental-car records. The suspect sketch hadn't turned up anything new, which wasn't real surprising. What you want in a suspect is someone with unusual features, something that stands out. Rau's description of the man she saw on the bluffs with Mary Pat Fitzgerald had been specific—but the suspect's routine good looks did not lend themselves to a readily identifiable drawing.

Nettie sat down in the conference room, staring at the pile of papers that wasn't giving anything up. "Any idea what happens next if nothing comes of this?"

"One thing I need to do is get back in touch with Bobby Fitzgerald. He might give us something on the drawing."

"The Prince girl said the drawing looked like everybody and nobody—is it likely Bobby Fitzgerald is going to know more people Mary Pat might have known than Becky did?"

"Probably not. In my gut, I think the only way an ID is going to work is if we can put Rau up against a lineup, real bodies or photos. In any event, I need to let Bobby know we've got a witness, so having Bobby take a look is worth a shot. You got his number? Can't remember when he said he'd be back from England, but it must have been around now."

Nettie spun around to her computer, then dialed. She talked for a moment, then passed the phone to Mars.

"Bobby? Mars Bahr in Minneapolis. How've you been?"

"Tired. Have been ever since I got back from England. I've been meaning to call you."

"Well, I called because we've had a bit of a break on your sister's case."

"Really?"

"We've got a pretty reliable witness who saw your sister with a guy on the bluffs shortly before she was murdered. What I'd like to do is fax a copy of the drawing that was made from the witness's description and see if you see any resemblance to anyone."

Bobby's end of the line was silent for a moment. Then he said, "Do that." There was another brief silence. "Mars, that's good news. . . . I'm wondering . . . there's something I wanted to talk to you about. I met with police here in Boston, but they weren't very encouraging. My parents' house is being sold, and I need to come out on that anyway. You available, say, early next week?"

Mars suppressed an urge to ask Bobby why he'd met with Boston police. Bobby seemed to be saying he wanted to talk face-to-face. "Sure. Anytime, just call when you get to town."

"So?" Nettie said when Mars hung up.

"Fax him the drawing." Mars thought for a while. "Something else is going on. He's coming out next week."

"Any idea what happens next if he doesn't have anything on the drawing?"

Mars looked at her. "I'm not worried about that. It'll come. What I am worried about is that you're never gonna take your vacation. Now might be as good a time as any. Why don't you take off?"

"I might just do that. But I'd be more comfortable taking leave if you'd give me a hint why you're so confident about clearing this case."

Mars smiled. "You've got fifteen seconds." He tapped his temple as he said, "Intuition."

"*The Fabulous Baker Boys.* Jeff Bridges to Michelle Pfeiffer when she asks him how he knows he's going to see her again. It's like the last line in the movie. Or close to the last line, anyway."

"*Very* good."

"I think we should retire *The Fabulous Baker Boys* to the Great Movie Lines Hall of Fame. Your last three lines have all come from the Baker Boys. I don't even have to think about it. I can just say, '*The Fabulous Baker Boys,*' and be right probably fifty percent of the time."

"It was a *great* movie. I'll never get over Jeff Bridges not getting an Academy Award nomination."

"This is also the one hundredth time I've heard you on the subject of Jeff Bridges not getting an Oscar nomination. We've got other things to talk about. Like where our next break is coming from on the case at hand."

"I can't tell you where. I can just tell you it's coming."

CHAPTER
16

It came with Bobby Fitzgerald.

Bobby called Mars first thing Monday morning from his hotel and arranged to come over to city hall almost immediately. He hadn't responded to the faxed suspect drawing, and Mars had assumed that meant the drawing hadn't rung any bells. But when Bobby walked into the squad room, accompanied by a sophisticated, cool-looking woman, he was carrying the fax.

Bobby said, "Mars Bahr, Ann Amundsen."

Mars shook hands with Amundsen, more perplexed than ever about Bobby's agenda. "You got the drawing, I see."

Bobby nodded. "I didn't get back to you because—well, Ann and I were in England last month. We were guests at the same house—" He stopped, looked at Amundsen, then started over. "I'll cut to the chase. Ann and I discovered on the plane back that we both had sisters who'd been murdered. When we started to talk about the murders, we thought maybe there were similarities in the murders that were just too unusual to be coincidence. Both women died from a single stab wound to the aorta, both women had high blood alcohol levels, both women were partially undressed but hadn't been sexually assaulted. What really concerned us, though, was that both women knew—well, *knew* probably overstates it a bit—

but both women had met the man whose house we were staying at in England."

Ann Amundsen said, "My sister was killed in my apartment in Boston. Neville Cook—the man who knew both sister—has an office in Boston. So, when we got back from England, Bobby and I went to the Boston police and told them about the two murders. They said they'd checked Neville out in the first week of the investigation—I'd included his name on a list of people who knew Holly or who'd had access to the apartment. They were interested, but they said he provided a very tight alibi. We felt a little deflated after that and decided that maybe we *were* seeing shadows. But when your fax came—well, it's a little too generic to be sure, but it definitely could be Neville. We at least wanted to get your reaction. . . ."

Mars sat back, clasping his hands together over the top of his head. He was more interested than he wanted them to know at this point. So he asked questions.

"What about motive? If it *is* Cook, why would he have wanted to kill either one of your sisters?"

Bobby said, "That's what the Boston police asked, and we didn't really have an answer. But Ann and I talked afterward and there was something." He glanced at Ann, looking a little apologetic. "Ann had been seeing Cook before her sister was murdered. But she'd broken the relationship off. After Holly was murdered, Cook showed up again. It was a vulnerable time in Ann's life, and Cook took advantage of that." Bobby paused. They could all feel that what he was saying was weak.

Ann interrupted. "It's a hard thing to explain. But Neville's relationship with me was obsessive. Granted, for most people it wouldn't make sense that someone would *murder* to make another person dependent on them. But if you knew Neville . . ."

Mars continued to listen without comment. Ann went on.

"And there were little things. A few weeks after Holly had been murdered, I ran into Neville in a restaurant where he would never go on his own. I think now that he had arranged with the person I was having dinner with to run into us. Then I find out that he'd established a business relationship with my boss, and used that relationship to manipulate my job in a way that served his purposes. . . ." Ann's voice trailed off.

Mars said, "Let's start this at another point. Do you have a picture of Cook?"

Ann slumped. "No. Nothing. You have to understand, a picture would fall into the general category of personal—and personal wasn't part of Neville's life."

Bobby said, "I do. I have a picture—it hasn't been developed yet, but you remember, Ann—the picture I took of the three of you in front of Charhill, the day I arrived. I've still got the film somewhere in my luggage."

Mars said, "I'm going to want you to get that film to me ASAP, and we're going to want to develop the film from here."

Tina Jerome, who was helping Mars with evidence administration in Nettie's absence, stuck her head in the conference room.

"Mr. Bahr?" She said Bear instead of Bar. Mars had long ago given up on trying to get Tina to use proper titles, much less pronounce names correctly. "Nettie on the phone for you."

"Have her hang on a minute." Mars looked at Bobby. "The film in your luggage. Is it out at your parent's house on Cornelia Drive?"

"My mother sold the house and moved my dad down to Florida. Ann and I are staying at the Marriott. I can get from here to there and back on the skyways in a half hour."

Nettie was experiencing separation anxiety. "Just wanted to check. Everything okay?"

"Interesting. Everything's interesting." Mars held back on telling Nettie about Bobby and Ann Amundsen. She'd probably hang up her vacation and be back on the next plane.

"How's Tina doing for you?"

"Better than nothing. Barely. She spends most of her time on the phone with her boyfriend, who's a real lowlife. But we'll manage. Even you are not indispensable."

"Sorry about that. Both of that: that Tina is—well, Tina—and that I'm not indispensable."

Bobby Fitzgerald was as good as his word. He was back with the roll of film in just under half an hour. Handing the film to Mars, he said, "Skyways are a goddamn lifesaver. It's raining crazy out there."

Mars gave the film—with explicit instructions as to who in the lab was to do the developing—to Tina. He had her repeat his instructions twice, her recitation accented with gum cracking, one of Tina's more refined motor skills.

Bobby Fitzgerald said he'd come in first thing in the morning to identify the photo. Mars would be in court in the morning, so he spent almost fifteen minutes beating into Tina the importance of having the picture up from the lab at the time Bobby would be coming in, and then getting the photo of Neville cropped and back down to the lab to be duplicated.

Tina nodded and blew a small bubble at the same time. Maybe, Mars thought, she had more talent than he gave her credit for.

To Bobby and Ann, Mars said, "Here's what I'd like to do, if the two of you can hang in there for the next couple of days. I'm going to start working with U.S. Customs to try and get records as to when Neville Cook was and wasn't in the country." Nodding at Ann, he said, "Then I'll need you to help me refine it, at least to the extent that you can reconstruct when he was in Boston or Minneapolis."

Ann said, "I know that Neville was in Minneapolis in April. I just don't have the specific dates. Sometimes he'd go somewhere, leave from there for a couple days, then go back again...."

"We'll take what we can get. What I'll want to do is get together enough for a court order on his credit card records. That'll help us pin down his whereabouts and—hopefully—where he rented cars when he was here. We haven't been able to nail down anything on the car the witness saw. At a minimum, I'm gonna have to get a positive ID on your photo of Cook from our witness. Soon as I get the photo back, I'm gonna set up a photo lineup. We get her ID, I'm pretty sure I can get financial-record access, and we're on our way."

After Bobby and Ann left, Mars sat at his desk, taking stock. Truth was, he missed Nettie like hell. Missed thinking out loud about where they were, with her listening. Missed knowing she was keeping track of loose ends without being asked. He took out a pad and made a list of loose ends.

1. Boston: check Cook's alibi for Amundsen murder.
2. Boston: check medical examiner's report on Amundsen body for match with MPF.

He stared at what he'd written. The big loose end wasn't there. In capital letters, he wrote:

3. MOTIVE????????

CHAPTER
17

The photo of Neville Cook was up from the lab by the time Mars got back from court. With the photo in hand, Mars spent the better part of two days setting up the photo lineup. Glenn Gjerde harped at Mars about the lineup.

"I'm gonna wanna see—at an absolute minimum—no less than a couple dozen other faces in the lineup. And I'm gonna want those guys' mothers to have a hard time telling their boys from Cook."

Mars made a face at Glenn. As any cop could tell you, part of the reason Glenn had never lost a case was that Glenn only took airtight cases to court. Most cops wished Glenn would take a flyer once in a while—go into court with a case that required perfect lawyering instead of perfect cop work.

Glenn caught Mar's look. "Mars, I'm telling you. Even with what it looks like right now, this is going to be a hell of a tough case to prosecute. It's all circumstantial. Every bit of it. Your one witness—provided she IDs the right guy—is a junkie who made a deal. And your suspect has resources to come back at us both barrels. This isn't gonna be your typical murder suspect shuffling into court in orange cotton, his hair all flat in back from not being washed in a month. In addition to which, he holds a foreign passport. We could have serious problems getting him extradited to stand trial, assuming we can get him indicted to begin with. So I want what we've got to be un-im-peach-a-ble. I mean *un*-im-peach-a-ble. You hear me? And I want to have to a look at that lineup before your witness gets near it. Understand?"

The photo lineup Glenn approved included thirty-one photos. All black-and-white. They'd printed Bobby's photo black and white from the color film. All candid shots, like Bobby's snap. No portraits. As much as possible, the subjects were face forward: to match Bobby's shot of Neville and to avoid the problems you ran into with left/right side differences in people's faces.

Mars got a little sweaty looking through the pics. They were too good. A couple of times he'd passed by Cook, had to stop and go back to find the right photo. And *he* knew exactly what he was looking for. *Damn.*

Evelyn Rau's back was to him as he walked into the same interrogation room where he'd first met her. From the back, her hair looked cleaner. From the front, Evelyn's face had the same expression of quiet composure that he'd found disconcerting first time around. This time, her eyes were clearer, and she was a shade easier, less touchy than she'd been. He guessed whatever she'd been taking when they brought her in was out of her system. And it showed.

Mars looked up to see if the video camera was running. The small green light was on. Outside, the rain, which was now into its third day, pounded on the windows. Lightning and thunder added drama to their little photo show. Mars glanced at Glenn Gjerde who'd just come in, then sat down across from Rau.

"I've got some pictures I'd like you to have a look at." He slid the stack of photos over to her. "I'd appreciate your going through those to see if there's anybody who looks like the guy you saw with Mary Pat Fitzgerald on the Father Hennepin Bluffs the morning of April third."

She looked across at him before looking at the pictures. "How's my deal doing?"

Mars made an effort not to wince. That question now on tape, he decided he'd better deal with it. Get his answer on the record while they were at it. "Too soon to say. The license plates you gave us were stolen before Mary Pat was murdered. So that looks like it's a dead end." Mars paused. "But it fit. And it got us started again. You're still in the game."

Evelyn kept her eyes on Mars's face for another moment. Then she pulled the pictures in front of her. She went through the stack at an even pace, boring in on each picture intently before sliding it to the bottom of the stack. She didn't blink much. Her hands, which Mars remembered liking from their first meeting, were shown to good advantage, the long fingers moving gracefully as she shifted from one photo to the next.

Neville Cook was the eleventh photo down, and Mars hadn't been able to stop himself from counting. His heart tightened at number nine and took a jolt when Evelyn flipped passed number eleven without breaking her pace. A seeping sense of disappointment started deep within his gut. To staunch the rise of the poison, Mars rose and walked casually around the table until he was standing behind Evelyn, a couple of feet back. He jammed his hands tight into his pants pockets, concentrated on trying to breath normally, and squashed the cigarette box in his pocket into a wad.

She'd gone through the stack once. She immediately recognized the photo she'd started with. She stopped, restacked the photos, and cracked them square on the table, like getting ready to deal a deck of cards. Then she started through the pile again. Faster, this time. She stopped at a picture that had stopped Mars first time he'd seen it, and looked at it closely, for maybe a half minute. Then, using the little finger on each hand, she blocked off parts of the face: first the eyes, then the nose, finally the mouth. She shook her head, and said, "Nope. Close, first time you look at him. But the eyes are spaced differently, the nose is a little short, and the mouth is thinner."

Mars looked over at Glenn, whose mouth was slightly open in admiration.

Evelyn resumed her sort through the photos, this time even faster than before. Mars had lost count, so he wasn't ready when she stopped and pulled one photo from the stack. She flipped it out and onto the table.

"That's him. I'm sure of it."

Faceup, on the center of the table, was the picture—cropped to show just the head and shoulders—that Bobby Fitzgerald had taken of Neville Cook.

Mars, still standing behind her, folded his arms across his chest. Reaching up with one hand, he pinched his tear ducts tightly with his thumb and index fingers to keep the tears from coming.

CHAPTER
18

The next time Mars felt like crying was Monday morning, four days after Rau had identified Neville Cook's photograph, when Mars picked up a phone message from Glenn Gjerde. Glenn's message was that the photo ID wasn't enough to get a warrant to go after Neville Cook's financial records. They both knew Mars needed the records to begin to build the case that Neville had been in Minneapolis on or around April third.

Glenn's message had been recorded at 4:30 A.M. The chickenshit didn't even have the guts to tell him live. Mars hadn't bothered to call Glenn back. He started off at a run from the third floor of city hall. Going outside at the first floor and across the street would have been faster, but he would have drowned in what weather reports were calling the rain of the century. Instead, he went down to the Hennepin County Courthouse tunnel, taking the escalator steps three at a time to get to the courthouse elevators.

Glenn Gjerde was just wheeling his seventeen-hundred-dollar racing bike into his office on the twenty-first floor as Mars, still winded, came up behind him.

"Got your message, Glenn."

Glenn started and turned. He was still wearing his bicycle helmet with a small mirror sticking out on either side, like insect antennae. There'd been occasions when Glenn had forgotten to take his helmet off and showed up in court with it still on his head. People around the courthouse were so used to seeing Glenn in his bicycle helmet that no one thought anything about it, except people who were in the courtroom for the first time. That no one else seemed bothered that one of the lawyers was wearing a bicycle helmet became just another reason why the judicial process, to a normal person, was like landing on the moon.

"Oh, hi, Mars. Sorry about that. I thought about your request all weekend. Decided it just wasn't going to fly."

"Do you mind giving me a little more explanation?"

Glenn took the keys out of his office door and motioned Mars in. The office wasn't big to start with, and Glenn had legal files stacked up like pillars all over the floor. They both walked delicately through narrow channels where, if you put the heel of one foot directly in front of the toe of the other foot, you could get by without knocking anything over. Maybe.

Glenn lifted his fourteen-pound titanium bike over his head and hung it on hooks he'd screwed into a wall bookcase. Mars stood, deciding the effort to clear a chair wasn't worth it. "I mean it. I want to know why you're not gonna go for the warrant."

"It's like I said. It wouldn't fly. We'll just have to figure out another way to get the job done. I went over what we've got and it's all too—too circumstantial, too many holes."

"You can't be serious. I've got Ann Amundsen's statement about Neville's association with her sister, Holly, and the similarity between the MO on the two murders."

"You've played this game too long, Mars, not to know without my telling you that there's no judge in this county who's gonna give us a warrant based on something a suspect might have done in another case, in another jurisdiction—maybe especially another case that's never even been changed."

"I've got a suspect whose lifestyle exactly matches what we'd expect for this type of crime. Highly organized personality, attractive to women, someone who they would start by trusting—"

"Weak. Very weak. And you know it."

"Okay. So I've got Dr. Karen Pogue's interview with Ann Amundsen, which is the basis for Pogue's conclusion that there is a psychopathological basis for suspecting that Neville Cook could be capable of committing the crimes given his obsessive behavior with Amundsen—"

"Bullshit. First of all, Pogue's conclusions are thirdhand. You know how the court is going to view that. Second, Pogue's got all kinds of qualifiers built into what she says, like she does not find it 'typical that the suspect would have been capable of normal sexual relations,' such as he had with Ann Amundsen."

It took effort for Mars to contain his anger. "Glenn, that totally disregards Amundsen's statement that she didn't view her sexual relationship with Cook as being anything like normal. Give me a break here. Did you or did you not see Evelyn Rau ID-ing Neville Cook? I've never seen a more impressive performance on a photo lineup. That should stand on its own. A judge should give us a warrant just on the basis of that ID. Rau is going to make one hell of a witness."

Glenn Gjerde shook his head. "The judge isn't going to be looking at a witness. He's going to be looking at a piece of paper that says a junkie drug dealer, making a deal to get out of jail, ID-ed a guy she saw once for less than three minutes. It's just not compelling in that context."

Mars decided he needed to sit. He leaned over, scooping

a pile of junk off the nearest chair, stepped over a pile of files, then eased himself down onto the seat. "So what are you suggesting would be compelling?"

Glenn pulled open a desk drawer, and sitting back in his chair, propped up his Nike clad feet.

"I don't see why you need a warrant for what you want, anyway. Why can't you get what you need from Amundsen? She was living with the guy for most of the period we're looking at, wasn't she?"

"I told you. We've already gone that route. She doesn't have any kind of records to document when she thinks he was in Minneapolis—hell, most of the time he didn't tell her where he was."

Glenn looked unperturbed. "Well, whatever. I just figured if she wanted to get this guy bad enough, she'd be willing to help out."

"Funny," Mars said. "That's what I'd figured about you." He stood to leave.

"One other thing," Glenn said, not looking at Mars. "I talked to the public defender about your witness. We're gonna have to release her. We're dropping the possession and accesory charges—nothing turned up from the crime scene to tie her directly to the drugs that were in the apartment and we got a plea from the shooter that lets her off the hook on the boyfriend's shooting. I suppose we could dink around and try hanging on to her as a material witness to the murder—but my guess is it's a smarter move to create a little goodwill. Keep her sweet. You've got your signed statement and the ID evidence. She told the PD she's willing to keep us informed of her whereabouts and not leave town as a condition of release—so, unless you can come up with a strong argument in the other direction?..."

Mars sighed. "Let her go. She may be the only doper I've

ever come across that I'm inclined to trust. And she's earned an out. She was damn brilliant on the photo lineup."

"She's outta here," Glenn said. He kicked the desk drawer shut and stood, stretching. "You come up with some solid physical evidence that ties this Cook guy to the scene—and a motive, a motive would be real nice—and we'll be cooking with gas. And now, if you will excuse me, I am due in court to oil the wheels of justice. Thanks for stopping by."

The brightest spot in Mars's deteriorating investigation was that Nettie came back from vacation three days early. Mars didn't even go through the motions of chastising her for cutting her vacation short. For her part, Nettie was disgruntled. It had rained the whole time she'd been in San Francisco and was raining even harder now that she was back in Minneapolis.

Mars briefed her on where they were on the investigation. "Boston sent us the case file on the Amundsen case—I haven't had a chance to go through that as yet—could you give it a go-over? I'm interested in matching what Boston's got with what we have on Mary Pat. And anything you can find in the written reports on Cook's alibi. I talked to the investigating officer who checked the alibi, and I have to say it sounds solid. Cook got called out of town unexpectedly on the morning of the day the Amundsen kid got killed. His flight departed two hours before Amundsen was last seen alive. And Boston confirmed Cook's arrival in Dallas with people he met there. Still, from what Ann Amundsen and Bobby Fitzgerald are saying, if there's a guy who could manage an airtight alibi, it's Cook."

Nettie said, "What's your thinking on Cook's motive?"

Mars grimaced. "We're looking at deviant behavior. A psychopath. It fits with the profile Karen Pogue had come up with—I was uncomfortable with that, given that until the Amundsen case turned up, we couldn't find any matching cases. Now, with the Amundsen case, I'm a little more comfortable. . . ." His voice trailed off.

"But it still doesn't feel right, huh?"

Mars stared, thinking back to the crime scene. "Not exactly. There was something too—too *neat* about the scene. I just didn't get any sense of *emotion* in what the killer had done to the kid. Karen says that the image of a drunken, partially undressed kid might have been what the perp was after—but, I don't know. That just doesn't quite do it for me. My impression of the scene was that it almost looked—staged. What I'd like to know is, did Cook have a motive for staging the murders."

"So. What next?"

"Well, Bobby Fitzgerald and Ann Amundsen are cooling their heels over at the Marriott, waiting for us get the search warrant for Cook's financial records. We should get together with them and decide if there's anything they can do, given we aren't going to get the warrant."

Bobby Fitzgerald and Ann Amundsen came down to city hall that afternoon. Mars gave them the bad news about Gjerde's decision not to go for a warrant. But Mars felt honor bound to confess his own reservations.

"What really gets me is that I kind of agree with Gjerde. All we've really got to go on is the witness who identified Neville from your photo and the association between the two murders. We get evidence with a questionable warrant, and we lose what we do have. Besides which, if the case isn't solid, if the search warrant is shaky, we're gonna tip Cook. He'll know what's going on. And nobody's saying this isn't a smart guy. We'll never get him back."

Bobby said, "How do you feel about the witness? Everything I hear about eyewitnesses is that they're notoriously unreliable."

Mars agreed. "That's exactly right. But our witness was impressive on the photo lineup—and it was as tough a lineup as I've ever given a witness. Admittedly, the witness has had some personal problems with drugs. . . ."

Simultaneously, Bobby's and Ann's brows furrowed. Mars held a hand up. "But my judgment is she got involved in an abusive relationship and ran off the rails. She's intelligent and articulate—she's been a graduate student in English at the U—any chance you have any contacts in the English Department here?"

Bobby shook his head. "Not anymore."

Mars pushed the transcript of his first interview with Rau across the table. Ann picked it up and started reading, but Bobby was preoccupied with other thoughts. He looked around the table, and said, "There is another way. Might be another way." To Ann he said, "Owen. We could ask Owen to help."

Mars said, "Owen?"

Bobby nodded. "Cook's younger brother."

Mars shook his head. "That wouldn't work. The chance that a brother is going to work with police against a brother—first of all he's not going to be willing to do it, and second, he's gonna tell his brother what's up. Then we're cooked. No pun intended."

Ann looked up from the transcript. "No. I think Bobby might be right. If you were suggesting we ask Neville's sister, Jocelyn, to help—forget it. Not a chance. But Owen? I think it might work. Owen has a soul. Unlike the rest of the family. Confronted with what we know about his brother, he'd want the truth as much as we do. Besides—even if he didn't have a conscience, he has motivation. If Neville's done this Owen's going to come into his share of Neville's share of the estate, which is the one thing Owen wants more than anything."

Bobby said, "There's something else. Owen is the one person, other than Neville's personal assistant, who pretty much knows where Neville has been over the last five years. They're in business together. The way they work is that when they're considering buying a property, Neville sends Owen out as an advance man to do the donkey work. Owen crunches the basic financial information, does the due diligence on the properties, checks out marketing data on the area—that kind of thing. Then Neville comes in to negotiate, to do the deal."

Mars said, "Would Owen have access to the company's files? Would he be able to document their activities?"

Bobby and Ann looked at each other. "I don't know why he wouldn't," Ann said. "He uses the Boston office, too. I'm sure staff there wouldn't think anything of his asking for records."

"Sounds good to me," Nettie said. She turned to Bobby. "Any ideas on how best to approach him?"

Ann interrupted. "Bobby—if you don't mind? I think it would be best if I made the contact. I think Owen trusts me. At a personal level."

Bobby nodded, and Ann went on. "The other thing is, I think Owen would feel less—less *threatened* by my confronting him. Let's get real here: a woman confronting him with this information is going to be less threatening than if it were a man. Am I right?"

Nettie said, "I think I agree with Ann. And you bring up something that I think is important. We don't want Owen to feel confronted or threatened. This should be a personal appeal. I don't think Owen should know—not at first—that you and Bobby have gone to the police. I think the approach should be along personal lines: You and Bobby had talked on the plane about your sisters being murdered. And after *you* started thinking about it, you started wondering if Neville could have been involved, and it's been bothering you. You'd feel better if Owen could tell you Neville couldn't be involved."

"That's good," Mars said. "I think if you start with the guy by saying that you've talked to the police and they think you've got something . . ."

"He's going to close up on you if you take that approach," Nettie said. "I don't care how altruistic he is, or how much he stands to benefit from his brother being in trouble. Starting with our involvement is going to make him defensive. Whereas if you talk to him one-on-one, in confidence, about something that you haven't articulated in any detail—well, that would likely be very effective."

"And it's consistent," Ann said, "with what our relationship has been in the past. From the first he's been—sort of a confidant. Somebody I could talk to. More than to Neville. He was somebody I talked to *about* Neville."

"Sounds good," Mars said. "The question is, how do you make contact with him?"

Bobby said, "He was going to Winnepeg on a property deal just after Ann and I left England. For all I know, he's still there." He thought for a moment. "That's only—what?— four hundred miles from here? What I could do is invite him to Minneapolis to talk about the Henry James piece he wanted me to write for the publishing venture he's trying to get off the ground. I'll say that I'm in Minneapolis wrapping up some family business, that Ann's here, and that she'd enjoy seeing him. I think he'd go for that."

"Sounds good," Mars said. "But it's important he not think that Ann has told you about her suspicions. The idea that you two are in cahoots would be as bad from his point of view as if he thought this were a police investigation."

"Not a problem," Ann said. "I'll tell him I'd like to see him alone, just the two of us. He'll assume I want to talk about Neville and that I wouldn't do that around Bobby."

"So," Mars said. "How do we want to proceed from here?"

"The simplest thing," Bobby said, "would be for me to call the Cooks' Boston office and tell them I want to get hold of Owen. I've done that before, and he's used that office to contact me."

The Cooks' Boston office gave Bobby a number for Owen in Winnepeg. "Cross your fingers," Bobby said as he dialed.

Their luck held, and Bobby had Owen on the line within minutes. The three of them could track the conversation just by listening to Bobby's side.

"Owen? Bobby Fitzgerald in Minneapolis—yeah—no, it was kind of sudden. My parents sold their house here, so I had to come out and settle some things. Right, right . . . No, the house is sold. I'm staying in a hotel downtown. I'm calling because I've been thinking about the James piece. . . . Yeah, I thought you would be, sure. . . . What I was thinking was, as long as I'm here, and you're up in Winnepeg—any chance you could get away for a day or two and we could talk more specifically about what you want. . . . You do that when? . . . Well, sure . . . No, that would work, that would be good for me. No problem . . . Owen? One other thing. A little awkward, but I wanted you to hear it from me. Ann Amundsen, your brother's friend . . . right, right . . . no, I did hear that she and Neville had split. In fact, I heard it directly from Ann. We ended up on the same flight back from England. The thing is, since then, we've been seeing quite a bit of each other and . . ." Bobby hesitated for the barest moment, his eyes lifting to the three of them, before he lied to Owen. "Anyway, she's out here with me, and when I mentioned to her that I was going to call you, she said she'd love to see you, so . . . right—no, no problem. Wednesday or Thursday would work for her, too. Great. Do you need a ride from the airport? Okay. Well, if your plans change, let me know. Sure. Sure. No, I look forward to seeing you then. Say, one-thirty, in the bar? That works. Great. See you Wednesday."

He hung up and looked at Ann. "We're having drinks with Owen in the bar at Palomino at one-thirty on Wednesday. He'll be here Thursday, as well, so you can try to meet with him then."

CHAPTER
19

Bobby was down at city hall by eleven-thirty on Thursday morning, the first day in almost five days when it wasn't raining. "I hope," he said to Mars, "you've planned someplace good for lunch. I'm starving and it's going to take a lot to get my mind off what's going on at Ann's lunch."

"How'd drinks go yesterday?"

Bobby paused. "Fine. But Ann's feeling pretty tense about having lunch with Owen today."

Mars looked at his watch. "You want to make book on when she'll be back?"

"Not a clue. Any more than I'd guess how Owen is going to respond. What's your guess?"

"About the same as yours. Not a clue. I would say this. The longer she's gone, the better for us. I think he'll either turn her off immediately or he'll go along and they'll talk it through. If he goes along, it's going to take some time."

"Which gives us plenty of time for lunch. Where we going?"

Nettie had decided lunch should be just the boys, and stayed downtown. Mars and Bobby took the Pontiac to Thirty-fifth and Cedar to Matt's Tavern.

Bobby looked around and made a face as they parked. "I

think I'd feel better about being here if this was a marked squad, and you were wearing a uniform."

"Don't tell me you were born and raised in Minneapolis, and you've never been to Matt's for Jucy Lucys."

"I was born and raised in Edina, six blocks from the Minneapolis city limits. There's a difference."

Bobby was right about the neighborhood. It had never been great. At its best it had been a working-class neighborhood. Its best was probably twenty-five years ago. In the last ten years it had slid into decay and dereliction. Matt's, however, had survived the change. It was a classic neighborhood bar: long and narrow, semidark, with the bar along one wall facing a mirror, a row of booths on the opposite wall. Down the center was a line of tables with four chairs at each table. Bobby picked up the single-sheet plastic-sealed menu and gave it a moment's consideration. Mars reached over and took the menu out of Bobby's hands.

"When you have lunch at Matt's, you have Jucy Lucys."

"I saw Jucy Lucys on the menu. I make it a practice not to order anything in a restaurant that's misspelled on the menu."

"At Matt's, jucy is the correct spelling."

Two things distinguished Matt's from other neighborhood bars: the clientele—which was an unmingled combination of locals, journalists, curious yuppies, and cops—and the Jucy Lucys, which brought the clientele in. Jucy Lucys were a distinctly retrograde menu choice. They were a high-fat variation on cheeseburgers, a double beef patty with a wad of cheese stuffed inside the two hunks of beef before the patty hit the grill. If you weren't careful when you ate a Jucy Lucy, the grease would roll down your arms into your sleeves.

Bobby was somewhere between amused and appalled. But being half-appalled didn't stop him from eating two Jucy Lucys and all the fries in the basket. "You come here often?" he asked Mars, looking as if he doubted that someone who came to Matt's very often would live to tell the story.

"Not often. I stop by now and again to pick up a basket for my kid."

"I didn't know you were married."

"Not married. Not anymore."

"I suppose being divorced is an occupational hazard for a cop."

Mars chewed for a few moments before saying anything. "True. But not true in my case—not if you mean that the stress of being a cop causes tension in the marriage. I married a woman who wasn't real emotional. I was a cop when we got married, she knew what she was getting into, and she isn't the kind of woman who changes her mind much. I was the one who changed. That, and I've been told by more than one woman I have 'intimacy problems,' whatever that means."

Bobby dropped the remains of his Jucy Lucy in the basket. With his mouth still full of greasy beef he sputtered, "Jeez. *Intimacy problems.* It's all you hear from women. Do me a favor: you ever figure out what women mean when they hit you with this intimacy-problem crap, give me a call. Day or night."

Bobby paused, then said, "I've meant to apologize to you about something. . . ."

"Apologize? To me?"

Bobby nodded. "When you called just before I left for England. To ask about my dad and Mary Pat . . ." Bobby traced his finger through beads of water on their table. "It was a hard time for me, and I'm afraid I responded—defensively." He looked up at Mars. "You did check my dad out pretty thoroughly?"

Mars nodded. "Everybody in your family. You included. Actually, your mother was the only one without an alibi."

"My dad. He checked out?"

Mars said, "Him we checked out backwards and forwards. Nettie went over your dad's alibi personally. It was tight."

"What's tight?"

"Well, we had people who could place him at the hospital throughout the day—from six-thirty A.M. through just after eleven P.M. The two pieces of information that were really strong, in my book, were patient chart notations—nurses' notes and your dad's orders in a couple of patient charts— and a statement by a parking lot attendant. The attendant had come in at seven A.M. Apparently they'd been doing construction, repaving or something, on one end of the lot, so by eight A.M. things had gotten jammed up. The attendant double-parked some of the docs' cars. Your dad's car was parked in from around eight A.M. until nearly three P.M. The attendant had checked with your dad to make sure that was okay, and he'd said no problem. He expected to be at the hospital all day. So we know he was there until at least three. And, we have a statement from the third-shift guard that your dad left just after eleven P.M."

There was no other way to say it. Bobby looked relieved. He looked Mars in the eyes for a brief moment, then looked at his watch. "One-thirty-five. Whaddya think?"

"I think Nettie would page me if Ann had come back. If she met Owen at noon—where did you say they were having lunch?"

"Not sure. Ann hadn't heard from Owen before I left this morning."

"Want to head back?"

"Might as well. Mind if I hang out with you down at city hall? I'd like to be there when Ann calls."

"Not a problem. I'll give you crayons and paper to keep you busy. I used to keep some in my desk for my kid, when

211

he was younger. They're probably still there. You can draw pictures."

Bobby snapped his fingers. "Damn. I keep forgetting. My mother asked me to pick up Mary Pat's senior picture, the one you took the first day you came out to the house."

"I'm sure Nettie is through with the photos by now. There were two pictures actually—the senior picture and a snapshot of Mary Pat with your Dad."

They exchanged eye contact. Bobby said, "Mom only mentioned the senior picture, but I'll take whatever you have."

Mars nodded, feeling that Mother Fitz had at long last broken her silence on what had gone on between Mary Pat and Doc Fitzgerald. "Sure thing," he said. "Just remind me when we get back downtown." He stood up. "I'm gonna hit the john. Meet you at the car?"

Bobby shook his head. "No way I'm going out there by myself. I'm waiting here for you and your gun."

Owen called Ann's hotel just after 11:00 A.M. He suggested lunching at a restaurant on the other side of the river.

"I'm staying at the Hyatt on the downtown side of the river. Why don't you walk to my hotel from the Marriott, and we'll walk to the restaurant from there," he suggested.

"Great idea," Ann said. "I've got cabin fever after all this rain. Looks decent out now."

The Nicollet Island Inn sat on a small island just up river from the falls. An old limestone building that had lived many lives prior to its current incarnation, the inn was over-decorated in a florid Victorian style. Ann and Owen arrived ahead of the lunch crowd and were rewarded with a choice table in a windowed area that looked out at the river.

Once seated, Ann said, "Has—has Neville said anything to you about me?"

Owen smiled an affectionate mocking smile. "Surely you know him better than that. I don't expect to live long enough to hear your name on Neville's lips. You've not told me how your farewell went."

The waiter came to the table for their orders. "You're ready, are you?" Owen asked.

"I'll have the veal piccata—and—a green salad. A glass of the house white wine would be good."

"That will do for me, as well," Owen said. The two of them sat silent for a few moments after the waiter left. Ann didn't want to start a discussion of Neville until after their food came, and an awkward pause fell.

Owen broke the silence. "So. You and Fitzgerald. I must confess, I thought you'd make a good pair when I invited him to Charhill."

Ann smiled. "I don't know that you'd say we're exactly a pair. . . ." There was nowhere to go with this, other than to say that they were bound at this moment in time by murdered sisters.

Their wine came, and shortly after their food. Ann ate with relish, in part because she was nervous about the conversation they would be having. "How did you know about this place?" Ann asked. "It's off the beaten path, I should think, for someone who doesn't know the city well."

"Neville and I probably know this part of the city—the riverfront—better than most of the residents. Cook Limited has considered property investments in the warehouses along the river."

Ann felt her breath catch. She said in a controlled voice, "Neville was in Minneapolis in April, wasn't he?"

"Yes. We came very close to doing a deal, ended up walking away. A Japanese firm came in after us. Will do badly on the deal, I should think. Another five years, and we should be able to pick up the same property later at half the price."

Owen looked at her. "You still haven't told me about the farewell."

Ann was trembling so violently she thought it must be visible to Owen.

"Owen, there's something I've been thinking about. Something—about Neville—that's bothered me since I left Charhill. I hardly know how to ask, but for my peace of mind, I must."

He was staring at her, but he didn't speak.

"When I told Neville I was leaving Charhill, I saw a side of him I wouldn't have believed existed. A capacity for emotion—rage. It terrified me. I was expecting him to resist what I was saying, but . . . he was violent. Physically violent. And I had the impression that it took every bit of self-control he had to keep that violence under control. As it was, he hit me so hard that I fell—but my impression then, and even now, remembering how he looked, was that the blow was only a bit of what he might do. . . ."

Owen said, "I won't pretend to be surprised, Ann. But to tell you the truth, it's more or less what I'd expect from him— given the right circumstances. And as I said at Charhill— losing control over you was something I thought he'd have a very hard time with indeed."

"But it's more than that, Owen. On the plane back . . . Bobby said he told you we came back on the same flight?"

"Yes. He said as much on the phone when he rang."

"We talked then—and found out that both our sisters had been murdered. That's a bit of a coincidence on its own, you'd have to admit. But there were other things, things that Bobby said about the circumstances of how his sister died . . ." She looked at Owen. "Owen, the things Bobby told me—I don't believe they could be coincidence. As I thought about it—if it's not coincidence, if in fact my sister and Bobby's sister were

214

killed by the same person . . ." She paused, hoping Owen would state the obvious, but he only stared.

"Owen, you must know what I mean. I'm saying that Neville was the only person who knew both sisters, who would have had an opportunity to kill them both."

Still he stared. Ann reached across the table, to touch his hand. "Owen, *I need to know*. And you can help me with that, if you will. You can help."

"*I* can help?"

"I know it's asking a lot, but I have to believe that, brother or not, you'd want the truth, too. The thing is, you'd know where Neville's been. When he's been there. Was he in Minneapolis in April? I thought he had been out of Boston when my sister was murdered—but for all I know, that could have been a lie. If I could just satisfy myself that there wasn't any way he could have killed Holly and Mary Pat—if you could help me look at expense records that would show where he was when they died . . ."

"And Bobby. What does Bobby have to say about this?"

She drew breath and sounded convincing, even to herself. "Bobby knows nothing. I couldn't bring myself to say out loud what I've been thinking—not without being sure . . . so I didn't tell him anything about how my sister died."

Abruptly, Owen stood. Digging in his inside jacket pocket, he pulled bills from a wallet stuffed with cash and dropped several bills on the table without looking at them.

"Ann, I don't want to have this discussion here. Let's walk, there are benches back by the bridge."

They walked in silence on the cobblestones for what might have been three or floor blocks. Ann spoke first. "Can you understand why I'm asking? I know it's not fair—that whatever your differences have been, Neville is your brother. But Owen, Holly was my sister. My only sister. If there's even

215

a chance that Neville was involved in her death, I have to know. I'm sorry if this shocks you. . . ."

They approached an open park area, with a sheltered bandstand on the bluffs directly over the river. Owen led her to a bench. They sat close to each other in the center of the bench. Owen remained quiet before saying, "You haven't shocked me." He turned to look at her. "You haven't said anything I haven't thought myself."

Owen's words chilled Ann. Until that moment her fears and suspicions had been abstract. Now she felt real terror. In a voice hoarse with emotion, she said, "But, Owen, if you thought he might be involved, *why* didn't you say something?"

Owen looked away. "I'd been out of town when your sister died. It had been my understanding that Neville would be in Boston while I was gone. When I came back and heard what had happened, the possibility that Neville was involved occurred to me almost immediately. It's what I said to you in England: I can't say why, but I've always felt Neville was capable of—well, evil is the only word for it. I agonized then over what I should do about my suspicions. But the police came to the office to talk to Neville—it wasn't until then that I found out he'd been called to Dallas on a property agreement that was going sour. So I put aside my suspicions— chalked them up to paranoia, I suppose—and forgot about it. And I didn't know about Bobby's sister until just now. Bobby's never said anything. Neville *was* in Minneapolis in April, Ann. And I agree with you, it's too much of a coincidence to be ignored."

Ann closed her eyes for a moment. Owen was as anxiety ridden over his suspicions as she was over hers. She drew a breath to gain courage. It was time to depart from the plan.

"I haven't been altogether honest with you, Owen." With Owen watching her closely, she said, "I haven't been honest

216

about who I've shared my suspicions with. I didn't want to feel that I was boxing you in a corner, I didn't want to go ahead unless I was sure that what I was thinking might be possible. . . ."

"You and Bobby talked."

Ann nodded. "Bobby feels at least as strongly as I do that Neville might be involved. But there's more. The Minneapolis Police Department contacted Bobby when we got back from England. They've found a witness—a witness who identified a photo of Neville as being that of the man she saw with Bobby's sister before she died."

Ann could see that this information had struck Owen with the same force she had experienced when she realized Owen shared her suspicions. It was one thing to hold a half-formed suspicion that someone you knew might be capable of murder; it was quite another to be presented with facts that supported suspicion.

Owen said, "A picture? How did they get a picture of Neville?"

"They contacted Bobby with a drawing of the person the witness said she saw. We gave the police the film Bobby had shot at Charhill. . . ." Ann gave a bitter laugh. "You remember the famous picture, when Neville didn't want to stand next to me, much less have his picture taken—anyway, that's the picture the witness identified."

Owen looked increasingly distressed. "That's all they have, after all these months—a single witness who says he saw Neville with the Fitzgerald girl before she died? I'm not going to risk going forward against Neville if all they have is a single witness—and what do we know about the reliability of the witness? You know as well as I what Neville is like. If we pursue him with flimsy claims, he'll destroy our charges. More to the point, he'll destroy me. He could use this as an excuse for excluding me as a trust beneficiary."

"The witness is a woman. And Detective Bahr—the lead investigator on the case—says she's impressive. He's very, very confident about her." Ann paused. She felt she needed to be completely forthcoming with Owen. "From what Bahr said, she got into drugs through an abusive relationship. But I read her witness statement, Owen. Evelyn Rau is smart—you can tell just reading what she's written." She gave Owen a little poke. "She's even an academic, a graduate student in English at the university. What more can you ask?"

Owen said, "But it's not enough—"

A little impatiently, Ann said, "That's the point, Owen. That's why we need your help. There isn't enough evidence to get a search warrant on Neville's financial records—but that's something you could find for us. With those records we can pin down Neville's whereabouts on the day Bobby's sister died—we may even find something about Neville's alibi for my sister's murder that Boston missed. Neville wouldn't need to know—unless you find incriminating evidence."

Owen sat stock-still. Something else was bothering him.

Ann pressed. "What is it, Owen?"

He leaned back heavily against the bench, putting his hand up over his face. His words were muffled. "There's something I haven't told you. . . ."

"What? I can't understand what you're saying."

His hand dropped. His revealed face looked worn. "There's something else. I don't know what it means, but my gut tells me it's important to all of this."

"*Tell* me, Owen."

"When we moved into our offices in Boston, there was a wall safe in Neville's office. I came back from an extended trip late one Friday. Neville was still in the office, and as I had a good bit of cash with me, as well as some important executed documents, I suggested to Neville that I put my cash and documents in the wall safe until Monday. He said he'd never opened the safe, didn't have the combination. I didn't think anything of it, at the time."

Ann prompted him, "But?"

"*But*—and this is what I'm just remembering—the day Neville came back from Minneapolis, last April, I walked into his office to ask him how things had gone. He was standing at the wall safe, and it was open. I probably wouldn't have thought anything of it, but he was so startled—and you know Neville—even if something did surprise him, he never showed it—it registered with me. He *did* have a combination to the safe, and he was using the safe. It particularly troubled me as Neville and I had had a very bitter disagreement over the annual bonus distribution the previous month. I felt that Neville had jiggled the numbers a bit to deny me my fair share. I suppose when I saw the open wall safe, I thought Neville might be keeping altered records in the safe...."

Owen sighed and sat forward before going on. "In any event. It troubled me. So the next time Neville was out of town, I looked about for a combination to the safe. I found it in Neville's desk...."

Ann's skin tingled at the prospect of what was to come, but nothing could have prepared her for what he said.

"When I first opened the safe, I thought it was empty. I put my hand in on the floor of the safe and felt about—and I found two small envelopes—glassine envelopes, we'd call them in England. You know, the kind of semiopaque envelopes your post office puts stamps in."

"Yes?"

"The thing is, all that was in the envelopes was—" He turned to her, and in almost a whisper, said, "*Pubic hair*."

"Pubic hair?" Ann's first reaction was incomprehension. Then a rush of understanding overtook her consciousness. In a safe in his office, a man she had lived with, a man she had slept with—had a small envelope that contained pubic hair from her dead sister. Ann gagged, then stood and moved away from the bench.

In a moment, Owen came up behind her, placing a hand softly on her shoulder. "We're both thinking the same thing, aren't we?"

Together they walked slowly over the Stone Arch Bridge, back toward downtown. Owen asked Ann to give him twenty-four hours to think through what to do next, how he should be involved.

"I promise. I will help—it's only a question of how best to do it. I want to think over everything we've talked about, try to remember things that may be useful. . . ."

"I want you to meet Mars Bahr. He's been great, Owen, and he's not going to force you to do anything you're not comfortable with—but he's really good at thinking through how to get information, what's important."

Owen shook his head vigorously. "The one thing I'm sure of just now is that my meeting with the police would make me feel like Judas Iscariot. For now, I'll cooperate, but I want to cooperate through you. Perhaps if I talk with Bahr by phone on occasion, I may develop the trust I need—but we needn't make that decision now. You'll be at your hotel tomorrow afternoon?"

"If that's where it's easiest for you to reach me . . ."

"I'll call you there."

Mars was the first to see Ann enter the squad room. He was startled by her appearance. Her usual paleness was gone; her face glowed with color. She must have walked at a fast pace back from lunch.

"Here she is," he said, standing in anticipation.

Bobby stood too. "So? My God, you look like you've been launched by a rocket—what is it?"

Ann gasped, pulled up a chair, and sat down hard. "I *feel* like I've been launched by a rocket. Let me catch my breath, I've been running...."

"Ann! C'mon! What is it?" Bobby looked like he was about to shake Ann's news out of her.

She drew deep breaths. "I need to think where to start."

Bobby said, "Just tell us. Is he willing to consider that Neville may have been involved—is he willing to help?"

Ann's eyes moved from Bobby to Mars to Nettie. She didn't speak, but, grinning, nodded her head yes.

It was more than they had expected—that Owen not only was willing to cooperate but that he shared their suspicions about Neville. The bizarre information Ann brought about pubic hair in a wall safe was confounding to everyone except Mars. To Nettie, he said, "Don't you remember? From Doc D's exam?" Mars pulled out the final medical examination report. Flipping through the pages, he found what he wanted. He read it outloud: " 'Exam of pubic area shows no evidence of'—blah, blah, blah, blah—here it is. 'There is superficial trauma to the pubic epidermis, including evidence of pinpoint bleeding, consistent with strands of pubic hair being removed at a vertical angle....' "

Nettie was on her feet before Mars could ask. She returned with the Amundsen case file the Boston police had sent. She flipped through the pages, pulling out the medical examiner's report. She skimmed the pages, her index finger tracing the words. On the last page, she looked up. "Nothing," she said.

Mars said, "That doesn't bother me. I looked at the body before Doc D did Mary Pat's exam—and I didn't notice anything. Doc D picked it up when he ran a magnifying glass over the pubic area—and even when he saw it, he didn't think it meant anything. It wouldn't have surprised me if he *hadn't* included it in his report."

Bobby Fitzgerald was pacing a tight path. He turned to Mars. "What next? Shouldn't Cook be put under arrest or something?"

"The first order of business," Mars said, "is to put hands on the two envelopes in Cook's wall safe. That's the missing physical-evidence link between our perp and the murder. Tie that to Neville Cook, who's been ID'd by our witness, and we are, as our prosecuting county attorney would say, cooking with gas."

Nettie said, "Doesn't the pubic hair also get us closer to motivation? If Cook is keeping pubic hair from the victim, doesn't that confirm deviant sexual behavior?"

Mars hesitated. "Yeah, sure. It does." Almost to convince himself, he added, "Deviant sexual behavior or not, keeping some object from the victim suggests we're dealing with a repetitive killer—a nut case, which is just about the only motivation I can come up with for Cook."

Bobby asked, "What about Neville wanting to make Ann more dependent on him by killing Holly?"

Mars nodded slowly. "If we were dealing with one murder, that *might* work—but it's a stretch. Then, you add Mary Pat's murder—it doesn't hold up."

"What if Neville *began* by killing Holly to get to me—and was excited by the experience, wanted to do it again?" Ann asked.

Mars shrugged. "Possible, I suppose—but almost impossible to take something like that into court. We're better off going full bore that he killed the women for psychological gratification. Look, we're wasting time. I don't want those envelopes in the safe in Boston to take a walk. Nettie—I need you to get hold of Glenn. At this point, even Glenn is going to agree we've got probable cause for Boston PD to execute a search warrant on Cook's office. If they find the envelopes in the wall safe, and can pull Cook's prints on the envelopes, I want them to take him into custody—"

Nettie frowned. "Are we going to run into some jurisdictional conflicts here? Once they have the envelopes, won't Boston want to hold Cook on the Amundsen case? At least until they double-check his alibi?"

"Probably," Mars said. "But Glenn can worry about that later. Right now I want to get those envelopes and keep Cook from getting on a flight back to England." Turning to Ann, Mars said, "I want to talk to Owen. We need to start pinning down in detail exactly what he knows and what he can do to help us—"

Ann shook her head. "He asked for time to think through what he should do next. He said he'd call me at my hotel tomorrow afternoon."

Louder than he meant to, Mars said, "No! Time counts on a deal like this. If he doesn't want to talk, I can have him brought in to talk. He wants to get a lawyer and stonewall us, that's another issue."

Ann was upset. "Please, Mars. I promised him we'd respect how he wanted to do this. Put yourself in his place. This is his brother. He's just found out that his brother is most likely a murderer—and that he's an important part of proving that. He said he feels like a traitor—at this point, he doesn't want to deal directly with the police at all. But I really think if we give him time—only till tomorrow afternoon—he's going to be okay. He was starting to soften on that as we talked. But I think if we pressure him now, he's going to back away."

"All right. He's got until tomorrow afternoon. It will take us that long to pin things down in Boston. But at that point, I'm not going to dance around with Owen Cook. He's got to either tell us he's not going to cooperate—in which case he risks becoming an after-the-fact accessory to the murders—or he's got to come forward." Mars paused, nodding to Ann and Bobby. "For now, the two of you can head back to your hotel and get some rest. Just let us know if you're leaving there at any time. Nettie and I need to get cracking on the Boston end."

Boston called back shortly after 1:00 P.M. the following day. Bobby Fitzgerald, who was too restless to hang out at the hotel, had come down to city hall. Mars, Nettie, Bobby, and Glenn took the call on a speaker phone. It was mostly good news. They had executed the warrant at 9:00 A.M. that morning. Neville Cook had been in the office and had denied having a combination to the wall safe. Boston police removed the lock from the safe and found the two envelopes from the safe. Cook professed having no general knowledge of the safe's contents nor any specific knowledge regarding the two envelopes or the envelope's contents. Cook had volunteered to provide the police with his fingerprints, and Boston police had confirmed just prior to calling Minneapolis that Cook's prints were on the envelopes.

"Couldn't have been better," the Boston investigator said. "Clean as a whistle, except for Cook's prints. The other good thing—some of the pubic hairs in each of the envelopes have roots. We're going to be able to do DNA tests to confirm the hair is from our victims."

"Outstanding," Mars said. "We appreciate how fast you moved on this. You've taken Cook into custody?"

"Absolutely. He's waiting on his lawyer as we speak. Denying everything. Mad as hell."

Mars said, "I asked yesterday if the person who conducted the medical examination on Holly Amundsen could be contacted regarding any evidence found suggesting that pubic hair had been removed from her body."

Another voice came through the speaker. "That would be me. Dr. Elton Mischke. I'm sorry, there wasn't anything. But remember, the Amundsen girl's body was badly decayed when it was recovered. The type of epidermal trauma you described on the Fitzgerald girl would have been obliterated."

"Oh, right," Mars said. "Hadn't thought about that. And it's not as important, anyway, given that we're probably going to have DNA evidence to prove the hair was taken from the victims. Look, we're going to initiate the extradition process to bring Cook to Minneapolis."

There was some mumbling on the line, and the investigator's voice came back on the line. "Uhhh—what I'm hearing from our legal people is that we're going to have a continuing interest in this case and may want to hang on to Cook here in Boston."

Mars made a face, and said, "Can't say that surprises me. Nonetheless, we're going to go ahead on our end. Do me a favor, will you? Two favors, actually. Let me know as soon as you get the DNA results—and once we've identified the Fitzgerald hair, I'd appreciate getting that transferred back to us. Then, stand on your heads to keep Cook from going out on bail, will you? And if he is granted bail, let us know immediately, okay?"

"No problemo," Boston said. "The Amundsen murder got a lot of press here. I don't think we're gonna have any trouble denying Cook bail."

After the call ended, Mars looked at Glenn. "So, Counselor. Are we cooking with gas yet?"

"High octane," Glenn said. "I'm going back to get started on the extradition shit. Don't mind telling you it's going to be tough. Boston's got the first murder in time and Cook's U.S. residence is in Boston."

"I'm going to let you worry about that. Right now I've got other stuff to do."

After Glenn left, Bobby said, "What do we do next?"

Nettie was looking at Mars. "You look like something's bothering you."

Mars rocked back on his chair, running his fingers through his hair. "There is something. I just can't put my finger on it. If it's important, it'll come. As for what's next, I'm going to return some long-overdue phone messages, including one that I made to U.S. Customs more than a week ago. Thought they might be able to give us something on when Cook was and wasn't in the U.S."

Bobby snapped his fingers. "Damn, I forget yesterday. Can I get those photos back? At least my sister's senior picture? I promised my mother—"

"Sure thing," Nettie said. "I've got all the pics we finished with in a photo file. Hang on a sec." She walked over to a cabinet and pulled out a file. She brought the file back to Bobby. "Everything's in here, including the pictures you took in England. Only thing is . . ." She opened the file, looked through the pictures, and pulled out a strip of negatives. Holding it up to the light, she said, "This is it. I want to keep the negative of the picture of the three of you with the photo of Neville we cropped and blew up for the evidence file. If I'd been here when the picture was developed, these negs wouldn't have ended up in the photo file." She dropped the file on the table in front of Bobby. "Take whatever you want."

Bobby started sifting through the file. "I never did see the other pictures I took in England. . . ."

Mars was on hold with Customs, one foot propped on his desk, when he noticed Bobby staring at one of the photos from the file. Still holding the photo, Bobby walked over to Mars.

Mars tucked the phone aside and said, "I'm on hold with Customs. What?"

Bobby dropped the photo he'd taken of Ann, Neville, and Owen on Mars's desk. "What do the red marks on the picture mean?" he asked.

"Grease-stick marks. It's like a red crayon. We use it to indicate how we want to crop a photo we're having printed. After the picture's been printed, you can wipe the grease-stick marks off with a tissue. No problem. Here . . ."

Thinking that Bobby was concerned about the photo being defaced, he opened a desk drawer to pull out a tissue. But Bobby, increasingly agitated, said, "No. That's not the problem. What I'm asking is—do the marks mean that's the person whose picture was used in the photo lineup?"

"Sure," Mars said. "Isn't that the picture you left with Nettie after you ID'd Neville?"

"Yeah," Bobby said, "the picture's right. But the grease-stick marks are around Owen, not Neville. I told the girl—it wasn't Nettie—I can't remember her name, but it wasn't Nettie—I pointed to Neville. She said something about the guy being good-looking and asked if the girl as the girlfriend, and I said yes . . . that was it."

Bile was rising in the back of Mars's throat. *"Tina."* He said. "Nettie was on vacation. You left the photo with Tina." Mars dropped the phone back on the cradle. He sat down at his desk and looked hard at the picture. Tina wouldn't have remembered for a nanosecond which of the two men Bobby had pointed to. And if you looked at that picture and asked yourself—which of the two guys is the boyfriend—you'd guess Owen. Owen and Ann were standing close together. Owen even had his arm draped loosely on Ann's shoulder. Neville was standing to the side, looking unconnected with the other two.

Mars closed his eyes to forestall panic.

Bobby said, "They must have used both pictures in the

lineup. I mean, there isn't any question that the witness identified Neville, is there? I thought you said she didn't hesitate. . . ."

"I said the witness didn't hesitate on the identification. But whether it was Neville or Owen—that wasn't the question. I put the photo lineup together. I don't remember—" Mars thought about the one picture that had been so close.

To Nettie he said, "Is it possible Tina had pictures printed of both brothers—and both photos were in the lineup?" Mars thought back to the one photo in the lineup that had looked so much like Neville/Owen that Mars had trouble telling them apart.

Nettie pulled the photos that were used in the lineup. The picture of Owen was plastic wrapped and already notated for evidence as the photo that had been identified by the witness as the individual seen with Mary Pat Fitzgerald on April third. Mars's palms were wet as he went through the rest of the pictures at a clip. The best he could hope for now was that Evelyn Rau had ID'd the wrong brother. But none of the other pictures matched the picture of Neville.

Mars looked up and spoke slowly and clearly. "We need to think about this very carefully. Is there anything we've been saying about Neville that wouldn't also apply to Owen?"

Bobby dropped to a chair. "My God. What Ann and I focused on was that Neville was the only person to know both sisters. But that wasn't true. Owen had met both Mary Pat and Holly. Only briefly—but not any less contact than Neville had with the girls. . . ."

Mars said, "I just figured out what was bothering me after the call with Boston. Boston said the envelopes were clean—only had Neville's prints. Owen would have had to have handled the envelopes when he found them in the safe. Where were his prints?"

"Meaning?" Bobby said.

"Meaning," Mars said, "that somehow Owen got Neville's prints on the envelopes with the intention that they have only Neville's prints. *Meaning* Rau didn't make a mistake. She didn't identify the wrong brother."

Mars sent a squad to pick up Ann at her hotel. She was confused when she arrived. "What's going on? I'm going to miss Owen's call—" She looked at Mars, Nettie, and Bobby. "What *is* it?"

Mars sat her down and told her what they'd discovered. "The more I think about it," he said, "the more sense it makes. My first—and lasting—impression of the crime scene was that it was staged. Someone was trying to make it look like something it wasn't. It makes perfect sense that if Owen committed the murders to implicate Neville, he was trying to make it look like a sex crime."

Nettie said, "Where does the blood alcohol level fit in?"

"My guess? Owen used alcohol to maintain control over the women—and to suggest to investigators how the women could have gotten themselves in a vulnerable position. He didn't know either girl well enough to know that heavy drinking wasn't something they'd do."

"And *motive*," Nettie said. "Does this mean Owen is the nut?"

Ann spoke before Mars could. Her voice was small and tired. The increasing evidence that Owen was the murderer was even more painful to her than if it had been Neville. "Owen's all but told me what the motive was. I just wasn't thinking. The only way he could get what he wanted from the estate was if Neville was out of the picture. He even mentioned a provision in his father's will where a trust beneficiary could be excluded if there were issues of 'moral turpitude'—he made a joke about Neville shitting at Buckingham Palace. He'd thought it through. He knew what

229

to do to get Neville excluded as a trust beneficiary." Ann made a cynical grimace. "Not, I guess, that any of this eliminates the fact that Owen *is* a nut. Someone who would kill two women for money could hardly be called sane."

Bobby said, "What about that—killing *two* women? Why not just kill Ann's sister, and leave it at that? Why risk another murder?"

Mars nodded. "We know the answer to that, as well. I think Neville's alibi is solid. He left Boston unexpectedly, and I don't think Owen knew Neville had left town until after the murder. He'd expected the police to discover the evidence in the safe during the investigation of Holly's death. But police don't keep looking at a suspect if an alibi is solid—unless other compelling evidence is available. So Owen needed to kill again. He probably thought he was strengthening the case against Neville with the second murder."

Mars walked around the room, thinking about the next step, trying to decide if it made more sense to arrest Owen immediately, or to try questioning him further before Owen realized he, not Neville, was the suspect. To Ann he said, "Something else. You said Owen didn't want to meet with the police—that could very well be because he was afraid we might recognize him, or that our witness would see him."

"Now that I think about it," Ann said, "he asked a lot of questions about what you did know. I read that as Owen wanting to be sure he wasn't implicating Neville unfairly. But as I think about it; I can see where he was really pushing for information—he even wanted details about the witness, how reliable she was. I told him she might be the only solid evidence you had at this point, but that she was a graduate student in English at the U. I thought that would impress him."

A chill slid across Mars's back. He said, "Did he ask the witness's name?"

Ann thought for a moment. As she thought, she realized

why Mars had asked the question. For the second time, the heat of emotion broke her pale color. She looked up at Mars. "He didn't ask. I said her name. I'd just read her statement, and I remembered the name. I said the name."

To himself as much as to anyone else, Mars said, "We need to get hold of Rau right away. Then we need to pick up Owen Cook."

CHAPTER
20

The English Department's student receptionist held the receiver against her chest, "Evelyn—call for you." Then, with a look that mingled embarrassment and accusation, she whispered, "It's the Minneapolis Police Department."

Evelyn looked at Rita Hoehne, who shrugged as if to say "*Who cares*." Evelyn didn't feel indifference. She was angry. Reestablishing herself as a graduate student was difficult enough when half the faculty and most of the graduate students knew her history. Having the police department identifying itself when calling her at the U didn't make life easier.

"Yes?" she said sharply into the phone.

"Evelyn Rau?" the man asked.

Again Evelyn said, "*Yes*." Sharper than the first time.

"Miss Rau, I'm Officer Olson calling on behalf of Detective Bahr. Detective Bahr would appreciate it if you could meet him at two o'clock on the Stone Arch Bridge. He wanted to walk through some questions regarding the crime scene."

"Why would he want to do that on the Stone Arch Bridge?" Evelyn asked, rolling her eyes at Rita. "I saw the guy on Main Street, in front of the Pillsbury A Mill."

"Detective Bahr didn't explain, ma'am. He just asked that we get in touch."

"Okay, okay." Evelyn looked up at the wall clock. As she did so, she looked out the window. It had started to rain again, and she hadn't brought an umbrella. Holding the phone aside, she said to Rita, "Is that old green-and-white-striped golf umbrella that somebody left still available as a loaner?"

"Still in the closet, only it's got a big hole and somebody spilled cranberry juice on it. So now it's green, white, and pink. Take it."

Into the phone, Evelyn said, "That's only a half hour from now, and I don't have a car. Tell Bahr I might be a little late."

When she hung up, Rita put a ring of keys in Evelyn's hand. "Take my car. You walk from here down to the Stone Arch Bridge, even with an umbrella, and you're gonna get soaked."

Evelyn put up a weak protest. "Rita, you've done too much for me already. You're going to rue the day you picked me up from jail."

Rita waved a hand at her. "Don't mention it. My life was boring. Nothing like a little criminal association to get your metabolism going. Just have the car back by four-thirty. I don't want to get soaked walking home."

Evelyn arrived at the east end of the Stone Arch Bridge before two o'clock. Parking on Sixth Avenue Southeast, she got out of the car, opening the umbrella as she walked toward the bridge. As she walked she felt a gathering sense of foreboding. It was, no doubt, a conditioned response to her being in an area where, in her previous life, she had often done deals.

Ahead, the bridge was deserted. Most of the weekday bridge traffic came early morning and late afternoon when people who lived on the east side of the river walked over the bridge to and from their downtown offices. And the rain had clearly discouraged casual walkers from being outdoors.

Evelyn was uncertain if she should wait at the east end of the bridge or walk across to the downtown side, which was probably where Bahr would be coming from. She looked at her watch and started walking slowly across the bridge toward downtown.

About halfway across the bridge, a man appeared, coming toward her. She was quite sure it wasn't Bahr. She didn't much like being isolated, out in the middle of a bridge with a strange man approaching. Her sense of personal caution had been highly developed in her days as a minor league drug trader and it had stayed with her. She tilted the umbrella forward, sheltering herself from the strong wind on the bridge and allowing her to keep an eye on the approaching figure through the tear across the top of the umbrella.

The approaching man seemed to be aware of her as well. While there wasn't anything in his appearance that was threatening, she nonetheless felt threatened. She considered turning and going back to her car. But she didn't like the idea of turning her back. Better to keep going, facing him.

It wasn't until he was within perhaps a hundred feet, when he called out, "Miss Rau?" She pulled the umbrella back, looking at him straight on. A gust of wind struck her as she recognized him.

"May I speak to Evelyn Rau, please?"

The young woman's voice said, "Who's calling, please?"

Mars hesitated. It could be awkward for Rau if he identified himself as being with the Minneapolis Police Department. Instead, he said, "My name is Marshall Bahr. I'm calling in connection with some information Miss Rau provided regarding the Father Hennepin Bluffs."

There was muffled conversation on the other end of the phone, then an older, more authoritative voice came on the line. "I'm Rita Hoehne. How may I help you?"

Mars said his piece about the Father Hennepin Bluffs again. Rita Hoehne said, "You with the police?"

Mars gave up being sensitive. "Yes, I'm Detective Marshall Bahr. There's no problem, but something's come up, and I wanted to talk to Ms. Rau—"

"You just missed her. She got your message about meeting on the Stone Arch Bridge and left about fifteen minutes ago. Probably down there already. She borrowed my car."

Mars felt like he'd been socked. Keeping his voice flat, he said, "Who did you say made those arrangements?"

"Don't know who, just know someone called from the Minneapolis police saying you wanted to meet her down on the bridge. Evelyn couldn't figure out why you wanted to meet on the bridge instead of over on Southeast Main."

"Thanks very much. I'll try to catch up with her on the bridge."

Mars turned to Nettie. "He's meeting her on the Stone Arch Bridge. They could be there now."

On recognizing the man coming toward her, Evelyn's mind clogged with irrelevant questions. How did he know her name? How did he know she'd be here? He could only know the answer to both those questions if he'd talked to the police. If he'd talked to the police, what was he doing here now? Why would he want to meet her? The first pertinent thought she had was the answer to that question, and she turned to run.

But her move had come too late. He was on her, one arm wrapped around her neck, his other hand grasping hair tight to her scalp. She struggled to turn the umbrella against him, but as she did so, a gust of wind blew it from her hand. An observer might think of them as a couple engaged in affectionate play. But he was pulling her toward the bridge rail, and Evelyn had no doubt as to his purpose. In the distance,

Evelyn could hear the wail of sirens. It was a poignant sound, knowing as she did how close she was to help—if only someone knew she needed help.

If I wait for help, I'm going to die. That thought was followed by the realization that her arms were free. They'd been free all along, but fear and shock had suppressed common sense. Evelyn reached up with both hands, digging her nails into his wrist below her chin. Forcing her chin down, she sank her teeth into the top of Owen Cook's hand. Startled by pain, his grip loosened, and Evelyn spun away from him—but she tripped, sprawling onto the bridge.

It was from that position that she saw a police squad car turn onto the bridge bed from the east bank. She looked up at Owen Cook and saw him see it at the same moment. They both turned toward the west bank end of the bridge. Two squad cars were approaching from that end. The passenger-side front door of the first car flew open, and Mars Bahr was running straight at them.

Owen Cook stood still. First he looked back at Mars, and then he turned toward the other squad. What Mars and Evelyn saw next appeared in slow motion.

In two long strides, Owen moved to the downriver side of the bridge, pulled himself up on the ledge, and with a mighty leap, threw himself into the air in a motion of deadly grace, his jacket flying open behind him. Mars opened his mouth to scream an involuntary "No!" The wind blew his cry into oblivion.

Mars was at the bridge rail within seconds. But there was nothing to be seen below other than the furious churning of a flooded river. He signaled with both arms for the squads to go down to both sides of the riverbank below. Then he sprinted to Evelyn Rau. She was on her knees where she'd fallen, dazed.

Mars put his hands on her shoulders. "You're okay?"

She nodded, looking up at him. "How did he ..."

Mars said, "Later. I'm sorry, but I'm going to have to get down to the river. I'll have an officer take you over to Hennepin County General. I want a doctor to take a look to you. I'll get back to you there later today."

Mars went back to the bridge rail, watching the activity below as he called Nettie on his cell phone.

"We've got Rau, but Cook went off the bridge. Call the Water Patrol and have them get boats out and set up squad patrols along both sides of the river between the Stone Arch Bridge and Lake Street. And have guards posted at Cook's hotel. Have Glenn get me a search warrant on his room. I'll be going to the hotel as soon as I finish here."

If it hadn't been for the clothes hanging in the closet, Mars would have guessed that Owen Cook had checked out of his hotel room. All surfaces in the room were bare: no antacid tablets, paperback books, or nail clippers on the bedside nightstand. No shopping bags or magazines lying about. In the bathroom, only Owen's leather monogrammed toilet case was on the vanity. Unzipping the case, Mars found dry, immaculate personal toiletries.

There were two suits hanging in the closet: a dark gray woolen pinstripe and a more casual tweedy brown suit. Three pairs of tree-horned leather shoes were precisely lined up under the suits. In a built-in set of drawers, Mars found a half dozen pair of rolled socks, three professionally folded shirts, and folded briefs of a soft Egyptian cotton. The briefs were unusual. There was a flat, handstitched seam around the waist; the fly buttoned. *God, this guy's life was complicated. Who the hell would want to unbutton his fly every time he took a whiz?*

At the far end of the closet was an expensive leather briefcase. Mars picked it up and carried it to the desk. The interior of the case was as spare and functionally ordered as the rest of the room: professional literature, an itinerary, and an airplane ticket. There was no passport.

Mars turned to the uniformed officer from the downtown command and the hotel assistant manager who had accompanied him. "Officer, I'd appreciate your having the room and personal items photographed—including the bathroom, then shots of the closet and drawers. After the photos have been taken, get an inventory and have everything delivered to the property room. I'd like a copy of the inventory delivered to me. We've already made arrangements to have room access controlled, right?"

"Yes, sir."

"I assume the hotel will be given a receipt for anything taken from the room?" The assistant manager was edgy.

"Yes, of course. The officer will see that you get a signed copy of the inventory."

"And what do we do if Mr. Cook shows up?"

"Our officers handling room control will take care of that. And they'll make arrangements with your reception staff regarding procedures to follow if Cook turns up at the front desk." Mars gave one last look around the room before leaving. If Owen Cook were alive, Mars didn't think there was a chance in hell he'd turn up here. There was nothing here worth the risk of coming back to the hotel.

It was dark before Mars got to the chief.

"I hear we had some excitement down on the bluffs this afternoon, Special Detective."

Mars slumped into a chair in the chief's office. He was more than tired. The day's events followed by hours along the river with the search crews had drained his physical and emotional energy.

"If Cook had done his dive an hour later we would have had the TV stations' traffic copters up over the Thirty-five W bridge, and they would've gotten the whole thing on the evening news. It would have given us a shot at finding Cook."

"Still no word from the search?"

"They worked for an hour after sundown. Problem is, with all the rain we've had, the water's high and running fast. He could be halfway to La Crosse by morning."

"Or we could find his body down on the flats, hung up on the undergrowth. Pretty well flooded over."

"That's a possibility." Mars rubbed his eyes.

"How's the girl doin'?"

"She's okay. Neck is stiff from how he was holding her, and she took a pretty bad bump to her head when she fell, but she'll be fine."

"We'll need to brief the mayor first thing tomorrow. I gather we're not going to have much to say publicly?"

"Not till I'm sure what's happened to Cook. We're going to release his photo and a contact number with a caution about approaching him. But nothing about the murders."

The chief shook his head. "Well, justice takes many forms. Many forms. Any way you cut it, you should feel good about putting this one to bed."

"Not really," Mars said. "I was off the mark on this one from day one. And this isn't the end I would have picked. I'd rather have taken our chances in court. It still feels like he got away from us."

"You're beat, Special Detective. I think you need a good night's sleep before you decide how this one came out. Why don't you head home."

The chief's steps echoed as he walked down the hallway. Mars turned, heading back to the Homicide Division. The chief's reference to home increased Mars's feelings of failure. Home wasn't a place. Home was grocery shopping with Chris.

Home was an investigation that was going well. Home was Nettie at the computer, making everything work. And on a night when Chris wasn't with him and when an investigation had run off the rails, what Mars felt as much as anything was homeless.

He was happier than he would have admitted to run into Nettie on her way out. And he was grateful when she turned and followed him into the lounge. Mars popped a can of Coke and dropped down on the battered lounge couch. He pulled out the cigarette pack, still rumpled from being crushed during the photo lineup, looked at it, then tossed it at a wastebasket across the room. It missed, sliding under a chair.

Mars looked sideways at Nettie, his head laid back on the couch, feet up on the coffee table. "You know what Glenn says. We would've had a hell of a time prosecuting even if we'd caught him."

Nettie made a face and started to say something, but stopped. Then she said, "Do you know what that wiseass kid of yours said to me on the phone this afternoon?"

"Not a clue."

"He asked me if I knew what Evian spelled backwards was."

Mars thought about this for a moment. Nothing came. His brain was suffering an oxygen deficit.

Nettie said, "Naive."

"That sounds more like Gloria than Chris."

"Gloria?"

"You haven't heard about Gloria? Chris and Gloria were a couple."

"How did I miss that?"

"Probably because there wasn't anything to miss. Except every now and then Chris comes up with something—I don't know, something *sophisticated*. It always traces back to Gloria. She's a whip. A real terror."

Nettie plopped her feet on the floor. "Well, maybe we could get her a job down here. She could replace Tina."

"*That* would be an improvement."

Nettie stood. "I'm gonna head out. When are you planning on coming in tomorrow?"

"I promised Chris he could go down to the river with me tomorrow morning. The search crews are going out at sunup. I should be back here around ten o'clock—unless we find a body. . . ."

Nettie took a deep swig of Evian, then looked down at Mars. "So. You think he's dead?"

The hands on the big wall clock jumped, making the only sound in the room.

Mars sat up, leaning forward, both feet square on the floor. He rolled the Coke can back and forth between his palms.

"No."

CHAPTER
21

What he wanted more than anything was to see the body first. To pull at his dad's coat, and say, "Over there, Dad," or, "What's that out on the water, toward the middle?" To be the first one to see Owen Cook's body.

Chris and Mars and a dozen others walked the banks of the Mississippi between the Stone Arch Bridge and the Lower St. Anthony Lock and Dam downstream. Three Hennepin County Sheriff's Department Water Patrol boats struggled with the current on the river. Attempts to drag had been postponed until the river dropped and slowed, maybe the following week or later. All they could do now was search for a body—or some remnant of a body—that had been caught in a vortex.

Chris's wish gave way to other thoughts. The fierce, dark water left him thinking about what it would be like to die in water like that. Of how it would feel dropping into the water from the bridge above. Would you see anything if you opened your eyes under that water? Would you touch bottom? Could you swim back to the surface if you wanted to? Would you hit bottom hard enough to break bones?

Mars's thoughts weren't much different. If the river had been at normal level, there wasn't any way Owen Cook would have survived the jump. But the river was up at least eight feet over its normal level, and it was moving so fast. Mars looked at his watch. Almost 8:00 A.M. He tapped Chris on the shoulder. "Come on. I made an appointment to talk with a guy who runs the locks in the U.S. Army Corps of Civil Engineers building, other side of the bridge."

Together they scrambled up the side of the bluffs to the east end of the bridge.

Halfway over the bridge, Chris said, "Is it a real waterfall, Dad?" Chris faced upstream, awed by the water's violent power.

"Yes and no. Remember when we toured Ft. Snelling, about five miles downriver?"

Chris nodded.

"Well, the original falls was there. But the bed of the river is sandstone, covered by limestone. What happens is, the sandstone washes out and the limestone crumbles. So the falls kept moving upriver. When settlers came here in the eighteen-hundreds, they didn't want to lose the falls. So they built a kind of platform under the water to stop the erosion. They tried to build a tunnel under the river to direct some of the water's force toward the other bank, toward the bluffs, but the tunnel collapsed, almost destroying the falls."

"Was anyone in the tunnel when it collapsed?" Chris's voice was tense with a mix of horror and thrill at the image of being in a collapsing tunnel under the force of water he saw before him.

"Don't know. Anyway, eventually a concrete apron was built to preserve the falls." Mars gave Chris a little pull. "Let's hustle. I'm late for my meeting."

The U.S. Army Corps building was just the other side of the bridge. Todd Richard met them at the door and walked them back up a tile stairwell to a big, windowed room that looked out over the falls and the bridge. It was the locks' control center and Richard's office. It felt a little like being on the helm of a ship.

"I saw that guy go off the bridge yesterday," Richard said. "Couldn't figure out what was up. Why were you guys after him, anyway?"

"He was a suspect in an investigation."

"Ha! You must have had the right guy. One hell of a guilty conscience to take a flying leap off the bridge, I'd say."

"Well, it doesn't look like we'll ever know the answer to that one. Like I said on the phone yesterday, I'd be interested in any information you can give us about what might happen with a body going off the bridge under these conditions."

Richard nodded. "Come over to my computer. After I talked to you yesterday, I called a pal of mine over at the university. A physicist. Me, I'm a hydrologist. Got an undergraduate degree in civil engineering, my Ph.D. in hydrology. A lot of the things you're going to want to know are more in the line of physics. So I called my friend, and he gave me a program we could use. I think you'll find it interesting. I'm kind of looking forward to playing around with it myself."

Richard slipped a disk into his computer. As the machine cranked, he said, "I paid attention to where the guy went over. Couldn't see much after he jumped, but I'll say this: He jumped over the eighteenth arch of the bridge, which is directly in line with one of the deepest channels in this stretch of the river. Two arches over, the bed of the river is higher. Even under these conditions, he'd have had a hard time coming out alive if he'd landed there. But where he went over, he had as good a shot as you're going to get when you do a damn fool thing like that. Other break he got, the river's highly oxygenated given how much turbulence there is. That creates a pillowing effect. If the water surface had been calm," Richard shook his head, "it wouldn't have mattered how deep the river was where he went off. The impact of landing from that height on a flat surface would have killed him."

Program images began flashing on the computer screen. Richard said, "Tell me the guy's height and weight."

"He was about six one, a hundred and ninety pounds."

"You see if he went in feet first, belly flop, or what?"

Mars shook his head. "We haven't been able to find anybody who saw him after he jumped."

Richard grimaced. "Makes a difference. Let's try this a couple of ways." He muttered under his breath, his right hand flicking a mouse back and forth. The image of a man standing on a level surface came up. Richard said, "I'm giving the program a description of your guy, the depth of the water, and the current velocity. And now"—Richard held his head up, looking down his glasses at the keyboard—"and now I'm gonna give your guy a little shove. . . ."

The figure on the screen moved from the top of the screen into the water. Under the water was a scaled topographical map of the riverbed below the bridge's eighteenth arch. Chris said, "*Cool,* Dad." The figure hit the water and the program made a splash. The figure went down fast, but at a perpendicular angle, dragged by the powerful flow of the river. The figure slowed as it moved down, touching the bottom in a gentle bounce.

"Dad!" Chris looked at Mars, uncertain what the image on the screen meant.

Richard said. "Well, like I said. As far as surviving the jump, I'd say your guy had a chance. But it would depend on a lot of things, most of which we can't capture with the computer—at least with the program we're using here."

"Like what?"

"Well, like wind direction. And that would be pretty hard to pin down. The river channel has a lot of draft variation, and it can shift dramatically in seconds. So we're not going

245

to be able to pin that down with any certainty. And I pushed him in feet first. If he went in, say, cannonball, back kind of flat toward the river, it would have slowed him down some. Even how he carried his weight could make a difference. How much body fat did he have?" Richard clicked keys and the mouse and the figure reappeared, this time in the shape Richard had described. Richard gave the figure another shove and it took another plunge. This time it didn't hit bottom.

"Cool!" Chris repeated.

Mars looked at him. "Number three." Chris blushed slightly and shrugged.

"Well, like you see, the position he was in when he hit the water would make a difference. Then there're other factors to consider, like how many layers of clothes he had on, the type of fabric—all that could make a difference between coming out of that jump alive or not."

Richard shoved his chair back and walked over to the windows. "But say he survived the jump. He could still get hung up underwater. Water as powerful as it is right now, that's a real possibility. Then you've got the Lower St. Anthony Lock and Dam just downriver. Given the volume of water coming through now, they've had the locks wide open and the grinders are off, but still, that's a real gauntlet for a body to pass. And you've got the cold. Our ambient air temperatures have been running twenty to twenty-five degrees below normal for the past few weeks, lower than that upriver. So the water's colder than normal. I'd say the guy would slip into serious hypothermia in—oh, maybe thirty, forty-five minutes, tops. Put it all together, and it'd take a small miracle for him to still be alive. Still, with the breaks he got, who knows..."

"Let's take a little walk," Mars said when he and Chris came out on the deck of the locks building. Together they walked downriver toward the Lower St. Anthony Lock and Dam. A gauntlet was a good description. Richard was right. It would take a miracle to get through that alive.

Mars stopped, looking out across the river, than back toward the falls. It was anyone's bet if Owen Cook had survived the jump and made it past the lock and dam.

Mars's money went with the miracle.

CHAPTER
22

Dead never smells good. And it never smells worse than when it's been wet for a couple days.

It had been scarcely more than forty-eight hours since Owen Cook had gone off the stone arch bridge, but Mars could smell the body when he was only halfway down the hill above the river shore. From that vantage point, Mars could see the County Coroner's Unit guys standing near what appeared to be a log lying on the shoreline. The CCUs were wearing face masks; the uniforms on the scene were holding gloved hands over the lower half of their faces.

Sliding sideways on the wet slope down to the sandy riverbank flats, Mars balanced himself by grabbing branches with his left hand, his right leg extended forward. Damn tricky. There might have been easier ways to get to the floater carrying Owen Cook's ID, but Mars was sure this was the fastest route. Behind Mars, Chris slid on his butt. Mars tried not to think about what Denise would have to say when she came across Chris's jeans in the laundry.

"Pee-*yew*!" Chris exclaimed as he caught the body's drift. Chris had seen—and smelled—corpses in a morgue. But in a morgue, refrigeration and chemicals mask the odor of decaying flesh. This was Chris's first nose-up-against-a-floater that had been marinating for a couple days in the rich sauce of the Mississippi.

"Breathe through your mouth, keep your hand over your nose and mouth," Mars called behind him. When he glanced back, he could see muddy fingerprints over the lower half of Chris's face.

"I can sort of taste it, Dad, when I breathe through my mouth."

"I think what you're tasting is mud—sure you want to come down? If you want to go back to the car, I'll throw you the keys."

Chris shook his head. "Nah. I wanna come." And he continued his slide.

Once on level ground, Mars slapped his hands together to shake off grit and slime. He waited for Chris to catch up, and said, "Stay by me. You know our rules—you got a question, you wait until we're back in the car." The caution wasn't really necessary. Chris had an innate reverence for crime-scene etiquette, and he understood intuitively how to modify his behavior to minimize questions about what he was doing there in the first place.

"Got your jumper, Candy Man." Nils Bergerson from the CCU grinned triumphantly as Mars approached. Nils held a dark, rectangular object in the air, flapping it at Mars.

Mars walked away from Bergerson, toward the floater. At best it was an abstract rendering of the trunk of a human body. No head, couple of stumps above where the elbows would have been, maybe five inches of thigh on the left, nothing on the right. If it hadn't been for the body's clothing, the notion that this *was* a body might not have been anybody's first guess. Mars recognized the fabric on the upper half of the torso as resembling the jacket Owen Cook had been wearing when he went off the bridge.

"How'd we find out the body was down here?"

Bergerson said, "Nine-one-one was getting calls about the stink. Nobody was saying they'd seen a body, but everybody was saying there was something above lock and dam number one that smelled to high heaven."

"Betty Johnson put it together?"

Bergerson gave a rueful grin, shaking his head at Mars's question. "You got it. She looked up the call log and saw there were a bunch of calls about the same location. Then *she* got a call from a guy who said what it smelled like was his mother's apartment after his mother hadn't answered her phone for a week."

"God bless Betty Johnson," Mars said.

"Betty Johnson thinks she is God," Bergerson said. "Other lucky thing—another half mile and your jumper would have run right into lock and dam number one. No way he's gonna get through that without ending up wood chips."

Mars pulled on latex gloves and folded open the wallet Bergerson handed him. The exterior of the wallet was swollen and slimy from being in the water. Remarkably, the wallet's interior was in fair shape, the contents clearly identifiable. Carefully, Mars opened the passport to the photo. The passport's pages looked like they'd been stained in tea, but the photo was easily recognizable. Owen Cook stared out at Mars, confident and unsmiling. Mars pried open the currency pocket and peered in.

Ding. Two—maybe three?—one-dollar bills. "This is it? You didn't find any more cash in the wallet?"

Bergerson looked ticked. "Meaning, did I find a thousand bucks and pocket it?"

"Not what I meant. My information is that our jumper was carrying a hunk of cash when he jumped. I'm wondering where it is. Thought you might have taken cash out and hadn't been able to get it back in the wallet, so you inventoried it. That's all I meant."

"What you see is what we got. We're damn lucky to have the wallet, much less identifiable contents. Only reason we've still got that, I'd guess, is that the guy's jacket was buttoned, which probably kept it together first few days."

Mars's head had come up sharply: Ding number two. "The jacket was buttoned?"

"You bet. Like I said, we're fucking lucky it was." Bergerson looked sideways at Chris, hearing himself say "fucking." A look of annoyance crossed his face. He was annoyed Mars was raising picayune questions on a sure thing. Jesus Christ. What did this fucking Homicide hot dog want? He has a guy who goes off a bridge upstream and CCU is giving them a floater with the jumper's ID. And Bergerson was annoyed he had to watch his language because the Homicide Division's number one hot dog had dragged his kid down to a recovery scene.

Mars wasn't paying attention to Bergerson. He was remembering Owen Cook's jacket flying—open—as he jumped from the Stone Arch Bridge. "You get video on the buttoned jacket?"

Bergerson's voice was tense. "Yeah, we got video on the buttoned jacket. We got video of the whole scene before we touched anything, including the body. Just like always." He couldn't stop himself. "Why the fuck you care if the jacket was buttoned or not. We're talking about a scene that fits perfect with your guy, and we've given you ID on a silver platter. What more you want, Candy Man? I can't bring him back to life so he can get down on his knees and give you a goddamn confession."

"Only because he hasn't got any knees to get down on," one of the uniforms said.

The other uniform said, "Knees ain't all he's missing. . . ."

They all laughed. Eyeing Chris for a reaction, Bergerson said, "Yup. It's a Bobbitt. Nothing a raccoon likes better than cocktail wieners before the main course."

Mars ignored them. He now knew the first question he was going to get from Chris back in the car. "I'm going to head back to city hall. Doc D in town?"

"He was in Friday," Bergerson said. "Didn't say anything about not being in town over the weekend."

"I'd appreciate your giving him a call. Ask him to come in and do the post on this one. I'll be at my desk at the division. Have him give me a call there. Then, if you could get the video and your recovery-scene summary over to me as soon as it's available."

"Will do," Bergerson said, no enthusiasm in his voice.

Mars knew the guys were already rolling their eyes and shaking their heads as he and Chris headed back up the hill. He called back, "Thanks, guys."

The passenger-side car door was barely shut before Chris asked the questions.

"What's a Bobbitt? What were they saying about raccoons and cocktail wieners?"

"Few years ago—I don't know, 1993, 1994—a guy named Bobbitt and his wife got in a fight. She cut his penis off. There was a lot of publicity about it. Since then, anytime we run across a male body that's missing the penis, somebody's gonna call it a Bobbitt. With cops, that's humor."

Chris's face was distorted with horror. Mars suppressed a grin.

"What about the raccoon stuff?"

"Lot of coons down by the river. They're real garbage pails. Eat anything, including dead bodies. I don't have a clue if coons ate this guy's penis." Mars couldn't stop himself. "My bet would be on a bald eagle. They're the real scavengers of the river."

Mars pulled out the car phone, and handing it to Chris said, "Do me a favor. Call Nettie. Ask her to meet us downtown. If she gets there first, ask her to pull up the Owen Cook files."

They were halfway downtown when Chris said, "Dad? At the river? It sounded like you didn't think it was the right guy."

Mars thought about his answer before replying. "There are a couple things that bothered me—odds are, it *is* Owen Cook—but I'm not willing to drop the hammer until I've checked some things out."

"Like what?"

"The woman with Owen Cook the day before he went off the bridge said he had a lot of cash at the restaurant where they ate lunch. I don't see him getting rid of that between the time he left the restaurant and the next day. The wallet we just looked at had a couple bucks. So where's the money?"

Chris grinned. "Dad, you've got fifteen seconds. 'Show me the money.' "

Mars grinned back. "Too easy. Cuba Gooding, Jr., to Tom Cruise in *Jerry McGuire*."

Chris's face tightened again with concentration. "What if someone found his body before you did, and stole the money?"

Mars reached over to ruffle Chris's hair. "Great minds think alike. I was just wondering about that. But think a little more. Someone comes across the body by the river. Number one, very few people are going to approach a dead body, much less go up to it and start digging around in the pockets. Number two, the kind of people who might do that are transients. On the river, transients hang out around downtown. I've never come across a transient on the river south of the Lake Street Bridge, and this guy was more than a mile downriver from Lake Street. . . ."

"So maybe he got robbed near downtown, and then the robber put the body back in the river?"

Mars nodded. "That could happen. But ask yourself, why would a transient rob the guy and leave a couple bucks in the wallet, put the wallet back inside the jacket, and button the jacket—which, by the way, is the other thing that's bothering me. I saw Cook go off the bridge. His jacket flew open when he jumped. It wasn't buttoned."

Chris's head started bouncing off the back of the car seat, a sure sign he was thinking hard and enjoying it. In a singsong thinking-out-loud voice, he said, "Soooo, Owen Cook came out of the river and buttoned his jacket because he was cold and then he remembered his money, so he checked his wallet—"

"*Unbuttoning* his jacket . . ." Mars said.

Chris's voice slowed down. "Okay, unbuttoned his jacket, looked at his money—then he starts to feel sick because he hurt himself jumping and he drops a bunch of the money and he feels too sick to bend over and pick it up so he puts his wallet back in his pocket. . . ."

"And buttons his jacket but walks away from the money?"

Chris sighed. "It's not working."

"I think you've put your finger on the only possible scenario for why the money wouldn't be in the wallet—and I also think you're running up against the same problems I've got in explaining why the wallet would still be in his jacket, with only a couple bucks, and the jacket buttoned."

"So how do you figure out what did happen?"

"Ask yourself this: Who really *needed* that money?"

Chris's answer was quick. "Owen needed it. To help him get away."

"I agree. So, let's say that the reason that the wallet on the corpse didn't have anything but a couple bucks is *because Owen kept the money.* Meaning?..."

Chris turned toward Mars. "Owen found a dead guy and put his stuff on that guy, except for most of the money?"

"Well, I suppose that's possible. But that would take a lot of luck—for Owen to be walking along the river and come across a dead guy—not to say Owen hasn't had most of the luck in this case. But I just think that's probably too much of a stretch. What I think is more likely is that Owen ran into somebody near the river, saw his chance, and took it."

"He killed someone else!"

"That would be my first guess."

"Dad, you know why else that makes sense?" Chris didn't wait for an answer. "Because there was still a little bit of money left in the wallet. Like you said, someone stealing the money would have taken all of it. But Owen would think the wallet would look funny if there wasn't any money in it."

"Outta the mouths of babes," Mars said.

Pulling into the underground garage at city hall, Mars said, "I'm gonna make a stop in the communications center before I go up to the squad room...." He paused. "Do you have some homework you can do in your backpack?"

"Yeah. And Nettie said she had a book for me to read."

"You won't get bored?"

Chris shook his head in a vigorous no.

Mars looked around the garage. He didn't see Nettie's car. "Looks like we beat Nettie coming in. You better come down to the communications center with me before we go upstairs."

The city hall communications center was in the bowels of the building, a huge room set in a below-floor pit and staffed by a couple dozen operators, all fielding 911 calls. Late afternoon on a Sunday, the phone volume was slow. Mars wound his way down the aisles, heading in the direction of a small, gray-haired black woman sitting on a slightly elevated platform in the far corner.

Betty Johnson, shift supervisor for city of Minneapolis 911 operations, and a legend in her own time. More than once Betty had figured out that information from various calls linked to a single perpetrator. Or that a call that didn't sound serious was a matter of life and death. Once she decided something was important, you'd better pay attention. You didn't pay attention, and one of two things would happen, neither of them good. Betty would either hound you to within an inch of your sanity, or you'd miss something that would make a big difference in a case. More likely, you didn't pay attention to Betty and both bad things would happen.

"Well, well, well," Betty said in her deceptively soft, slow drawl. "The prince of Homicide graces us with his presence. Do tell, Special Detective. To what do the likes of us owe this honor?"

"Just paying my dues to the queen of nine-one-one," Mars said. "Wanted to thank you for giving a push on the stink down by the river. Turns out we got a floater that connects to a case I had last spring, the Edina girl found dead on the bluffs."

Once given her due, Betty always affected modesty. "Oh, my. Well, I had no idea, I'm sure. Perhaps you should mention your gratitude to your colleagues in the Third Precinct, as well. After all, it only took me seven calls and a personal appearance to get them to dispatch someone down there for a look-see. Always quick off the dime, those fellows from the Third." Betty bent back in her chair and looked around Mars. Chris was hanging behind.

"That your little man, Special Detective?"

Mars beckoned to Chris. "Betty Johnson, my son, Chris."

Chris stepped forward, holding his hand out. Mars was used to his son's smile until he saw Chris use it on other people. The kid was a heartbreaker.

"What a handsome boy," Betty said. "Just like his daddy. And nice manners, too. Like his daddy."

"Gets good manners from his mother." Mars bent over and kissed Betty's forehead. "Thanks, kiddo."

To the other operators, all of whom were paying close attention to what was going on between Mars and Betty, Betty called out, "Hope you all saw what happened just now. I've been sexually harassed, I have. You all are witnesses in my lawsuit."

A fat, bleached-blond operator sitting kitty-corner from Betty called out, "In your dreams, Betty, in your dreams. Hey, Homicide. You wanna harass me sometime, just dial nine-one-one and ask for Rhonda. And ten years from now I'll take calls from your little sidekick."

Mars and Chris exited the communications pit to a chorus of laughter. Chris walked fast, his face bright red.

By the time they got to the squad room, Nettie had arrived.

Chris said, "You remember the book you were going to borrow me to read?"

Nettie winced. "*Lend* you. Yes, I did." She handed Chris an old, hardbound book with a red cover.

Chris looked at it. "*In Cold Blood*. What did you say it was about?"

"Good people with really bad luck. So, Mars. What's up?"

Mars reached over and took the book from Chris. He looked through it quickly. To Nettie he said, "This okay for him to read?"

"Not half as bad as the stuff he sees following you around. Scary, though—the people who get murdered are about as

257

unlikely victims as you're gonna find. And speaking of unlikely victims..."

"They've pulled a floater out of the river. Owen Cook's
ID was on the body."

Chris said, "The guys down there called it a Bobbitt."

Nettie rolled her eyes. "So what you're saying is, the guy
was missing his, uh, male part."

"He didn't have a head or arms or legs, either. The guys
said the raccoons probably ate the penis." Chris was making
the most of his newfound knowledge.

"I just *love* it," Nettie said. "You've got, like, six men—
all professional crime-scene guys—standing around a corpse
that has no head, no arms, no legs. And what they talk about
is, Where's the dick?"

Chris said, "Dad doesn't think it's Owen Cook."

Nettie looked at Mars. "How could it *not* be Owen Cook?
I mean, you've got a body in the river after Cook jumped
from the bridge and the body has Cook's ID—who else is it
going to be?"

Mars walked her through the ideas he and Chris had
talked about in the car.

"I think I see where I come in on this action. You want
me to do a missing-persons search, right?" Nettie asked.

"Exactly right. And while you're doing the missing-
persons search, I'm going to go over the incident reports we
got from officers patrolling the river area after Cook jumped."
Mars looked at Chris who'd sat down at a desk and was
already deeply engrossed in his book. "We should probably
eat something. Anybody want pizza?"

Chris nodded without looking up. Nettie said, "Hey. I
almost forgot." She dug around in her purse, pulling out a
candy bar, which she tossed over to Chris. "Try this. I had
one yesterday and thought it was pretty good—and a lot
cheaper than Ghiradelli or Godiva."

Mars said, "That's a felony: contributing to the chocolate addiction of a minor. Chris, save the chocolate for after pizza."

Doc D called shortly after the pizza arrived. "I've got a rotten piece of meat over here my people tell me you want cut up."

"Remember the homecoming princess from Edina who got killed on the bluffs early last spring?"

"Fitzgerald. The one with the classy watch . . ."

"The same. And the guy we think killed her jumped from the Stone Arch Bridge on Friday. Your piece of rotten meat was carrying the perp's ID. But I've got some doubts. Any chance you can do the post sooner rather than later?"

"You available right now?"

"I can be over there in ten minutes." Mars hung up. To Nettie he said, "I'm going over to the morgue. Doc is going to do the post now. That's not going to leave me time to pull the incident reports—they on-line?"

Nettie shook her head. "Haven't gotten to that level of document yet. The only links we've built are with arrest reports and case summaries." She pushed up out of her chair and walked over to the files. "Go on. I think they're filed up here and that they're together. I'll have them ready when you get back."

"Don't want to take you off putting together the missing-person stuff—"

"Won't happen. Get on over to blood-and-gutsville."

Normally Chris would have been bouncing up and down begging to go with Mars to the autopsy. Mars glanced at him. Chris wasn't paying attention to Mars and Nettie. Mars recognized the surefire signs he was concentrating hard: Chris's pupils were big and black and his cheeks were pink.

"Chris, I'm going over to the morgue. You okay here?"

Chris nodded but didn't look up.

Doc was wearing a face mask when Mars came in. He handed one to Mars, shaking his head.

"Wish we had more time to chill this one out. What's on your mind?"

"I've got some doubts that this guy is my jumper. I'm thinking it's possible that my jumper survived and that what we've got here is an opportunistic killing—that our perp used this guy as a decoy to cover his trail. I'd just like to get a closer look at the body to see if there's anything that points us one direction or the other."

Doc D said, "Well, given the condition of the corpse, I'm not optimistic. But let's have a look."

With delicacy, he pulled away the outer layers of clothing from the body. He stopped. Mars was staring at a remnant of fabric around the torso's waist. "What?" Doc said.

"Can you use your scalpel to clear off right around here—" Mars pointed. "I want to look at that fabric under . . ." The scalpel pulled off a chunk of suit pants with a frayed belt loop. Directly under the suit pant's fabric was what was clearly the remnant of the elastic waistband of a pair of briefs. Mars could make out three faded letters woven into the band: H-A-N.

Ding. "Hanes," Mars said.

"Say again?" Doc asked.

"Our suspect's shorts would have had a flat waistband, button fly. This isn't my jumper."

"How'd the autopsy go?" Nettie asked when Mars came back to the division. She was still at the computer.

Mars shook his head. "I don't know yet how I'm going to prove it, but our floater is *not* Owen Cook. Remember that underwear we brought back from Cook's hotel room?"

Nettie thought about it. "Oh, yeah. Bone buttons on the fly."

"Exactly. Our floater was wearing Hanes Jockey shorts. Owen Cook would rather *be* dead than wear briefs you buy in a plastic three-pack." Mars stood behind Nettie at the computer. "Where, by the way, is Chris?"

"He went back to the lounge. Was gonna read on the couch. You get any material that looks like we can draw a DNA profile from the floater?"

"Doc said that shouldn't be a problem. Just need a family member—either from Cook's side or the floater's side, provided we can prove the floater's not Cook." Mars sighed. "I need to get started on the patrol incident reports—"

"On your desk."

"How we doing on our missing persons?"

Nettie grimaced. "Nothing yet. The connection is slower than mud."

Mars stared at the stack of sixty-seven patrol reports on his desk. Within a half hour of Owen Cook's jump, four police squad cars had been dispatched to patrol West and East River roads between the Stone Arch Bridge and Ft. Snelling. With the incident reports, Nettie had included a copy of the patrol assignment the Downtown Command had issued. Mars read through the assignment before starting on the reports.

Patrolling officers are instructed to question all males found on foot on the assigned surveillance route meeting the following general description: Caucasian male, early to mid thirties 6'–6'2", 190–200 pounds, wavy light brown hair of medium length, eyes green to hazel, no identifying facial features, wearing tan dress slacks and a brown herringbone tweed jacket. Search subject is a British citizen and may speak with an English accent. The search subject jumped from the Stone Arch Bridge at approximately 13:30–14:30 on

August 14. The subject may have visible injuries and his clothes will show evidence of having been in water. Any subject meeting this description should be asked to show identification and should be detained pending further questioning. Patrol officers are instructed to file incident reports on all subjects questioned, including subjects that are not detained, with the duty officer, Downtown Command. The patrol will continue until further notice. Officers are advised that the search subject may be armed and should be considered dangerous.

Mars exhaled heavily after reading the patrol assignment. Looking up from the computer, Nettie said, "What?"

Mars stared at the paper in front of him. "I just reread the patrol assignment issued to the squads that patrolled River Road after the jump."

"And . . ."

"It's—fine. In fact, a good piece of work given how fast the Downtown Command got squads out after the jump. Thing is, it's almost too good. Too much detail. *Great* detail if the guy you're looking for hasn't changed his appearance. But the scenario I'm checking—that Cook disguised himself using another guy's clothes—a description like this can mean a patrol would exclude someone who should have been included."

"They used the description I gave the squads that went down to the bridge to back you up when you went after Cook."

Mars shook his head. "Not sure I would have done any better at that point. Probably wouldn't have anticipated this scenario, would have thought the search assignment looked great. And it probably doesn't matter anyway." He put the patrol assignment aside and restacked the incident reports. "This," he said, "is going to be a lot of fun."

It took him a few minutes to decide how he was going to review the reports. As he flipped through the pages something written across the top of one report caught his eye.

Jumper?

Mars's breath caught. Why would a patrolman write "jumper?" on one of—Mars flipped through the reports with the officer's signature—why would Officer Danny Borg write "jumper?" on only one of eleven incident reports he filed unless there was something special about that subject that made Borg think this guy might be the jumper? And, if there was something special about that subject, why hadn't the subject been detained for questioning or, at a minimum, why hadn't the report been forwarded to Homicide?

Mars traced his finger over the report for anything unusual. The incident reports had been formatted with pre-printed search items to minimize the time patrolmen had to spend writing interview summaries. Danny Borg had checked height, weight, eye color, and age as matching. He had not checked any of the special features—English accent, wet appearance, injuries, clothing description—Mars stopped. There was the start of a check on injuries, but it had not been completed. And the space that followed "specify" if injuries had been checked was blank. There was no information under identification verification, meaning Borg hadn't asked for identification. Which meant Borg hadn't thought there was any reason to ask for identification.

This was probably nothing. Borg had probably been doodling on the report when he wrote "jumper?" If Mars spent this much time with each report he'd never get through all sixty-seven.

Nettie said, "I've got a live one."

"I could use a live one."

"Here we go. How about this? An attorney, Andrew Shard, age thirty-seven, five feet eleven. Went missing—get this—Friday, reported yesterday morning. Nada since then, except for his car turning up, a red Volvo station wagon."

"Who's the investigating officer?"

Nettie peered at the screen. "Dale Nelson."

"Do me a favor. Talk to Nelson. Number one, see if there's any reason Shard would have been in the vicinity of the river Friday afternoon. Number two, find out why the car was left where it was." He stopped, his eyes dropping down to the incident report with "jumper?" written across the top. "One other thing. See if you can get me a number where Patrolman Danny Borg can be reached. He works out of the Downtown Command. I've got a question about one of the incident reports."

Danny Borg was in a deep sleep after working seven days in a row, a double shift the last day. He jumped, answering the phone before he was awake; his girlfriend, Fay, still sound asleep at his side.

A slow, easy voice on the other end of the line said, "Patrolman Dan Borg? Mars Bahr, special detective in Homicide. Sorry to call so late, but I'm following up on a floater we pulled out of the river this afternoon."

Borg's heart was pounding. He sat bolt upright on the edge of the bed, squeezing his brain into action. "No problem, sir, how can I help?"

"I've got an incident report you filed on your patrol—one of your incident reports had the word 'jumper' written across the top. A question mark after the word. Just wondering if there was anything special about that subject that made you write 'jumper'...."

"Oh, geez. I mean, God. I must've filed a dozen reports from that patrol...."

"Eleven, actually."

"Eleven sounds right. Ahhhh. And you're saying I wrote 'jumper,' on just one?"

"That's right."

Borg could hear the interest draining out of Bahr's voice. He broke out in a light sweat. "God, I'm really sorry, but..." He was tempted to tell Bahr about the last hellish thirty-six hours of work since he'd completed the River Road patrol. About the drunk at Cub Foods that had been waving a gun. The drunk who, after Danny had single-handedly disarmed him and gotten him cuffed, had shit in the backseat of the squad car. Danny knew going into detail would only make things worse. Finally composed, he said, "I'm really sorry. I can't come up with anything...."

"Not a problem," Bahr said. "It was a long shot. Just wanted to make sure it didn't mean anything. Sorry to bother you. Let me give you a couple numbers where you can reach me if you think of anything."

Not about to make Bahr wait for him to get paper, Danny wrote the numbers on his pillow with a tube of lipstick from Fay's makeup bag on the nightstand. Then he said, "Detective Bahr? Could you just tell me the address where that report was taken?"

"Uh—let's see. Little north of the Lake Street Bridge. West River Road."

"Thanks, sir. Sorry..."

Bahr said good night and hung up.

Danny Borg dropped to his knees next to the bed and pounded the floor with clenched fists. "Jesus fucking christ! Goddamnit all to hell. Damn, damn, damn!"

Fay sat up on one elbow and squinted at Danny. "What is it? What happened?"

"I just fucking ruined my career, is what happened. Jesus. I didn't give him one single thing—I can't even remember the guy I talked to, much less . . ."

Fay dropped back down on the bed, hands over her eyes. "I don't get it. What could you possibly have done in a two-minute phone call in the middle of the night that could ruin your career?"

"On the phone. Just now. That was Mars Bahr. He's a fucking legend in the department. Special detective in Homicide. Handles all the big cases. And one thing everybody knows is that if you help him out on something, he remembers. He's given a lot of guys a hand up. You do a good job, and Bahr sees you do it, it can make a big difference on moving out of a uniform and into a suit. And Jesus. He calls *me*, and all I come up with is, '*Dub?*'"

"You were sleeping, for God's sake, Danny. . . ."

Danny suddenly scrambled up and started pulling his clothes off the chair.

Fay propped herself up on two elbows. "What are you doing now?"

"I'm going to drive the patrol again. Something may come back."

He drove all the way downtown to where he'd started the patrol Friday afternoon. Then he reversed direction and turned left off Fifth toward West River Road, picking up the road just below Portland Avenue. As he headed south he could feel it coming back. He remembered the first two guys he'd stopped. Couple guys who worked downtown, out for a run. Except for clothes, they fit the general description, but—not a chance. Next stop was just north of the Franklin Avenue Bridge. The guy was at least twenty years older than the search subject.

It wasn't until he passed Twenty-sixth Street that he remembered the guy who'd made him write "jumper?" on the incident report. What he remembered was that a couple of blocks south of Twenty-sixth, he'd noticed a beat-up red Volvo station wagon illegally parked. The Wellstone bumper sticker had caught his eye, and he'd considered pulling over to ticket the car. He fucking hated all those bleeding-heart liberals, and Paul Wellstone, Minnesota's senior senator, was the worst of the lot. But when it came down to simple civil obedience, these were always the guys who broke the rules. Like parking their fucking Volvos—which was the car they always drove—in a no-parking zone.

Danny Borg caught himself. How would it look if he turned in a parking violation ticket when he was supposed to be patrolling for a missing suspect. He refocused, and as he did, he saw the guy coming up the hill. Right height, weight, age looked good—but nothing else fit. Danny slowed and pushed the power window control.

Looking up at the guy, he got a good look at his face. The description—which could have been just about anyone— fit. And this guy had a gash across the top of his nose that ran down to his cheek. Danny felt uneasy. But the guy sounded cool, had a reasonable explanation for the injury, didn't have an English accent, and was dry as a bone.

Now, two days later, in the dark, Danny Borg pulled over and rolled his window down to get a better look at where he'd seen the guy. Night air filled the car—Danny shivered. And then Danny remembered. It had been unusually cold the afternoon of the patrol, and the guy he'd stopped only had on a jogging suit. Danny had said something about needing to keep moving to stay warm. And the guy had said something about "wearing a jumper." As Danny had pulled away, still feeling uneasy about this one, he'd scribbled, "jumper?"

on the incident report. Not for any special reason, just because he felt a little uneasy. What the hell had the guy meant about *wearing* a jumper? What he thought was he'd probably misheard; Danny had been thinking jumper and the guy had said something else.

It wasn't a lot. But at least he'd remembered something. Should he call the number Bahr gave him when he got back to the apartment?

Nettie picked up, then handed the phone to Mars. "For you. Patrolman Borg."

As Mars reached for the phone, Chris, tired but still bright-eyed with interest in his book, came into the squad room. "Dad? Is there a dictionary? I need to look up a word."

Mars covered the phone with one hand and pointed to a bookcase against the wall. "If we've got one, it would be with those manuals on the wall." He brought the receiver up to his ear. "Yeah, Borg. You thought of something?"

"Well, sir, I thought it might help if I redrove the route." There was a mixture of pride and embarrassment in Borg's voice. "And I did remember the guy—and why I wrote 'jumper' on the incident report. I'm just not sure it means very much. . . ."

"I appreciate the extra effort. Tell me what you do remember, whether you know what it means or not."

"The guy fit the general description, sir. Which could have been anybody. But none of the specifics fit—I mean, he was dry as bone, had on a jogging suit, didn't sound like any Englishman I've ever heard—so I didn't think I had cause for detaining him. . . ." Danny thought about the gash across they guy's nose, and the same sense of uneasiness he'd felt on the patrol came back. "Thing is, he did have a—well, like a cut—across his nose, ran down on his cheek. But when I asked him about it, he didn't even seem to know it was a problem. Said he'd hurt himself doing yard work and it must have reopened while he was running. I didn't see any problem with that. . . ."

"He was just walking along the road—you didn't see him come up from the river?"

Danny thought about it. "Thing is, sir, I had been . . ." Danny hesitated, not wanting to say he'd been thinking about the bleeding-heart liberal's illegally parked car and hadn't noticed the guy until he was almost on him. "There was a car illegally parked on the road, and I was considering inspecting the car, sir, when I saw the guy on the road—" Danny stopped. "Actually, sir, the guy told me himself. He said he needed to piss, so he'd gone down toward the river. Made some sort of joke about it. . . ."

Mars pulled over the notes he'd made when Nettie called about the missing lawyer. She'd said something about a red Volvo. "Borg? The parked car. You have a description on that?"

"Pretty much a beater, sir. I'd say late eighties Volvo red station wagon. A Wellstone bumper sticker—"

"And 'jumper?' on the incident report, Borg. You said you remembered why you wrote that."

"Right. And this part still doesn't make sense to me. As I was pulling away, I said something to him about keeping moving because it was cold—and all this guy had on was a jogging suit. What I *think* he said was, 'I should have worn a heavier jumper.' I think I must have been thinking about the search subject, sir, and misheard him. Anyway, I wrote it down, just sort of thinking on it—not meaning anything. . . ."

"His words to you when you commented on the cold were 'I should have worn a heavier jumper.' "

"Like I said. That's what I thought I heard. . . ."

"Doesn't make any sense to me, either—but this has been helpful. Could I ask you to come over to Homicide tomorrow and look at some pictures?"

Danny was scheduled for his first day off in over a week, but he didn't hesitate before saying, "Absolutely. First thing, sir."

"Thanks again, Borg. I look forward to meeting you."

Mars sat thinking for a moment after hanging up with Borg. Nettie looked up. "Anything good?" she asked.

"Yeah. I think we're going to be able to tie the missing lawyer's car to River Road. Need to follow up on some details, but from what Borg said, it looks probable. And Borg may be able to identify our photo of Cook as being a guy he ran into while doing patrol. He still can't figure out why he wrote 'jumper?' on the incident report. He thought the guy said he was cold and should have worn a heavier jumper—but that doesn't make any sense. Why would he take note of that?"

Chris dropped the dictionary on the desk next to Mars with a heavy thud. "Dad, you know what c-o-n-n-o-t-e-d means?"

"Yes, I do. And when you look it up in the dictionary, you'll know too. How's the book."

"Pretty good. But it's got some hard words. And I don't understand what the dictionary says. Listen to this." Chris's finger followed the words on the page. "It says, 'Imply additional meaning,' and then its says, 'Two. Imply as a condition. . . .' I still don't know what it means."

"It's like if I said, 'I think it's too late for you to be up reading your book,' I would also mean you need to stop reading and start sleeping. Why don't you sack out on the couch— I'll try to finish up here in the next hour."

Chris said, "First I'm going to look up 'jumper.'"

Mars said, "We know what jumper means, Chris. We just

270

don't know why the guy would use the word the way he did."

Undaunted, Chris turned pages in the dictionary. Then his face twisted. "It has jumper twice, Dad. The first one is 'a person or animal that jumps.' But then, the next one says, 'One, sleeveless dress worn over blouse.' Then it says, 'Two, Brit. A pullover sweater.' What does b-r-i-t period mean?"

Nettie and Mars looked at each other. Nettie said, "British usage."

CHAPTER
23

By noon on Monday Danny Borg had identified Owen Cook's photo as the man he had talked with on River Road on Friday. The photos he had looked at included a shot of Andrew Shard, but Borg hadn't even blinked at Shard's picture.

Shortly after Borg's identification, Nettie confirmed with the Missing Persons Division that Andrew Shard's red Volvo had a Wellstone bumper sticker. The Volvo had two parking tickets on the windscreen. The first ticket was issued Saturday morning, the second had been issued after the ticketing officer had noticed the first ticket and called in the plate numbers to find that the car's owner had been reported missing. Nettie had checked with both the Minneapolis Park Patrol and the Third Precinct on other parking tickets that had been issued in the area on Friday. Tickets had been issued along West River Road Friday morning, but nothing on Friday afternoon. The next ticket issued had been Saturday morning when Shard's Volvo got the first tag. What that gave them was strong evidence that Shard had parked the car between noon and the time Danny Borg saw the car Friday afternoon. In other words, Shard arrived at the river during the critical time period.

"Time to talk with Mrs. Shard," Mars said. But first he called Sgt. Dale Nelson in Missing Persons to let him know where they stood on the floater. Nelson was a workmanlike cop who liked regular hours and avoided getting emotionally involved in his cases. He was delighted that it looked like the floater was going to clear the Shard case.

"I'm just about to call Janet Shard," Mars said. "Anything I should know before I do that?"

Nelson laughed. "Good luck. All I can say is, if I were married to that woman, I'd be missing too."

Janet Shard picked up on the first ring. Her voice was tight, edgy.

Mars said, "Mrs. Shard? I'm Special Detective Marshall Bahr with the Minneapolis Police Department. I'm calling in connection with a case that may be related to your husband's disappearance. . . ." Without being aware that he'd done it, Mars had pronounced her name Share-ed.

"If you're going to have a shot at finding my husband, Detective Bahr, I think you should start by pronouncing his name right. It's Shard, not Share-ed. You go around town asking about a guy named Share-ed, and you're not going to get a lot of right answers."

What a pisser, is what Mars thought.

"Actually, Mrs. Shard—"

"I prefer *Ms.* Shard."

Mars paused. "Actually, *Ms.* Shard, I'm not directly involved in investigating your husband's disappearance. As I said, I have a case that may be related. I'd appreciate a few minutes of your time for some questions that may—"

"Detective, I really don't have time to solve other people's problems."

Mars said, not meaning it, "I can understand your frustration."

"No, you can't, Detective. I went from being a vested member of the upper middle class to having enough debt to

273

keep me homeless until I die—all thanks to my husband. Between you, me, and anybody else who cares to know, I don't give a flying fuck what happened to the guy. You want to find him or anybody he knew, I suggest you run a nation-wide search on blood banks. That was how he got walking-around money and change for the quarter slots at Mystic Lake Casino. I told the same thing to Sgt. Nelson. From where I sit, he doesn't turn up, I'm in debt for the rest of my life. He turns up a suicide, and I've got enough insurance that maybe I'll be out of debt by menopause. Now, if you can find he died a natural death—then I might just be ahead of the game financially, and you and I might have something worth talk-ing about."

Mars said, "How you feel about his turning up a murder victim?" He'd caught her off guard, which gave him consid-erable satisfaction.

Her words were sarcastic, but her voice was serious. "I'd have to work real hard to keep from jumping for joy."

Mars quickly went through the connections he had between Cook and Andrew Shard. Janet Shard asked, "Okay—so what do you need from me?"

"I'll want you to confirm some details, and I'd like to know if there's any reason your husband might have been near the Lake Street Bridge and West River Parkway on Fri-day afternoon."

"That's easy. Andrew rowed. It was one of the few things he kept up—other than playing blackjack and the slots—and he was a member at the Minneapolis Rowing Club. The boat-house is, like, a half block north of the Lake Street Bridge on River Road."

Which is where they found the car, Mars thought, but did not say. What he had to say next was easier because Ms.

Shard clearly wasn't going to be blown away by the possibility that her husband was dead.

"Ms. Shard, I think we have some pretty strong circumstantial evidence that our suspect killed your husband. What would be very useful would be locking that likelihood down with DNA analysis. Our County Coroner's Office has ordered a DNA profile on the body we found. What I want to do is create a profile for your husband, which will show he was the victim, not our suspect. You have children, Ms. Shard?"

Her answer was slow. "This is the first time I've regretted *not* having children with Andrew...."

"Other relatives? Mother, father, siblings..."

She was silent. "This might be a problem. I've been married to Andrew for seven years. He said his mother died when he was in grade school and his dad died the year he got out of law school. His father's second wife had a kid from a previous marriage—but there weren't any other kids."

"Were the parents buried?"

"His dad was cremated. His mom? I don't know. I can try to find out."

Mars bounced a pencil on its eraser a couple times. "Do that, Ms. Shard. In the meantime, if you'll give us permission, I'll have a technician come out to your house and collect any personal belongings of your husband's that might provide cells for testing—hairbrushes, razors—things like that."

"That's gonna be real easy. I dumped anything he'd ever touched into cardboard boxes. They're stacked in the garage."

Definitely a pisser, is what Mars thought as he hung up. He sat by the phone for a while. He'd better hope Ms. Shard turned up some blood relatives. He didn't want Glenn Gjerde going into court arguing that the DNA match between Andrew Shard and their floater was based on trace evidence from a razor that had been found in Shard's garage.

He heard the rattle and slosh of Nettie's Evian bottle behind him. He looked over his shoulder. "Just talked to our floater's wife."

"That must have been a little rough."

"Not really. She's pissed. Sounds like he was a gambler, left her chin-high in debt. She'll stand on her head to help us prove her husband was murdered, and won't shed a tear while she's at it. Problem is, we may have a tough time coming up with relatives for DNA analysis—" Mars stopped. "Jeez." He sat forward and redialed Ms. Shard's number.

"Ms. Shard? Special Detective Bahr again. Sorry to bother you, but I started to think about what you said about your husband being a blood donor. You have any idea where he was donating?"

Nettie took over tracking where Andrew Shard had been donating blood—and, if where he donated blood could be located, determining if Andrew Shard's donated blood was still available for DNA typing.

"We get blood," Nettie said, "then what?"

"I'm not waiting for blood or for the results of DNA analysis," Mars said. "We need that for court, but as far as I'm concerned, we have solid evidence that Owen Cook is alive. My priority right now is to find Cook before he leaves town."

"What makes you think he's still *in* town?"

"Well—first off—nothing's turned up from the net we set up on Friday at the airport, Amtrak, the bus depots, and rental car agencies...." He held up a hand to keep Nettie from challenging what he'd just said. They'd faxed alerts with photos to all public transportation sites in the seven-county metropolitan area on Friday. In addition, they'd put holds on Cook's credit cards. But Mars knew the net wasn't fail-safe. "What we've really got going for us is that I think Cook is going to be real edgy about trying to get out of town while he thinks we're still actively investigating his disappearance. I think he's smart enough to know that, for now, we're going to be looking for him at all the places he needs to go to get out. So I think he's going to lay low for a few days."

Nettie said, "That I can buy. So we're going to rely on our net to catch him when he decides to make a move?"

Mars bounced the pencil on its eraser again. "Not much else to do at this point. Right now, I'm going across the street to get a commitment from Glenn Gjerde to support us legally on anything we need to locate Cook."

Nettie pulled a face. "Good luck."

Three things surprised Mars about his meeting with Glenn Gjerde. First, Glenn's office—which was normally stacked floor to ceiling with legal files and Glenn's athletic equipment—was bare. Second, Glenn was wearing something that vaguely resembled a suit. And third, in Glenn's own words, the case Mars presented sounded "one hundred percent copacetic." Mars should just give Glenn a whistle if he needed search or arrest warrants, extradition orders—whatever.

"So you're on board on this." Mars felt a little like Charlie Brown looking at Lucy holding the football.

"Like I said. One hundred percent. God, the evidence you've already got? I could take this into court this afternoon, and I guarantee you, half hour into our evidence, the jury would rise en masse and scream, 'Enough already, let the sucker swing.'"

"That's assuming I had the sucker in custody by this afternoon and that the state legislature held a special session in the next two hours to enact a capital punishment statute—"

"Admittedly a bit of a stretch. But you get my point. You're on solid ground, Detective. I can prosecute this one blindfolded with my shorts on backwards. Bring me Cook, and you've got drive-through justice."

Mars nodded, still feeling like there was something more he wanted to do. He'd come prepared for an argument. Looking around Glenn's office, he said, "What happened in here, anyway?"

"I got busted. County has a cleaning contract with a company that hires South American immigrants to clean. Don't speak English. In fact, I'm going to check into it. I'd bet anything they're illegal. Anyway, for as long as I've been in this office, I've had a sign up on the door saying that cleaning staff is not to enter. First day on the contract, these South Americans come in and decide nobody's gonna notice if they have a cigarette—like, I wouldn't *smell* it immediately in the morning. So they're sitting in here smoking, and a live ash lands on one of the legal files. A fire starts. Fire department comes. Fire department puts out the fire. Hardly *any* damage. Fire department issues a complaint saying my office was a fire hazard. Gives me thirty days to get it cleaned up...."

"What did you do with all the stuff?"

"Friend's got a pickup. Loaded it all in the pickup. Took it home."

"Took it *home*?"

"Wait. You haven't heard anything. Fire department's complaint gets reported to country administration. They hold a review hearing with the Hennepin County District Attorney. I mean it. With Jill. The DA herself. The review concerns my fucking professional conduct. Not my conviction record, mind you. But whether my office is neat, whether I dress appropriately in the courtroom, the fact that I bring my bike into the building. Really important stuff. Then I get a disciplinary notice: clean office, no bike in the building, suit in the courtroom. To her credit, Jill said she was sorry, but the precedent argument—you know, if one county employee does this stuff, everybody can do it, except it would be unmanageable if everybody did it so nobody can do it. Bottom line: I've gotta walk around looking like Donald Fucking Trump...."

Mars, who had heard more than enough about Glenn's lifestyle change, backed toward the door. "Don't worry, Glenn. You don't look anything like Donald Trump."

CHAPTER
24

Working with Ms. Shard, Nettie found more than thirty receipts from the two Twin Cities blood banks where Andrew Shard had been donating blood. The immediate problem was that he'd used different identities at each of the locations.

"Start with the location where he used his own name," Mars said. "It'll save us a pile of trouble proving that it was Andrew Shard who donated."

"Bit of luck, there," Nettie said. "He used his own name at a blood bank on University Avenue. And that was his most recent spill—which, I hope, will give us a better chance his blood is still around."

"Spill?"

"I made that up," Nettie said. "Thought it sounded like a cool way to describe blood donation."

By late afternoon on Monday, Nettie was back. "How would you like some bad news–bad news–bad news–good news?" Nettie was giving Mars the kind of grin she used only when things were going very, very well.

"One out of four ain't bad."

"Bad news: the blood Andrew Shard donated was used three weeks ago in a kidney transplant."

"I'm having a hard time figuring how you're going to get from that to good news."

"You're going to love this. I'm thinking, maybe the blood bank transferred the blood to the hospital, maybe the patient is still there, and maybe the hospital is holding on to some of the blood in case the patient needs another transfusion. I call the hospital with the ID information I got from the blood bank. Bad news: the blood's gone. Not even an empty plastic pack in the fridge we could scrape. I hang up. Then I start thinking *really* creative. You transfuse a guy with another guy's blood. What's the chance that if we drew blood from the patient, we'd see a DNA profile for the blood donor?"

Mars sat up straight. "Damn it, Nettie. Before you're done, you're going to make one hell of a street cop."

Nettie raised a hand to hold him off. "I call the transplant surgeon, tell him what I'm thinking. The guy was blown away—but, bad news: in three weeks' time, there's not going to be any donor blood in the patient. We would have had to draw blood within eight hours of the transfusion to have a fair shot at finding any cells for the donor."

Mars was into it. He slapped both hands on the desk. "So then you said."

Nettie nodded emphatically, her grin wider than ever. "I said, 'Well, wouldn't you draw blood on a patient right after they had major surgery, and like a couple more times in the next eight hours?' And the doc says, 'You bet we would. And what's more, this was a protocol patient,' meaning they're using specific treatments that require record retention for research purposes. The doc said we had a very good shot that the blood drawn immediately following surgery was being retained under the treatment protocols."

"And the good news: you've confirmed that it is."

"Exactly. But we're not home free. Separating donor cells

from the patient's cells is not going to be a cakewalk. I talked to the state crime lab just before you got back. They won't touch it. Recommended we send our blood to a lab in Richmond, California. Even then, no guarantees they can do the separation without damaging the cells."

"Why the hell not? They do it all the time when we have two victims' blood at crime scenes."

"You're forgetting. Shard was a donor for this patient because they had the same blood type. Apparently that complicates separation. What we have working for us is we've got plenty of blood to work with. But it's going to take time."

"Time is what we've got, given that we don't know where Cook is."

"More to the point is that we don't know how we're going to find out where Cook is."

Mars had a dinner scheduled with Karen Pogue for the following week. Wanting the stimulus of discussing the case with her, he suggested instead that they meet that night at the Village Wok. It was a straight shot for Mars from city hall to the Wok on Washington and just around the corner from Karen's university office. Karen was there ahead of him and had ordered for them both: duck in black bean sauce and a whole steamed walleye.

"What's on your mind?" Karen asked, between chopsticks full of duck.

"We're finally getting solid evidence on the Fitzgerald case."

"Oh, God. I really led you down the garden path on that one, didn't I? How bad did I screw you up?"

Mars shook his head. "What you said was on the mark for what I described. And our suspect set the crime scene up to look like a sexual perversion was the motive. The problems were on my side. We just didn't have what we needed on motive until three days ago. Now all I've got to do is find our suspect. He went off the Stone Arch Bridge Friday afternoon. Yesterday we found a body downriver that suggests our suspect survived the jump and killed another guy to use as a decoy. The question is, if he did, how do we figure out where he is?"

"Good question," Karen said. "What *does* a guy like that do if he survives? How does he even get out of town?"

"He had cash. We know that. What happens next is up for grabs."

Karen tapped her chopsticks on her plate. "How is it I haven't seen anything in the paper about the guy he killed?"

"We've been holding back on that. Waiting for positive identification on the floater we pulled out of the river yesterday."

Karen said, "I bet your perp would love to know you found his decoy. Probably break his heart you didn't fall for it."

It came to Mars all at once. He knew exactly what he needed to do. Despite his late arrival he needed to leave early. He picked up the check as he went. "I'm really sorry—but what you just said. I've got something I've got to do right away. This one's on me," he said, squeezing Karen's shoulder.

Karen called after him, "Let me know what happens."

Mars drove back downtown over the Washington Avenue Bridge, turning left off Fourth Street onto Portland. With any luck, he'd catch Ray Bunt putting tomorrow's edition of the *Star Tribune* to bed.

Bunt was a hard-edged former police-beat reporter for the *Strib*. He had, in his own words, been kicked out of the real world and was senior editor of the Metro-State Section of the paper. Every time Mars saw him, Bunt was heavier, grayer, and more cynical.

"Hey! The heat is here!" Bunt called out when he saw Mars coming across the city room of the paper. "Please, please, say you're here to tell me my second wife has met an untimely death. . . ."

Mars said, "Cracks like that can get you in trouble down the road, buddy."

"Some trouble is worth having. I take it you're not bearing glad tidings?"

"Need a favor. Somewhere we can talk?"

Seated in a glass cubicle, Mars said, "I need you to run something in the Metro-State Section, as soon as possible."

Bunt squinted at Mars across the desk. "You asking me to run something that isn't true in my section, *my paper*?"

Mars said, "I'm asking you to run something that *is* true right now. My guess is that in the next few weeks, it won't be true. But based on evidence in hand right now, it's one hundred percent true."

"You're gonna have to tell me what it is you want me to run and what basis you've got for saying it's true right now."

"I want you to run a piece that says a body's been recovered from the Mississippi. That identification on the body indicates that the victim is Owen Cook, a British citizen who is known to have fallen from the Stone Arch Bridge last Friday. That's it. Couple paragraphs will do just fine."

Bunt stared at him. "And you think in a couple weeks you're going to have evidence that the body *isn't* Cook?"

"That's it exactly."

"But Boy Scout's honor, *as we speak*, evidence suggests it is Cook."

"Well, his undershorts didn't look right to me, but other than that . . ."

Bunt took this as a joke, which is what Mars intended. Bunt waved Mars away. "Don't see why we can't do that."

He turned his wrist to look at his watch. "We've missed tomorrow's paper. Wednesday is gonna be the earliest we can go."

Mars said, "I could use one more day to get ready. Wednesday is fine."

Bunt said, "Am I gonna be interested in who the floater is when your new evidence comes home?"

"There's going to be a lot to keep you interested when my new evidence comes home."

"And I assume your call list is in alphabetical order?" Meaning, that the *Minneapolis Star Tribune* would get a call before the *St. Paul Pioneer Press Dispatch*.

"Count on it," Mars said.

CHAPTER
25

Mars woke before 3:00 A.M. on Tuesday. He hadn't gone to bed until after midnight, but there was too much to do, too much too think about to sleep. He took a quick shower, dressed, and headed back to city hall.

In a case that had been fogged in for months, Mars finally felt like he knew what was ahead. He had every confidence in Cook's ability to think and act defensively. In fact, Cook acting rationally was what Mars was counting on. As Mars saw it, there was only one way Cook was going to get out of town, and that was by bus. Cook would have to use a credit card and have photo ID to fly or rent a car. Amtrak had only four trains leaving the St. Paul station on Wednesday, making it an easy stakeout. Mars knew he could count on Cook to figure that out. What was left was the bus station.

They had a planning meeting scheduled for 10:00 A.M. Mars planned on being there along with Glenn, Nettie, the chief, two other Homicide detectives, and four guys from the Downtown Command. Mars, impressed with Danny Borg's initiative on Sunday, had asked Danny to join them as well.

Mars began the meeting by passing around a copy of the news story that would run in tomorrow's *Strib*. "The newspaper story is the trip wire. Our expectation is Cook is checking the papers to see if the body has been found, and when he confirms that it has—and that we're accepting that it's him—he'll try to get out of town ASAP."

"Page one of the Metro-State Section?" Glenn asked.

"No," Mars said. "Page three, right column in the Metro-State Section. I think it would look like bait if it ran on page one of the section—it's just not enough of a story to get carried on page one. Now, let me run through the overall plan. Starting at midnight tonight we're backing up personnel at Amtrak, the airport, and the major rental-car locations."

Jim Risser, one of the Homicide detectives, said, "Spell that out."

Nettie said, "In addition to the instructions we've provided staff at those locations, we've arranged to have Minneapolis police personnel at each of the security checks at the airport. They'll question any individual that meets our suspect's general description. We'll also have police personnel at Amtrak and the rental-car locations with the same instructions—particularly for any traveler attempting to purchase a ticket or rent a car using cash."

Mars said, "We feel pretty confident that Cook will use the bus station to leave town. He can pay cash for a ticket, it's always crowded, and there are a lot of departures. For that reason, we're putting most of our resources into covering the bus depot between six A.M. and midnight tomorrow." He looked around the table. "In addition to myself, two of our Homicide investigators have volunteered to assist, along with several officers from the Downtown Command. We'll also have uniformed officers covering all entrances and exits at the depot as well as the restroom. Of the surveillance team, both Danny Borg and myself have seen the suspect in person—although my contact was at a distance and Danny's contact was brief. We are anticipating that Cook will have altered his appearance—so it's important that you focus on basics: height, weight—someone who seems unusually aware of his surroundings. You all know the type. Now, this is key. We think the most distinguishing characteristic is going to be an injury to the suspect's nose and cheek." Mars held up the photos they'd distributed, on which the injury had been superimposed. "Patrolman Borg noted such an injury in his encounter with the suspect. The injury would have been fresh then. Since Friday, there may be swelling and discoloration, as well—"

Risser interrupted. "How is it Borg had an encounter with the suspect and the suspect isn't in custody right now?" Risser's eyes moved around the room, looking for support. Then he stared at Borg with a disdainful look. Danny Borg had flushed, keeping his eyes on the floor.

Mars had to work at it to control his temper. It was stuff like this that kept him from liking Risser, who in all other respects was a first-class investigator. Risser always had to put other people down, preferably in public. And Risser always looked for a chance to exacerbate the internecine battles between uniforms and suits.

In a flat, controlled voice, Mars said, "Borg's decision not to detain the subject was absolutely right based on the patrol assignment we issued. And the patrol assignment was my responsibility. Let's get back to the business at hand." Mars shot Risser a hard look before he continued. "I will observe any suspect being questioned. If I remain seated, assume that the subject being questioned should not be detained. If I stand up and begin to approach the subject, other members of the surveillance team should take position. Any questions?"

Risser asked, "What chance is there this guy is going to be armed?"

Mars nodded. "Meant to cover that. We're pretty confident the suspect does not own or carry a firearm. He may be carrying a knife, so he should be approached with caution. If, as we've covered, I stand and approach a subject, the officers covering the perimeters of the facility have been instructed to move in and begin to move other passengers away from the area."

"And," Risser said, "what happens if no one turns up between six and midnight?"

The room was quiet. Looks were exchanged. Mars said, "We'll be keeping backup personnel in place at all locations throughout the week."

"What's our chances here—you pretty confident tomorrow's the day?"

"That's why I'm going to be there," Mars said. "This is one arrest I want to make personally."

Mars hated the bus depot. It made him worry about the future of the human gene pool. He and Risser entered the waiting room shortly after 5:30 A.M. Standing slightly behind him, Risser looked around, and said, "Doesn't leave much of anyone home to watch *The Jerry Springer Show*, does it?"

"My thoughts exactly," Mars said, moving off to a plastic molded chair that faced the front door and the ticket counter. The toughest thing about an assignment like this was keeping your concentration sharp and focused without looking like someone whose attention was sharp and focused.

Early morning traffic was heavy, with a bus departing for points east and Chicago first off after 6:00 A.M. The passengers were a mix of young black men dressed in low-slung, over-sized jeans, young mothers with small, tired-eyed kids in tow, a scattering of teenagers in UW sweatshirts, probably making a drop in Madison, and a bunch of old guys who didn't look like anybody would be expecting them when they got where they were going. There wasn't anybody who looked remotely like Owen Cook.

Between six and ten, roughly a dozen guys were pulled aside for questioning. None of them got Mars off his chair.

But he felt good about how the interrogations had gone. Nothing that drew the attention of any of the other passengers.

Around ten-thirty, Mars went to a machine to get a Coca-Cola. Coke in hand, he turned, just as a male figure moved into the curtained photo machine booth located to the right of the depot's front door.

Mars felt a slight jolt at the sight of the figure. He called back into his mind's eye what he had seen in the brief glimpse: right height, build seemed similar, glasses, a hooded sweatshirt, hood down, over a T-shirt and jeans. *A shaved skull.* Nothing altered appearance like removing all the hair—not color, not cut—nothing like no hair at all. Mars hadn't seen the face clearly, but he thought he'd seen a bandage across the guy's nose.

Mars stood up and walked over toward where Danny Borg was sitting. Danny was making a good show of working a crossword, and as Mars approached, Danny tipped his pencil in the direction of the photo booth. Mars sat down two seats away from Danny. Seated, he leaned forward, rubbing both eyes with his knuckles. As he rubbed, he said, "Wait a couple minutes. Then walk over to the photo machine. See if you can get a look at the guy inside."

Danny waited more than five minutes. Then he got up, stretched, and slapping the folded newspaper against his thigh, walked in the opposite direction from the photo machine. Mars leaned back in his chair, stretching his legs. He let his head turn toward the photo machine, eyes mostly closed, but open enough to tell if anybody came out from behind the curtain. Next thing he saw was Danny Borg walking near the machine, doing an impatient little pace, looking at his watch, then sitting down in a chair near the machine. Danny was in the chair for probably ten minutes, working the crossword again. And still nobody came out of the photo booth.

Mars saw Danny shove himself up, then amble back. Sitting down in the row of chairs that backed the row Mars was sitting in, Danny said quietly, "He's just sitting in there. Couldn't see his face. But it looks like he's watching the room from the booth."

Outside the station, Rebbie Baker grabbed her two-year-old daughter, Leesha, and Leesha's stroller out of the car's back seat, snapping the stroller into position as it hit the sidewalk. Stuffing Leesha into the stroller, she said to her husband in the driver's seat, "Man, if your dawdlin' around this morning makes Zita miss that bus, there's gonna be hell to pay." To Zita, she hollered, "I'm gonna run ahead with Leesha. I wanna take pictures of her and me at one of them machines for you to take to show Momma. Momma hasn't had a picture of Leesha since her first birthday." Rebbie peered in the car at her sister, who had the visor mirror down. Zita was putting on lipstick. "Girl," she said, her voice mean, "this is the last bus to Omaha today. You miss this one, there's no way I'm gonna haul you down here again tomorrow. So you hustle your butt, hear?"

Rebbie struggled to get the stroller through the station's front doors. Two cops were standing to the left of the front doors, but they were too busy talking to each other about what Art Bell had said on last night's broadcast to offer any help. She gave them both her dirtiest look, and said loud, "Thank you so much, *gentlemen*." They'd looked back at her without interest.

Once inside the station, Rebbie paused for a moment to look for the photo booth. It was maybe ten steps away, just to the right of the station's entrance. Rebbie headed directly for the booth, then stopped cold. *Damn.* Someone was in there—and Rebbie had less than ten minutes before Zita's bus was scheduled to leave. To make a point, Rebbie rolled the stroller back and forth in front of the booth, saying in a loud voice, "You just be patient, baby. 'Nother minute and whosoever is in there gettin' their picture taken will be out, and you and me will take the prettiest picture ever for your grandma."

Zita came in while Rebbie waited. Over her shoulder she said to Rebbie, "Girl—you don't have that picture taken yet? You better hurry it up 'cause I'm getting' on that bus soon as I got my ticket."

Rebbie's slow burn accelerated. What was really making her mad was that she could see the guy in the booth was just sitting there. Not taking any pictures. Zita was now second in line at the ticket counter, and they had seven minutes until the bus was scheduled to leave.

Rebbie clenched her fist and banged on the side of the photo booth. "Hey, in there," she called. "We don't got all day. You gonna be outta there anytime soon?"

A voice from within the booth said, "Move it, lady. I'll out when *I'm* ready."

Rebbie waited another minute, then banged again. "C'mon. I gotta do this now or we won't have the picture in time. You've had your turn, clear out." Rebbie waited to a count of ten. When nothing happened she pushed Leesha's stroller to the side of the booth and with both hands pulled the curtain back.

The man was sitting on the little bench at one side of the booth facing toward Rebbie, instead of looking into the camera straight ahead. And why would someone with a big old Band-Aid right across the front of his face want his picture taken anyway?

"You're a selfish bastard, is what you—"

Before Rebbie could finish what she had to say, the man

292

came at her, pushing her aside with a single, furious word: *"Bitch!"*

Mars and Danny Borg exchanged glances when they saw what was, so to speak, developing at the photo booth. Simultaneously they both stood, moving toward the booth. The rest of the surveillance team was confused. They hadn't seen the man go into the booth and didn't know what Bahr and Borg were up to. In a horrifying moment, Mars realized he and Borg were probably fifteen seconds away from the photo booth, with luggage and stretched legs creating a natural obstacle course between them and where they needed to be. And Owen Cook was only five good strides from the front entrance, with none of the team alert to his presence.

What Mars didn't know was that he had Rebbie Baker on his team.

At first Rebbie was too startled to do anything, but when the man ran straight into Leesha's stroller as he headed for the door, catching his foot in the stroller spokes and nearly tipping over the stroller with Leesha in it, Rebbie sprang into action. She leaped onto the staggering man's back, hanging on with one arm while she pounded the back of his head with her free hand.

It was Danny Borg who bellowed, "Minneapolis police! Everyone! Stay where you are!" Borg had assumed a firing stance, his gun drawing a bead on Owen Cook's head. Owen Cook's head was flat on the bus depot floor, a cigarette butt someone had walked in from outside stuck to the blood from the open wound on his cheek. Rebbie Baker was sitting on his back. For the first time in a long time, she was subdued, turning her head slowly to take in the circle of men surrounding her, all with pistols drawn. One of the guys was next to her on his knees, clipping handcuffs on the guy she was sitting on. Rebbie heard him say, "Owen Cook, you are under arrest for the murders of Mary Pat Fitzgerald and Andrew Shard...."

"Murder!" Rebbie Baker said, hopping off Owen Cook's back in one fast move. "I *knew* he was a *nasty* man. *And* he made me miss gettin' our picture taken before my sister's bus leaves."

Turning Owen Cook over to four uniformed officers, Mars said, "Which bus is your sister taking, ma'am?"

"Zita's goin' to Omaha, provided she ain't already missed the bus."

Mars turned to Danny. "Go out and flash your badge at the Omaha bus driver. Tell him to hang on for a VIP passenger."

Rebbie smiled. "Well, thank you very much. And I hope that nasty man goes to jail for a very long time."

"That's the plan," Mars said.

CHAPTER
26

Denise called on the Friday before Thanksgiving week.

"You're picking Chris up at James's around nine tomorrow morning?"

"Okay by you?"

There was a brief silence. "No problem for me, but there are some things I wanted the two of us to talk about—without Chris. Could you come over here first?"

"Sure. I'll come over around eight."

Nothing ever changed in the house Mars had lived in for the five years he and Denise had been married. The furniture in the living room had been bought as a set, and looked as good ten years later as it had the day they'd bought it. Looked *good* as in looked unused. Mars hadn't much liked the furniture ten years ago and liked it less every time he'd been in the house since. Anytime there wasn't company over—company being anyone other than Chris, Denise, or Mars—there were cloth things that Mars called blankets and Denise called throws over the furniture. About a year ago, Mars had gone in to give Denise a check, and Carl and the throws were on the couch in the living room. Mars had known then that the relationship was serious.

At eight o'clock that Saturday morning, the throws were

in evidence but Carl was not. Mars was a little surprised, because nights Chris slept over at friends' houses were the nights that Carl stayed over.

Denise handed him a Coca-Cola, cold with no ice, as soon as he sat down at the table in the kitchen. She poured herself a cup of coffee, swiping the counter with a damp dishcloth on the chance that a drop of coffee had been spilled in the process. She folded the dishcloth precisely before she sat down across from him.

"You and Chris need to work out something different on the time you spend together."

Mars looked at her, puzzled. She spoke again before he could ask what she meant.

"Chris is starting to not do things he wants to do with friends because he feels he has an obligation to spend as much of the weekend with you as you have time to spend with him." She frowned a little after she said that, sipped her coffee, and said, "I didn't say that very well. Do you know what I'm saying?"

He knew immediately, and realized he'd seen signs himself, signs he'd chosen to ignore.

"Two nights ago, Chris was on the phone with James when I was in his room putting his laundry away. And I heard him tell James that he couldn't go to a party tonight because you and he were going to *The Godfather* at the Oak Street Cinema, and you'd been talking about that for weeks. You'd be really disappointed if he didn't go. And I could tell Chris was really feeling bad about missing the party."

Mars sighed. "I'm sure you're right. I should have figured it out myself. I'd been telling him that I'd pretty much decided to take the job setting up the Metropolitan Division of the Cold Case Unit at the State Bureau of Criminal Apprehension and that it would mean I'd have a more regular schedule, more time to spend with him. Now that I think about it, he didn't exactly jump with joy."

"That's going too far. He's crazy about you, Mars. If he could spend every hour of every day with you and still have time for—"

"I know what you're saying. It's natural, at his age, to want to be on his own more. It just means he's a happy, normal kid. Thanks for bringing it up. I'll take care of it."

Denise looked at him quizzically. "So you *are* going to take the new job?"

Mars gave a self-mocking laugh. "It's the job I should have had when Chris was younger. I haven't made a final decision, and the legislature hasn't approved funding yet—so who knows. Nettie wants to do it, and she'd be just what they need—but she won't go without me. That, and the chief maybe taking an offer in San Diego. They've appointed an interim chief with the understanding the chief will move in another year. He goes, I go." There was a hollow pit in Mars's stomach at the thought of doing a nine-to-five job.

Mars decided to seize the moment and make an immediate change in the breakfast routine. With Chris in the car, he said, "Turns out I've got a bit of a time crunch today. Okay with you if we just go over to the Modern for breakfast and then I drop you back at the house?"

Chris was untroubled at the change in plans. In fact, Mars thought he detected something like relief.

The only thing wrong with the Modern, a small restaurant in Northeast with tile floors and dark wood booths that were original to the 1950s, was that it was too small to really get away from the smoking section. Chris loved the food, which was also circa 1950. It relied heavily on potatoes: hash browns, garlic mashed potatoes, thick-cut french fries.

297

Chris asked for fresh tomatoes with his hash browns, sunny-side-up eggs, and two strips of bacon. He had a Coke to wash it down. Mars was in no position to object.

Once into their food, Mars said, "My agenda. I've been thinking we should maybe change how we organize our time together."

Chris looked up at him, wary. "Like what?"

"Like at your age you're going to have more and more things that you need to do on weekends. I think we should set a schedule based on other things you're doing. Even if we've planned to be together, if something comes up for you, we can always reschedule."

Chris was staring at him. "So we wouldn't have breakfast Saturdays?"

"That would depend on what else you had going on Saturday mornings. Maybe we'd have breakfast Sundays, if Saturdays didn't work for you."

"Church."

Mars made a gesture of indifference. "Whatever. Nothing says we can't do breakfast after church, right? All I'm saying is—I don't want you to miss things a guy your age should be doing because we're locked into a schedule we don't have to be locked into."

Chris's face was smooth with pleasure. "That probably would be good." Then, sounding cautious, "When do you want to start? I mean, changing from trying to spend all day Saturday together?"

"I thought what we could do is go over what you've got coming up. Like today. Then plan around that. We can just kind of play it by ear."

"Yeah, but tonight is *The Godfather*."

"Well, it's up to you. There'll be lots of times we can see *The Godfather*. We could even rent the video."

"You said seeing it on video wouldn't be as good."

"I guess I think that seeing it in a theater would be the best way to see it, but video would be okay, too. So, if there's something else you need to do, we'll just plan on seeing it another time." Mars was careful to say *"need"* to do, rather than *"want"* to do.

Chris hesitated, then he said, "Actually, I'd sort of forgotten. But there is a party tonight I should probably go to. Gloria's having a bunch of kids over. Could we do something together tomorrow afternoon?"

"Sure. I'll come over around one, we can decide then what we want to do . . . Gloria? Are you still going with her?"

Chris looked confused for a moment. Then he shrugged. "I don't know. I don't think so. I think we must have broken up."

Chris called around six-thirty that night. "What are you doing tonight, Dad?" There was anxiety in his voice.

Mars said, without even thinking about it, "I may just go to *The Godfather.*"

"By yourself?" The anxiety in Chris's voice intensified.

"I used to go to the movies by myself all the time, Chris. Before you were old enough to go with me. Your mom never liked movies much, and I got so I liked going by myself." What Mars didn't tell Chris was about all the times he told Denise he was going out on an investigation and instead had gone to the movies.

But it had been a long time since Mars had gone to a movie by himself, and he'd sort of lost the hang of it. He felt a little self-conscious about going by himself and probably would have skipped it if Chris hadn't called again just before he left the house for his party.

"I wanted to see if you went to the movie."

"I was just on my way out the door." So he went.

The thing about the few theaters around that still showed old movies was that they ran on a shoestring. As the cashier at the Oak Street Cinema gave him his change and tore his ticket, she said, "We've got a problem with the projector. The movie'll probably start about a half hour late. Maybe a little longer."

Mars made a face and thought about asking for his money back, but it was a request that would make a scene. It was easier to stay. He moved into the lobby, already half-full of college students.

It was then that he saw her. It was the intensity with which she watched him that first drew his attention. But more than how she looked, it was that she was watching him—watching him with a small, ironic smile. It struck him that not only did she seem to know who he was but she did in fact look familiar. He gave her a slight nod to acknowledge the attention she was paying him. She had been leaning against a wall, and after he nodded, she pushed off, coming toward him, the small smile unchanged.

"Hello, Special Detective."

Mars nodded again, struggling to put the various components of the woman's appearance into an identity. She lifted a hand to draw her hair back, her eyes still on him, and he noticed her hands. They were beautiful hands, small, fine boned, with long fingers . . . and he remembered.

"Evelyn . . . Evelyn Rau. Good God. I almost didn't recognize you. Sorry—I haven't seen you since the trial. What are you doing here, anyway?"

She shrugged. "You mean, why am I here instead of in jail? I thought I'd go to the movies is all."

"No, that's not what I meant."

"You must be pleased with how the trial went?"

Mars shook his head. "Relieved it's over and that Cook got the maximum. But the County Attorney's Office did some follow-up with the jurors. We came damn near having a hung jury. Cook's defense—that his brother was the perp in Fitzgerald's murder and that Shard's death was self-defense—kicked up a lot of dust. Three of the jurors felt there was reasonable doubt on the Fitzgerald murder—and Shard's history of financial problems and erratic behavior made Cook's claim that Shard tried to rob him seem possible. Frankly, without your testimony and the information you provided on the vehicle which we were finally able to tie to Owen Cook—we might have lost it. The other thing that helped was Cook luring you down to the bridge. There just wasn't any way he could explain that in a way that was believable. The three uncertain jurors were prepared to believe that your identification might be wrong or that Owen Cook killed Andrew Shard when Shard tried to rob him—but when we added Cook's attack on you at the bridge—well, it's what we call critical mass. . . ."

"You know what I've never understood? Why he bothered to come after me."

"Makes perfect sense, really. Once he knew there was a witness, there was always the risk you'd see him and recognize we'd made a mistake. *His* mistake was thinking it would be easy to implicate his brother. And he had a piece of bad luck: his brother's schedule changed at the time of the first murder and that change gave the brother an alibi. If Neville hadn't had an alibi for the first murder, Owen's scheme might have worked. The second murder was too good—we didn't have anything to tie either brother to the scene. So, Owen brought the brother and sister of the two victims together in England in hopes they'd see a connection to Neville. And they did. Then Owen caught a real piece of luck. We got the photos of the two brothers mixed up. From the standpoint of the investigation, your ID was the linchpin for all the evidence."

"Nice to know something good came of out of the mess

my life was then." She looked at her watch. "Can I buy you a cup of coffee while we wait?"

Mars hesitated, then took the path of least resistance. "You can buy me a Coke."

They walked down to the coffee bar on the corner. It was crowded with other moviegoers waiting out the delay. Mars and Evelyn stood for a while, until a table opened up. There wasn't much to say, but being quiet with her was easy. That was something he noticed. He never found talking with women difficult, but a good silence was hard to come by.

After they were seated, he said, "What have you been up to? I take it you're back in graduate school?"

"I had one option when I got out of jail. I called a woman I'd worked with in the English Department at the U. I said, 'Rita, I'm in trouble and I need a place to stay.' She said, 'Where are you?' and when I said the Hennepin County Jail, she said, 'Don't move. I'll be there in fifteen minutes.' And she was."

"What have you been doing with yourself since then?"

"I'm going to finish my degree, get my Ph.D. Just for the sake of finishing what I started." She stopped. "Well, that's history. Somehow, going back just to meet my own personal goals feels right. If I can get myself to England in the next year to finish some research, I'll get my degree within the next couple of years. Then I'll probably just do freelance writing. Keep my eyes open for a chance to do a book, if the right subject presents itself. And you. You're going to be a cop forever?"

"For now." He didn't bring up the possibility of moving to the Bureau of Criminal Apprehension. Mars shifted, looked down at his Coke. "Ask me six months from now." He regretted saying it right away; he didn't want her to think he was suggesting anything.

"When your partner took my statement . . . the first time you interviewed me?"

Mars nodded. "Yes?"

"Afterwards, I saw you leaving with a boy. Your son?"

"Yeah. I guess Chris was with me. We'd just left the movies when I got paged about you. He lives with his mother, but she was out of town that weekend, so I brought him along."

"You're divorced?" It was just a question, with none of the coyness he'd gotten from other women asking the same question. He started feeling a little more comfortable about her expectations.

"Since Chris was three. Chris's mom is fine, we have a good relationship. Better now than when we were married. But I just couldn't make it in the marriage. My problem, not hers." Mars shifted a bit. "My partner says I have an 'intimacy problem' with women. Not that I've ever figured out what that means, but I've heard it from more than one woman, so there must be something to it."

Evelyn Rau looked away from him for a moment. Then she said, "Let me take a shot at it—not that I can give you a definition—but I think a couple of examples will make the point." She grinned. "I'll even use movies as a teaching aid— to make sure you get it. Have you seen *Klute*?"

"Sure. Great movie."

"The scene where Jane Fonda and Donald Sutherland are wandering through a fruit market late at night?"

"Yeah . . ."

"And she puts her hand on his back . . ."

Mars nodded.

Evelyn pointed a finger at him across the table. "*That* was intimacy from a woman's point of view. And the movie *When Harry Met Sally*? The scene where Harry and Sally are on the phone, split screen, watching a late-night movie together, each in their own apartments..."

Mars nodded again. This was definitely making sense. Evelyn said, "*That* was intimacy, whereas the scene where they have sex, was, well, *anti*-intimacy."

Mars said, "You're onto something. You should publish that."

"Maybe I will." She looked at him closely. "You know, I'd think after solving a case like the Fitzgerald murder—you'd be jumping up and down. But you aren't quite as—satisfied—as I'd expect. You almost seem sad when you talk about it."

"Resurrection syndrome," Mars said.

"Say what?" Evelyn asked.

"I should be dancing a jig. But sometimes, after a long, frustrating case, you almost feel worse when it's over."

"Why?"

Mars ran both hands back through his hair. "Have you seen the old Otto Preminger movie *Laura*?" Evelyn nodded. "Well, it's kind of like that. When you start the investigation there's no attachment to the victim. You deal with the victim's friends and relatives who are in denial about the victim being dead. Then you spend months finding out everything there is to know about the victim—the victim kind of comes alive for you. You start feeling like you own that person, who that person *was*. Then you solve the murder, and by now, the victim's family is accepting that the victim is dead. All they want is justice. But for me, at that point, the victim is the most alive they've ever been. And it's kind of an emotional shock to realize that after everything you've done, everything you've been through—that none of that has changed the fundamental fact that the victim is still dead. Resurrection syndrome."

Evelyn said, "Did you go to Mary Pat's funeral—or to her grave?"

Mars shook his head. "No. There really wasn't a funeral. The family had a private interment ceremony at Lakewood Cemetery—and about four weeks after that there was a big memorial service at her high school. Edina PD covered that— thought they'd have a better shot at spotting something out of the ordinary."

Evelyn looked at her watch. "We should probably get back to the theater—" She stopped, hearing "we" the same way he did. "I'm sorry, I've kind of horned in on your evening—would you rather go on your own from here?"

"No, I'm fine as is," Mars answered, not at all sure that he meant it.

It was almost midnight before Mars headed back to his apartment. Seeing Evelyn Rau reminded him he hadn't touched base with Bobby Fitzgerald since the trial. He reversed direction and drove down to city hall. A new Homicide detective was hanging around the squad room when Mars walked in.

"Hey. Candy Man. What brings you in? Number forty-three hit the city's murder list?"

Mars shook his head. "Nope. Just needed a phone number." He rooted through a desk drawer, pulled out a notebook, said good night, and headed back to the apartment.

In the apartment, he dialed Bobby Fitzgerald's number. It was a little after 1:00 A.M. in Boston, and Bobby's voice was sleep laden when he picked up.

"Mars Bahr in Minneapolis."

"Geez. Mars. Don't tell me Cook's out on the appeal?. . ."

"No, he's still our guy. But I think maybe I have an insight about what women mean when they talk about intimacy. You and I made a promise to get in touch immediately if we figured anything out on that score."

"Let's have it."

"You've seen the movies *Klute* and *When Harry Met Sally*?"

"Sure. Liked them both."

"Okay. The scene where Jane Fonda touches Donald Sutherland's back when they're in the fruit market, and the scene where Harry and Sally are watching an old movie together, only they're in separate apartments, watching the movie on the phone?..."

"Sure..."

"That's it. Those two scenes represent intimacy from a woman's point of view."

The other line was quiet for a moment, then Bobby said, "You know, that makes sense. This is very helpful."

"You want another piece of good news?"

"Always."

"Owen Cook has been served with notice that Neville Cook had petitioned the English courts to exclude Owen as a beneficiary of the trust on the grounds that Owen has breached the trust's moral turpitude clause. The same clause Owen was going to use when Neville was convicted of murder."

"That is what is known as poetic justice."

"I'll tell you what's poetic justice. Owen had pledged his interest in the trust as collateral to retain a top-flight criminal defense lawyer for the appeal. With his interest in the trust subject to litigation, his top-dollar lawyer took a walk. Owen's going to have to use a public defender."

Bobby let out a small moan of appreciation. "Ahhh— there is a God, Mars. And he is just."

CHAPTER
27

Headed south on the freeway Sunday afternoon, Mars did a double-take on the Thirty-sixth Street exit. He thought about what Evelyn Rau had asked last night about whether he'd gone to Mary Pat's funeral or grave. Mars glanced down at his watch, and on an impulse, took the exit.

Lakewood Cemetery is prime Minneapolis real estate. It's bordered by West Thirty-sixth Street, Lake Calhoun, and hills. The gently rolling hills of the site are populated by hardwood and evergreen trees. This November, with no snow, the evergreens were the only things in sight that looked alive.

Mars slowed the car to a crawl as it passed a faux Byzantine chapel. Could he find Mary Pat's grave site without going in to ask? A cemetery maintenance man came around the side of the building. Mars rolled the window down and asked for directions. The man went into the building, came back out, and pointed Mars to a fork in the road that ran to the right, toward the lake. Mars's memory held an image of a newspaper photo of the family standing under a canopy by the graveside. As he drove, Mars looked for something that matched the memory.

He was concentrating so hard on where he was going that he didn't pay much attention to the sleek black Mercedes that passed, too fast, on his left. Mars braked as the Mercedes slowed ahead of him, pulled to the right, and stopped, its hazard lights flashing.

The driver's-side door swung open, and a young woman in big black sunglasses, designer jeans, and a parka, got out of the Mercedes. It wasn't until she pulled her sunglasses off that Mars recognized Becky Prince.

Becky took broad, jumping steps toward Mars. "Detective Bahr! What are *you* doing here?"

Through the opened car window, Mars said, "I thought you were going away to school in September?"

"Thanksgiving break." She held her hand up to shade her eyes, peering at Mars.

Mars said, "I'm probably here for the same reason you are. Except I'm not sure where the grave is. Can I follow you?"

Becky was already by the headstone when Mars pulled up to park. Coming up behind Becky, Mars saw that she had embedded a small bouquet in the dirt below the stone. Stuck in among the flowers were Tootsie Roll pops.

"Mary Pat liked Tootsie Roll pops?"

"Ummm. Her only vice." She glanced back at Mars. Her eyes were unreadable behind the big black glasses, but there were no tears on her cheeks. She said, "Can I confess something to you, Detective Bahr?"

"I'd make a lousy priest. And I hope to God you're not going to tell me something I don't want to hear about this case. . . ."

She smiled and shook her head. "I guess 'confess' isn't the word. It's more like 'admit.' And it doesn't have anything to do with the case." Becky looked away from him, back down at the gravestone. "You know I'd do anything to bring Mary Pat back. But the weird thing is, as much as I love her—in a way my life is better now. I mean, Mary Pat was always better than everybody else at everything. And I always felt sort of second-rate, by comparison. If Mary Pat had lived, I think I would have lived the rest of my life comparing myself to Mary Pat—where she was, what she was doing. And I know I would never have matched up." She looked up at Mars. "Am I an awful person to feel like that?"

Mars stepped forward and, putting an arm around Becky, gave her a quick hug. "I'm going to share with you the only wisdom I've gleaned from my years as a Homicide cop. Murders change lives. Most of those changes are bad. If you can squeeze something good out of Mary Pat's death—do it, and don't look back."

Becky extended her arm around Mars and squeezed back. "Thanks." She pulled away. "I gotta go. Lunch at the club with my parents." She rolled her eyes and walked back toward the Mercedes, throwing Mars a small wave before she got into the car.

Mars stood alone by the gravestone for a moment longer. The engraving on the stone read, Mary Patricia Fitzgerald. Beloved Daughter, Beloved Sister. You couldn't help but notice what was missing. Being a daughter and a sister were all she'd had time for.

The warmth of the car felt good. He reversed gears and backed out. When he looked in the rearview mirror, the grave was out of view.

Keep reading for an Excerpt from
KJ Erickson's Newest Mystery

THE DEAD SURVIVORS

Coming soon in Hardcover From
St. Martin's Press

At four o'clock on that December afternoon, the dim winter sun cast a shallow light across Joey Beck's apartment. Outside, the sound of heavy traffic was steady as the Friday rush hour began. Joey glanced at his watch, then at the beckoning couch. He had two hours before he was due to meet his dad for dinner. Bone weary, he stretched out on the couch.

It was the darkness of the room and the silence from the streets that wakened Joey five hours later. He sat upright as if shocked, his heart racing. His hand groped in the dark for the stem on his watch. The green light on the watch face flashed on. It was after 9:00 P.M. More than three hours after the time his father had said he'd call.

Joey clicked on a lamp, stretching and shaking as he rose, using physical motion to assert conscious control over the netherworld of sleep. What had he forgotten? *Was* it Friday night? Hadn't they planned dinner for sometime after six?

No message light flashed on the answering machine. Joey punched the menu on the phone to check the call log. Maybe his dad had called but hadn't left a message. Rapidly, he clicked through all the calls. Only three calls all day—none from his dad.

He dialed his dad's apartment. Four rings and the answering machine picked up. Joey hesitated, then said, "Dad. It's Joey. Am I missing something? Thought we were having dinner tonight. I'm at my apartment. Call."

Now fully awake, Joey still felt the shock, like something was wrong. For all his faults, Frank Beck didn't change plans without letting you know. Joey paced, wanting to take a shower, but not wanting to miss his dad's call. It struck him that he didn't know who to call to check on his dad. Six months ago he would have called his mother, and she could have told him with certainty what was going on. Six months ago he could have called any one of a half dozen of Frank Beck's friends, all of whom would likely know where Frank was and what he was doing.

But a lot had changed in six months. A wife of 30-plus years, friends, an older son and daughter—all had gone on one-too-many roller-coaster rides with Frank Beck. Six months ago when the roller coaster went down—went down steep—they'd all opted off. Everybody except Joey.

Joey hesitated for a moment, then dialed his mother's number.

"Hi, Joey." Mona Beck had gotten caller ID after the separation. She wanted to be sure that when she answered her phone, Frank Beck wouldn't be on the other end of the line. She'd told everybody she knew: "You call and I don't know the number or it comes up 'private name' or 'unidentified'—I don't answer." What she didn't admit to anybody was that she wouldn't answer Frank's calls because she didn't trust herself not to see him again.

"Mom—I know you don't want to be involved in anything with Dad . . ."

"That's right, Joey." Her voice was hard, just on the edge of mean.

"The thing is, Dad and I had plans for dinner tonight, and he didn't call. I worked a double shift starting at midnight last night and didn't get home until almost four this afternoon. I laid down, expecting to wake up when Dad called at 6:00—we were going to decide where to meet when he called. But I just woke up and he hasn't called . . ."

Her voice was tight, impatient. "I told you, Joey. Your father is no longer my problem. If you don't expect anything from him, he can't let you down."

"Mom, you know he never says he's going to do something with one of us and then just doesn't show up. He always calls. That much you can count on."

The line was silent for moments. She knew that Joey was right. "You called his apartment?"

"Of course. I left a message." She didn't ask if he'd called his dad's cell phone, which meant she knew Frank Beck no longer had a cell phone. Frank Beck had been the first person Joey knew to use a cell phone, and the cell phone was as much a part of Frank Beck as his right arm. It was when Joey found out his dad hadn't been able to pay his cell phone bills that he knew things were irrevocably bad.

"And you tried the office?" His mother's voice was now a little worried around the edges.

"The office? He still has the office?"

"I ran into Phyllis Quinn at Lund's a couple weeks ago— maybe longer—" She stopped. He knew they were both thinking the same thing. His mother couldn't afford to grocery shop at Lund's. Old habits die hard, and she was feeling guilty. "Anyway, Phyllis said she'd run into your dad coming out of the Dachota Building the day before. She'd asked him if he still had his office there, and he told her that the leasing agent was letting him stay through the end of the year. No phone. Probably no electricity . . ."

"Phyllis said there was no phone?"

She was slow in answering. "I checked. I just wanted to know . . ."

"Maybe that's it, Mom. Maybe he started working on something, forgot about the time, and not having a phone handy . . ."

"Your guess is as good as mine, Joey. Probably better."

The heater was out in Joey's car, and he shivered all the way downtown. Joey wished his dad's office was anywhere other than in the downtown Minneapolis warehouse district. On a Friday night, the district's bars and restaurants would be full and parking would be at a premium. Then Joey remembered. His dad used to park in the alley behind the Dachota in a space that came with the lease. If his dad's car were in the space it would make sense to go to the trouble of parking and going up to the office.

Joey hit First Avenue North just as traffic from a Target Center concert was getting out. Joey's car crawled, his anxiety building with each traffic light that changed before he made it through an intersection. Couples ran across the street between the cars, women dressed for a night on the town. The women clung to their boyfriends for warmth and to balance themselves on spike heels. These were people his own age, but Joey felt no connection to their high spirits. He resented that any problems they had were easy enough to be obliterated by the energy of a Friday night.

Finally reaching Fifth Street North, Joey swung right, drove a half block, and pulled into the alley behind the Dachota. Without streetlights, it was like driving down a hole. But even in the dark, Joey could see the dim gleam of his dad's silver Jaguar. A wave of relief washed over him—but seconds later he realized the car behind the Dachota didn't explain why his dad hadn't called. All the parked Jaguar meant was that the bankruptcy settlement hadn't taken place yet.

Joey pulled up behind the Jaguar. If you parked here on a weekday during business hours, you'd get towed before your engine cooled. But after ten on a Friday night, with First Avenue traffic backed up, Joey had all the time he needed to get up to his dad's fifth floor office and back to the car.

Getting out of his car, Joey looked up toward the fifth floor. The windows were dark. Which meant one of two things: the heavy black blinds in the office were down or the office lights were out. Joey thought about what his mother had said about the electricity probably being off. If that was the case, what would his father be doing in a dark office with no lights, no phone, or no functioning computer?

Walking toward the back door, Joey checked his key ring. The office key, which he hadn't used in months, was still there. Turning the lock, Joey pushed open the heavy metal door. Immediately he was hit with the particular smell of the Dachota's back entrance: unvarnished wood floors, indigenous dust, and uncirculated air that collected under the high ceilings.

Frank Beck had been among the first businessmen in town to renovate office space in one of the handsome old buildings in the warehouse district. He couldn't afford Class A office space for his start-up wireless electronics business, but after he saw the Dachota, it didn't matter. In its first life, the Dachota had been a warehouse that supplied farm implements to the prairies west of the Twin Cities. Beck had signed a lease minutes after opening the door to the vast, derelict fifth-floor space and within a month had gutted the Dachota's top floor down to brick walls and exposed vent work. He'd covered the high, broad windows with heavy black shades. When the shades were up, there was a spectacular 360 degree view that took in the downtown skyline in one direction and the Mississippi River in the opposite direction.

Within weeks of Beck Electronics moving into the Dachota, a half dozen other businesses had signed lease agreements and the warehouse office boom was under way. Frank could have taken an option to buy the Dachota and two other warehouse buildings for less money than a single lease in the Dachota was going for by year end. But as usual, his too-scarce capital was tied up in a venture that was long on concept and short on business plan. So he'd passed on an opportunity that would have made a fortune even Frank Beck would have been hard-pressed to blow.

The back halls of the Dachota were badly lit, and the silence of a late Friday night did nothing to relieve Joey's anxiety. He wound his way through the labyrinth of hallways to the freight elevator, pushed the up button, and heard the immediate clank of the elevator's lifts. The slow grind of the elevator's gears filled the empty corridor, ending with an echoing double *thunk* as the elevator landed on the first floor. The double steel doors slid back, and Joey stepped forward, pulled the metal gate to the side, and headed up.

Two things were wrong when the elevator doors opened. The first thing was the black lacquer door to Beck Electronics. It was partially open, and no light was coming from behind it. The second thing wrong was the cold air Joey could feel coming from behind the partially open door, even before he was off the elevator.

The cold hit him with a physical force as he stepped into the office. Without thinking, he pulled the door shut behind him, closing off the single ray of light in the space. Into the darkness he called, "Dad?"

His voice hung in the air for seconds before it was sucked into the void. With his right hand, he felt along the wall for the light switches. He flicked all the switches, but no lights came on. He turned to reopen the door to regain the shaft of light, but already the deep darkness had caused him to lose his bearings. He reached again for the wall, finding only empty darkness.

He forced himself to stand still to quell dizziness. Joey thought about the layout of the office. It was open with four space dividers and a couple dozen workstations scattered across the polished hardwood floors. The only thing he could think to do was to follow the river of cold air to what must have been an open window. Once he got to the windows, he could raise the shades and let in some street light. You wouldn't be able to read by it, but at least you would see the basic outlines of what was in the office.

Joey started a careful shuffle in the direction of the cold. He had taken a half dozen steps when he struck something. It moved away from him as he reached for it, then swung back at him. He couldn't think of anything in the office that hung from the ceiling. Reaching out, he stabilized the object.

The first shape he recognized was a man's hand.

The message was on his desk when Mars Bahr walked into the squad room of the Minneapolis Police Department Homicide Division.

Call Danny Borg.

He looked at it for a moment before turning to see his partner, Nettie Frisch, coming across the room from the employee lounge. The message wasn't in her handwriting, but he asked her anyway.

"You know what Borg wants?"

"Wasn't here when he called." In front of her computer, Nettie immediately focused on the monitor. She took a big gulp from a partially frozen bottle of Evian water and said, without looking at him, "He probably just wanted to hear your voice."

Mars sifted through stuff on his desk that had come in while he'd been out. Nothing urgent. Things were slow. Minnesota Nice was in ascendance and the city was in danger of losing its hard-earned sobriquet, "Murderapolis." He dropped papers back on the desk and glanced over at Nettie. It struck him that something was wrong. It took him a minute, then he said, "You're wearing denim, Nettie. What happened to the black-and-white-only rule?"

"Denim is consistent with the rule. The reason I made the only-wear-black-and-white rule was to keep my life simple. Denim doesn't make my life complicated. *Plaid* would be complicated. What I want to avoid is having too many options."

"There's no such thing as too many options, Nettie. Not in our business." Mars shifted his attention back to Borg's message, the only thing on his desk with any promise of being interesting. He stretched back in his chair and dialed the downtown command.

Mars had worked with Borg on another case and had been impressed by Danny's hustle. Borg wasn't the most sensitive guy around, but Mars had liked his commitment and energy. Some cops, even good ones, went for the easy answers in an investigation. Borg focused on hard questions.

The duty officer in the downtown command said Borg was out on patrol, but offered to page him. Mars hung up and looked at his watch, making a bet with himself that Borg would call back in less than five minutes. Mars got up to walk back to the lounge for a Coke, but his phone rang before he'd made it out of the squad room.

Danny Borg's voice was breathless. "Special Detective Bahr? I apologize for missing your call."

Mars shook his head. One of Borg's endearing characteristics was a deep capacity for reverence, which was fine except that Mars had become the object of Borg's worship. He'd told Borg to drop the title and call him Mars almost a year ago. Borg's response had been, "Yes, sir. I'll do that, sir."

"Not a problem, Danny. What's on your mind."

Danny Borg's voice lowered. "Do you recall hearing about the guy who hung himself in his office last week? There was a big article on the front page of the Metro/State section on Monday."

"I remember seeing the article. Sounded like a slam dunk suicide. This is the guy who'd gone bust, right?"

"Yeah. Frank Beck. He'd lost his business. Most of his family kind of backed off on him—and the ME's office found out he had colon cancer when they did the autopsy."

"Yeah. I definitely remember reading about it. Homicide never got a referral—at least, it never came to me. And it would definitely be my kinda case if someone thought it was a homicide."

Borg didn't answer right away. When he did, his voice had dropped another octave. "No, there wasn't any referral to homicide. My sergeant's decision. I was the investigating officer on the scene. Got sent over when the nine-one-one call came in." Borg hesitated again. "The thing is, sir, I did recommend a referral to homicide, but my sergeant said 'No way.' And on the face of it, I can understand that. It's just that there were a couple things I thought merited a second look. But my sergeant is saying to leave things as they are. He's probably right."

"Tell me why you thought it should have been referred."

"There was a number written on the guy's arm, and I couldn't find anything that connected to those numbers. No bank accounts, pin numbers, nothing. That, and I couldn't find where the guy got the fabric for the noose. For that

319

matter, I couldn't find anyone who knew him who said Frank Beck knew how to tie a hangman's knot. What everybody said about him was that Beck wasn't a detail guy. He was a big idea man. Was sloppy about doing anything that required a long attention span. So I have to ask myself, how'd a guy like that tie a picture-perfect hangman's knot?"

Mars didn't say anything right away. He bounced a pencil on his desk and thought about it. His first reaction was that if Danny Borg had a gut feeling something wasn't right on a death, that in itself was enough to bring homicide in. And he agreed with Borg that questions about the number and the noose should be resolved.

"Let's do this. Send me a copy of your report from the scene, the medical examiner's report, and anything you took from the scene. I'll look it over. If anything comes out of our review, we'll open an investigation. No promises, but I agree with you. It sounds like we should know more than we do about the number and the noose."

"I really appreciate that, sir. The other thing is, Beck's youngest son was pretty torn up about what happened. Either way—it stays a suicide or you find out something that makes it a homicide—the kid is going to feel better being sure. He's a good kid, just started college last fall. The only one who stuck by his dad when things got really tough." Borg hesitated again, then said, "I hate to put you on the spot, but can we handle this without a formal referral? I mean, without the paperwork and everything? Like I said, my sergeant hasn't authorized ..."

"Don't worry about it. Just send me what I asked for. We'll worry about paperwork if we decide to open an investigation."

Without looking at Mars after he hung up with Borg, Nettie said, "What was that about?"

"Remember reading about the guy who hanged himself in his office—about a week ago?"

Nettie gave Mars a look.

Mars ignored the look, and said, "Borg thinks there are a couple of issues we should review before closing the file."

Nettie put words behind the look. "C'mon, Mars. There was nothing—*less* than nothing—to suggest this might be a homicide. And lots to support suicide. From what I read, this guy had every reason to die and nothing to live for."

Mars nodded. "I agree—from what I read at the time. Nothing that raised any flags, that's for sure. But I also remember from what I read that the family was pretty devastated. First the financial losses, then the suicide, then finding out after the fact that the guy had cancer. And Borg said Beck's youngest son is taking it pretty hard. I don't mind taking a look at the file and talking to the kid. If it'll make him feel any better."

Nettie said, "I know what's happening here. You're projecting."

"I'm *what*?"

"You're projecting. You're thinking, 'What if something happened to me, and Chris needed to talk to someone about what happened?' "

Mars made a face. "So what you're saying is I make decisions about work priorities based on stuff that I connect to my ten-year-old son? I don't think so. If my taking an afternoon to look at the file helps a family accept the medical examiner's conclusion, I'd say the public interest is being served. Chalk it up to goodwill. Something the department needs as much of as it can get."

"What I'm saying is the First Response Unit is already having credibility problems, what with the murder rate being down nearly seventy percent since we got the FRU assignment. Chasing around trying to make a big deal out of a case the downtown command has already called a suicide isn't going to win us any friends."

Mars shifted in his chair and turned away from Nettie. "Winning popularity contests has always been my weak suit. If we can't keep our enemies off our backs, we might as well make them happy by giving them something to whine about."

"Project away if it'll make you feel better," Nettie said.

Mars was on his way out of the squad room when the phone rang. He walked back to his desk, looked at the caller ID, and picked up.

"Hi, Karen. Dinner off?"

"Nuh. Just that I've had a hell of a week. I want to go someplace really nice. Someplace with cloth napkins and good wine."

"Fine with me. As long as they don't water the Coca-Cola. You've got somewhere special in mind?"

"Restaurant Alma. It's new. On University between Fifth and Sixth Avenue. Ted and I had dinner there a week ago with some of his clients. It was sublime."

"So I'll meet you there at seven?"

Karen was silent for a moment. "Mars, you've got to promise me something."

"Depends on what it is."

"Dinner tonight is on me . . ." Mars started to protest, but Karen came back at him fast. "I mean it, Mars. I know how much you make and I know what your child support payments are. You can't afford to eat at Alma. And I don't want to stint on what I order because I'm worrying about what you can afford. I want to have salad, an expensive entrée, dessert, coffee—I want to order whatever I want without thinking about it. And the only way I'll do that is if you do the same and I pay. Don't be a bonehead about this, Mars. If it were the other way around, we wouldn't even be discussing this."

"It's my son you should be having dinner with if you're bent on charity. He could bankrupt you in two courses without even ordering a glass of wine."